AS167250
D1150710

Dumfries and Galloway Libraries, Info[illegible]nd Archives

This item is to be returned on [illegible] date
shown belo[illegible]

NIK[illegible]GAN

AND

THE ARMY RANGER'S RETURN

BY

SORAYA LANE

A KISS TO SEAL THE DEAL

BY

NIKKI LOGAN

DID YOU PURCHASE THIS BOOK WITHOUT A COVER?
If you did, you should be aware it is **stolen property** as it was reported *unsold and destroyed* by a retailer. Neither the author nor the publisher has received any payment for this book.

All the characters in this book have no existence outside the imagination of the author, and have no relation whatsoever to anyone bearing the same name or names. They are not even distantly inspired by any individual known or unknown to the author, and all the incidents are pure invention.

All Rights Reserved including the right of reproduction in whole or in part in any form. This edition is published by arrangement with Harlequin Enterprises II B.V./S.à.r.l. The text of this publication or any part thereof may not be reproduced or transmitted in any form or by any means, electronic or mechanical, including photocopying, recording, storage in an information retrieval system, or otherwise, without the written permission of the publisher.

This book is sold subject to the condition that it shall not, by way of trade or otherwise, be lent, resold, hired out or otherwise circulated without the prior consent of the publisher in any form of binding or cover other than that in which it is published and without a similar condition including this condition being imposed on the subsequent purchaser.

® and ™ are trademarks owned and used by the trademark owner and/or its licensee. Trademarks marked with ® are registered with the United Kingdom Patent Office and/or the Office for Harmonisation in the Internal Market and in other countries.

First published in Great Britain 2011
by Mills & Boon, an imprint of Harlequin (UK) Limited,
Eton House, 18-24 Paradise Road, Richmond, Surrey TW9 1SR

© Nikki Logan 2011

ISBN: 978 0 263 88894 2

23-0711

Harlequin (UK) policy is to use papers that are natural, renewable and recyclable products and made from wood grown in sustainable forests. The logging and manufacturing processes conform to the legal environmental regulations of the country of origin.

Printed and bound in Spain
by Blackprint CPI, Barcelona

Nikki Logan lives next to a string of protected wetlands in Western Australia, with her long-suffering partner and a menagerie of furred, feathered and scaly mates. She studied film and theatre at university, and worked for years in advertising and film distribution before finally settling down in the wildlife industry. Her romance with nature goes way back, and she considers her life charmed, given she works with wildlife by day and writes fiction by night – the perfect way to combine her two loves. Nikki believes that the passion and risk of falling in love are perfectly mirrored in the danger and beauty of wild places. Every romance she writes contains an element of nature, and if readers catch a waft of rich earth or the spray of wild ocean between the pages she knows her job is done.

For the real McMurtrie family and for the
Cape Saunders colony of New Zealand Fur Seals.

To my friend Kate, whose research formed the basis of
the background for this story. Her family farm sits on a
stunning peninsula on the South Island of New Zealand
and is home to abundant wildlife, including a colony
of seals as depicted in this story.

CHAPTER ONE

*R*ESPECTFULLY *yours…Kate.*

Grant snorted. Since when had any part of Kate Dickson's dealings with his father been respectful? She and her travelling band of greenies were single-handedly responsible for crippling Leo McMurtrie's farm. And for his death that had followed.

The town might believe old Leo had had a dicky heart, but there were three people who knew otherwise: Leo's best mate the mayor, the town doctor and Grant—the only child who had found his father in the front seat of his idling vehicle. It hadn't even run out of fuel yet.

Kate Dickson's letter was still open on Leo's kitchen benchtop. Grant had left it, and everything around it, untouched until the doctor had made his declaration and the funeral was over.

He ran his eye over it now.

Negotiate the buffer zone… Protect the seals… Limit farming activity… Regretfully…

First respect, now regret.

Right.

What was respectful about hounding an old man into letting you onto his land and then putting the wheels in motion to have tight conservation restrictions slammed on twenty-eight kilometres of his coastline? About repaying a favour by screwing over the man that had given it to you? Kate Dickson called herself a scientist, labelled her work research, but she was nothing more than a bleeding heart with her eyes on making a name for herself.

At his father's expense.

The irony that he found himself in his father's corner for the first time now, only after he was dead, that their only common ground should be beyond the grave, didn't escape Grant. Or was it that he just hadn't been willing to appreciate his father's perspective while he'd been alive and so staunchly defending it?

He balled the delicate handwritten letter—who wrote by hand these days?—and erased the irritating Kate Dickson from his conscience. Then he let his head fall forward onto the hands that fisted on his bench top and took a shuddering breath.

And then another.

A shrill call made him lurch; he snatched up the phone before thinking. 'McMurtrie.'

The uncertain pause sounded long-distance. 'Mr McMurtrie?'

Grant understood the confusion immediately. 'McMurtrie junior.'

'Oh, I…I'm sorry. Is your father there, please?'

A road-train slammed hard into his guts. The man who'd raised him had never really *been there* for him and never would be now. 'No.'

'Will he be back today? I was hoping to discuss…'

Breathless. Young. There was only one female that he could think of who hadn't been at Leo McMurtrie's packed funeral yesterday, that hadn't brought a massive plate of country cooking for his orphan son. That would be oblivious to his death. His eyes fell on the letter. 'Miss Dickson, I assume?'

'Ms.'

'Miss Dickson, my father passed away last week.'

Her shocked gasp sounded genuine. So too the agonising pause that followed and the tightness of her voice when she finally spoke. 'I had no idea. I am so sorry.'

Yeah, I'm sure you are. Just as you'd been getting somewhere with your crazy plans. If he made a sound, he would say exactly that. So he said nothing.

'How are you?' she asked quietly. 'Can I do anything?'

The country courtesy threw him for a second. This woman didn't know him from Adam but her concerned tone was authentic. That boiled him more than anything else. 'Yeah. You can keep your people far away from this property. You and your microscope brigade are no longer welcome.'

The voice sucked in a shocked breath. 'Mr McMurtrie—'

'You may have sweet-talked my father into letting you on his land but that arrangement is now void. There will be no renegotiating.'

'But we had a commitment.'

'Unless your commitment is in writing, and has the words "in perpetuity" in bold print, then you have nothing.'

'Mr McMurtrie.' Her voice hardened.

Here we go...

'The arrangement I had with your father was not just about him. It has the backing of the Shire Council. There's district funding attached to it. You cannot simply opt out, no matter how tragic the circumstances.'

'Watch me.'

Slamming the phone down was the most satisfying thing he'd done all week. It gave him an outlet. It gave him focus. Blaming someone helped; it meant he didn't have to blame the man he'd lost. The man he'd been estranged from for nineteen years.

Nothing Grant did could bring back the father he'd walked away from as soon as he'd hit legal age. But he could do one thing for him—the thing his father had died wanting.

He could save the farm.

He could not run it. He was no more equipped to do that now than the day he had walked away from it when he'd been sixteen. But he could keep it ticking over. A week, a month, however long it took to get it ship-shape and ready for sale to someone who could make it great. Probably not what his father had left Tulloquay to him for, but he'd never buckled to his father's demands before and he wasn't about to start now.

He'd never been farmer material growing up and Leo McMurtrie dying hadn't changed one part of that.

Kate Dickson had stood on this rustic porch one time too many, readied herself for this argument once too often. It had taken twelve solid months of negotiating—almost pleading—for Leo McMurtrie to agree to let her team conduct their three-year research study on his property. And now in the final, crucial year of operations she was right back where she had started.

Up against a lawyer, no less.

An hour on the internet had tracked down Leo McMurtrie's only son, Grant. He was some contract specialist from the city, and he was angry and still grieving, if his manner on the phone last week was any indication.

Hopefully the personal touch would do the trick.

She knocked on the freshly painted timber door then smoothed her hands down her best business outfit. Pencil skirts and fitted blazers weren't really her thing but she had two of them in her wardrobe for occasions just like this one.

The door didn't move. Kate glanced around nervously. Should she have called ahead or would he have just ignored that? Someone was home; she could hear the thump of loud music coming from deep inside the farmhouse. She knocked again and waited.

'Come on, McMurtrie…' she mumbled.

When the son still didn't materialise, Kate tested the door. It swung happily open and the music-level surged.

'Hello?' she shouted down the long hallway over the *doof-doof* of heavy metal. 'Mr McMurtrie?'

Nothing.

Cursing under her breath, Kate moved down the hall-way towards the deafening noise. The smell of paint hit her immediately and she saw old floral-patterned sheets draped over furnishings in the freshly coated rooms that she passed. The sheets struck her as incongruous on a property belonging to a man's man. Leo McMurtrie had been as tough as nails. Even once they'd finally come to an arrangement regarding access for her team, he'd still been as surly as a mule, with a sailor's vocabulary. The fact he slept on old-fashioned, floral sheets just didn't fit with the man she knew.

Then again, she barely knew him at all. Leo hadn't wanted to be known.

'Hello?' *Jeez.* Lucky there wasn't an emergency or something. She tiptoed forward.

'What the hell—?'

Out of nowhere, a solid-rock wall stepped out and slammed into her, sending her reeling backwards, a damp weight dragging on the front of her suit. Kate lunged for the paint bucket that tipped between them just as a pair of masculine hands did the same, and the two of them ended up half-crouched on the floor like a badly-gone-wrong game of Twister. But they did manage to right the bucket and stop any more paint from sluicing down onto the timber floorboards.

The second thing Kate noticed—after subliminally absorbing the sensationally manicured pair of hands that relieved her of the bucket—was the intensity of a pair of eyes the colour of sea grass. They blazed at her from under a deep frown.

She struggled for something else to focus on. Paint pooled at her feet, dripping wildly off her clothes onto the floor.

'Oh…'

'Don't move!' Leo McMurtrie's son barked, blocking her passage with his body and placing the tin carefully to one side. It took him a few minutes to wipe up the worst of the mess at her feet with a series of cloths but, as fast as he wiped, she dripped. Paint thickened and blobbed off the pointed seams of the tailored fabric.

'Get that jacket off.'

Kate bristled at his autocratic tone but couldn't ignore the fact that her jacket had taken most of the paint and it was very clearly still streaming onto the floor. She stripped it off, bundled it up with no further concern and tossed it over to the growing pile of paint-covered rags in the corner.

Two sets of eyes went to her beige-stained skirt.

'That stays on,' she said unequivocally.

His tight lips wanted to twitch but his scowl wouldn't let them. Kate saw it all play out on his face in the seconds before he masked it. He crouched before her and, without so much as a word, he hand-scraped the paint off the tight fabric of her skirt, off the thighs underneath that stiffened with surprise, reaching around behind her legs to hold her steady as he did it.

Kate stood compliant and mortified until he'd finished, feeling every bit like the child she'd worked so hard to grow out of. The girl who just did what others told her. McMurtrie junior straightened up and glared at her. Those captivating eyes were evenly set in an oval face framed at the top by short, sandy-blond hair and at the bottom by a matching two-day growth. His eyes perfectly matched the khaki shirt that flared open halfway down his chest and which revealed a gold band hanging by a leather thong around his neck. More sandy-blond hair scattered across his tanned collarbone.

His lips tightened further as he noticed the direction of her gaze.

Desperate to get things back on a professional footing, Kate pushed her thick hair back from her face and wedged her 'game on' glasses more firmly up her nose. She straightened as best a paint-covered woman could and held out her hand to shake his.

Too late, she noticed the slap of wet paint on her right hand—which meant it was on her hair and probably her glasses too. The hand dropped limply.

Nice one, Kate.

But the pragmatist in her whispered that what was done was done. Nowhere to go but up. 'Mr McMurtrie…'

'Never heard of knocking?' He glared at her, unimpressed.

Her eyes narrowed. Maybe he wasn't grieving. Maybe he was just an ass most of the time. Like father, like son. Even if she'd come to feel great affection for McAss senior, he'd been pure hard work at the beginning.

'Never heard of a perforated ear-drum?' she shouted back, eyebrows lifted.

It was only then he seemed to realise that the stereo was still pounding out. He turned away and killed the sound with the flick of a nearby switch. It took her heart a few beats to realise it had lost its synching rhythm. When he returned, his shirt was fixed two buttons higher. The tiniest part of Kate mourned the loss of that manly chest.

'Thank you,' she said, her voice overly loud in the new silence. 'Do you always enjoy your rock at full blast?'

'Better than drinking.'

Kate frowned. How were the two remotely connected? She took a deep breath and started again. 'I'm Kate Dickson. I assume you're Grant McMurtrie?'

'You must be top of your game with scientific deduction like that.'

She ignored the sarcasm. 'You haven't returned my calls.'

'No.'

'Or my email.'

'No.'

'So I came in person.'

'I can see that.' His eyes drifted lazily over her paint-spattered blouse. 'Sorry about your suit.'

Kate shrugged. 'I don't like it anyway.'

'Then why wear it?'

'Societal expectation.'

He stared at her, assessing. 'What would you prefer to wear?'

'A wetsuit.'

'Ah, that's right. Your seals.'

Kate quietly congratulated herself for getting things neatly back on topic. She had a lot to lose if this meeting didn't go well—more than just her project. 'I need to continue my research, Mr McMurtrie.'

'Then you'll need to find another beach, Miss Dickson.'

'All the early research was done here, I can't simply change locations. Neither can the colony I'm studying. They've been returning to that little cove for years.'

'I know. I grew up here.'

Oh, that's right. A spark of excitement flared through her. 'Do you remember the colony when you were a boy?'

His lids dropped. 'I should. I spent part of every day with them.'

Kate froze. 'No. Did you?'

He stared at her overly long. 'Don't get your hopes up, Miss Dickson. It doesn't mean I have any information for you and it doesn't mean I'm going to say yes. My answer is still no.'

'Why?'

'I don't need a reason. It's the beauty of Australia's freehold system—my land, my rules.'

Kate brought out her big gun. Her only gun. 'Actually, it's not.' His face grew thunderous but she pushed on. 'Technically speaking, it's not your land. Not yet.'

His eyes narrowed. 'Is that a fact?'

'I've been told it will take six to eight weeks for probate and to settle the estate according to the terms of Leo's will. Until then, this farm still belongs to your father. And the contract stands.'

God, she hoped so. She'd had to have dinner with a loathsome octopus in order to get some certainty on that. His price for helping her.

The fury on Grant McMurtrie's face had her crossing her arms across her chest, just in case he reached right through her ribcage and snatched at her heart with that big fist. He glared at her and it fluttered even faster.

'You doubt I have enough connections to get it pushed through? I'm a lawyer, Miss Dickson.'

'Ms!' she hissed.

'Actually, I imagine it's *Dr* Dickson, if we're being formal. Why not use that?'

'Because Dr Dickson was my father. And because I prefer Ms. If you can't manage that, then just call me Kate.' She took a breath. 'But that's besides the point. I've been told that even with fiddling probate won't take less than six weeks.'

The hostility switched to offence. 'I do not *fiddle*, Miss Dickson. I merely apply the law.'

Uh-huh. The octopus had been a lawyer, too.

His expression changed. 'What do you imagine will change in six weeks?'

'Maybe nothing. But maybe you'll come to see that the work we are doing is important.'

'To whom?'

'To science. To understanding the role of predators on fish stocks. To the future ecology of the oceans.'

'To you.'

Her chest rose and fell twice. 'Yes, to me. This is my life's work.'

And all she had.

His half-smile, half-snort managed to be engaging and offensive at the same time. 'Play that tune in a few years when *life's work* means something more than five or six years.'

'*You're* not exactly Methusela. What are you…forty?' She knew he wasn't.

His nostrils flared. 'Thirty-five.'

Young, to be the success the internet hinted he was. He must have been very driven. She appealed to that part of him. 'When you were younger, didn't you care about something enough to give up everything for it?'

Grant glared and buried his paint-encrusted hands in his pockets. When he'd been young all he could think about was getting away from this farm and the certain future that had felt like a death sentence. Finding his own path. It had taken him the first ten years to realise he hadn't found it. And the next nine waiting for some kind of sign as to which way to go next.

That sign had come in the form of a concerned, late-night call from Castleridge's mayor that his father had missed the town's civic meeting and wasn't answering his phone or his door. He'd driven a three-hour drive in two and they'd broken his father's door down together.

Grant stopped short of the door in question—newly replaced, newly painted—and let *Ms* Kate Dickson walk ahead. Without her destroyed jacket, her opaque crème blouse hid little as the Western Australian light blazed in the doorway. Her little power-suit had given him a clue to the fit, lean body beneath. Now here was exhibit A in all its silhouetted glory.

His gut tightened.

Not that she'd played it that way. Her attire was entirely appropriate for a business discussion. Professional. *His* shirt had revealed more than hers, even though she had cleavage most women in her position would have been flashing for leverage. It had felt positively gratuitous as her eyes had fallen on his exposed chest. He certainly wasn't dressed for company.

Then again, she wasn't invited, so she'd have to take what she got. 'Don't ask me to empathise with you, Miss Dickson.'

'Ms!'

'Your life's work destroyed my father.'

The sun was too low behind her for him to see whether she lost colour at that, but her body stiffened up like the old eucalypts in the dry paddock. She took an age to answer, low and tight. 'I'm sure that's not true.'

'I'm sure it is.'

She seemed genuinely thrown for a moment. Her blouse rose

and fell dramatically and his conscience bit that he'd struck that low a blow. He'd only just stopped short of saying 'took my father's life'.

But that was a secret for only three people.

She ran nervous hands down her skirt and it reminded him instantly of the soft feel of her legs under his hands just moments before. He shoved the sensation away.

Her voice, when it came, was tight and pained. 'Mr McMurtrie, your father was a difficult man to get to know, but I respected him. We had many dealings together and I'd like to think we finally hit an accord.'

Accord. More than he'd had with his father at the end. All they'd had was estrangement.

'The suggestion that my work—the work of my team—may have contributed to his death is…' She swallowed hard. 'For all his faults, your father was a man who loved this land and everything on it. He came to care for the Atlas colony in the same way he cared for his livestock. Not individually, perhaps, but with a sense of guardianship over them. Responsibility. I believe the seals brought him joy, not sadness.'

'Wishful thinking, Kate?'

She turned enough that he could see the deep frown marring her perfect face.

He struck, as he was trained to. 'My father was served a notice just a month ago that said sixty square-kilometres of coastland was to be suspended while its conservation status was reconsidered—a two-kilometre-deep buffer for the entire coastal stretch. That's a third of his land, Kate.'

Her body sagged. She chose her words carefully. 'Yes. I was aware of the discussions. Aware our findings were being cited as—'

'Then it should be no surprise to you that it might have pushed him—'

Grant clamped his mouth shut, suddenly aware of what it might do to a person to be told they were responsible for someone's suicide. Someone like Kate. Especially when he didn't know that for a fact. Yet. 'That it might have stressed him unduly.'

Her nod was slow, her face drawn. 'If it wasn't what he wanted, yes, I could imagine. But he was working with us.'

For what reason, only his father would know. But Alan Sefton had a thorough and detailed will sitting in his office, completed just weeks before Leo's death, that gave Grant responsibility for Tulloquay. And that will didn't say one single word about seal protection or participating in research. And, where Grant came from, legal documents like that spoke infinitely louder than words.

'There's not a snowball's chance in hell that my father would have willingly signed over one third of his land to a bunch of greenies. He loved this farm.'

Her eyes dropped. 'He was not a man to do anything by halves.'

It dawned on him finally that his father and this woman had had some kind of relationship. Not conventional, he was sure—his father just wasn't that easy to get on with—but her shock on the telephone and her sadness now finally registered. And his own grief and long-repressed anger lifted just enough for him to see how the passing of Leo McMurtrie might impact a young woman who'd spent several days a week for two years on his farm.

But he couldn't let compassion get the better of him. That was probably what his father had done in the end—compassion and a healthy dose of male paternalism. He looked again at the small, naturally beautiful woman before him. Possibly male something else.

And look what it had led to.

He stiffened his back. 'The moment probate goes through, your team needs to find somewhere else to do your study. Ask some of the farmers up the coast for access.'

'You don't think I would have done that rather than negotiate with your father for so long? This site is the only one suitable. We need somewhere accessible that allows us to get quickly between the seals and the water. The cliff faces to the north are even less passable.'

'Then you'll have to get creative. The moment it's in my power, I'll be closing my gates to your seal researchers. Fair warning.'

Even without being able to clearly see her face against the glare, he knew she was staring him down. 'Warning, yes. But fair? For all his faults, your father was at least a man of integrity.'

She turned and gracefully crossed the veranda, down the steps to her beat-up old utility truck. Hardly the sort of vehicle he would expect a beauty to travel in. She slid in carefully and swung her long legs modestly in before quietly closing the door.

In that moment he got his first hint as to why his father might have relented after a year of pressure. Not because she'd used her body and face to get her way…but because she hadn't.

Kate Dickson was an intriguing mix of brains, beauty and dignity and she clearly loved the land she stood on.

No wonder his father had caved. It was exactly what he had loved about Grant's mother.

CHAPTER TWO

STRIPPING bare in an open paddock was the least of Kate's concerns. The looming threat of every visit being her last made her suddenly want very much to visit her seals. Just socially, despite the timing being wrong.

Wrong shoes, wrong clothes, wrong time of day. But she was doing it anyway.

These animals were the most stable thing she'd had in her life in the past few years and the idea of losing them filled her mouth with a bitter taste.

An arctic gust blew in off the Southern Ocean as she peeled off her ruined skirt and blouse and hauled her wetsuit on in their place—the closest she'd ever get to being a seal, albeit twenty kilos too light. No wonder sharks sometimes mistook surfers for their favourite blubbery food-source when they were in full wetsuit. She'd relied on the same confusion to get closer to the Atlas colony the first time.

On a usual working day she ditched the wetsuit for serviceable, smelly overalls, about the most comfortable thing ever invented—warm, dry and snug. But also the least attractive.

Unless you were a male wool-sack.

Her beat-up old utility gave her the tiniest bit of privacy against the baleful stares of thirty sheep that scattered like freckles across the dry, crunchy paddock. It was not really suitable pasture for sheep grazing, but they had a ready food source in feed stations dotted around the farm. They were more interested in the engagement and social aspects of grazing as a flock than in what little nutrition the salt-stiffened grass afforded.

The sheep had seen her half-naked plenty of times and were about as uninterested as the rest of her team to whom boundaries, and gender, meant nothing. Sifting through seal vomit for six hours a day had a way of bringing a team closer together. But sift they did, and then they studied it. Such a glamorous life; no wonder gender and modesty came to mean nothing to any of them. Kate couldn't remember the last time she'd actually felt like a woman.

How about twenty minutes ago?

Even angry, Grant McMurtrie had made her body resonate in places she hadn't thought about for years. It was still thrumming now; something about the insolent way he'd sized her up. It had boiled her blood in one heartbeat then sizzled it the next. She'd been insanely pleased to be wearing a skirt and blouse for once, even if she'd been covered in paint. Imagine if his first impression of her had been her usual working attire…

The sheep turned away, bored, as she tossed her ruined clothes and shoes into the back seat of her car for later and reached back over her shoulder to snag the zip-tether and pull her rubbery wetsuit up tighter against her skin. She picked her way barefoot over the edge of the bluff and down a near-invisible crease of sand in the painfully sharp rocks, their oft-trodden pathway down the cliff face to the rocky cove below. The trail had been worn when they'd found it, hinting at use over generations. A mercy for her poor feet, but trickily narrow, just wide enough for a slight woman.

Or a small boy.

Her mind immediately went to one in particular. Grant McMurtrie must have come here a hundred times in his young life, hard as it was to imagine the imposing man as a child. What adventurous little soul wouldn't find his way to the dangers of open cliff-face, gale-force wind gusts and wildlife galore? Envy as green as his eyes bubbled through her.

He might have had the seals before her, but she had them now. They'd been hers for the past two years and, if she played her cards right, they'd go on being hers for the next year. Longer, if the Conservation Council ruled in her favour. They were already extremely interested in her research.

Two-dozen dark heads lifted as she negotiated her way down the crease. These seals were used to the arrival of humans on their beach now. They were not trusting—definitely not—but accustomed. Only a couple of heads remained raised at the unusual sight of just a solitary human; the rest flopped back onto the rocks to continue their lazy sunning. Kate smiled at the typical scene. A gang of rotund pups mucked around by the water's edge, vocalising and chasing each other and play-fighting, as though they needed to use up all their energy now before they grew up and became biologically sluggish like their mothers, scattered lazing around the rocks.

Or their older brothers, hanging out in bachelor groups further up the coast. Or their fathers, who did their own thing most of the year but came together with the females for breeding season.

Families. They came in all shapes and sizes, and if those pups got lucky they'd have theirs for a lot longer than she'd had hers. Kate frowned. She'd had a long time to grow accustomed to being on her own but it had never really grown any easier.

One of the pups squealed and drew her maudlin focus back to them.

It was amazing they tolerated human presence at all, given Kate and her team caught them up once a month and piled them into wool sacks for weighing. But the young seals seemed to view it as a regular part of their lives, a game to be had. More than one pup dashed straight back into the wool sack after release, keen to be back with its mates. Looking into the sack was one of the rare true pleasures of her job, as four pairs of enormous, melted-chocolate eyes in brown furry faces peered back out at her.

It got all her maternal instincts bubbling, yearning, until she shushed them. When your colleagues barely noticed you were female, and when colleagues were the only men you met, kids weren't an immediate issue on the horizon, no matter what her biology was hinting.

Plus they were just one more thing to love and lose. And what was the point?

'Hey, Dorset,' Kate murmured to one of the seals she could recognise by sight as she settled herself on a suitably flat rock. The large female was one of five wearing the monitoring equipment this month. The time-depth recorder captured her position above sea-level every five seconds when she was dry and every two seconds when she was wet, twenty-four-seven. They rotated the expensive recorders monthly across the whole adult colony, to get a good spread of data from as many animals as possible, in order to determine information for their study: where the seals fed, for how long and how deep they went.

What they were eating was a different matter. There was no convenient machine for that, hence the vomit and poop-sifting.

Dorset gave an ungracious snort and turned her attention back out to sea, sparing the briefest of glances for Danny Boy, her pup. Seal mothers were shockingly fast to abandon their pups when threatened; that made it much easier to catch up the young for weighing, but it bothered Kate on a fundamental level that these babies were often left undefended.

She knew from experience how that felt.

She'd made a pledge to herself back when she was young that she'd never let herself get in that position again—exposed, vulnerable to the capricious decisions of others. Without control. Without any say.

It must have occurred to the seal species in the ancient past that the loss of the baby meant the loss of only one, but the loss of a fertile mother meant the loss of an entire genetic line. Pups were expendable. And entirely, tragically vulnerable.

Danny Boy looked straight at her and then dashed off, barking in grumpy high-pitched tones. Sad affection bubbled through her. As far as the fishing communities along the west coast were concerned, seals and man were hunting the same fishstocks. And, when that industry was worth millions of dollars a year, anything or anyone threatening supply would not be tolerated. Her research was showing that, whether by good design or dumb luck, seals were hunting totally different fish from humans. If only she could prove that to the people of Castleridge. To the government. To the world.

'Don't suppose you guys would consider going vegetarian?' she quietly asked the wary mass of seals.

Close by, one mother trumpeted her displeasure at that idea, and Kate scrabbled away from the ensuing stench; beyond disgusting.

Her chuckle was half-gag. 'Go on. Get it out of your system now. I need you guys to be charming the next time I come down.'

With McMurtrie junior in tow. It was the obvious next step. If he was going to throw legalese at her, then she'd fight back with the only thing she had—history. If Grant McMurtrie had cared for these seals as a kid, maybe she could use that and try to change his mind about her access. She wasn't above begging, or conniving.

Whatever it took to snatch back a bit of control.

Not only did she have three funding grants riding on this, but her professional reputation as well. She didn't want years of work to be wasted because somebody had a chip on their shoulder about conservation programs. She had her university, the Fisheries Department and the Castleridge Town Shire to remind her of that. They were expecting results in return for their contribution and it was her job to get them, come hell or high water.

Or hot, surly city lawyers.

* * *

'So, what was the good news?' Grant drained the last of his coffee and stared meaningfully at Castleridge's mayor.

Alan Sefton chuckled. 'Twelve weeks is pretty short for probate settlement, as you know. You should be thanking me.'

Three months before he could legally boot Kate Dickson and her team off his land.

'Thank you for agreeing to be Dad's executor,' he allowed.

The older man smiled sadly. 'I was aware that he wouldn't… That you and he…' Grant lifted one hand and Alan gratefully picked up the cue to move on. 'Did you know he'd left you the farm?'

'I had no idea.'

'You were still his son. His only heir. Time couldn't change that, nor distance.'

'It wouldn't have surprised me if he'd left the farm to those greenies just to spite me.'

Alan frowned. 'Spite is not a trait I connected with Leo. Belligerence, absolutely. Selective hearing, sometimes. But he was not a man who wasted time on petty grudges.'

Grant let that sink in. 'Perhaps he mellowed in the twenty years we were apart.'

'Or perhaps you did.'

Silence fell. With no other customers this early in the Castleridge café, the tinny radio coming from the kitchen was the only other noise.

Alan cleared his throat. 'How are you doing, son?'

Son. It had been a long time since anyone had called him that—since his mother had died early in his life. His father had called him exclusively by his given name growing up, his school teachers by his surname, and his staff tended towards 'sir'. Just hearing the phrase 'son' brought a certain familiarity to the discussion. If anyone else had asked him how he was getting on, he would have moved the conversation quickly on.

But discovering a body together had a way of forging a bond

between strangers. The genuine question deserved a genuine answer.

'I'm…getting by.'

'How are you finding being in his house?'

'It's fine.' And, surprisingly, it was, despite everything. 'It's been so long since I lived there with him; it's not like the walls are infused with his spirit, you know?'

Alan nodded.

'Unlike his tobacco,' Grant said. 'Twenty years didn't change that habit.' The memories of his distinctive brand made it too hard to sleep. 'I had to repaint the whole place to get rid of the smell.'

A dark shadow crossed the mayor's face before he masked it.

Grant moved the conversation on. 'What else did you want to tell me?'

Alan caught the eye of the teenage waitress and interrupted her nail-varnishing session at a far table to indicate it was time for the bill. 'Not *tell*, so much as ask,' Alan hedged.

Grant waited but nothing further came. 'Shoot.'

'I know you don't have a lot of connection to Castleridge these days.'

Not a lot, no. But he'd been floored by the number of people who had attended Leo's funeral, and the amount of prepared dinners that had graced Leo's freezer when he died. The locals were still looking after their own. 'I grew up here, remember? There's still a lot of familiar faces.'

'Well…that's good. Makes what I'm about to say that bit easier.'

Grant frowned. 'Just say it.'

'It's about the research team…'

He snorted. 'If you can call a bunch of science types counting seals *research*.'

Alan nodded thoughtfully. 'Leo had reservations for a long time before deciding to work with them.'

'I'll bet.'

'It took him a year of discussions before finally relenting to—'

'I've met Kate Dickson. I can well see what he relented to.'

Alan's weathered face creased. 'Kate came to see you?'

'Last week.'

'How did she seem?'

Seem? Too beautiful for a scientist. Too young to have shadows beneath her eyes. 'She seemed hell-bent on getting her way.'

'Yes. That would be Kate. She wouldn't let her sorrow detract from the work she's doing.'

Grant tightened his jaw. He had thought he had an ally in Alan Sefton but the man was every bit as smitten with Ms Dickson as his father had apparently been. 'The only thing she was sad about was me shutting down her access.'

'Ah.' Alan nodded. 'I wondered what your choice would be.'

'There is no choice. Introducing the buffer zone will cut the farm's profitable land by a third, and its valuable coast-access completely. I have no interest in helping the people who tore my father's farm out from under him.'

Alan's clear blue eyes held his. 'Oh, now you care about the farm?

Grant had spent too many years across negotiating tables in the corporate world to let his shock show. Instead, he swallowed back the shaft of pain and fixed Alan with his hardest stare.

The older man glanced away first. 'I'm sorry. That was unnecessary. But I'll ask you to remember that twenty years of your father's life may have passed for you, but I lived them. Here with Leo. Listening to his stories. His dreams.'

The lost dream of passing Tulloquay on to his son. A son with passion and aptitude for running stock. A son made of different stuff from the one fate had served him with. 'Life wasn't always his to dream with,' Grant said simply.

'True enough. But he made his choice freely when he decided to support the university's program.'

Grant snorted. 'Right. No-one wore him down…'

The older man flushed slightly. 'I won't apologise for the stance I took,' Alan said, straightening and reaching for his wallet.

What? '*You* took?'

'Your father has always been slow to change but, like this land, he responded best to consistent, evenly applied pressure.'

He leaned forward. 'You support the conservationists?'

Alan tipped his head. 'I support Castleridge and the people in it. This program comes with significant grant-monies. And, if it helps us to understand our fisheries better and protects our tourism, everyone wins.'

Are you serious? 'Uh, except the McMurtries. We lose a third of our land.'

Alan pursed his lips. 'To grazing, yes. But it opens up all kinds of possibilities for eco-tourism.'

Grant couldn't help the sound that shot out of him. It was a cracking impersonation of one of Kate Dickson's fur seals. Every disparaging thing his father had ever said about the landholdings in the district opening up to eco-tourism flashed through his mind. 'My father would have died before letting a single tourist step foot on his property.'

And maybe he had.

Alan stared at him sombrely. 'When was the last time you recall Leo McMurtrie doing something just because someone else wanted him to?'

Grant stared. He'd tried—and failed—his whole young life to get his father to budge once he'd set his mind on something. Maybe he'd just had the wrong tools. 'I have a theory.'

Alan Sefton's face said 'enlighten me'.

'Have you met Kate Dickson?'

The older man ignored his sarcasm. 'Yes. Several times. Lovely girl. A little closed-in about her work…'

That threw him briefly. '"Closed in" how?'

'Oh…' Alan waved a careless hand 'I just got the feeling that she doesn't have a lot else going on in her life. You know—family. Children.'

Grant snorted again. He was becoming an honorary member of the Atlas colony. 'I imagine *Ms* Dickson would take issue with your concerns in that regard.'

'Never met a more dedicated and conscientious professional,' Alan amended quickly. 'But Leo knew people. And Leo saw something in her that… Well, in how she is with the seals—so fiercely protective. So single-mindedly determined to help their cause.'

'What are you, the president of the Kate Dickson fan club? She's the opposition, Alan.'

'This is not about sides.'

'It is when it's your farm under threat.'

Oh, now you care about the farm? He didn't need to say it again. It was glaringly obvious and not all that unreasonable a comment. Grant sighed.

'I walked away from Tulloquay nineteen years ago because I knew I couldn't be a farmer. My whole teenage life, I lived through my father's recriminations that I wasn't interested in the land he'd built up.' He cleared his throat. 'He let me leave rather than witness one more example of how useless I was with the most basic agriculture tasks. How much I had failed him. I cannot believe for one second that he left me the farm with any intent other than wanting me to sell it for the best possible price to someone who could make a go of it. Quite frankly, I'd believe he'd had a personality transplant before I'd believe he'd willingly excise off a third of it to a bunch of tree-huggers.'

And if he did he would have put it in his will.

Plus there was the glaring matter of his father taking his life over the pending conservation-order. What more evidence did he need? But he wasn't ready to say the *s* word out loud just yet.

'Alright, then.' Alan sat up straighter. 'Then, as you are the man who will soon inherit Tulloquay, I'd like to communicate to you my support as mayor—in fact, the town's support—to this fisheries program and the investment it represents in regional relationships, science partnerships and eco-tourism. We urge you to give it—give us—your support.'

Grant lifted one brow. 'That's quite a speech. Take you long to prepare it?'

Alan smiled. 'A couple of hours two years ago when I first had the discussion with your father.'

Grant blew out a carefully moderated breath. Did Kate Dickson and her fur seals have the whole town wrapped around their flippers? But Mayor Sefton was no more a soft touch than his father had been. In the short fortnight Grant had known him, he had seen an astute businessman and a strong leader. Which didn't mean Alan didn't have his own priorities.

Grant slid from the booth. 'I'll take that under advisement.'

The mayor dropped a handful of bills onto the table and stood, clapping Grant on the shoulder. 'I can't ask more than that.'

'I'm sure you could.'

And probably will.

CHAPTER THREE

THICK arms crossed against a broad chest, which was thankfully fully covered this time, less likely to distract. Grant glared at her from his barrier position in the doorway. Still hostile. Still handsome.

'Why would I need an invitation to visit my own cove?'

Kate's mouth opened and closed like a stranded fish. 'Not your cove, our *work*. I thought if you saw it…'

'I might be overcome with fascination and empathy?' His grin was tight. 'You don't know me that well, Kate, so I'll forgive the assumption that I would have the slightest interest in what you're doing down there.'

Kate glared. 'I'm sure you didn't get where you are in business without knowing the first step in a successful negotiation is to know thine enemy.'

'We're not negotiating.' *But he didn't deny they were enemies.* 'That would imply some leverage on your part. As far as I'm aware, you have none.'

She stiffened her back. 'I have twelve weeks.'

His eyes darkened. 'News travels fast.'

'It's an important time frame for my team. Of course I checked.' She'd been calling the probate authority every few hours until the timeline had been announced.

'What's stopping me from shutting this door and only opening it in three months when your time is up?'

Kate's heart hammered. *Absolutely nothing*. 'The hope that

there's a decent human being in there. And that bullying people is just what you do for giggles these days.'

His left eyelid twitched but he didn't move otherwise. '*You* came to *me*. Twice now.'

A hiss squeezed out past tight lips. 'Mr McMurtrie, I don't enjoy debasing myself. I don't have the luxury of walking away from all of this, much as I might like to.' She swallowed hard. 'I'm fighting for my life's work here.'

It's all I have.

Her heart pounded the words out in Morse code and she shoved the prickle of concern down deep. Somewhere in her subconscious, she knew that she needed to get some life balance back. That she'd put her whole life on hold for this project and that, somewhere in the past three years, it had started to feel normal.

But life balance could wait. Changing Grant McMurtrie's narrow mind was what mattered now.

He stared at her long and hard. 'I'll give you one hour.'

Kate almost sagged with relief. 'Thank you.'

He turned for the house. 'I'll just get my keys.'

Her hand shot out to curl around his wrist. Warmth pinballed between them. 'Uh, can I ask you to take a shower first?'

He turned back slowly. Deliberately. She swallowed hard.

'I've been battling the artesian pump,' he said darkly. 'I wouldn't have expected the seals to be bothered by a little honest sweat.'

'Actually, it's the opposite. You smell too good.' Heat blazed high into her cheeks as the words tumbled from nervous lips. 'I mean, too *human*. We don't wear deodorant or fragrance or even perfumed shampoo in the field. It helps stop the seals from scenting us coming.'

If any more blood rushed to her head she was going to pass out. *Ground, open up and swallow me now.*

'That explains a lot.' Those green eyes bored into her, but

then they softened. 'If I have to smear seal dung all over myself to disguise my scent, I'm not coming.'

The humorous murmur was like a lifeline tossed into the Sea of Mortification; Kate grabbed it with both hands. 'Of course not. That would be a criminal waste of a perfectly good sample.'

His straight lips opened to speak and then twisted in the closest thing to a smile she'd seen him offer. 'Give me fifteen minutes.'

'I'll see you out there.' Standing around compliantly while Adonis took a shower was not part of her plan. 'Do you know where to come?'

'Dave's Cove?'

Kate nodded and turned for her car but, before she could relax even a bit, he called after her.

'The shower is coming off your sixty minutes.'

With every breath, the power seemed to shift further and further away from her. Sheer bravado kept her walking. She flicked her hand in the air as though dealing with gorgeous, clever, angry men was an everyday occurrence and called back over her shoulder.

'Bill me!'

No deodorant. No perfume.

Grant hadn't been kidding when he'd said that explained a lot. He'd been trying to pin down something about Kate Dickson since the day she'd stood in his house covered in paint. Back then the paint had masked it but today, as she'd stood just feet away from him in the spring sunshine, it niggled at him. She looked completely different today from her last visit. The power-suit was gone and she'd replaced it with a baggy T-shirt and cargo shorts. Really dirty cargo shorts. All that thick, dark hair was pulled back in the most serviceable of ponytails. No make-up. No deodorant. No perfume.

Just one-hundred-percent clean, pure woman. With killer bone-structure.

She had to be the most natural, open woman he'd ever met. And as she'd stood there, playing the worst game of negotiation he'd ever witnessed, showing her entire hand in an easy second, he'd found himself wanting to help her. To teach her how the game was played. To save her from herself.

Kate Dickson and her greenies needed someone like him in their corner or they were going to get absolutely screwed by this world. But the idea of playing Sir Galahad to her helpless maiden appealed a little bit too much—given what she'd done. What she was still doing.

He shut off the water with a slam and yanked a towel from the rack.

Yet she'd walked out of here with the very thing she'd come for. He might disagree with her technique, but he couldn't fault her results. Maybe he had more of his father in him than he realised if a few nervous smiles and a charming blush from an *ingénue* could have him eating out of her hand. Or maybe *she* had more of *him* in her than he gave her credit for. An innate talent for spotting someone's weakness.

In his room, he yanked on a fresh set of jeans and a denim shirt before shoving his feet into well-worn paddock boots. His father's, but a reasonable fit. Leo McMurtrie would flip in his grave to see his city son pulling on his battered work-boots and heading out into the paddocks.

He snatched his keys off the kitchen bench, slid an expensive pair of sunglasses on and sprinted to his car, eager to catch up with the virginal Ms Dickson and get the balance of power back on track between them. She and her team might sit on beaches all day getting a killer tan and counting bobbing seal-heads in the water—or something—but he was about to show them just how pointless it all really was. Probably better in the long run, given they'd be moving on soon, regardless of what the district mayor wanted. If Alan Sefton was so fired up about their success, then he could work with them to find a new location.

Tulloquay was off-limits.

He pulled his car up next to Kate's battered ute right on the fifteen-minute mark and looked around. There was no sign of anyone up here, but a third vehicle was parked a few metres away. Six sheep sat curled happily in its shade, the only shade as far as the eye could see. He'd forgotten what a barren, blustery spot this was.

A healthy gust blew the fine sand from the cliff face back up at his skin and he found himself tempted to turn his rump to the wind like the sheep did. So much for the royal treatment. Looked like he'd have to show himself around.

He peered over the edge of the bluff and then gaped at what he saw below.

Kate lay full-bodied on a big, round seal, kitted up in elbow- and knee-pads, her dirty cargos and the filthiest shirt he'd ever seen. Her long, brown legs were hiked up hard and pressed into the sides of the seal, pinning its powerful flippers to its side and holding it immobile. Two rangy young men, as mucky and wet as Kate, worked hard at the front of the seal, fitting something to the vacant space between its shoulder blades. She contained the protesting seal just long enough for them to fit the small black box and test its fixings. Then the men backed off across the cove to join two other researchers there. Nearer to them a couple of other seals looking after a group of babies shifted nervously from side to side.

Grant held his breath.

These weren't bull seals, but females could still give a nasty bite and they were known to carry toxic bacteria in their mouths. One bad contact and Kate would be under medical attention for the rest of her three months. Even he knew that, and it had been twenty years. She worked with these animals every day.

What the hell was she thinking?

Below him, Kate seemed to gather herself for a moment,

and then in one lithe move she sprang sideways, rolling and crashing onto the rocky outcrop as the seal lurched away from her into the sea and disappeared under the waves. Grant felt the crack of bone against rock from his eagle-nest position, and was sure he heard her agonised groan as she flopped over onto her back and stared up at the sky.

Right at him.

From his high position, he could see the small track he used to take to get down to the water where it came out near the waterline of the rocky inlet known as Dave's Cove. Two decades dissolved away as muscle memory took him to where he knew the top opening of that trail was. It was a lot harder getting down as a grown man than it had been as a fearless, fleet-footed boy but he stumbled out onto the rocky base just as Kate was pulling off an elbow pad. Bloody scrapes marred those perfect legs.

Adrenaline made itself known at last. 'What the hell was that?' he growled.

She stopped, stunned. Three of her team looked up. 'What?'

'Seal-riding is part of your research protocols, is it?'

Her mouth dropped open. 'I wasn't riding it, I was restraining it.'

'Kitted out in rollerblading gear?'

She stopped and looked down at herself for a moment, astonished. Then she straightened and stared at him as though he were mad. Which at this moment he'd be prepared to believe.

'I got back from your place and Stella was onshore. We've been waiting to get her alone for a week now. I didn't have time to change into overalls.'

That was when he noticed the rest of her team was dressed alike in terrible blue overalls. At least, it could be blue, under all the filth. Hard to tell.

'What were you doing to her?' His seals. From years ago. *His* seals. Just when he would have sworn he didn't care for any part of this farm.

'We were fixing the TDR to her back. She'll carry it for the next month'

Feeling like an idiot didn't help his mood any, and it was starting to sink in that he'd made a mistake. A big one. He frowned, but softened his voice with effort. 'The what?'

She eyed him cautiously. 'Time-depth recorder. It collects data on their foraging habits.'

He looked out to sea where Stella had disappeared and then back at Kate. An odd feeling very close to grudging respect began to nibble in his belly. 'That was dangerous, Kate.'

'Don't worry, you're not liable; we have our own insurance. We know what we're doing. And it doesn't hurt her.' At his sceptical look, she relented. 'Well, maybe her pride. A little. She'll forgive me; they always do. They're very resilient. We've been doing this a couple of times a month for two years.'

'So this is what you do down here? Track seals?'

Kate laughed and someone on the other side of the cove joined her. 'Uh, no. That was the exciting part.' She glanced at the huddling young who were starting to relax again now that the drama was over. They opened their dark mouths in a belated show of group bravery. 'Sometimes we catch up the pups to weigh them and check their condition. But mostly we just take samples.'

'Samples?'

Kate stripped the other elbow pad off but left the knee pads in position. 'Come on over, we'll show you. You might like to help.'

Let the sell-job begin. He had sudden visions of lifting traces of fur samples from the rocks, CSI style, and studying them for genetic variation under multi-million-dollar microscopes. Or extracting blood samples from the cute little fur-balls blinking at him. 'Sure, why not?'

Kate threw him a pair of rubber gloves and a couple of plastic bags then handed him a large spatula as he grew close. 'What do you want—vomit or scats?'

One of her team snorted. Grant just blinked at her.

'Sorry.' She was all innocence. 'You did say you wanted to help?'

He had a sudden recollection of her joking about not wasting a valuable sample on smearing him with seal poop. 'You cannot be serious?'

She sank onto one hip and braced long slim wrists on her waist. 'Were you hoping for something sexier? Sorry; seal riding's all done for the day.'

With a sarcastic smile, she bent down and artfully scooped a mountainous pile of silvery black gunge into her plastic bag, taking care to get every last bit. Grant's stomach turned. She handed the bag to an assistant who labelled it for her and put it into one of three eskies over near the limestone cliff-face.

'You're not kidding.'

She straightened and looked at him. 'Do I strike you as a comedian?'

No. Not at all. But he was damned if he was going to be shown up by a greenie. He glanced around the rocky beach. The way he figured it, what came back up *had* to be better than what had gone all the way through. 'I'll take vomit.'

Her smile, instant and genuine, was at least as dazzling as the sun burning down on them. It stole his breath almost as much as the odour from her sample, which reached him in the same moment. His stomach lurched again.

'If you puke, do it away from our samples. We don't want any contamination.' With no further discussion, Kate turned back to her collection and left him in the dubious care of one of her team, who showed him the basics of vomit scooping.

He only gagged twice, which he was pretty proud of. And he collected three whole samples before he reluctantly gave in to his curiosity.

'Why are we doing this?'

Kate worked hard to disguise the tiny, triumphant smile. But she wasn't fast enough. Weirdly, it didn't bother him. Instead, it birthed a warm kind of glow that something he'd done had finally pleased her. A rare enough sensation, when it came to her.

'Our study relates to the foraging habits of these females so we can determine what level of threat the seals pose to commercial-fishing harvests.'

'And collecting the foulest substance known to humankind will tell you that how, exactly?'

Kate straightened and zip-locked a particularly feral sample into containment. 'Beaks and ear bones.'

Don't ask. Curiosity, real and genuine, blazed. *Do not ask!* He stared at her, burning, determined not to speak.

'OK, go ahead and tell me,' he blurted and the power slipped further.

Kate's face exploded with life, earnest passion glowing past the smears of dirt and goodness knew what else on her flawless skin. 'We sift the faecal samples to isolate the otoliths—ear bones—of the food in their stomach. Then we pair the otoliths up, identify and count them, and it tells us how many fish each seal ate and of what species.'

There was no chance on this planet he was going to admit to the unconventional brilliance of the plan. How else could you figure out what the black goo once was? 'You do realise it's absolutely disgusting?'

'Oh, completely. But sensationally effective.' She shrugged. 'Everything else digests.'

He scraped another sample into a fresh bag, mouth-breathing the whole time, still fighting back the stomach heaves. When he spoke, he sounded vaguely like he'd been sucking helium. 'And the vomit?'

She moved to the next sample, closer to him, and squatted to attend to it. 'Squid and octopus beaks get stuck in their sphincters. Make the seals regurgitate.'

Of course they do. When had his ordinary day taken such a surreal twist?

'Wouldn't want to miss any ear bones.' His voice sounded tight, even to him, as he lifted a sample bag and braved a look.

She seemed genuinely pleased that he'd caught on so quickly. 'Exactly. Let me show you something.'

If it wasn't from a seal's body, and if it got him away from this stench, he would follow her into the mouth of hell. He offloaded his sample to one of Kate's assistants and followed her over to a far dry corner of the cove. She rummaged a moment and produced a laminated photograph of a small, glossy fish with googly eyes and fluorescent spots on its dark silver face. A particularly unattractive fish, but from the distant recesses of his memory he realised he knew that animal.

'Lanternfish.'

Her brown eyes widened. 'Right.'

'You forget, I grew up around here.'

'Still, not a common catch. It's a deep-sea fish. How do you know it?'

Grant frowned. His father's face swam in and out of his memory just as fast, but he couldn't hold the elusive memory. 'I have no idea. Why are they special?'

'My research shows that ninety percent of the fish coming out of these seals is lanternfish.'

'And?'

'And humans don't eat lanternfish. Too oily.'

It hit him then, why this mattered to her so much. 'The seals are no threat to human fisheries.'

'None. In fact they probably help it, because *our* fish and *their* fish prey on the same smaller species. So by keeping lanternfish numbers down the seals help ensure there's more smaller-prey fish to support the fish we haul up by the netful.'

'Thus protecting a multi-million-dollar industry.'

'Exactly.'

Well, damn. The seals were probably essential to Castleridge's thriving fishing industry. The same kind of feeling that he got when he found the weak link in a competitor's contract hit him, a mini-elation. Except hot on the heels of the rush came a dismal realisation, and this one sank to the bottom of his gut. 'Who knows about this?' he asked carefully.

'So far? My team. Leo knew. And now you know.'

'Is that why my father gave you his support?'

'It was your father that put me onto the lanternfish in the first place.'

His gut clenched and it had nothing to do with the stench. 'Bull.'

She seemed surprised by his vehemence. 'He never believed the seals were a problem. He'd watched their habits. He grew up with them too.'

True. How could he have forgotten that? Had Leo spent the same lazy days he had as a boy, hanging out with the forbidden seals? Had he sought sanctuary there when *his* father went off at him?

Her eyes gentled. 'He was stoked when the results started coming in showing he was right.'

That was what she'd want him to believe, to improve her case. 'You're telling me he was happy his land was going to be accessioned?'

Her eyes dropped.

'I thought not.' *Look at what he'd done as a result.*

Brown almond eyes lifted to his. 'He was conflicted, Grant. He wanted to do what was right. But he knew what it would do to the value of the farm.'

The almighty farm, the god to which Leo McMurtrie prayed. It had always been his beginning, middle and end. 'And now you expect me to simply follow suit?'

Kate frowned and clutched the photograph. 'I thought…'

'You thought this would make a difference? Why?'

'Because you're a lawyer. You pursue justice. These animals are being unjustly persecuted and we hold the evidence in our hands.'

'I'm a contracts lawyer, Kate. I don't do the whole "scales of justice" thing. I lock down minor details, I screw down better deals, I hunt for loopholes and make sure no-one can get out of something they've committed to. Or, in this case, I'll be doing my best to get *out* of the agreement my father had with you.'

Kate paled. 'But how can you, now that you know? You can protect these seals. Help save them. Your whole property could become a sanctuary.'

Her naïve idealism was like a foreign language to him. 'I can't protect anyone, Kate. They won't be mine to protect.'

She blinked. 'What do you mean? I've been watching you improve the place. Getting it back in shape. Giving Tulloquay its life back.'

'To sell, Kate. I'm doing it up to sell it as soon as it passes into my name.'

She seemed to stumble briefly but caught herself on a rocky outcrop. 'You're selling your farm?'

She said it as though he'd announced he was going to slaughter the seals for their coats. 'My father's farm. It was never mine, even when I lived here. I'm not a farmer. I'm a lawyer. I never wanted this.'

And Dad knew it. The final irony—leaving it to a son who wouldn't want it, making all of this his problem.

'But the seals…'

'Three months, Kate. I did warn you. You'll just have to wrap up early.'

The panicked glitter to her eyes wheedled its way straight into his subconscious. He didn't like distressing her. 'We can't wrap up early. Breeding season starts in two months and we need to establish where that happens. It's a key piece of the cycle to ensure we have a full year of foraging behaviour established for this year.'

'Then you should have done it before now.'

Colour roared high along her cheekbone. 'Do you think we didn't try? We've been searching for two seasons to work out where they go. It's unusual for any group to breed somewhere other than their rookery, but these ones do. The TDR's don't record positioning, only depth. We've lost the colony two seasons running during breeding season.'

'Then who's to say you wouldn't have lost them again this year? I'm sure the bulk of your research will still stand. Whatever you have now has got to be more than science has ever had before. Two years is not a bad innings.'

She stared at him with eyes as big as the seal pups'. 'How can you be so different to your father?'

His head came up like whiplash, his gut sucking up as tight as the vacuum-seal lid on the eskies. 'Whatever you think you know, Kate, you're wrong. My father gave his life to this farm. He wouldn't have stood by and watched it get carved up.'

Her mouth gaped. 'Yet you're going to sell it off to some stranger?'

'As a going concern. To someone who'll work it the way it was meant to be.'

Her colour rose with her voice. 'It wasn't *meant* to be a farm. It's meant to be a delicate coastal ecosystem for all creatures to enjoy, except we came along and colonised the south coast for ourselves and filled it with hard-hoofed livestock!'

'People don't buy delicate ecosystems.'

Hurt and disappointment washed over her face. 'Shutting us down early makes it harder for me to get my results finalised, but it doesn't invalidate the study completely. The research will still go through. You can't stop it.'

In the moment when he should have been saying something, he saw the lightbulb come on over her head.

She gasped. 'But it will stall ratification by the conservation commission. You're going to rush this sale through before the conservation status changes.'

His choices were reflected back to him in the disgust in her pale expression. Infinitely worse than the hard, callused glares of some corporate types he routinely nailed down. At least there the playing field was relatively equal. Discomfort burned low in his throat.

'I told you, Kate. Loopholes and weaknesses are what I do. You've shown your hand too early.' He peeled off his gloves and tossed them into the bag at her feet, feeling about as worthy as the slimy muck that splattered off them.

'You have three months.'

CHAPTER FOUR

FOR the next month, Kate's days started at half-past four in the morning as she drove out daily to Tulloquay, arriving just after sunrise and staying until dark. The looming deadline of the settlement of Leo's probate pressed down on her relentlessly—and now the addition of a possible new owner to negotiate with. How many times would she have to fight this battle? How many times would she see her world slide into disarray?

She hated it. When her parents had died, her life had been ripped comprehensively out of her hands. She'd been voiceless amongst strangers making decisions for her, people who'd thought a pre-teen wouldn't have a problem with having a brand-new life mapped out for her. But she had.

A big problem.

It was why she'd picked science for a career—cause and effect. Logical progression. Predictable results. Her work rarely spun out of control the way her life had.

Until now.

Not that she wasn't doing her best to drag it back into some kind of order. She'd split her team into half so that three of them could stick to the analysis of the samples in their lab in the city while she and two others continued collecting what samples they could on ever-lengthening shifts. She assigned herself the longest ones of all. It was exhausting and discouraging work and she was dreading the day they'd have to walk away, unfinished, from their study. From the seals. From everything they'd built. All on the very unlikely *maybe* of a future owner letting them resume their work.

But she backed up the new team rotation by working on a report late into the night that would hopefully show the Conservation Commission that the seal population was no threat to Castleridge's fisheries, and, by extension, the rest of the region. Maybe that would be enough to get some protections put in place for the seals.

She tried hard not to think about the better use that her team could be putting all that driving time to—three hours in the morning and three in the evening. But, unless Grant McMurtrie planned to relent on his determination to sell Leo's farm, there was no real option. They needed to increase the number of field days and they just couldn't afford the kind of trailer-based accommodation infrastructure that went with remote postings.

It was bad enough fretting about the twenty-thousand-dollar TDR still fitted to the back of Stella, who was missing. It would eventually fall off the seal as her fur grew out, but for Kate's project it would be a significant financial blow if it wasn't recovered. Plus it carried a month's worth of crucial data.

The most useful thing she could do to try and put the brakes on her madly spinning world was to stay down here overnight, mitigate all that time lost to travelling. She had a tent but last night she'd had no energy to erect it. She'd sat awake, long after her team mates had gone home, staring out at the glittering sky and watching the reflection of the stars shift on the ocean surface. Exhausted and discouraged, she'd curled up in the cramped back seat of her ute. She'd knocked off a whole report chapter—freehand, on her lap—before falling asleep, chilled and miserable, in her sleeping bag.

Now she stumbled back up over the edge of the cliff where she'd found a private spot to relieve her bladder after a long night in the car.

'Tell me you didn't sleep on the beach.'

She leaped clean off the ground at the unexpected voice,

deep and close. She was more conscious than ever of her smelly seal-clothes, extra rumpled after a night squished up in her car. And the fact he'd just busted her peeing, albeit out of view.

'Grant.' Her hands went to her loose hair, blowing in the ever-present wind, before she could stop them. She scanned the desolate coastal paddocks until she spotted his truck in the far distance over near the sheep's water supply. 'What are you doing out here so early?'

'I wanted to check the drinkers before it got too blustery. I saw your ute.' He glared into the tiny extra-cab of the ute. 'Did you sleep here, Kate?'

'I was just too tired to drive last night.'

He narrowed his eyes and really studied her. 'You look terrible.'

Again her hands twitched to attend to her shabbiness. He, of course, looked every bit the fresh-from-the-shower Aussie farmer, even though she knew he wasn't. Clothes, it appeared, really did maketh the man. Every time she saw him those shoulders seemed to get wider. 'We have so much to try and finish. Every minute counts.'

His lips thinned. 'Where's your team?'

'I'm only bringing half of them; the other half are in the lab rushing the samples through.' She could hear the tension in her own voice and smiled brightly. 'But we're getting there. It's all good.'

He pulled his hat down harder over his eyes against the rising morning sun. 'No, it's not. Not if you're wearing yourself out and sleeping in your car.'

Frustration hissed out of her. 'Sadly, my budget doesn't really run to portable labs and campers. I'm just working with the parameters I've got.'

'Would that help? A lab down here?'

'Talking in hypotheticals sure won't.'

He stared at her steadily.

'Fine. Yes, it would help. We would run the samples during

the hottest part of the day and move our contact hours to morning and late afternoon. I could get my whole team back down.'

Grant looked out to sea for moments and then brought his clear green eyes back to hers. 'What sort of a building do you need? Does it have to be hospital-grade?'

Her heart-rate picked up. Was he serious? Was Grant McMurtrie offering to *help* her? He was built near enough to a gift-horse. 'No. Just dry, lockable and pest-free. As long as the equipment can be sterile we can work anywhere with power.'

'How about my garage? It needs a good clean-out but I'm not using it.'

Grant drove a top-of-the-range Jeep Wrangler and it sat out weathering most days. 'You need that for your car.'

His eyes darkened. 'No. It's not…suitable.'

She stared at him. 'It's a garage.' *Of course it's suitable.*

'Do you want it or not?'

Kate's breath whooshed out of her. 'Why would you do that? You want us gone.'

His gaze was steady. 'Despite what you believe, I'm not completely heartless. I grew up with these seals and don't want to see them persecuted any more than you do. The way I figure it, you can't get a complete year's worth of data no matter what happens, so me making your daily tasks more comfortable isn't going to hurt me, particularly.'

He was right. Volume made all the difference in the world to her, to the validity of her research. But depressingly little difference to him or to the Commission, who were holding out for something more persuasive.

'What if you're wrong?'

'I wouldn't be offering if I thought there was a chance of that.'

The smug confidence should have infuriated her. But all it did was remind her how much she was drawn to a capable man, with a good mind.

His eyes softened. 'And I don't like seeing you hurt yourself. Have you even had a day off since I last saw you?'

And a kind heart, as it turned out.

Kate shuffled. She didn't want to think well of the man whose self-interest was sending her life into chaos. 'The clock's ticking. I'll have nothing but time off when it's all over.'

He frowned, knowing full well he was the cause of the rush. 'You're welcome to my garage, Kate. Make the best of it that you can.'

Relief hung, suspended and pendulous, waiting for her mind to make a decision. She briefly tossed around the idea of declining, maintaining a high moral ground. But practicality won out; she was nothing if not practical.

The relief released its iron grip as soon as she had the thought and whooshed in a free-fall through her body. 'Thank you, Grant. That will really help.' She chewed her lip.

He saw it. 'What?'

In for a penny… 'Would it be okay if I set up a camp in one of your sheltered paddocks? With the lab here it would make more sense for me to stay, too. My team can bring things in and out as I need them. Most of them have families to get home to.'

'You don't?'

Kate kicked herself mentally for opening the door to that line of enquiry. Gentle warmth flamed up her throat and the contrast between it and the arctic breeze sent a blizzard of tiny lumps prickling down her flesh. 'Only my Aunt Nancy,' she hedged. 'And I don't really see her all that often these days.'

Mad old Aunt Nancy. She'd got Kate to adulthood after her parents' accident, but only barely, and mostly by luck. It had been more a case of reverse parenting in the end. Still, Nancy had provided food and shelter and access to a decent school after Kate had lost everything. She'd done the rest herself, miles from the town and countryside she'd loved so much. It had been the beginning of a lifetime trend. She didn't like to leave anything to chance. Chance had a way of turning around and biting you.

'Your parents?' His words were casual enough, but his gaze was intense.

How had they got here? She shook her head knowing there was no way to not answer such a direct question. But her chest still tightened like a fist. 'Died when I was a kid. Road accident.'

Grant said nothing for a moment. 'Where were you?'

'School. I didn't know until the principal came to collect me at the end of the day.'

'Lucky you weren't with them.'

Kate felt the familiar stab deep inside. Her voice thickened. 'That's the consensus.'

But some days her personal jury was still out on that one.

She'd stayed with the country-school principal for three days until Aunt Nancy had arrived from the city to collect her—her mother's whispered-about sister. A woman she'd never met. Someone had packed all Kate's belongings for her and shipped her up to the big smoke in a matter of days. Her family farm and everything in it was sold by solicitors and the money left over after the debts were settled had been put into trust for when she was eighteen. She'd never even been allowed to set foot on her property again. As an adult, she realised everyone had done what they thought was the best thing at the time. But losing your parents, your home and your community in one hit had been brutal on a young girl.

Although, it had taught her how to plan, how to make sure there were never any variables outside of her control. And how good it felt to be standing on land again.

'It's tough, being on your own so young.'

She looked at him. Really looked. 'You sound like you're speaking from experience.'

'I left the farm when I was sixteen. Dad and I… It was time for me to make my own way.'

'What did you do?'

'Anything I could for the first couple of months. I worked part-time in a timber yard to keep a roof over my head and I put myself through the final year of high-school at a community college. An advisor there got me into a scholarship program for business and law and the rest is history.'

Self-schooled, self-housed, scholarship grades and partner by twenty-eight. This man knew something about being driven. And about being busy.

'Look at that—something in common! Who'd have thunk it?' Awkward silence fell and Kate blew the cobwebs away. 'Anyway, are you happy for me to camp?'

'No.' Grant seemed almost surprised by the word he'd uttered. He shoved his hands into deep pockets. 'I have room in the house. You'll be more comfortable.'

Kate stared. 'I can't stay in your house. I barely know you.'

He shrugged. 'So? It's a working arrangement.'

'But what will people say?'

'Do you care?'

The glint in his eye said he already knew the answer.

'No.' Not when her deadline ticked maddeningly in her head.

'Look, Kate, I put the toilet seat down and I'm kind to puppies. Despite being on different sides on this, I'm not actually trying to sabotage your work.'

So her jibe from a month ago had stung. Good. She chewed her lip. 'It would make things go much faster here.'

His eyes narrowed again. 'How much faster?'

Her lips twisted in a sad smile. 'Don't panic. Even if we worked twenty-four-seven we can't get the buffer ratified. Not without identifying the breeding ground.'

'That would make that much difference?'

Why did she keep trusting this man with information? He stood between her and her project. Her mouth opened without her consent. 'I believe so, yes. The Conservation Commission would accept partial research results if we could also hand them a site of significance.'

He looked undecided. Was he about to change his mind about helping her?

'Don't worry; I'm no closer to knowing where it is than I have been for two years. Your plans for world domination are safe.'

He matched her smile and the sorrow reached all the way to his eyes. 'This isn't personal, Kate. It's business.'

She looked at him long and hard. 'I'm prepared to believe it's not personal between us, but this is very personal between you and your father. Why are you selling the farm? He left it to you.'

His face shut down hard before her eyes. 'Because I'm no farmer. That's become abundantly apparent to me this month.'

'You've kept the place running for weeks now.'

'Barely. I know nothing about stock. Short of feeding them and keeping them watered.'

'I'm sure there are people who can help you. Teach you.'

'Like who?' he said.

'Like any of the farmers in the district. Leo was a very popular man.'

'I'm hoping one of those farmers will be champing at the bit to get an outfit this size when it comes on the market. I don't want to seem desperate.'

Kate realised. 'You're trying to build the farm up, make them think you have it all under control, so you get a good price.' She had to give him points for controlling his environment.

'Bingo. If they sense the vulnerability, they'll go for the jugular.'

'You're trusting me not to tell them?'

His regard was steady but tainted with a hint of confusion, as if it hadn't occurred to him until that very second what he was trusting her with. 'You don't strike me as someone to play games.'

'Unlike you, you mean?'

'Very unlike me. We couldn't be more different, Kate.'

She shook her head. 'Crazy world you live in.'

'It's human nature, Kate. If they know how much I need to sell, the price will drop.'

'I wouldn't have thought you needed the money.'

'This isn't about the money. This is my family's farm. It's about dignity. The Tulloquay name. Keeping the farm intact. Making sure the person that buys it values it.'

Conservation restrictions would reduce the size of the landholding and diminish the forward-investment value. Who would want a coastal farm with no usable coastal strip? Apart from her, that was. Without the valuable coastal kilometres, the remaining land would most likely get carved up for paddocks for adjoining farms.

He wanted Tulloquay to stay a farm, no matter who ran it, even if he didn't want the property for himself. Leo McMurtrie would have approved of that part, at least.

'Maybe I could help you? As a thank you for the lab space and room.'

His sceptical expression shouldn't have surprised her. 'You know about farming?'

'My father was the town doctor but we lived on my mum's dairy farm. I remember the seasonal rotations, the basic preventative care for the stock.'

'You barely have time for your own work.'

'I'm not proposing I do it all; you're a big boy. I'll just give you some pointers. The rest is up to you and the internet if you're so determined on the smoke and mirrors.'

It was his turn to frown. 'Why would you help me? You think I'm a jerk.'

Ass, actually. Kate held his gaze against the flush she could feel rising. 'It's in my best interests to keep you amenable. And your father gave me two years of access to the Atlas colony, which I consider priceless. I owe it to him to help you.' She glanced around. 'Plus, I've grown fond of these sheep and don't want to see them starve.'

'Have they starved yet?'

Her laugh was gentle. 'No. But they're going to need drenching soon. Have you got that one covered?'

He tipped his head back as he realised he hadn't. 'How do I know you won't sabotage me?'

Oh, Grant. Is that really the world you live in?

'You don't,' she sighed. 'You'll just have to trust me.'

Intense eyes blazed into hers as his mind worked with that concept. He had a lot to lose if she betrayed him. Kate fought the tremor that fluttered up her spine and forced her body to remember that this was the man that stood between her and her project. Possibly between the seals and their survival.

There could be no flutters. And if she had to hold her breath then it would be awaiting the outcome of his decision, not waiting to see if he trusted her.

'Room and lab space in return for some farming advice. *Confidential.*'

She rolled her eyes. 'If you think it's necessary.'

'It's necessary.' His eyes grew serious. 'You specialise in seal vomit, I specialise in human nature.'

'Interesting analogy.' Kate took a deep breath. 'But you have yourself a deal. On one condition.' His left eye twitched and its brow lifted. Did no-one challenge him in his world? 'The AC-DC stays below eighty decibels.'

In the split second before he remembered who he was and who he was with, Grant gifted her with the most spectacular of smiles. She saw more perfect, pearly teeth in that brief moment than she'd seen the whole time she'd known him. A throaty chuckle escaped, and his green eyes creased and reached out and whomped Kate clean in the solar plexus. She couldn't even suck in a shallow breath, let alone a deep one.

Just when she'd wondered if he couldn't do more than twist those serious lips.

But as quickly as the smile came it died, and Grant dropped his head so that the sparkling eyes were lost in the shadow cast by his akubra hat. Kate felt the temperature drop around them. As if to punish himself—or maybe her—for the smile, he gravely thrust out his hand toward her and barked a curt, 'Deal.'

Goose bumps prickled all over her skin as she slid her chilled hand into his furnace-warm, Goliath one. It swallowed hers completely and Kate had a moment of unease; the image aptly represented their parts in this situation.

He might tolerate her presence, he might humour her research, he might even help her in ways that didn't hinder him. But ultimately Grant McMurtrie held all the power here.

For now.

Her mind went to the nearly finished report for the Conservation Commission, sitting in the back seat of her ute. She straightened her spine and closed her fingers defiantly tighter on his. 'I'll move in tonight.'

CHAPTER FIVE

'YOU do realise you smell appalling?' Grant scrunched his nose.

Her grin was way too sexy to be good for him. After only a few days, Kate's presence felt as ingrained in the house as his father's tobacco.

'Occupational hazard. The smellier we are, the better the seals like us.'

His nostrils flared. 'Then they must be ready to adopt you as one of their own today.'

The grin burbled over into a full laugh and those dimples flashed enticingly beneath a layer of dirt and muck. His gut kicked over, and not from the smell. That was happening way too often. He swallowed past the tight ball.

'We had a good day today, got a heap done. Enough that I can spend all of tomorrow setting up the lab.'

An overflowing carful of her gear had been dropped off by two of her team earlier in the day. It sat intriguingly on the verandah now. As though realising that sharing her joy about having made good progress was not entirely appropriate, two frown lines formed between her brows. The dimples flattened out.

'I'll go take a shower and leave my work clothes in the lab,' she said. 'Hopefully that'll keep it contained.'

The lab formerly known as the garage.

He'd thought about making it a store room, but then realised he wouldn't be able to go in and out of there for stuff, so he'd left it empty. Better a science lab than empty as a tomb—although, the latter was more appropriate. Would Kate freak out if she knew? Part of him thought no—she was a scientist and used to much more grisly things than that—but part of him remembered that she'd been fond of Leo.

'How often did you see my father?' he asked a little later, when she was back to smelling like a clean, natural woman. She was trucking things from the verandah around to the double-doors of the garage. He lumped one of the bigger boxes as he followed her.

Kate paused and thought about it. 'Maybe three times a week?'

For two years. That was a lot—compared to him. Yet she could still whack on the pressure when she had to. 'Must have been tough while he was against your project.'

Kate smiled, and he realised how much he waited for those peek-a-boo dimples to show up. How he lightened just for seeing them.

'He was no picnic even after he came round.'

I'll bet. 'Came round?'

'Reconciled himself,' Kate corrected.

Grant's feet locked up at the roll-door to the garage. No way he was going a step further into that space. 'To giving up his land?'

Kate dropped her box and straightened, frowning. 'To giving up his dogged stance. I think he was just being belligerent out of habit toward the end there.'

Grant snorted. 'He always was contrary.'

She thought about that. 'No, I think he was lonely. Dragging out the negotiations gave him regular contact.'

Pain sliced unexpectedly low in his gut. He shot up straight.

'I'm sorry,' Kate rushed to make good. 'That's none of my business.'

'My father didn't really *do* lonely, Kate,' he said, lowering his voice, critically aware of their location. Leo McMurtrie had liked nothing better than to be alone with his thoughts when Grant was a boy, sitting out high on a bluff somewhere. Leaving his son to find his own amusement.

'I know he filled his spare time with committees and doing odd jobs for friends,' she said. 'But I think you can be busy and still lonely.'

'Speaking from experience, Kate?' Her eyes rounded and darkened with pain, then flicked away carefully. Grant gave himself the fastest of inner lectures.

She rushed on. 'Just as some people can be bored but think they're content.'

Was that a dig at him? No, she couldn't know… 'Bored is not a phrase I associate with Dad, either.'

'No.' Did that gentle smile mean she forgave him his snappy response? 'No shortage of tasks when you're running a farm single-handed.'

Grant winced. Everywhere he turned there were reminders of the future that his father had wanted for him. He should have been here with his dad, running the farm. Maybe then he could have headed Kate's research off before it had even started. Maybe then there would have been no question of the surety of their property. Maybe then his dad would still be alive.

And maybe he'd be arguing loudly with an impossible man right now instead of talking quietly with a woman who was intriguing the hell out of him.

They added two more loads of gear to the pile at the roller-door. Grant knew the moment was coming when he'd need to press the remote and open it. There was nothing in there now but dust and storage boxes. But still his pulse began to hammer.

Kate turned to him. 'Could I ask…?'

His heart squeezed painfully. *No, don't ask. Don't make me say no.*

She nodded towards the garage. 'Just some of the bigger pieces?'

An icy sweat broke out along his spine. He called on every boardroom tactic in his arsenal to keep it from showing on his face, and then he really scraped the barrel and called on desperate humour.

Not his strong suit.

'What happened to your fiery independence *Ms* Dickson? Does it only last until there's heavy lifting to be done?'

He saw the impact of his words in the dimming of her eyes, in the stiffness of her shoulders. He kicked himself, while at the same time acknowledging that his sarcasm was still better than what he wanted to do: turn and sprint for the hills.

It was stupid not to have anticipated this moment. He should have left her to her unpacking and made himself scarce instead of hanging around like a blowfly waiting for her to smile again. Now he either had to forever position himself as a jerk in her mind or walk into the room he'd found his father in.

'Sorry,' she said, clipped, frosty and calm. 'You must have things to do. I'll be fine.'

He knew that. If he hadn't been here, she would have managed. All she had to do was take a few things out of the heaviest boxes. She didn't actually need the help. Whether she knew it or not, she'd been making overtures of friendship since she'd walked in his front door with her paltry belongings two nights ago.

And he'd just thrown it back in her face.

Suck it up, kid. The voice in his imagination was a hybrid of his father's and his own.

'Kate, wait.' He stopped her as she would have turned completely away. 'That was a bad joke. I'm sorry.'

'No.' She shook his hand free, her eyes low. 'You've been more than generous with your offer of lab space and a room. I don't want to take advantage any more than—'

Grant silenced her by bending and intentionally taking the

biggest of the equipment boxes. 'Can you get the door?' While he had an armful of box, he couldn't operate the remote; something told him that was a button-press he simply could not make.

Even if Kate was with him.

That thought brought his head up sharply. Since when had Grant 'the Closer' McMurtrie needeed someone to hold his hand? Since never. But, as he watched Kate's delicate index-finger activate the remote control and that enormous door began to rumble upwards, he'd never in his life been so grateful for the presence of another human being.

With no chance of stopping himself, he moved one step closer to Kate. Sweat broke out across his top lip.

'Oh, it's fabulous!' She swept in ahead of him, into the large, open space. His heart pounded against his ribs and he forced his feet into action. Alan had rallied some volunteers to tow his father's car away and help clean the garage out after his death. Only the mayor had known the significance of what they were doing. The resulting space was clean, empty and entirely innocent of the terrible thing that had happened here. The garage was as much a victim of his father's decision as all of them.

It was due a reinvention.

'Will this do?' Only those who knew him best would spot the slight break in his voice.

'Do? It's perfect. It's fully plumbed.' Kate moved around the large space, checking out the features. 'It has a fridge.'

'Dad's old beer-fridge.' Beer and, for some reason, bowls of the most disgusting liquid covered in damp tea-towels and foaming away beneath a pancake layer of thick fungi. 'I think Dad was working on his own laboratory experiment in here.'

At Kate's quizzical look, he explained what he had found. Not when or why, but what.

Her face softened. 'Kombucha tea. I'm glad he finally gave it a try. I put him onto it.'

'What tea?'

'Kombucha. It's a fungus. It grows on the top and the tea below ferments and forms a naturopathic cider. It's good for you.'

'I can't imagine how. It looked and smelled disgusting. I imagine the only thing it was good for was the compost heap.'

Why the hell had a grumpy, acerbic old farmer been talking herbal recipes with a gorgeous greenie? How much had the man changed in twenty years? And what kind of a relationship had he had with Kate Dickson? Every conversation Grant had with her led him to imagine the two of them had been more than just business colleagues.

Friends.

Kate's enthusiasm for her new lab chased more of the shadows away from this place; she was just so excited. But still she turned to him, eager to give him a last chance, presumably.

'You're sure you don't want to use this for your Jeep?'

Not in a million years. 'It's all yours. Just don't blow anything up.'

'I think you're over-imagining what kind of work we do here. It's mostly microscopes and sifting.'

Ah, yes—the vomit. *Charming.*

Wide brown eyes turned to him. 'You're welcome to come in and have a look any time you want.'

He crunched his nose as she turned back to the mountainous boxes. 'Don't be offended if I pass.' For more reasons than one. He couldn't imagine himself ever getting comfortable in here.

Kate smiled as she hauled more boxes into the lab.

This really was perfect. She couldn't imagine why Grant wouldn't want to keep his precious car in here, but his loss was her gain. She'd downplayed the difference having an on-site lab would make to her program, because he was still so sensitive to their progress and because his offer really was a gift from the research gods. The truth was it would make an enormous difference to their ability to process samples and with the hours saved she could dedicate some time to searching up the coast for the seals' primary breeding-site.

All she needed was a boat. And someone to sail it.

How hard could that be to find in a fishing community? First chance she got, she'd head into town and see who she could rustle up. Things were beginning to go her way again. Kate could feel rightness returning to the world.

'So when do farming lessons begin?'

His voice was still tight but his body looked more relaxed than when he'd first entered. You'd have thought he was being escorted to the gallows. She'd given him one last chance to opt out if he was that reluctant to have her lab in his house—or maybe to help her project out, after all—but he hadn't taken it. And, although he'd been painful about helping her move her stuff in, he was certainly applying himself and all those compounding muscles admirably to the task. Super-quick, in fact. Like he couldn't wait to get out of here.

Kate sighed. It would be easy to trust him and believe that he had the Atlas colony's interests at heart; that he was trying to offer a compromise that meant they both got what they needed. But at the end of the day that was navïely futile. No way could they *both* walk away from this situation equally happy. Grant was going through the motions out of courtesy, but everything in his manner said he couldn't wait to be out of here. After the rocky start they'd had, courtesy was something, but just because she was starting to like the man didn't mean it was mutual.

This was Leo all over again. Look how long it had taken him to warm to her—although once he had it had almost been like becoming family. When the McMurtrie men bonded, they really bonded.

Which was not something she should be thinking in Grant McMurtrie's presence. Not when he stood between her and her nicely ordered world, her nicely ordered future.

So when *should* farming lessons begin—if at all?

'Without the travelling time I should have a few hours each evening,' she said carefully. Dinner. Conversation. The intricacies of sheep castration. Nice and neutral. 'Could that work for you?'

'Night school…' Jade eyes considered her. 'I like it. It'll fill those long evenings.'

Right. Another subtle reminder that this was business to him. As it should be to her.

'Would you mind if we postponed Friday night's tutorials? I was hoping to go into Castleridge.'

His reply was immediate. 'Into town? Sure. I'll come in with you.'

That brought her head around. 'Why?'

Charming lines furrowed his brow. 'Uh…'

Kate smiled. 'Getting used to the company, Grant?'

He slid one last box onto the work bench. 'Maybe I'm looking for a better class of company.'

She would have been offended if she'd thought for a moment that was true. While she might not be the best reader of men on the planet, she did know sharp conversation when she found it, and her discussions with Grant so far had been diverse and free-flowing. Almost scintillating. Especially when you threw in the healthy dose of chemistry that zinged around between the words.

In between remembering they were on opposite sides of this awkward situation.

Her smile widened into a full tease. 'Well, then, perhaps we'll both get lucky in that regard.'

He muttered something she couldn't hear but then decided she didn't want to. She'd kid herself a little longer that there was a mini-friendship brewing here; she wouldn't go bursting her own bubbles just yet. Life had a way of doing that for her—with terminal impact.

'I'll come along to keep you out of trouble with the locals.

They might not take kindly to a conservationist in their territory.'

Kate grinned. Finally something they agreed on. 'If there's something I know all about, it's territorial mammal behaviour. Especially the bulls.' She kept her gaze innocent and open, but his narrowed eyes told her she wasn't fooling anyone. 'Do you think we'll need some kind of secret signal if I get in trouble?'

'No need,' he assured her, a tasty twist to his full lips. 'I'll hear the sounds of the gallows being erected and come running.'

Kate bent for the final box of equipment. 'To help them with the finishing touches?'

His gaze smoothly shifted from her back end to her face as she straightened. 'That remains to be decided.'

She held a cupped hand to her ear and tipped her head towards the floor. 'Why, I do believe that's the sound of ice cracking in hell.'

His indulgent smile shouldn't have been steamy, but it was. Somehow teasing Grant was turning into a specialty of hers, even when she didn't mean to. How could it not be, with positive reinforcement like that? When she teased, he smiled. And those smiles were rewarding in a way she was only just beginning to understand.

'The only thing cracking around here is my back under the weight of these boxes,' he grumbled. 'What's in this stuff? Gold bullion?'

Kate paused a moment, deciding whether to let him retreat from their flirtatious exploration. But then reality came creeping back in and she realised that putting things back on a professional footing was not only wise but overdue.

Even if it was also a lot less fun.

Grant stood directly between her and her project. He was the man robbing her of the choices she'd worked so hard to assure, taking control out of her hands.

And no-one was doing that again.

No-one.

CHAPTER SIX

EVEN though they'd joked about the townsfolk stringing her up, Kate hadn't actually believed it would happen. But here she was, metaphorically at least, being marched to the gallows by the fishing fraternity of Castleridge. She'd come to find a man with a boat. What she'd got was a whole lot more complicated.

'Not a single hour free in the next month?' She gaped. 'Seriously?'

Joe Sampson was the fourth fisherman she'd tried. How could they all be busy?

'Not for the sort of job you want.'

Oh, here we go. 'You charter your vessel. Isn't a job a job?'

'Not around here, love. I can afford to pick and choose.'

Another person ripping options out from under her. 'So why are you choosing to turn down my charter?'

Joe turned his grizzled face and his beer breath her way. The whites of his eyes were stained as yellow as his nicotine teeth. 'I told ya. I'm busy.'

Kate narrowed her eyes and raised herself to her full height. She raised her voice, too. 'Not too busy to find time to get drunk with your mates, I see.'

Two of those mates laughed, booming, gusty guffaws; Joe Sampson turned and glared at them. When he came back to her, his eyes were sharp like a fox. 'That's right, love, I like a drink. The last sort of person you want driving you up the coast.'

She'd heard that about him. She planted her fists on her hips and glared at him. 'Beggars can't be choosers.'

His friends burst into fits of laughter again, one of them coughing and spluttering with the effort. Kate distantly wondered whether he'd ever tried kombucha for *his* lungs.

Out of nowhere, a steely hand closed around her upper arm and pulled her away from the fuming Joe Sampson. 'Kate,' a familiar, velvety voice said. 'Sorry I'm so late, got a call from the city. Let's get our table, shall we?'

The words triggered a delicious tingling through her body. She spun around to face Grant. Table? What was he doing here?

'She's a guest on your land, McMurtrie,' the old fella wheezed. 'And it's out of respect for your father that I haven't told her exactly what she can do with her request to charter my vessel.'

'Joe…'

Grant and the bar manager spoke at the same time but the older man wasn't deterred. 'Leo might've gotten himself all addled by a piece of city skirt, but not everyone is as easily swayed as he was.'

Kate spun around again, not sure which insult boiled her blood more. 'Easily swayed? Had you *met* Leo McMurtrie?'

Joe finally put down his beer, ready for a battle. 'I grew up with him, love.'

Then something else hit her. 'And I am *not* a piece of city skirt. I grew up in a town smaller than this one.'

'Good for you,' Joe snapped. 'Why don't you head back there? Your kind is not wanted here.'

Even his own mates stepped in then, taking Joe's beer from the bar and moving away from their seats as if he'd follow, pied-piper style. They underestimated him.

She straightened to her full height. 'Is that so?'

'Kate...'

Grant's warning was warm against her ear but she was too far gone to care. She ignored his plea and shot back at Joe. 'And what kind is that, exactly?'

The whole bar stopped to listen. People peered in from the dining area next door.

'You greenie mob. More interested in saving a bunch of thieving sea-dogs than the lives and livelihoods of the people living here.'

Grant's hand tightened further on her upper arm. He slipped his body closer to hers and tried to nudge her away from the bar with it.

Kate leaned around him. 'Those *sea-dogs* have more right to be here than you do. They've been fishing here for millennia.'

'Rubbish! I've been around a lot longer than you have, love, and there were hardly any when I was a boy. Just those few out on the McMurtrie farm.'

'That's because morons like you hunted them nearly to extinction. They're only just now getting back to—'

'Kate! Enough.' Grant physically pushed his way between the two opponents and forced her back a step.

'Get out of my way.' Her verbal warning was for Grant, but her narrowed gaze and her furious attention were all for the ageing fisherman at the bar. Although not so much she didn't feel the strength of Grant's body pushing back against hers.

He dropped his head low against her jaw and whispered warm against her skin, 'Don't do this, Kate. You're not going to do yourself any favours.'

Behind him Joe Sampson snorted. 'Oh, not another bloody McMurtrie man addled by a nice pair of legs,' he sneered, before turning back to the bar and speaking too loudly to be to himself. 'Or what's between them.'

Grant spun faster than Kate could blink and his body was hard up against Joe's. Both the old man's friends stepped in, hands raised, to head off the conflict. Joe stumbled backwards off his chair and looked every year of his considerable age.

Grant caught him and held him with the steeliest grip Kate had ever seen. 'Apologise.' His voice was low and hard, and she got her first inkling of what he might be like as a boardroom opponent.

'I'm not apologising to no city skirt.'

Grant shook the older man and spoke low and hard. 'I'm not talking about Kate. She can look after herself. Apologise for what you implied about my father.'

Kate held her breath. So did the rest of the pub.

Joe Sampson eventually dropped his gaze from Grant's. 'Yeah, all right. I shouldn't speak ill of the dead, I s'pose.'

Kate stepped up behind Grant and put her hand gently on his back, moral support, for what it was worth. He didn't even notice. Furious heat radiated through his shirt.

'My father negotiated access with Kate's team. As was his right on *his* land. Nothing more.'

'That we know of,' Joe threw out stupidly.

Grant's whole body tensed but one of Joe's mates stepped into the simmering tension. John Pickering, the one with the bushy beard. 'Look, I'll take her out. I don't mind,' he said.

Joe turned on his mate. 'Traitor!'

'Let it go, Joe. What's one boat trip to keep the peace?' Pickering looked past Grant at Kate. 'This has gone far enough. Take this as my way of saying sorry for not stopping it sooner. I'll take you out tomorrow afternoon if that suits. Half price.'

Kate just nodded dumbly. The bearded man matched it and then steered the belligerent Joe Sampson away from her. Grant straightened up but didn't turn back to her. He spoke quietly to the bar manager over the counter, who nodded and then wandered off to wipe down a surface at the far end of the bar.

Kate stared pointedly at Grant's back. Eventually, he turned and faced her. She lifted both eyebrows.

To his credit, he didn't even pretend to misunderstand. 'You would have made things so much worse.'

'You were right when you said I can look after myself. I don't need your help.'

'Kate, you were warming up to a bar fight. With one of Castleridge's longest-standing residents.'

'He's an idiot.'

'*Moron* I think was your professional estimation.'

Smiling now would be a mistake, but Grant with his super-solemn face was hard to take seriously. Her lips twitched.

'I'm serious, Kate. You could have ruined everything you've worked for.'

'By having a vigorous discussion on a subject I can argue convincingly in a room full of potential allies?'

He stopped and stared at her. 'You did it on purpose?'

'Not stir up Joe Sampson—although I'm glad I'm not getting on a boat alone with him now that I know what a misogynist he is. But it wouldn't hurt if word began to spread in town that the seals aren't threatening human fish-stocks.'

Green eyes blazed. 'You actually think that's a good idea?'

Whose side was he on? *Oh, wait...stupid question.* 'Why are you here?' she asked irritably.

'I told you I'd come if I heard the sounds of scaffolding being erected.'

'From the other room? You were supposed to be at the movies.'

'A man's got to eat.'

'Dine alone often, do you?'

He shrugged. 'It's Friday night. Always someone to meet.'

He looked entirely innocent. If he was lying, he was good at it. 'There really is a table?'

'There was. If you haven't got us banned.'

Kate smiled and followed him into the dining hall. All eyes

were on them, which barely registered, because her eyes were entirely on Grant.

Kate can look after herself.

Uncertainty nibbled. On one hand, it was enormously validating to have someone like Grant McMurtrie display such confidence in her ability to handle herself, after years of being talked down to as a pretty, young woman in the male-dominated scientific community. But, on the other hand, feeling Grant's hard body slide in between her and danger had generated a heady, primitive kind of rush, and the tingles it caused were still resonating. Kate stared at the back of those broad shoulders crossing the dining room and remembered how they'd shielded her from Joe Sampson.

She smiled. Or perhaps protected Joe from her.

'Table for two?' A tall, toothy waitress appeared from nowhere with two menus. She gave Kate an approving wink before placing the menus on a neatly laid table and parting on, 'Hope the company's more agreeable in here.'

It couldn't be hard. Still, for all the drama, at least she was walking away with a boat and someone to captain it. So something positive had come from the evening.

A few moments later they were settled and seated and everyone in the bar had gone back to minding their own business. Mostly. Kate could feel Joe Sampson's malevolent stare on her back from across the adjoining bar-room. Her heart slowly got back to its normal rhythm.

'So, you weren't kidding about being farming blood. You're a country girl,' Grant said by way of a conversation-starter.

Kate looked up. 'Sunbrook. We ran dairy, mostly, but had sheep and some alpacas.'

'What happened to the stock when you moved to the city?'

'Sold, apparently.'

'Apparently?'

Her hands tightened under the table. 'I never asked. I never wanted to know. Two of those alpacas were like pets to me.'

Grant shook his head. 'And no-one asked your permission? Asked you what you wanted?'

Defensiveness surged through her for the people who'd been left with the awful task of sorting out her life. The people who'd done their best. But deep down she knew that Grant only voiced the same question she'd had her entire adult life. How hard would it have been to ask her what she needed?

She shrugged and studied the menu. 'I was twelve. What was I going to say? There was no way Aunt Nancy would have moved onto the farm, so what choice did I have?'

Conversation stalled while they ordered meals and their drinks arrived—a tall beer for Grant and a wine and soda for Kate.

'It's funny,' he finally said, breaking the silence. 'While I was doing everything I could to get out of this place, you would have given your life to go back to your farm.'

Kate sipped carefully then lowered her glass. 'I still would.'

'Did you ever go back?'

She'd driven south especially to see it a few years back but, even with the shielding of time past, it hurt too much. 'Only once. I couldn't bear to see someone else's children climbing my trees. Someone else's washing on Mum's line.' Her voice cracked slightly and she took another sip. He hadn't touched his beer; his attention was completely on her.

'What did you do with the money?'

'Most of it went back to the bank to pay off the agricultural loan. Some of it went to Nancy for taking me in. What little was left I got when I was eighteen. I used it as a down payment on my apartment.' She folded her hands on the table and leaned towards him. 'Grant, why are you selling Tulloquay? I completely understand your desire to keep it in one piece, but why sell it at all? Why not lease it, or get a caretaker in? Keep it in your family?'

His lips thinned. 'What family?'

That was right; he had as little as she did now that his father was gone. 'Your future family. Someone should look after it. Until you need it.'

'Angling for a new job, Kate?'

She didn't laugh. 'No. But I would give anything for a chance to come back to country living, to have something to call my own: land. A future. A home. I can't understand how selling it is better than keeping it. Even if you kept it empty.'

'An empty farm is soulless, Kate. I'd rather see a stranger take it and make it great than let it run fallow.'

Her heart softened. She considered not voicing her thoughts. 'Every now and again I look at your face and I see Leo staring back at me.'

He stiffened.

'I meant that as a compliment, Grant. He was a complicated but dedicated man. And he was determined to strengthen Tulloquay, to keep it relevant.'

'Then he should have left it to someone else.'

'Because you're not interested?'

'Because I'm not a farmer.'

'That's not the first time you've said that. Do you think farmers are born knowing what to do?'

'They're raised. Trained.'

She frowned at him. 'Leo didn't teach you?'

He thought about that long and hard, staring into his beer. Eventually he lifted his head. 'I didn't want to learn.'

The dark shadows in his eyes called out to her. 'You didn't want the farm—even then?'

'I didn't want my future mapped out for me. If he'd said he wanted me to go into the army, I probably would have wanted to be a farmer. He pushed too hard.'

The two lines that creased his forehead told her he'd said more than he meant to. She nodded. 'I can see that. He had a very forceful way about him. Particularly after he… Well, at the end there. When he thought he was out of time.'

Grant's forehead creased further. 'What do you mean?'

Kate rushed in to fix her insensitive gaffe. 'I'm sorry. I just meant that he must have felt the pressure following his diagnosis. The urgency to get things in order.'

Grant's face bleached in a heartbeat. His body froze.

Kate's stomach squeezed into a tiny fist. *Oh please, Leo... Please have told your son...*

His already deep voice was pure gravel. 'What diagnosis?'

Kate's eyes fell shut. 'Grant, I'm so sorry. I had no idea you—'

'Kate!' The bark drew stares from the other diners. 'What diagnosis?'

Empathy bubbled up urgently. Memories of that awful discussion in her principal's office bled through her. Memories of Mrs Martin's pale face. Her shaking fingers, having to break a child's heart with unspeakable news.

She groaned. 'Grant...'

'Tell me, Kate.'

'Lung cancer.' The words rushed out of her. 'Terminal.' She took a deep breath. 'You didn't know?'

Grant's chest rose and fell roughly and his gaze dropped to the table.

Damn you, Leo... To tell a stranger and not his son...

She reached across the table and slid her fingers around Grant's icy ones. His Adam's apple worked furiously up and down as he struggled to compose himself. Her focus flicked nervously around the dining room and caught the cheerful waitress as she smiled her way towards them with two steaming meals balanced carefully on her forearm. Kate's eyes flew wide and she shook her head subtly.

Effortlessly, the waitress spotted it, interpreted the tension at the table, turned on the balls of her feet and whipped the meals back into the kitchen. Kate had a horrible feeling they wouldn't be eaten tonight—at least, not by them. She slid

Grant's untouched beer towards him. Then she just waited, her fingers still wrapped tightly around his. He clutched them back, holding on tight.

Holding himself together.

'Are you ok, Grant?'

When he finally lifted his shaking head, his colour was back but his eyes had faded. 'I didn't know, Kate. I'm sorry that you had to…' His words ran out.

Tears prickled embarrassingly behind her eyes. She shook her head, unable to speak.

He seemed to realise where his fingers were and he gently extracted them, sliding them into his lap, dragging the napkin with them to disguise their trembling. Distancing himself.

Kate cleared her throat. 'He told me last August—in case anything happened to him. Because I was on the farm so often.' It sounded exactly as lame as it was.

He told me. But not you.

'Something did happen to him. But you weren't there.'

Kate's eyes dropped, her guilt surging back. 'No. I was on a conference. It was terrible timing.'

His frown was tortured and angry at the same time. 'You weren't his nurse. He wasn't your responsibility.'

'He was my friend.' Grant's loud snort drew more eyes. 'You doubt me, but you weren't there.'

His eyes blazed. 'I had a life to lead.'

She gentled her tone and didn't bite. The man was suffering enough right now. 'I meant you weren't there to judge the friendship. But clearly you two weren't—' she changed direction at the last second '—in touch, so he told…a friend. I imagine Mayor Sefton knows, too.'

Grant's nostrils flared wildly and his eyes darkened. 'If he does, he'll have some explaining to do.'

Kate frowned. This was more than just a horrible surprise. Grant was really struggling. What did he think his father had died of? 'Let me take you home, Grant.'

His distracted eyes scanned the dining room. 'Our meals…'

'I'll make you something at home.'

She stood and held out a hand to him; it hovered, ignored, in space and Kate fought the flush that rose as she let her fingers drop back to her side. The gesture had been automatic, but now, more than ever, was the last time a man like Grant McMurtrie would accept a gesture like that from her. Yet his world had just imploded so very publically and he was desperately trying to pull himself together.

She softened her voice. 'Come on.'

He stood unsteadily on his feet and dropped a handful of notes—way too much for what they'd ordered—on the table. Kate smiled an apology to the waitress through the servery window and led Grant out into the cool night.

At the car she stopped him. 'Keys.'

'I'll drive.'

'You'll drive us into a ditch. I have a research study to finish and I imagine you have—' she suddenly faltered '—someone to get safely home to when this is all over.'

He tossed her his keys with an accuracy that suggested he was quickly recovering his wits. 'No someone. No family. Not now.'

Lord, did she sound that morose when speaking of her long-dead family?

'Well, aren't we just a pair of poster children for "misery loves company"?' she offered lightly. It seemed to work; his face defrosted a hint more. She pulled open her door. 'In the car, McMurtrie.'

Grant desperately needed a few minutes in the darkness to gather his composure. He slid into his passenger seat and sank into the familiar, comfortable leather, breathing deeply.

Cancer. Lung cancer.

A whole bunch of things flashed through his mind and suddenly made sense: Alan's awkwardness when Grant had mentioned the stink of tobacco in his father's house. The freaky, hippy health-concoction in his beer fridge. The fact he'd more or less got his affairs in order before…

Grant took a deep breath.

He'd even waited until Kate was away before taking his life. He glanced at the face, so serious with concentration, watching the road ahead. Had Leo not wanted such a gentle woman to find him? To discover the horror? He was willing to bet big bucks that his father wouldn't have expected his only son to find him, either, in a million years. Grant had a sinking suspicion he'd been counting on his old mate Alan Sefton to do the honours.

Cancer.

It had had nothing to do with Kate's project or the land grab. Something very close to relief rushed through him, stumbling and falling over the latent grief still clogging his arteries. He should have been here. He should have made more than one call a year. He should never have let so many years go by. And neither should his father.

I see Leo staring back at me. Were they truly that similar? Would he end up grumpy and alone and sick enough to end it all? There wasn't much else stopping him, just his work. Just the same rigid discipline about his job that his father had had. That Kate had.

He cleared his throat and turned to the woman whose hands gripped the steering wheel brutally. She knew, first hand, how he was feeling yet she hadn't taken advantage of his weakness. She'd just been there for him. Is that the kind of quality his father had seen in his young friend's character?

He cleared his throat. 'Kate, thank you.'

Her eyes flicked to his, wide and anxious. 'How are you?'

He nodded slowly. 'I'll survive.' She wanted to ask something. He could see it in the way her teeth worried her lips. 'Go ahead, Kate. Ask.'

The words practically exploded from her. 'Did it not say on the certificate—the cause of death? Or did you not see it?'

His chest tightened up. Could he tell her? She and Leo had been friends. 'I saw it,' he answered carefully.

'Yet tonight was still a surprise?'

Anxiety ravaged her sweet face. Knowing would only hurt her, and lying couldn't hurt Leo. Or him; not any more. Yet he couldn't let her go on feeling bad for letting the truth slip, either. He reached over and slid a hand onto her cool arm.

'I'm glad you told me. Imagine if you hadn't…'

Her brows dropped and she thought about that. 'I just…I would have approached it so much more carefully if I'd known. Obviously,' she finished flatly and shook her head.

'It hasn't been the best night for you—assaulted by the local fishing mafia, accosted by me and now digging your way out of the deepest of social *faux pas*.'

Kate's laugh shriveled. 'Oh no; that's pretty typical of a Dickson night out. It's why I prefer to stay in.'

'Well, looks like you've got your wish.'

She hit the indicator and turned off the highway into Tulloquay's long access-road.

'It feels weird, coming here at night.'

But also strangely right. Grant had the sudden flash of them driving home from a night out at the community centre, grey and old, chatting about town affairs, about their grandchildren. Their hands old and weathered, tightly entwined. Just like his father must have always wished for with the wife he had lost so young.

And then to lose a son, too…

They didn't speak until Kate pulled up in front of the house. She killed the ignition and then turned to peer at him from the half-shadows. 'What did he die of, Grant?'

Damn her intuition and her curiosity. 'Kate…'

'I've been thinking about it all the way home. I assumed it was the cancer—but there should have been hospitals, a decline.

His lungs weren't really any worse when I saw him the week before.' Beautiful brown eyes appealed to him. 'Please, Grant. I know you must not want to talk about it but the question is going to eat at me.'

He studied her hard. No matter what he said, she was going to sit on her guilt for not being here. That Leo had died alone. The same guilt he was nursing. 'It was the cancer, Kate.'

Tears filled doe eyes. 'You're lying—which means it was worse. Was it his heart? Did something happen to him? Was he hurt?'

Her anxiety was only going to increase if he didn't put an end to this. He tightened his lips and swore inwardly. 'Did Leo ever lose stock?'

Thrown off-balance momentarily, she blinked back at him. 'Sure. Sometimes. He hated finding them out in the paddock, suffering. He hated shooting them, too, but he did what he had to do.'

'He never could abide anything suffering. Any*one*.'

Kate frowned and waited for him to continue, but in his steady, loaded silence her beautiful face blanched and the liquid wash of her eyes spilled over as she pieced together Leo's puzzle.

'He did what he felt he had to do, Kate.'

She fought so hard to keep from losing it in front of him, almost visibly willing those tears back under the privacy of her eyelids. But she couldn't sustain it; they leaked, unauthorised, down her face. Grant cursed and reached out to gently curl his hand around the back of her neck. She let herself fall into the support of his shoulder. Immediately his nostrils filled with the scent of clean, unadorned woman. Even going into town, Kate hadn't broken the no-perfume rule. Her hands slipped up to control her descent, one curling around his bicep and the other bracing on his chest. They burned through his wool-blend sweater and branded his skin, setting off a chain reaction of tingles.

But his hormones weren't his priority right now.

He threaded his fingers through the thickness of her hair and pressed her against his shoulder, murmuring comforting sounds. She wasn't a sobber, but her silent tears were almost worse. They matched her perfectly—stoic and dignified.

'I should be comforting, you,' she mumbled between tight shudders.

'It is comforting, knowing he had a friend who would cry like this for him. Honour him.'

She sniffed. 'I hate that he felt he had to do it, but I understand why.' Grant stroked her hair. 'Maybe it was the last thing he could control—how he left us?'

Us. That sounded way too good on Kate's tear-puffed lips. His eyes lingered on them—fuller and redder than usual—even in the half-darkness.

The tears surged back. 'He was so difficult,' she squeezed out. 'But so lovely.'

'I know,' he murmured against her hair.

Except he didn't. 'Lovely' was not a word he ever would have associated with his father.

'It's like losing Dad all over again,' she croaked.

Nothing she said could have cut him more deeply. Here was a woman who would give anything to have her father back, to have a farm to call her own, to have sheep and alpacas and… bloody seals. And he'd thrown it all away decades before, as though it had no value.

To him, it hadn't.

'I was born into the wrong family,' he murmured, not really expecting her to hear. She curled her fingers tighter in his sweater and it was strangely reassuring. 'I bet you would have traded with me in a heartbeat.'

She nodded silently against his chest. His next words crawled out of his deepest subconscious. 'I might have stayed if you'd been here.' Tear-streaked eyes raised to his, but she didn't speak. She just studied him in that all-seeing way of hers. His explanation was more for his own benefit than hers. She wasn't asking anything of him, not tonight. 'Having someone who I could connect with—identify with—it would have helped.'

'Helped how?' It was more hiccup than anything else.

'Made me feel less alien.'

Her sympathetic hand slid up to his shoulder. 'You didn't feel like you belonged here?'

Not until this month. 'Never.'

Kate sighed, long and deep. 'So sad. We've both lost so much of our lives.'

Somewhere deep in his brain he knew what she meant—that they'd both suffered loss. But the words echoed around the car, blew a trail through her loose hair, mingled with the wholesome scent of Kate, and all he could think about was not wasting one second more…

His left hand cupped the back of her head more comfortably and his right pressed against her cheek and tipped her face up towards his. He knew then that he'd been thinking about this for days—specifically *not* thinking about this for days. About how she would feel. How she would taste.

How she would react.

But she surprised him. Although her body stiffened against his initially, she didn't pull back as he lowered his mouth gently onto hers. It was soft and salty from her tears, but full, honest and courageous like the woman it belonged to.

Kate's head spun a lurching figure of eight at his closeness. His strong, distinctive cologne seemed to shimmy around her like scent released from the heat of a candle. She held herself suspended, lips gently parted against his first touch, assessing, and then leaned infinitesimally towards him, gently increasing the pressure of their kiss. Heat burst through her and crackled out to lick at the place their lips joined. Her mouth slid across his, tasting, breathing his air, melding perfectly.

He nipped and nibbled, sucking her bottom lip between his, then releasing it to slide across the neglected top lip. His big hands forked up through the waves of her hair, messing it around her face until it hung, wild and natural, like it sometimes did at the end of a long day on the rock-shelf.

She pulled back to gaze into eyes darkened with green heat. His thumbs learned the delicate line of her cheekbones and rubbed the last of the tears from her damp lashes.

She sucked in a breath to speak, but he slid one thumb down to silence her lips, closing the gap between them and taking her mouth with his again. It blazed against hers, his tongue hot, confident and branding its possession. Her skin burned wherever it rubbed against his which, squeezed as they were in the front of his car, was just about everywhere.

Her breath grew thin and desperate deep in her chest, but freeing herself for air was the last thing on her mind. Grant's hands slid down over her shoulders and found their way to the sides of her ribs and under her arms. Then he pulled her more comfortably against him, sliding himself sideways to give her more room, freeing her to climb that masculine chest and latch on more firmly to his talented lips.

Heavy eyes simmered into hers and Kate suddenly grew shy, uncertain. His large, work-roughed hand stroked up her throat to rest under her chin and encourage her gaze back to his.

'You will always look like this to me,' he murmured thickly, kissing her brow, her jaw, her lips. Making her lashes fall to her cheeks. 'Wild. Hot.'

Kate let her head fall back and Grant mouthed his way up her throat. Just as well she was lying half-across him, because there was no way she could have kept standing. Feelings she'd begun to think she'd forfeited for life came surging forth in sharp, exquisite lances deep in her body. Her fists clenched high on his open-necked sweater, giving her strength but letting her fingers spread to tangle in the scattered hair there, against the furnace that was his flesh. The forbidden feeling of the skin she'd tried not to ogle that first day made her smile and Grant's lips moved instantly to the deep dimple that formed on her left cheek.

His tongue dipped in and out, his smooth teeth sliding against her cheek as he matched her smile. 'I've wanted to touch those since I first saw you.'

Not that she wasn't unexpectedly thrilled to hear such sentiments but, while she was busy making sense of words, she wasn't drowning in the pleasure sensations of his body moving against hers. His mouth feasting on hers. She speared her fingers up into his short hair and forced his head back so she could glare into his eyes meaningfully. 'That's lovely, but you want to talk or you want to kiss?'

His answer was practically a growl.

And then it was on—both of them clamouring for the best position, the most access, surging, devouring and consuming each other. Grant reached down to the side of his seat and activated the recliner and both of them mechanically lowered until they stretched almost into the back seat. Kate lay across Grant's chest, along his straining body; his hands had free access, at last, to the rest of her. They slid up and down her length, from shoulder to hip, rib to thigh, learning her contours. Blood rushed, thick and molten, through her arteries keeping her hyper-sensitive cells acute and full of oxygen, and keeping her grey matter thoroughly distracted about what the rest of her was doing.

And with whom.

Then suddenly, with no warning, the vehicle shot forward with a lurch.

Kate managed to suck in a breath and expel a scream at the same time. Grant yanked on the handbrake, crunching into Kate's hip painfully, and then jammed the automatic gearstick into park position. Dimly, between the heaving breaths she drew in, she realised she'd pushed the automatic vehicle into gear with her hip as she crawled more fully onto Grant's prone body.

Oh my God...

Heat surged into her cheeks as the full picture they presented finally dawned on her: sprawled out in his Jeep like a pair of sexed-up teenagers, her dress hiked up, shoes kicked off. She reached blindly for the steering wheel, anchored herself to it to haul herself back into the driver's seat and then sat, puffing, as Grant moved his seat back up into the upright position.

Reality ran in rivulets down the car's windows where they'd seriously fogged them up in the hot, sultry minutes that had just passed. Kate cracked her door open and sucked in the cold night air. There were two ways out of this and neither of them offered much in the way of a dignified exit. She could cry foul and leap from the car with indignation or she could be flippant about what had just happened and try to extract herself with as much dignity as possible, as though she did this kind of thing every day.

Or she could just be honest.

'Holy cow.'

Grant's lifted eyebrows and equally stunned expression told her she'd spoken for them both. He blew out a long, controlled breath. Kate fumbled for the door handle then paused when she found it.

'Will you walk me to the door?' *Assuming I can walk at all...*

His sexy smile made her want to fling his seat back again, but she contained herself.

'I have to,' he said. 'It's my door too.'

Kate frowned. 'Can we... Could you give me a few minutes' head start? Let me maintain the illusion?'

His smile was pure indulgence. 'Sure. I could use a few minutes in the dark anyway.'

Everything in her wanted to look down, but she hadn't made

it to the top of her field without having *some* self-discipline—even if it seemed to be largely AWOL tonight. She kept her eyes locked on the front door where the little welcome-home light glowed.

'We never had dinner,' she said simply, running shaking hands through her hair to tame it.

His smile twisted up on one side. 'We can eat tomorrow.'

She turned her eyes to his, certain they'd be as wide and dazed as she felt. 'Are you going to want to talk about this?'

His face grew serious. 'Not tonight. Let *me* maintain the illusion.'

Kate's smile was half-hearted as she pushed open the car door. A wall of frigid air rushed in, dousing the last of the latent flames. Grant climbed out behind her and caught her up near the steps to the house. He followed her up onto the verandah and paused with her under the light. His hand came up to stroke a lock of hair back from her flushed face.

'Well, goodnight, Kate. I can't say the first part of the evening had much to recommend it, but the last part certainly surpassed all my expectations.'

The blush returned furiously. But he wasn't making fun of her. 'Me, too.'

'Can I kiss you goodnight?'

The gentle request touched her deep down inside where no-one went. After everything they'd just done… Still, she nodded.

In slow motion, his hands came up to softly frame her face. He shifted closer; the warmth from his body hadn't diminished at all since getting out of the warm car and she leaned into the heat. His lips, when they finally lowered to hers, were chaste and respectful but trembled with barely repressed passion.

If it had been their first kiss, she might have passed out. But, despite the fact she'd just been crawling across his lap, giving him a manual tonsillectomy, his simple kiss still made every cell in her body sing out.

'Goodnight,' she whispered as he finally lifted his head. Her tongue slipped out to taste the last moment.

Grant groaned. 'Go now or I'm coming in with you.'

That got her feet moving. She opened the house door and slipped quietly in. Behind her, Grant moved to the balustrade of the verandah. He was seriously letting her go inside alone. He turned just as she swung the door closed and she captured the look like a photograph in her memory.

Hot. Bothered. Confused.

But mostly hot.

And that bothered her very much.

It took her just minutes to strip out of her dress and into her warm pyjamas. She didn't dare go out into the bathroom to brush her teeth or her tingly body would keep walking and end up in his room—and that was not a good idea. But sliding straight into warm sheets with un-brushed teeth meant that she could fall asleep with the taste of Grant still on her lips. Could enjoy the kiss—and him—just a little longer. That would guarantee they'd both populate her dreams.

Which was pretty much where she should quarantine any further contact between the two of them.

If someone had told her heading into town tonight that she'd wind up wrapped around Grant McMurtrie with her dress hiked high, she'd have laughed— Possibly fantasised about it for a week, but still laughed. They just didn't have that kind of relationship. Even if, for a few precious minutes tonight, they'd offered a cracking impersonation of it.

She let her breath out in a carefully controlled sigh.

It was just sex. They'd both been overwhelmed with emotion tonight after she'd so horribly blabbed about Leo's cancer. And when emotions got bubbling, so did tension, and it had found a natural physical outlet in the front seat of his car. The man was sex on a stick, and he had a dangerous effect on her good judgement even during the day when he wasn't even standing particularly close. Tonight, she'd had no chance.

She touched her still-tingling lips.

Staying put was more than just a good idea—it was vital. Grant was actively trying to hamper her project. Trying to keep Tulloquay intact and sell it to someone who would farm it, as Leo had before he'd got sick. Trying to keep it a working farm. Which wasn't in the seals' best interests.

Kate punched her down-pillow to make it more comfortable and burrowed into it. On the other hand, he'd given her lab space and a room, and had followed her to the pub to make sure she didn't get into any trouble.

She frowned into the darkness.

Those weren't the actions of a man who was entirely indifferent to her.

She heard the click of the front door, exaggerated in the night silence, and realised he'd been as good as his word, giving her a head start so they could both pretend their night had ended more like a traditional date.

And less like a steamy, irrevocable mistake.

CHAPTER SEVEN

THIS had seemed easier when he was nine.

Grant shoved hard at the bracken and thick scrub that barred his way and used his shoulder to bully his way through the tangle of branches. Sure, there'd been over twenty-five years for the coastal scrub to grow thicker, but…

Come on…. He shoved again. Harder.

A branch struck back, whipping high across his cheekbone and making him glad for the thick sunglasses he hadn't removed. Another snared his T-shirt, grabbing hard and tearing a small hole.

Of course, it probably would have helped if he'd had some decent shut-eye last night. Even plant life seemed too complicated this morning, after the revelations of yesterday. After hitting on Kate…

He paused midway through the bracken and asked himself for the third time if this was worth it. But, yeah, he needed to know if his suspicions were correct.

It would change everything.

He pushed onwards. His foot felt the change of land but—just in case he missed the signs—gravity sent him on a slow, gravelly slip for a few feet; those thick bushes gave him something to grab onto. They slowed his slide and let him gently lower himself to a more familiar feature.

The pathway. Unless twenty-five years of erosion had taken a toll, then this little trail would take him right down to the flat area near the water. Not a Sunday stroll, exactly, but doable. Lucky he'd kept himself in hiking condition instead of boardroom condition or this would have been a whole heap harder.

He might not have bothered.

It took around ten minutes for Grant to pick his way carefully down the ageing trail in the brutal cliff-winds. It levelled out at the base and he looked left and right, saw some familiar landmarks and remembered. Definitely right. For another ten minutes he worked his way carefully across an expanse of large, ancient rocks, with bigger waves occasionally soaking his boots. The same curled spit of land that obscured this spot from view from the sea stopped it getting hammered by the ocean's force.

No wonder the seals loved it here.

No wonder he had, when he was a boy. If ever there was a spot destined for buried treasure and ruined pirate-ships, this was it.

A moment later and he was there. Stepping into the comparative darkness of the cove, overhung by a limestone canopy older than mankind, he lifted his sunglasses and let his eyes adjust before climbing up higher on the rocks and sliding down behind the cover of a large boulder. It was only dim but, after the bright glare of the limestone cliff-face, his pupils were the size of pin-heads. And, after what had happened the last time he'd been here, he wasn't taking any chances. He'd been young enough to be curious and stupid enough to be careless, but swift enough to get away safely when two-hundred kilos of angry, sexed-up bull seal had come lurching towards him, hell bent on seeing off the interloper. Or possibly killing him. Who knew how bull seals thought?

Kate probably did.

Kate…

The woman he'd snuck out on in the early hours of this morning, delaying the inevitable moment when they would talk about what had happened the night before. He'd faked important work on the far side of the farm—as though she'd buy for one minute that anything that important could be fixed by the anti-farmer—and had taken off like a thief in the night just as the sun had wiggled its golden fingers over the eastern horizon. Because it had been easier than facing her after he'd kissed her last night. Because it had been easier than thinking about how much that kiss had rattled him. Excited him.

Centred him.

He couldn't afford to be centred by Kate Dickson. He had a legal partnership that needed all his attention and a full life in the city to lead. Never mind that his partnership tended to take up most of his life or that, increasingly, a night in with a good book was about all he had energy for at the end of a long day.

A Technicolor image intruded into his mind: Kate curled up at the opposite end of his enormous modular sofa, her lip between her teeth, lost in something on her laptop while he read the latest bestseller. If he stretched out an imaginary foot he could just about touch hers…

He shook the image loose.

Kate was farming stock. It didn't matter where she lived or what she did; farming was either in your blood or it wasn't. And in his case it wasn't, even though technically it was. That was more than enough reason not to get involved. Plus, he wasn't good relationship material, as so many women had found out over the years. He'd been wedded to his work for a decade.

Not that she was exactly picking out engagement rings. She'd thrown herself into that kiss with as much gusto as he had, but she knew full well how different they were and how they stood at polar ends on the issue of Tulloquay and the seals. At least, she thought she did.

She had no idea what these seals *actually* meant to him. What sanctuary they'd offered him as a child. That they were important to more than one person for more than one reason.

But not necessarily as important as keeping his farm intact.

It was yet another of those moments in life when you realise you can't have everything. That you have to choose priorities.

He was choosing the farm. She was choosing the seals. And she was fighting hard for them.

The state Conservation Commission was already interested in her colony. If he knew her at all well, Kate would be banking on them ratifying conservation protection on the strength of her partially completed research alone. But, on her own admission, her request would carry more weight if she could sweeten the pot with a site of extra significance—a breeding site, for instance.

A secret breeding site, for instance.

A site pretty much like this one.

Grant peered around the large boulder to see who was home. Two bull seals and a number of smaller females lounged around, barely noticing his presence. Both bulls sported bloody, superficial wounds but their relaxed posture told him neither animal had been serious about killing the other. Only one of them lay near the females—the victor. The one who had won mating privileges. The other, stretched out on its back, its small flippers waving in the gentle cliff-base breeze, looked like it was just all too hard.

He sighed.

No question about it—this was Kate's breeding site. What she needed to put all the pieces of her puzzle neatly together and change the way the town, the government—the world—thought about fur seals. What she needed to guarantee a conservation zoning on his land.

His eyes fell shut. What she needed, he couldn't give her.

In so many ways.

The lab was one thing, something he could do to help her that wouldn't really make much of a difference in the long term. Something he could give her to help take some of the weight off her shoulders.

But handing her the ammunition to make sure no serious

investor would ever want Tulloquay? Not an option. He may be the lousiest farmer ever to grace the south-west, but the last useful thing he could do for his father would be to find someone who would love the farm as much as Leo had. And to do that he had to have something worth selling.

And, as the incident at the pub last night had made entirely evident, there weren't too many folk in Castleridge who thought the words 'seal' and 'worth' had any relation to each other.

Except maybe his father. He'd been so convinced that his dad had filled his lungs with carbon monoxide rather than face losing, to greenies, the farm he'd spent his life building up. But it turned out his lungs had been filled with something much more sinister all along—the same disease he'd lost his wife to when Grant had been little, although a different organ. No way strapping Leo McMurtrie was going to let himself grow as weak, frail and airless as his beloved wife had.

Opting out must have seemed the most humane option.

And, for a seventy-year-old man living alone three hours from his only family, maybe it had been.

Grant let his lids flutter closed and finally allowed the blocked out memories to gurgle to the surface: those idyllic early years before Leo had grown disappointed with him, before Grant had discovered the father he worshipped had clay feet. Back when he still had a mother, the first happy years of his life. Just a man and wife blissfully in love and the young son they'd tried so hard for growing into the man he would one day be.

At least the man they'd wished he'd be.

Go on then, go! You've added no real value to this farm, so it might as well run without you.

That awful last day when Grant had packed his bags and prepared to leave for good shoved its way into his memory: the mottled red of his father's anger. The hurt in his eyes.

If I'd known what sort of a kid you'd turn into, I wouldn't have encouraged your mother to try so hard to have you. Maybe she'd still be with me today.

Old anger sliced sharply below Grant's ribs.

Even as a sixteen-year-old he'd recognised the pain in his father's words, but they'd burrowed down and festered in his subconscious nonetheless. Maybe there were drugs his mother could have taken if she hadn't been pregnant, or therapies. Maybe being pregnant *had* drained her of the life-force she needed to fight off the disease that eventually took her life. He'd wondered about that often enough, growing up.

But to hear it so baldly from his father's angry lips…And then the final cut.

I would trade you for her in a heartbeat.

He forced his eyes open and stared down at the seals. Well, he had his wish now. Somewhere up in heaven Leo McMurtrie and the love of his life walked the land hand-in-hand once again. Hard to know whether a lifetime alone might have mellowed his father; if not, he had a whole after-life to find out whether he was capable of it.

Grant turned away from the peaceful seals to face the steep climb back up the long, narrow track. The treacherous, torturous climb in gale-force winds suited his mood perfectly. Somehow he'd made such a mess of all of this, despite his best efforts. Kissing Kate was just one more in a series of questionable decisions.

But as he turned to cross the shore towards the pathway back up the cliff, something small caught his eye. One of the females had a bloodied patch between her shoulder blades—not surprising, if childhood memories of graphic seal-mating served him well—but a few feet from her he could see something out of place, about the size of a pack of cards. Black. Durable.

Expensive.

Kate's time-depth recorder. Her assistants carefully clipped the fur below the TDR to remove it; clearly, bull seals weren't so courteous when they only had one thing on their minds. If the recorder had been sandwiched between a seal and two-hundred kilos of male, it might not even work. But he had to try and retrieve it. Those things were twenty grand each, she'd said, and Kate was responsible for them.

If she couldn't even afford a caravan to make their work easier, Grant was certain she couldn't afford to replace a twenty-thousand dollar electrical device.

Damn

The bull seals grunted, grumbled and rolled over in the gentle breeze. They were settling in for a decent post-coital nap. He had two options: wait it out and hope the males went for a restorative swim later, or make the treacherous climb back to his Jeep and then return later today, when there'd be no guarantees the group would have shifted at all. Or that more bulls wouldn't have appeared.

Or that the TDR wouldn't have been knocked off the rock shelf into the inky depths.

He glanced at his watch, knowing he'd miss Kate, who would be up and gone within the hour, but conscious of the value of the little device lying out in the open on the rocks. To her.

He backed out of the cover and climbed higher for protection and for a clear view of what the seals were doing. Then he crouched down to wait.

Stinking coward.

Never mind that she'd gone to bed without brushing her teeth rather than face him so soon; the fact she woken to an empty house and no decent morning-after conversation after she'd lain awake so long thinking up her part of it…

Not that it was the morning after much. A kiss, that was all. OK—a killer kiss. A kiss that definitely would have led to more if her butt hadn't intervened and sent the car lurching. Which would have made Grant's no-show act this morning doubly despicable, because intimacy only prevented by accidental gear-engagement still counted as intimacy by proxy. The intent had been there.

And they both knew it.

'Coward,' she mumbled again as she hauled on a pair of tight leggings to go under her baggy field-shorts, warding off the cooling weather. Never mind that she hadn't really perfected her blasé response before falling into a sweaty, turmoil-filled sleep—she deserved a chance to deliver it. Never mind that Grant being absent was about as effective a cool-off as she was ever going to get. Never mind that cooling off was what she wanted…

There was a principle at stake.

Decent men didn't kiss someone living under their roof and then leave them hanging. Who did that? Complicated men. Complicated, conflicted men. And who was the poster child for complicated and conflicted? Grant McMurtrie.

Today of all days.

Not only was she still heart sore from discovering the truth about Leo's suicide, and confused from the kiss she'd shared with his son, she was also thirty years old today.

Her toast popped in the kitchen. OK, she'd dallied as long as she could, hoping he'd return from wherever. She was now officially pathetic—thirty and pathetic. She wolfed down her toast, cleaned the kitchen quickly and threw her gear into the back of her ute. She had a full day ahead of her, after losing all of yesterday to the lab set-up. Her seals needed her attention.

The uncomplicated, unconflicted, comfortably predictable Atlas colony.

Who were all in attendance for once, she realised, emerging down on the rocks at Dave's Cove fifteen minutes later. Except for Stella, of course, but that was normal these days.

It was bad enough worrying that something had happened to one of the longest-standing members of the colony without also worrying about her twenty-grand TDR fixed to her back and possibly lying on the bottom of the ocean. Or in some shark's belly.

She worked steadily, alone, until a carload of her team arrived.

'Hey, Happy Birthday, old lady!'

Her lips tightened into the serene smile she'd spent a long time working on. 'Thank you, Artie. I can always rely on you to remind me when I'm getting older.'

Her field assistant chuckled and threw her a small parcel wrapped in tin foil. Kate stared at it, then at him.

'I believe it's customary amongst your kind to exchange a gift.'

'Amongst humans, you mean?' Artie was the result of puberty gone wrong, super-long legs and arms that gave him a rather alien appearance. He traded on it. 'I think you're finally learning to understand us,' she joked.

She unwrapped the gift as he recited an ode out loud for the amusement of the rest of the team. 'Things that are older than Kate…'

It was a triple-chocolate cake, small, with melted chocolate inside and the richest of chocolate icings outside. She'd had this before when Artie's mum had sent supplies to one of their most remote field locations.

She clutched it as though it was a bundle of precious gems and interrupted his oration. 'Artie, thank you!'

The whole team laughed. Every cell of her being wanted to just gobble the chocolate delight, regardless of what was on her hands, but she held off long enough to strip off her gloves, rub alcohol cleanser all over them for good measure and pour herself a steaming hot coffee from the flask.

Once that was done, the cake lasted about six seconds. It was as light, moist and to-die-for as the first one she'd ever had. She probably should have nibbled it. She probably should have savoured it. But after last night, she practically inhaled it.

Fuelled by cake, and feeling infinitely better surrounded by the relentless banter of her team, Kate got back to her sampling. Even the putrid collection couldn't spoil the happy feeling of a belly full of chocolate cake. She even forgot about Grant for a few minutes.

As they worked amongst the lazing seals and nearly mature pups, a large wave washed up and onto the rocks, bringing a mercury-slick mass with it.

'Stella!' Kate's heart lifted as she saw her long-missing female come lurching up the rock-shelf. She scrabbled the last of her sample into the bag and then tossed her stained gloves in favour of a crisp new pair. They snapped into place as she reached for the medical kit.

'She's wounded,' Artie needlessly pointed out; the blood was streaming from a wound on Stella's back.

Together, the team worked to isolate her from the other seals for treatment. She wasn't happy about it, but she lay still enough. Kate examined her thoroughly; the surge of blood had been caused by the movement of her powerful fore-muscles pushing her up onto the rocks and made worse by the water that streamed off her. On closer inspection, it wasn't more than a surface wound and some lost fur. No stitches were necessary, just some antibiotic gel.

But there was no escaping what had caused it. Kate's heart sank as life delivered one of its stomach-curdling twists: Stella's TDR was missing.

'That's an expensive haircut, girl,' she whispered, gently applying the gel and wondering whether they'd affixed the recorder badly, whether she'd snagged it while hunting along the reef edges or whether something bigger and nastier had torn it from her.

Whatever, it was not good.

Kate saw her research bonus shrivel before her eyes. Mind you, given that she wasn't likely to finish her study before Grant evicted her, even that was looking dicey. No completion bonus meant she'd have to sell her apartment to raise the money to cover the cost of the missing TDR, as per her contract. Her gut plunged.

'Hey.'

Then it flipped in on itself.

Oh, yay. Just when a birthday couldn't get any better.

Kate twisted her face up towards the deep voice. 'I hope you've come to pitch in. You've used your one free spectator-pass.'

Grant's eyes narrowed and he chose his words carefully—smart man. 'I can help, if you like.'

She released Stella, who eyed both her and Grant balefully and lurched off, back into the water. Given how long she'd been absent, and given how she'd been man-handled the moment she'd arrived, Kate knew it was likely she wouldn't see her again this season. And, under the circumstances, that meant ever. Her stomach squeezed.

She stood stiffly and glared at the most convenient outlet for her frustrations. 'You know what would help? Let me finish my research.'

'Kate…'

'Thought not.' She marched away from him to repack the medical kit carefully. 'Then I think my team has everything covered here. I'm sure you have a lot of things to do to get the farm ready to sell.'

In two months. Just a matter of weeks. Panic began to nibble at her spine. She wasn't ready. She wasn't done. Her research was sound but it wasn't complete. She'd been crazy to take her eye off the ball, to let her growing friendship with Grant influence her work. She should have fought harder. Should have pushed the Conservation Commission; maybe it wasn't too late.

Somehow the hurt expression on his face only infuriated her more. He was the one who had skipped out before talking everything through this morning.

'What?' she all but barked.

The hurt morphed into confusion, then something closer to amusement. 'I… You have…' He frowned at her mouth. 'Actually, I'm not sure what it is. You look a little like The Joker. Is that Vegemite?'

Kate's fingers rushed to her lips which tingled where his green gaze touched. She could feel the dark frosting that had marked her skin left and right of her mouth in a macabre chocolatey grimace. Heat flared up her neck and she scrubbed at the offending stain with her long sleeve.

'Kate and chocolate cake cannot co-exist simultaneously in time and space,' Artie helpfully piped up as he passed them *en route* to a nearby sample. 'It's a well-known scientific principle.'

'Cake.' Those eyes became carefully neutral. 'You guys celebrating something?'

He thought they'd had a research breakthrough. Kate could see a darkness lurking deep and it only served to reinforce how impossible their situation was. How opposed their positions were. 'Birthday, actually.'

'Whose birthday?'

She shook out a clean plastic sample-bag with a snap and turned to locate a convenient pile of ick. 'Mine,' she murmured.

He followed her, carefully stepping between the unfussed seals. 'It's your birthday?'

'Pretty sure we just covered that.'

'And you didn't think to mention that last night?'

She straightened on a huff and whispered furiously, 'When was the right time, Grant? Just after I told you your father had cancer? Or when you had your tongue in my mouth?'

Artie straightened and hurried his sample over to the storage hamper.

Grant's frown doubled. 'Are you always this caustic on your birthday?'

She slapped a sealed sample into his hands. 'No, Grant. I'm

not. In fact, I don't usually even do birthdays. Not since I was a kid.'

'Why not?'

'Because Aunt Nancy didn't believe in birthdays; she only marked obscure made-up observances no-one else had ever heard of.' And because Kate had stopped counting birthdays the year her parents had died.

'So, can I assume that this fine mood you are in today has something to do with me?'

Kate crouched for another sample, her lips as tight as her words. 'That's why you get the big bucks, McMurtrie.'

'You're angry that I wasn't there this morning.'

Bits of seal waste went flying as Kate flicked them fractiously into the sample bag, then she steadied herself and tried to collect the disparate particles, like a good scientist. She took her time, taking more care, and then stood and extra-carefully took the first sample from Grant. She glanced around. Her team was well occupied on the other side of the cove.

Too well-occupied. Clearly the excellent acoustics of rocky Dave's Cove had done its job.

She turned back to Grant and lowered her voice. 'I would have thought we had something to square off today.'

'I had something I had to...' Even he must have heard the lie in his voice. 'OK, yes. We should talk.'

She rounded on him. 'What makes you think I still want to?'

'Because you're a scientist. You don't like loose ends.'

Loose ends. 'Is that what I am?'

His eyes narrowed. 'Kate, what's going on? It's not like we slept together.'

In her periphery, her team got busier and practically climbed the cliff face trying to get further away from the two of them.

Great.

'I don't...' She pressed the heel of her hand into the space between her eyes, trying to dispel the tension headache thumping away there, then she lifted tired eyes to him. 'I don't trust easily, Grant. I wasn't prepared for you not to give a damn this morning.'

His focus dropped for a single breath then lifted back to hers. 'Kate, I'm sorry. I wanted to give you some space, and there was something I needed to...check.'

She lifted one miserable eyebrow.

'OK, look— I needed to think some things through too. Last night was not something I'd meant to happen and I wanted time to review it.'

'Looking for loopholes?'

'I don't need a loophole, Kate.' He said firmly. 'We don't have any kind of commitment—implied or otherwise.'

That stopped her cold. True enough; his kissing her wasn't a guarantee of anything further developing between them. It was just a result of the simmering chemistry between two people. Simple cause and effect, like all good experiments.

An experiment she'd been a willing participant in.

She sighed deeply. 'Grant, I'm sorry. I discovered I lost an expensive piece of equipment today, I don't like birthdays and I slept—" *barely a wink* "—badly last night. You should go. I'll see you later.' *She'd barely slept a wink.*

'Is this what you were looking for?'

Kate turned and nearly fell from the rush of blood to her body core. The TDR sat comfortably in Grant's large upturned palm. She took it from him with shaking fingers. 'Oh my God. Where did you...?'

'It was here when I came onto the rocks.'

She turned disbelieving eyes up to him. 'Here?'

He kept his gaze just shy of hers. 'Well, over there, actually, just as the path widens out.'

Six highly trained scientists had all missed a twenty-thousand-dollar piece of equipment lying on the rock shelf...?

The hairs on her neck shot up. 'Show me. Exactly.'

Grant frowned but turned back towards the path. As he got

close he veered closer to the edge of the water. He pointed vaguely in its direction. 'I guess it washed ashore.'

A tight ball grew in her belly. She lifted her eyes back to his and masked them carefully. 'Well, thank you. You just saved my apartment.'

'You're welcome. Will I see you at dinner?'

A tight breath squeezed through her. 'Sure.'

'We'll have something special. For your birthday.'

Her ponytail swung. 'I don't do birthdays.'

'For mine, then.'

Her head came up. 'Yours? When's that?'

'In a few months, but since neither of us will be here…' He seemed to realise, too late, what a dismal pronouncement that was. He let his eyes shift out over the ocean.

Kate swallowed back an ache. 'I'm going out on the boat this afternoon, to search for the breeding site. Not sure what time I'll be back.'

His face snapped back to hers. 'The boat—what time?'

She shrugged. 'Not sure. He only said afternoon.' They'd hot-footed it out of there before she could get concrete details from John Pickering.

'I'd like to come along—since you're searching my property,' he added, when she was about to decline.

What could it hurt? One more pair of eyes. She could ignore him as thoroughly as he'd ignored her this morning; that would be satisfying. 'I'll text you when we see the boat.' Any vessel from Castleridge had to pass Dave's Cove on its way to Tulloquay's jetty, closer to the homestead.

'OK. See you then.' Grant waved farewell to the rest of the team and turned to scale the access path, his long legs giving him a climbing advantage and taking him out of sight in no time.

Kate stared at the place he'd identified, at the two little starfish clinging to the rocks where the water surged on and off the granite shelf. At the pools of water left behind that couldn't drain away. Her eyes shifted to the TDR in her hands.

Bone dry. And not a shred of blood or fur on it. As though someone had carefully cleaned it up. Her eyes lifted to the path Grant had just disappeared up. Why would he?

And, if he had, why would he lie about it?

CHAPTER EIGHT

GRANT braced his legs against the roll and toss of the fishing boat *Nautilis* as the captain swung her around. They'd started twenty kilometres up the coast, just past Tulloquay's boundary line, and had chugged their way back towards Dave's Cove bay by disappointing bay.

Kate had grown more and more despondent as she meticulously notated a coastal map and ruled out every site they'd visited: too steep. Too barren. Too rocky. One was a maybe, given two seals lazed on the sandy shore, but they were both females, so Kate wasn't encouraged.

Grant had always had excellent sea-legs so the churning of his stomach had to be a mix of empathy for Kate's growing distress and nerves as they drew closer to the site he knew she was looking for. Alone, she wouldn't have been able to spot the disguised entrance from the sea. But a seadog like the captain; there was no question he'd see it. And he'd take Kate there.

Outside the bar and away from his grouchy mates, John Pickering was a pretty decent bloke and a good sailor. He chatted to Kate throughout the afternoon, sharing his experiences and listening genuinely to hers. The man wasn't about to join the Seal Protection Society, but he was definitely open to believing seals and humans hunted different fish species.

Which meant he was open to working hard to help Kate. He was no more immune to those enormous, optimistic eyes than Grant was.

'This is horrible.' Kate flopped onto the gunnel of the *Nautilis* next to him. 'And it's getting us nowhere.'

'You think a shore search would have been more effective?' he suggested, confident that she'd never find the bay from the landward side.

'I don't know. What if it's not even here? It's unusual for the males to choose a site a long way from the female's territory, but it's possible.'

Temptation scraped at his conscience. She'd be busy for weeks if she started looking further up the coast—plenty of time for probate to settle, for him to put Tulloquay on the market and sell it. The bleakness in her eyes was so different from the passionate sparkle that usually inhabited her brown depths. It would be so easy to whisper demons into her ear when she was in this mood—flat, despondent. It was exactly the sort of doubt he targeted in the boardroom.

And he wasn't called 'the closer' for nothing.

He could probably convince her to look elsewhere. But something about the way she ran the back of a weary hand across her eyes had him tightening his ribs against the desire to lean into her. To lend her strength.

Resignation leached through him. 'Finish the day, Kate. At least then you'll know, one way or the other.'

They were that close to the breeding site now it was really a question of when, not if. It would take a miracle for sharp-eyed Pickering to miss the entrance to the tiny cove. Grant had the sinking sun on his side; he knew from childhood that the seals generally disappeared from shore in the late afternoon and evening, preferring to laze around in the warmth of the morning when the east-rising sun blazed directly on their beaches.

Pickering took the *Nautilis* closer to shore and Grant noted the changing structure of the rocks. This bay looked a lot like his hidden one, only more open, exposed. The breeding site had to be close. Maybe it was the next bay around? Kate used her field glasses to search every bit of the new site.

'Nothing.' She shook her head heavily, then turned to Pickering. 'Are we wasting our time, John? Leo told me lanternfish school on the ocean floor this time of day. The seals will be deep-diving now, if they're hunting at all.'

And that meant they wouldn't be in the cove. Grant's heart set up a steady thrumming, but he kept his body language relaxed.

John glanced up at the lowering sun as he swung the *Nautilis* back around to proceed. 'It's not dusk yet. One or two could still be onshore. Let's wait and see.'

Kate moved to stand in the centre of the boat, field glasses raised, eyes on the rocky cliff face as they motored parallel to it. Grant's spine ached from the rigid set of his back. The topography was definitely looking familiar, even from the ocean side. His pulse hammered more definitely as his focus ping-ponged between Pickering and the shore.

Any second and they'd motor straight past it.

'Well, I'll be blown!' Pickering exclaimed.

Suddenly, the *Nautilis* spun round. Kate lost her footing and lurched towards the edge of the boat, her binoculars clattering to the deck. Grant shot up and into her path, catching her against his body and steadying her before she hit the gunnel and flipped into the water. Her hands slid up his arms for support. Out of nowhere, a flash of her stretched out and pressed against him in his Jeep hit him and, two seconds behind that the memory of her mouth, hungry and hot against his. His lips tingled in sympathy.

Her eyes flicked up to his, wide and aware. But then the twin brown depths carefully masked over and she straightened onto her feet. 'Thank you,' she murmured, before lowering her lashes.

Every part of him tightened. Maybe her memory was just as vivid as his. It had only been a few hours.

'Sorry, love,' Pickering laughed. 'Nearly overshot this one.'

He pointed to shore and Grant knew, without turning round, what he'd found: the opening to the breeding site.

Kate's graceful neck stretched as her head tilted and her eyes narrowed. 'Is that an opening?' she asked Pickering.

'Yep. Well disguised.'

She bent to retrieve the binoculars. 'How close can we get?'

He spun the wheel and motored forward. 'Let's find out.'

Damn; trust a seadog to like a challenge. When he got closer, Pickering would see that he could get right in.

Kate moved to his side at the front of the boat. 'Slow down, John. Just in case.'

The boat slowed and Grant's stomach churned. They were going to round the opening and the bay was going to be full of seals having a frat party; he just knew it. Kate was going to find the site she needed to slap a conservation restriction on his land and his chances of selling Tulloquay as a going concern was going to be shot. The whole plan fizzled right before his eyes.

His heart started hammering.

He'd been crazy to let her stay. He should never have fallen for those big eyes, or let himself be affected by her idealistic dreams. If he'd booted her out that first day he would never have found himself torn between wanting to hinder her and help her. Never have been so eager to make her smile, half-devouring her in his car, all the while trying to keep her from finding the one thing she really needed.

Even now, the two sides of him warred. He could imagine the look on her face when she found what she'd been looking for all these years. He wanted to see that expression in her eyes. He wanted to see this lonely, focused woman get something that meant so much to her.

Yet, he didn't…because of what it meant for Tulloquay.

He studied her as she studied the map, trying to isolate the cove's location. Her hair blew out behind her in a blazing tangle in the offshore breeze, natural, wild.

She'd burst to flame in his arms last night the same way Tulloquay's parched fields did when the firebreaks were burned into the land—as though she'd been thirsting for it for years. And he'd blazed right along with her, more of his heart in those kisses than in his last five sexual encounters put together.

A careless slip.

Hearts had no bearing on what simmered away between himself and Kate Dickson. Given what had gone on between them, it couldn't for her either. She was a woman of singular will, she'd never allow herself to develop feelings for the man standing in the way of her dream. It had been an emotional night, that was all. And the two of them had a positively incendiary chemical thing going on fuelled by mutual sorrow.

That was all. Kindred souls for a precious moment.

Kate lifted her eyes to the coastline, a worried tightness to her lips and a deep sadness in her eyes.

It's here, Kate.

The words trembled unsaid on his tongue. One side of him just wanted to throw it out there into the mix, deal with whatever came. The same insane, roaring desire to help her that had made him offer her lab space in his father's house. That had returned the TDR. His subconscious was finding a hundred ways to justify making the sort of decisions that would get him fired in the boardroom.

It'll be too late.

I'll sell before it matters.

The Conservation Commission will make their decision anyway.

He had the burning need to help make someone else's dream come true, whether or not it made his own needs more complicated.

All he had to do was say the words: *it's here, Kate.*

But, just as the letters sorted themselves into a cohesive

sentence on his lips, his father's face swam in his memory; those gnarled hands, old even twenty years ago, worn to calloused stubs working the land that he loved. The land he'd lived for.

He glanced at the shore.

Only seconds now…

*Thump, thump, thump…*A heavy beat beneath his jaw-bone.

Pickering deftly manouvered the *Nautilis* towards the edge of the rock face, ready to reverse sharply out if conditions turned treacherous. But the water was deep and free of reef, and in moments he nudged the bow straight towards the opening.

'I'd best not get us any closer, love,' he apologised. 'Not if we want to get back out again.'

Without a moment's hesitation, Kate clambered up onto the gunnel and edged her way right out onto the *Nautilis's* bow as far forward as she could stretch. The advance location put her almost in direct line with the rock shelf from where Grant had retrieved the TDR. She raised the binoculars. His chest squeezed so tight he couldn't draw breath. Every muscle coiled tight and painful as she finally turned back to them and called out.

'Empty.'

Shaking her head, she let the binoculars drop again and shuffled back along the bare edge of the boat, puffing slightly with the disappointment. 'It's a good site, though. Impossible to tell from this distance whether they come here or not. I would if I was a seal.'

So would I.

'You could swim in?' Pickering offered.

Kate studied the deep, dark waters around them. 'Too much risk of shark.' She circled the site on her map and marked it with a bold asterisk. 'I'll try it from the landward side next week. Before noon; before they start hunting.'

When Grant knew it would be full of seals, like this morning—bulls and cows. And there'd be no question about its purpose. But he let out a slow, controlled breath. She wouldn't find it easily on land; spotting the access was near impossible and getting down there even harder. It would still take her longer than he needed for probate to settle.

As if he'd read Grant's mind, John Pickering caught his eye as he turned to reverse the *Nautilis* out to clearer waters. 'Is it true you're looking to sell Tulloquay?'

'Why? Are you looking to buy?'

The larger man laughed. 'Me, on land? No fear. I'm happiest with wet feet, mate.'

Kate slumped down on one of the boat seats, and Grant eyed her from behind the privacy of his sunglasses. Deep creases had formed between her eyes; the tension played out on her miserable features. He directed his response to their captain. 'Fair enough. Spread the word; yes, I'm looking to sell.'

Kate looked everywhere but at him.

'Should get a decent price. Your father did a good job with Tulloquay. Considering.'

That got Grant's full attention. And Kate's. 'Considering?' they said in unison.

Pickering swung the boat round and continued south. 'Considering he was more of a fisherman.'

Grant laughed. He'd fished with his father off the jetty only twice in all his childhood, pretty much the only time he could recall his father having anything to do with fish. Then again, those two memories were amongst the best of his childhood. His father had been rarely relaxed and content. The laugh settled into a wary frown.

'He did know a lot about fish stocks,' Kate murmured. 'It was him who put me onto the lanternfish, remember?'

'There's no question,' Pickering said. 'It was a joke amongst the seadogs—that we'd lost him at land.'

'At land?'

'Some people get lost at sea. Leo McMurtrie got lost on shore. He was a natural fisherman.'

In Grant's periphery, Kate turned and look at him strangely, cautiously. It only tensed his spine more. 'My father was a farmer,' he said flatly.

'It was what he did. But not what he *was*. A man can spend a lifetime being something he's not.'

I should know. Outwardly, he only said, clipped, 'He was a farmer.'

Pickering's eyes softened a hint. 'Were you at his funeral?'

'Of course.'

'I was there too. One of the six men carrying his coffin.'

Grant remembered. That was where he'd seen John Pickering before. But something held his tongue.

Kate asked the question for him. 'Who were the other five?'

'All seadogs, love.'

Grant remembered the tanned, weathered men in their dated suits. One of them had had fish scales on his Sunday-best shoes, as though he'd thrown in a quick line before setting off to bury his mate.

Kate stepped closer, almost imperceptibly, but he felt it. He needed it. Again. But he had no idea why. A deep vibration started up in his gut. 'So he hung out with the fishing fraternity. So what?'

'So he was one of us, mate. No matter where he spent his days. And there's a lot of loyalty amongst the fishing community.'

'And?'

'And your father gave up his life for that farm so that you'd have something to call your own. Some land to grow roots in. And you're going to toss it away, like those seventy years have no value.'

His muscles jerked back to full tension in a heartbeat. Had Kate somehow primed Pickering to say this? 'I'm going to sell it to someone who can run it like it should be run.'

'There is no Tulloquay without you on it. It's just land.'

Grant frowned. 'It's some of the best coastal land in Castleridge.'

'It has no value if it passes out of McMurtrie hands. It was your great-grandfather's, then your grandfather's, then Leo's. It only exists because of you.'

Grant clenched his fists where they rested on the gunnel. Kate stepped into the breach. 'How about we keep our focus on finding the breeding site?' she gently hinted.

John Pickering threw her a speculative look from under grey, bushy brows but turned back to his wheel. Grant stared long and hard at the man's broad back, his mind churning.

Did everyone think he was letting his family down by selling Tulloquay? He was trying to do the exact opposite—keep the property's soul intact, honour its heritage.

Why would his father have spent a lifetime building up Tulloquay if the sea had truly been his mistress? Once he had lost his wife, his son, what had stopped him from selling up and pursuing his own dream?

Nothing. So it couldn't have been what he wanted.

He had a lot of fishermen mates—so what? Most of Grant's own friends were in construction, not law. Who a man chose to have a beer with didn't mean a thing.

His brow folded again. Unless it did?

Grant turned his back on the uncomfortable conversation except to note how effectively it had distracted Kate from thoughts about the breeding site. Her focus was well and truly on the next bay on her map, a kilometre closer to the homestead.

At least they were moving in the right direction. If his luck held, she'd forget all about the empty cove half-hidden from view.

If his luck held.

CHAPTER NINE

'YOU cook?'

Kate looked up from four bubbling pots. 'I live on my slow-cooker at home. I thought I'd give the theory a crack on a country stove.' She frowned. 'It's not really working out.'

Just one more thing she couldn't get to go her way. Everything was slowly slipping out of her hands.

Grant peered into the fiercest of the simmering pots. 'Smells fine to me. And it's not from a tin, so I'm already sold.'

'You don't cook?'

'Not for one. I'd rather eat out and have someone who actually knows food make mine. Or have something at my desk.'

'You're still at work at dinner time?'

'Sometimes. It's quiet after five; I get more done in those couple of hours than the rest of the day.'

The campus lab was exactly the same. Kate stirred the most vigorous pot and then reduced the heat and sat the lid on top. Grant reached around her for the bottle-opener which hung on a peg under the overhead cupboards. They didn't touch, but she was more aware of the gentle heat coming off him than from the furnace she'd coaxed to life in the country oven in front of her. And that smell….

She sighed.

'This was supposed to be *your* birthday dinner. You shouldn't be making it,' he said, snagging two glasses from the shelf above.

'I was serious when I said I don't do birthdays. Consider this a thank-you for finding the TDR.'

His footsteps behind her slowed and her eyes flicked to the polished stainless steel of the fridge. His reflection paused, half-turned back, but then moved on, crossing to the wine-rack, whatever he'd been about to say lost. 'Red or white?'

Kate released the breath she only just realised she was holding. 'Absolutely no idea.'

'What are we having?'

Kate frowned at the meal that wasn't really going to plan. 'Beef Surprise'.

Grant chuckled and reached for a red.

Kate put the lids on all the pots to keep simmering, wiped her hands and then turned to him boldly. This was a conversation she much preferred to lead, even though she didn't really look forward to it. 'I'm just making good on my promise to cook you something after I dragged you from the diner last night.'

Openings didn't come more obvious than that. He didn't look surprised that she'd handed it to him—if anything he looked impressed. Had he not expected her to have the guts to be direct? He took his time pouring an inch of blood-red Merlot into two large glasses. He passed Kate one then leaned on the kitchen island. 'You have nothing to make good for. I appreciate the fact that you got me out of there until I'd pulled myself together. I wasn't really *compos mentis*.'

Her chest tightened. 'It was a lot to take in. For both of us.' She paused. 'Is that why you…?' Her newfound courage failed her.

Grant held her eyes. 'No. I knew what I was doing.'

'So it *was* intentional?'

Thick lashes dropped over those green eyes and Kate realised, looking at Grant, that they reminded her of the place the forest met the jade waters of an inlet lagoon. The kind of place she liked to go to do her thinking. Was that why she felt so comfortable gazing at him? Yet so intensely uncomfortable.

One brow quirked. His eyes pumped out heat. 'You think my lips stumbled and fell onto yours?'

A warm stain raced up her throat and she stepped away from the stove. 'No. But I did wonder…because you were upset…'

'Did I kiss you because I was in shock about my father?'

Yes, exactly. Her fingers shook as she swirled her wine. She glanced up at the steady eyes that carried so much hidden thought deep in their depths. How could he be so composed?

He placed his wine glass down after an age and stepped towards her. 'I've told myself all day that was why—that we were both upset, that we were both seeking comfort.' He stopped just shy of bumping against her and her heartbeat tripped over itself. 'Is that why you kissed me back? Because you were upset about Leo?'

Any chance of blaming it on that, or of pretending the kiss had been one-sided, flew out the window like a rogue, deflated balloon. But before she could answer he stole the words straight from her subconscious.

'I kissed you because we were alone, confined and because all I could smell was you.'

Physical attraction. Her heart took a few seconds to collect itself and get back up—that, at least, she could still control. Somewhat. She threw out a breezy chuckle. 'I hope it was better than my usual *eau de* fur seal.'

The two pools of green focussed on her seemed to swirl and intensify while she waited for his answer. 'Immeasurably.'

She took a deep breath. 'What are we going to do about it?'

His mouth twisted seductively. 'This kitchen island looks like a pretty good place to continue where we left off…' He patted the top of the carefully crafted timber island behind him.

Kate's lungs squeezed into a tiny ball before she could take a proper breath. Excitement and outrage felt like close cousins when she was this close to Grant's masculine tug, but sense returned with the airflow and she opened her mouth to tell him exactly what she thought of that idea. They were in a professional working relationship. Supposedly.

He headed her off. 'Relax, Kate. That was a joke.' He twisted and reclaimed his wine. 'You have the worst poker face I've ever seen.'

The umbrage leaked out of her on a carefully released breath. 'You think this is funny?'

His gaze grew serious. 'No. But you're wound as tight as the coils running the artesian bore. I just wanted to let you release some of that, so we can properly talk.'

Oh.

'My question's still the same,' she persisted. 'What are we going to do about it?'

The glinting flash of speculation filled his gaze. 'What do *you* want to do about it?'

Kate couldn't have this discussion with them crammed like sheep into Leo's small kitchen. She crossed round the opposite side of the island and moved to the dining table. Having its width between them was a blessing, even if it did mean Grant's long legs brushed against hers as he sat across from her.

'Nothing. It can't happen again,' she said.

He pursed his lips and nodded slowly. 'Kisses like that don't come along every day.'

Kate forced air up her tight throat. 'Are you saying you—?'

'What we *want* and what we *do* are different things. It's what makes us a civilised species. I'm just playing devil's advocate, making sure we look at this from all angles.'

'Covering all contingencies?'

He lifted his palms in front of him. 'It's what I do best.'

She begged to differ. There were probably a number of things this man could do brilliantly. Kissing, for starters. She took a breath. 'OK, I'll play. Sure, it was a good kiss.' Then, at his expression, 'OK—a *great* kiss. So what?'

'So we have to take that into account.'

Her eyes narrowed. 'Like a scientific variable?'

He laughed, and the sound was a hot blow of breath down her spine. 'If you insist on de-romanticising it, sure.'

There was nothing romantic about the careful way he was keeping his emotions hidden from her. 'I thought we were talking about attraction, not romance,' she challenged.

He raised his glass. 'Spoken like a true scientist. Actually, we were talking about kissing.' He leaned further towards her. 'But, since you mention it, yes, let's talk about attraction.'

Kate knew she'd opened the door but shoving it closed wasn't going to be easy. Not when this thing pulsed between them thick and hard-to-miss even now.

'Lust.' Kate straightened up and faked confidence she was far from feeling. 'It's straightforward enough. My pheromones and yours are mingling. Our receptors are connecting.'

He smiled. 'Is that right?'

She shrugged, though it wasn't convincing. Even to herself.. 'I can practically feel the norepinepherine doing its job.'

The smile doubled. 'And what job's that?'

She kept her face impassive. 'Sweaty palms. Racing heart. Dry mouth. Inability to think clearly.'

Burning need to crawl right over this table…

Green eyes blazed into hers, complicated and speculative. 'Really? I'm doing that to you right now?'

The air was sucked clean out of her body and her brain instantly felt the loss of oxygen. 'I…um… We were talking theoretics.'

The gorgeous grin graduated into a full chuckle, and he sat back and took a long sip of wine. Kate's gaze clung to the way the red liquid stained his full lips.

'You live in a horrible, sterile world, Dr Dickson,' those lips informed her.

The ancient need to defend her occupation bubbled up. 'It's good to understand these things. Keep them in perspective.'

'Or what?' His eyes blazed into hers. 'Seriously. What's the worst that could happen?'

'We could misread this. Make bad choices.' If he'd noticed her unintentional 'we' he wasn't saying.

'Some things are beyond our control. Where's the law that says we can't just enjoy each other while it lasts?'

The implication bristled. Was any kind of more meaningful relationship so unlikely? 'There's a lot at stake.'

At last, his eyes sobered. 'True enough. Have we done much damage already?'

'Nothing irreparable.'

Liar.

He nodded, slowly. 'Good. I wouldn't want to make this any harder for you.'

'Me? What about you?'

He shrugged those enormous shoulders. 'I don't care about me. I'll survive.'

And somehow she knew the first part of that, at least, was one-hundred-percent true. But, even though common sense said she should, she couldn't let it go. Something deep down said that she should push this. Explore it, like a good scientist. 'That suggests you might care about me?'

The pause was telling, given this man's skill for repartee, his rapier-sharp verbal swordplay. 'I don't want you to be hurt, no.'

'Why?'

Those expressive brows dropped again. 'Why? Because you've done nothing to deserve it.'

The Beef Surprise bubbled in its pot.

'Are we friends, Grant?'

The change of direction threw him. 'You were a friend of my father's. More than I'd realised.'

She sat up straighter. 'I never had dinner with your father. I never slept in his house.' Parrying with a verbal swordsman was almost thrilling.

But it couldn't last.

'I imagine you didn't slide all over him in a car, either.'

That shut her down more than effectively. Heat flooded her neck.

Grant continued. 'You and I are a different creature to you and my father.'

'You hope.' She couldn't resist poking the angry bear, just a bit

He shook his head. 'I *know*.'

'How can you know? You two never spoke. Maybe we had some kind of December-May thing going on.'

He visibly winced. 'I know because I saw how he felt about my mother. That kind of love never ends.'

'He had a long life without it.'

'There's the tragedy.'

'I wouldn't have picked you as someone who believed in true love.'

'Maybe I'd have been better off never recognising it. Makes it hard not to notice its absence elsewhere.'

The comment so perfectly fitted her own views; Kate had to force a light laugh. 'Love isn't all it's cracked up to be. It didn't save either of our parents.'

Nor their children.

'True enough. But we weren't talking about love. We were talking about why I know you never shared red wine with my father.' Grant swilled what was left of his wine in its glass and brilliant shards of ruby light bounced into Kate's eyes. 'I've spent enough time with you to see what kind of a woman you are.'

'And what kind is that?'

He sat back in his seat and tilted his head, studying her. As though he hadn't needed to put the concept into words until now. 'Direct. Loyal. As easy to read as a billboard. You're passionate about the things that matter to you and selective in what you let that be. You like everything to be ordered. You're not what I expected at all.'

Kate forgot to be angry at his cut-glass assessment. 'What did you expect?'

'Someone harder. Ruthless. Someone with no goodness.'

The ball in her throat expanded. 'Someone more like you're used to dealing with?'

'Pretty much. I don't always know what to do with you, Kate.' His eyes dropped briefly. 'Or how to be.'

That hint of vulnerability limboed straight under her defences. She swallowed the tiny lump that formed. 'Just be like this. No matter what happens, I'd rather face it openly with you—' *together* '—than try and second guess what you might think or mean.'

'It can't work like that, Kate. We're on opposite sides of the table.'

In that moment, the timber slab laid out for dinner for two might as well have been as wide and impassable as the Simpson desert. 'Just because it hasn't happened doesn't mean it can't,' she muttered.

He shook his head. 'It never happens. Not for real, only as strategy.'

Kate sighed; game playing just wasn't in her repertoire of life skills. She leaned forward. 'I don't want to spend all my time dancing around you, Grant. I have too much to do and, quite frankly, there's too much pressure already. It wears me out. So, regardless of what you choose, I'm choosing to stay open.' She finished her wine in one big gulp. 'And in the interests of that…' She'd never seen a human face shut down as fast as Grant's did as she paused to take a breath. 'Tell me about the TDR.'

His face went from freshly closed to ancient granite in a blink. 'What?'

'The data logger confirmed it. Early this morning the TDR

captured a range of diving behaviours from Stella, but then it started recording unusual variations.'

His jaw hardened impossibly further. 'Variations?'

'A sharp climb above sea level, then a long flat period, then a sharp drop again. All five seconds apart, so that tells me the TDR was dry.' She leaned forward. 'In fact, it hasn't been wet since very early this morning; the sensors never recorded moisture.' She paused for effect. *'Any.'*

They both knew the place he said he'd found it was the better part of a puddle.

He clenched his teeth hard enough to see high in his jaw. 'What are you suggesting?

'I'm not suggesting anything. I'm trying to make sense of the data. The data tells me that the TDR didn't wash up at Dave's Cove.'

'There's probably an error.'

'Twenty grand's worth of equipment doesn't make errors.'

Grant surged to his feet and moved to the kitchen to refill his glass. 'Careful, Kate. I might start to think you're calling me a liar.'

Kate followed him, tucking her trembling fingers out of view and peering up at him, but held his gaze. 'Whether you lied or not doesn't interest me. What interests me is *why* you felt the need to.'

His eyes hardened and his arms folded across his chest. 'I assume you have a hypothesis, doctor.'

She smiled, delighted for once to see him so thoroughly on the back foot. 'Why, yes I do, thanks for asking.' Then she got down to business. 'Returning the TDR makes very little operational difference to our project beyond the financial impact of having to repay twenty big ones unexpectedly. Thank you again for that, by the way.'

He tipped his glass at her, though his mouth remained tight. His voice was pure sarcasm. 'You're welcome.'

But she didn't let it faze her; the thrill of the hunt was too great. 'So I figure there must be something important about the way you found it that you didn't want me knowing. Something that would help us.' She tilted her head, thinking out loud. 'Something that would damage your plans to sell.'

His jaw flexed. His silence screamed.

'No.' Kate gasped as she realised. 'Not the *way* you found it. The *place*.'

She locked on fast to Grant's gaze. He stared her down but she saw the faintest hint of colour stain his jaw. Her eyes narrowed. 'You're blushing.'

He towered over her. 'That's a sexual response, not an admission of guilt. I'm having a bit of a norepinepherine reaction of my own right now.' He leaned in closer. 'You're very hot when you're thinking.'

She couldn't help the stumble—more of a blink, really—but regained her visual hold. 'You're trying to distract me.'

His eyes positively smouldered. 'When I begin to try you'll know it.'

Certain she'd be matching his flush, Kate held on for dear life, recognising that this moment mattered. What happened in this kitchen was going to change their flawed, awkward relationship for better or worse. She really hoped it was better.

Grant stepped up hard against her. His eyes simmered into pools of molten green. 'Make me, Kate. Make me try. I haven't had this much fun in years.'

The heat spread downward from her cheeks, pouring over all her most sensitive points as he brought out the big guns of distraction. His hand lifted to tangle in her hair. Every part of her tingled, especially her intuition.

It had never, ever failed her.

Her eyes shot wide open. 'Oh my God…'

Grant backed her into the fridge. 'You should see your pupils, doctor. They're the size of dinner plates.' His breath tickled her hair.

'You found the breeding site,' she whispered as he lowered

his face close. 'Didn't you?' Her lungs started to heave, desperate for air. She knew she was right but needed to hear it. 'Didn't you?'

His next words would make or break her career; every part of her throbbed from anticipation. From excitement. From raw, senseless attraction. Grant rested his forearm against the fridge door and leaned on it until his mouth paused dangerously close to her ear.

He stood frozen there for an eternity.

Then he pressed his blazing, soft mouth to her ear and she struggled to remain upright. She felt his lips open and the rush of breath as he whispered.

'Yes.'

Her legs did give out then and he caught her with his free arm. Everything she'd worked for, everything she'd dreamed of accomplishing clicked into place as her arms snaked up around Grant's neck to hold herself upright. He consumed the flesh of her throat, her ear, biting and mouthing his way. She hung on for dear life, the sensual bliss of his mouth and the intellectual buzz of this amazing gift keeping her weak.

'If I'd known you'd react like this I would have told you immediately.' He pressed into the ear that was rapidly becoming the centre of her sensory universe.

She held her own but barely. 'No, you wouldn't. You wanted to drag it out longer.'

His chuckle was like the most wicked chocolate ice-cream, except hot against her cheek.

She peeled herself out from under him. 'Seriously. You found it?'

He took a huge breath in and blew it out slowly, looking resigned to the inevitable. 'I did.'

'When can we see it?' Anticipation zinged hot and bubbly around her body.

'I'll have to think about that.'

Disappointment thunked, dull and heavy, at her feet. 'What's to think about?' He couldn't mean… 'You're not seriously going to keep it to yourself?'

'If I hadn't returned the recorder you'd be none the wiser.'

Kate stared. It was true. He could have tossed it out to sea and said nothing. 'Why did you return it?'

He shrugged. 'Because you needed it.'

'I need this more.'

His wide shoulders slumped. 'I know.'

'Grant…'

'I'm going to need some time, Kate. You understand what you're asking me to do.'

To kill his hopes of selling Leo's farm. 'You don't *need* to sell it, Grant. You only want to.'

'You don't *need* the breeding site, you only want it. Your research will stand without it.'

'It's not the same.'

'It's exactly the same.'

Kate stared, long and lonely. The excitement that had blazed through her so gloriously congealed into a thick, disappointed glug. In him. In herself. That he could seriously wave her life's dream under her nose and then just whip it away. That he could possibly barter with her future. But he wasn't playing; this wasn't sport for him.

It was business. And when it came to business, she was woefully outclassed

'We can't both have what we want, can we?'

His eyes hardened. 'Doesn't look like it, no.'

Of course not. Why had she expected any different? Had she thought that the universe was going to cut her a break just because she'd met someone that filled her with life? Just because she'd let her heart start to thaw?

What a timely reminder of the reasons she never let herself care for someone like this.

Life had a way of ripping her away from anyone she dared to care about.

Maybe she should be grateful that it happened sooner rather than later with Grant. Before she gave any more of her heart and soul to someone who didn't deserve it.

She carefully placed her wine glass on the counter and turned back, as composed as she could be. 'I think I've lost my appetite. Enjoy dinner.'

She turned for her bedroom and steeled herself to keep walking in case he called her back. But she needn't have bothered. When he spoke it wasn't to say *Kate, come back, I'm an idiot.*

It was simpler, more brutal; whispered into the night.

'Happy birthday, Kate.'

CHAPTER TEN

KATE sagged back onto the ratty old swing chair she'd found out the back in a shed. For some reason she felt very at home in the lab, and in this chair—infinitely more than inside the house with Grant, as though she was in safe hands in here. As though she was surrounded by friends instead of the enemy. She shook her head. Both those thoughts were crazy.

The pressure was definitely getting to her.

Grant was just a man who wanted something a pole away from what she wanted.

She spun round and round in the chair, the hypnotic movement helping her think, helping her remain objective. It was Sunday, supposedly a day of rest, but when the clock was ticking rest could wait. Most of her team had families and so she released them on Sundays and worked alone in the lab to get ahead on processing the samples and analysis of the TDR data. Before now, it had been the lab at the university. But now she only had to walk down the hall from her bedroom and she was there. There should be no reason for this lethargy, this inability to focus. She had an esky full of samples and a rogue TDR awaiting attention.

And absolutely no inclination to do it.

Just one more thing to curse Grant for. She'd lain awake long after the moon had passed overhead, for the second night in a row, her thoughts vacillating between exhilaration that he'd identified the breeding site and memories of the feel of his hot breath against her ear as he confessed to it. The way his hips had pushed hers back into the fridge. How she'd been excited, not threatened. How she'd wanted him to touch her for ever.

How it had come so close to distracting her from his discovery. Would he have told her if she hadn't pushed, if his body language hadn't given him away?

She lowered her feet to change the chair's direction.

Could he truly withhold the location of the breeding site? Would he turn out to be that kind of man?

Not for the first time, she wished the TDR recorded position as well as time and depth, then she wouldn't be reliant on a man with an agenda to find the breeding site. She could try and triangulate the location by the number of time readings that the TDR was above sea level, but how fast had he been driving? How slow? Did he go anywhere else first? The two differentials alone were no use to her beyond recording Stella's hunting and foraging activity before the TDR came off.

Once again, Grant held all the cards. Except this time he'd made sure she knew about it.

Maybe he was that kind of man.

He'd accused her of having a terrible poker face; his must be absolutely perfected, because he'd given nothing away yesterday out on the water. They'd probably stopped at the breeding site and he'd never so much as twitched.

More and more was slipping out of her influence. Just like when she'd been twelve and the world was happening to her, not with her.

She snagged the map off the bench top and stared at the long stretch of Tulloquay coast. Which one of the thirty or so pockmarks in the cliff face on the map was the one? There were six marked with an asterisk indicating likely seal territory, yet only one had any animals on it at all. Without Grant, it could take weeks to find it.

A few months ago that wouldn't have bothered her much. She'd learned to be extra patient where seal research was concerned, but she no longer had the luxury of patience. The calendar had now turned onto the same page as the big, ugly red circle marking E-day: Eviction Day. That meant less than a month and her access to the Atlas colony would be shut off, for good.

She let the chair slow to a halt and then reversed direction absently.

Unless she could negotiate with the future buyers. It was possible, but why would new owners be any less concerned about conservation restrictions than Grant was? She'd got lucky with Leo. She'd come along at a time when he was reassessing many of his life's decisions, and, unwittingly, she'd brought him the one thing that he couldn't have said no to.

At the time Leo's deep knowledge about the fishing stocks in the region hadn't seemed unusual. But, in hindsight, she'd never met another landholder who was so informed about the stocks of a species beyond his fence lines. Maybe Leo saw her project as his last opportunity to make a difference to the industry that—if John Pickering was to be believed—he'd secretly wished to be part of.

Maybe it was true. Kate had wondered if his heart was truly in agriculture. No matter what his son thought, Leo McMurtrie had hardly been Super Farmer. He'd grazed his sheep too hard on the more arid parts of his property and he hadn't planted the right tree species to reduce salinity. And after his diagnosis he'd started to run his stock levels down and spend less and less time out in the paddocks.

Kate sucked in a breath and halted her relentless spinning.

And he'd spent more and more time sitting on the blustery bluffs of his coastal paddocks staring out to sea.

'Oh, Leo!' How sad if he'd never felt free to pursue his true calling.

'Kate?'

She spun towards the voice that had the same inflection

as his father's. The same fatalistic sadness in his gaze. Grant stared at her long and hard then held the door open for her.

'Come on.' He was reluctant, resigned. 'I've got something to show you.'

Her stomach lurched. *The breeding site.*

Heart in mouth, Kate pushed out of Leo's chair, silently pressed past Grant in the doorway and led the way out into the sunlight. Part of her was excited by the possibility of seeing the breeding site, another part—almost a bigger part—was heart-in-mouth that maybe, just maybe, the man she'd just convinced herself was irredeemable was about to do the right thing.

The right thing turned out not quite the way she'd expected. They drove the length of the coastal strip, right along what she estimated was the inland perimeter of the proposed conservation buffer-zone. He talked about his memories as a child, of what used to fill the now-empty paddocks, of growing up on the farm before he learned to hate it. The more he spoke, the harder it was to stay angry at him. Her body ate up his closeness. Her starved heart gorged on clues to the person he'd been.

'It was a great life for a boy,' he murmured from behind the shelter of his dark sunglasses, still careful after the way last night had ended. 'Wildlife. Space. Adventure.'

'Danger?'

He smiled. 'Definitely danger. And if I couldn't find any I'd make my own.'

'It's a pity you never had siblings to play with.'

'Mum got sick before they tried for another.'

'How old were you when she died?'

'Three.'

A sharp pang bit deep and low at the slight crack in that single word. 'I'm sorry.'

'Me, too. A lot might have been different if she'd lived.'

'Different how?'

He shrugged. 'If there'd been other kids. Or if I'd been older when she died. Maybe Dad wouldn't have fixated so much on me. The farm.'

Grant inheriting the farm.

'Maybe she could have been a cushion between us as I grew up,' he went on. 'There was a lot I loved about my early life here.'

'But not enough to stay?'

He shook his head, almost invisibly. 'I wanted more than the farm. I wanted more than some land to define who I was.'

'You think that's how Leo defined himself?'

'I know he did. It was his whole world.'

Yet he'd harboured a secret love for the ocean. 'What if it wasn't?'

Those dark glasses locked onto her. 'What are you saying?'

'I'm just asking the question. What if he really wanted to work at sea, doing what he loved?'

Grant pulled the Jeep to a halt and turned to her, sliding the glasses up. Revealing those fathomless eyes glinting with pain. 'Fishing?'

Kate shrugged. 'Maybe.'

'What stopped him after I left?'

'That's not a question I can answer. I wasn't there. What do you think?'

White tension showed at the corner of his mouth and the jade in his eyes seemed to darken. 'I think it would suit you if I changed my mind about selling Tulloquay.'

The simple truth burned deep like a poker from the fire. But the fact he still thought she would trade on that, or that he would use that to distract her from this conversation…

Her breath shuddered. 'It would make my job easier, yes. But so would a lot of things that I haven't done.'

'Like?'

'Like calling in favours at the Conservation Commission to get the application fast-tracked. Like letting them know I've

ID'd possible breeding sites.' She took a breath. 'Like calling on Castleridge's council to halt the sale until our contract is concluded.'

A tic pulsed at the corner of his eye like a tiny heartbeat.

'You didn't think I knew about that avenue?' she asked. He didn't answer. 'I don't screw people over, Grant. I'm not one of your boardroom negotiations. I don't think that way.'

'You don't want to protect your site?' The disbelief in his voice sliced even deeper.

'I do. Desperately. But not enough to play dirty.' *Not enough to wound a lonely little boy grown into a shut-down man.*

'Exploiting available tools is not playing dirty. It's playing the game.'

'In your world, perhaps. I'd rather sort this out the old-fashioned way.' One look told her what he imagined that to be. Heat roared into her cheeks. 'Not that, either. A handshake. Like adults.'

'How do you imagine we'll find a middle ground that we're both prepared to accept?'

'I have no idea.' *Yet.* 'But I'm not prepared to do anything that forces your hand.'

His eyes briefly softened. 'Trying to show me the error of my ways, Kate?'

'No. I'd just rather you willingly do the right thing.'

'What if the right thing for you is the wrong thing for me?'

Her breasts heaved with the chore of sucking in air. She'd asked herself this question over and over into the small hours of the morning. 'Then you shouldn't do it.'

He squinted his disbelief. 'Really? Even if you could force my hand with one phone call to Mayor Sefton?'

'*Especially* because I could force your hand.' She tucked her hands together out of view. 'That's not who I am. I lost my whole life when a road-train took away my choices. I'm not about to do that to someone else.'

Incredulous eyes blazed at her. 'You liken this to losing your parents?'

Her breath was tight enough to ache. 'Grant, this means a lot to you, or you wouldn't be fighting so hard. I don't have to understand it to recognise it.'

Silence fell thick and loaded.

Grant shook his head. 'You're a strange creature, Kate Dickson.'

'I know. But I'd like to think there are more people like me than…' Her words dried up.

'Than like me? Is that what you were going to say?'

'No. I was going to say than like the woman you think I am.'

He stared at her long and hard, to the point she wanted to squirm from the scrutiny. Then he simply turned to the steering wheel, slid the car into drive and moved off across the paddock on a sharp tangent towards the coast.

Kate sat quietly for the ten minutes it took to drive across the buffer to the coast, her trepidation growing. Without her map she had no hope of knowing exactly where they were. She'd been too sensitive to Grant's closeness on the way out to pay more attention to things like distances and landmarks. Out here, one bleached kilometre looked much like another.

He stopped the car and turned to her

Her heart raced. 'What are you doing?'

'I'm trusting you.'

She stared at him, her mind racing through the many ways this could be a trap.

'I think I started trusting you a long time ago or else I wouldn't have told you about the site last night—no matter how good you smelled.'

Still shc could say nothing.

He dropped his gaze to the dials on the dashboard then lifted it to meet her eyes once again. 'I'm tired of being the bad guy, Kate. I spent the first part of my life being the kid who disappointed his father, the next part being the man who abandoned his heritage and the most recent part being the guy who nails people to the cross contractually. I don't want to be the man who ruins your life, too.' Sincerity stained his pained glance. 'So I'm abdicating the responsibility. Giving you the power.'

Kate's throat tightened up. 'You're making *me* choose? What makes you think I won't just choose the seals?'

'You're a scientist. I trust you to look at all the angles, weigh everything up and make the best decision.'

Her frown turned to a scowl. 'You can't just opt out, Grant. I wanted…'

'What?'

'I wanted to give you the chance to make the right choice.'

'To see if I failed or not? I've spent more than enough of my life being a disappointment to people, Kate.'

She had to choose. She had to make or break one of them. She wanted control of her life but…like this?

Careful what you wish for.

'It might not even be the breeding site.' Ironic that she could even hope for that a little bit after all this time.

Grant cracked his door open and snapped off his seatbelt. He met her eyes. 'Only one way to find out.'

Her eyes were as big as any child's on Christmas morning despite the new pressure Grant had given her. She knew she should probably strive for more professionalism, that clinging to Grant's arm was inappropriate at best. But she didn't care. Anticipation raced through her like a drug, drawing her focus to just one thing.

The seals.

She was about to find the missing piece of the puzzle. Cap off her research study. Get her future firmly back in her own hands.

Maybe. Depending on what she decided.

It was a hellish journey through bracken and the most brutal and most effective coastal scrub she'd ever seen, and then over the cliff face onto a heavily eroded and dangerously exposed path. Grant led her carefully down and her legs and chest ached when she finally reached the bottom from the brutal descent, from the torturous anticipation. And from the weight of her heart at having to make this decision for them both.

'This way.' He took her hand again and helped her over the rocks, catching her elbow as she stumbled and guiding the way over the easiest parts. She clung to his strong fingers. It felt strangely right to be discovering this together, to have someone by her side at one of the most exciting moments of her life. Not just someone—him. Every moment before it suddenly seemed meaningless because Grant hadn't been there to share it. She frowned.

That wasn't good.

Physical pull was one thing, but how long had this been building? How long had she been slowly forming a list of qualities in him that she was drawn to, nurturing growing tendrils of attraction and admiration? She lifted her head and watched him move carefully and surely over the rocks. How long had it taken before even the shape of him walking away from her had become burned into her psyche? The breadth of his shoulders, the taut, narrow waist. The firm, strong legs built for climbing rocks, built for pinning her to the mattress…

She gasped out loud.

He turned and placed a finger to his lips and Kate squeezed her windpipe shut, not even daring to breathe, and mentally shook the uninvited thoughts free as they stepped quietly around a limestone spur covered in tufts of coastal spinifex.

And then there they were.

Her heart muscle seized. Her feet stuck to the rocks as though it was quicksand and not millennia-old granite she stood upon. Adrenaline flooded her system. Only the tug of Grant's reassuring hand got her moving again, let her turn her head to scan the rock shelf by the water.

Four bulls and eleven females, all lazing around, two bulls making furtive sport of play-fighting. It was hard to tell from this distance whether any of the Atlas colony was here but chances were good they were.

Grant towed her up behind a large boulder and helped her climb to its top. From there she could watch the colony in safety. She slid down to a comfortable resting position, braced against Grant's strong length, her eyes glued to the mammals below.

'There's more males than last time,' he whispered.

Last time? How many times had he been here?

'He's like a sheik with his harem.' She indicated the largest of the bulls who scanned the group looking for interlopers, alert for dissent. 'The lesser males will fight each other for the privilege of the big guy's cast-offs, or whatever they can steal while his attention is on rutting another female.'

'Not much dignity in being a fur seal,' Grant murmured.

'Nope. Not for any of them. Then again none of us make our best choices when our hormones are surging.'

Wasn't that the truth?

The big male lurched over to a female half his size. She saw him coming and the chase was on, the bull hitting amazing speed for a body so cumbersome, for rocks so sharp. The young female gave him a good run before his biological imperative won out. He caught up with her, subdued her and clambered on top, practically obscuring her from view.

Kate dropped her eyes as the alien grunting began, and the terrified squeals.

Grant leaned closer, a strange tone in his voice. 'After all the disgusting things you do every day, *this* is what gets to you?'

She winced. It sounded too much like fear, like pain. The scientist in her said it couldn't be because the rest of the colony lay relaxed and unconcerned. But a deeper part of her…

'That could be one of my girls,' she hedged. 'I don't like seeing them brutalised.'

He snagged her hand and tucked it into the warmth of his. 'Isn't it nature?'

'Unfortunately, yes.'

'How long will it take?'

'Not long.' As Kate said the words, the male lurched off his flattened mate and she bolted to the far side of the shelf, vocalising her protest loudly. Kate hurt for the confused little seal now tending its various injuries.

'Well, I'm feeling a bit rubbish about being a bloke right now,' Grant muttered next to her and she couldn't help the watery laugh that broke free. Several sleek, brown faces snapped in her direction, including the giant male, who didn't seem to be any sleepier for his exertions. Grant pulled her closer to him, out of their view, and the two of them lay there, unmoving, breathing in synch and waiting for the seals, attention to be diverted.

Kate's eyes drifted closed as her lungs filled with Grant's close scent. Clean and masculine. It was a darned sight better than the odours wafting all around them. She happily pressed her face into the warmth of his shoulder while the legitimate opportunity presented itself. He was every bit the opposite of that lumbering, savage bull-seal. If he made love to a woman, it would be tender and gentle, generous and protective.

That last quality, particularly, cracked her heart just a little bit more.

Not that anything like that between them was particularly on the cards. For all their progress, the place they'd reached was barely more than where other people started—civil neutrality. Despite some random kissing here and there, she was no closer to knowing Grant's heart than when they'd met two months ago. Except to know she wasn't in it.

When he released her moments later, she pressed cool fingers to her warm cheeks. 'I'm sorry. That was really unprofessional.'

He smiled. 'Kate Dickson, the seals' champion.'

She stared at the young female seal. 'If I was Mother Nature there are a few things I would arrange differently.'

His eyes held hers, warm, soft. 'I can't think of anyone more suited to the job,' he said.

His smile deepened and Kate took a moment to enjoy the rare, natural moment. She stared up at him, lost.

He broke free an eternity later, flicking his eyes back to the seals briefly. 'How much do you need to see?'

'That's about it. There's no question this is the breeding site.'

He stared at her. Hard. 'So what happens now?'

Kate measured his mood and then twisted sideways to face him more directly. 'Don't sell the farm, Grant. Please.'

Disappointment flooded his eyes. 'Kate, we've been through—'

Desperation made her rash. 'I'll run it for you. I'll make it profitable.'

'What's left of it after the buffer goes in? Good luck with that,' he snorted.

'I'll find a use for the conservation zone.' Apparently she wasn't above begging, whatever it took to get a mutual agreement. So she didn't have to choose.

'Isn't that the whole point of a buffer zone? That it's livestock-free?'

'I'll think of something.'

'How, Kate? With what money?' His reasonable tone only tolled certain doom. Was she so pathetic he couldn't even be angry with her?

A deep frown cut into her vision. 'You'd have to float it at first, of course, but if we can make a profit…'

'You can't be a scientist and a farmer, Kate.'

'Why?'

'Because you're good but you're not super human.'

The stark common sense ate like acid into her desperate

plea. What was the point of killing herself keeping the farm going if she couldn't keep up with her study?

'No.'

He watched her carefully. 'Will you report this to the Conservation Commission?'

This find would put the signature on a buffer decree. The land would be accessioned and a caveat would be put on Tulloquay's title. Grant would be legally obliged to declare it which meant he'd probably be unable to sell the farm to a decent buyer. At best, he might be able to get the zoning changed, sell what was left of it to hobby farmers.

Slice it up like a pizza into ten-acre lots.

Along with his soul.

She looked at him and remembered how she'd felt when her life had been sold off in auction lots to strangers. That made her decision clearer, if not easier.

She shook her head and damped down the ache in her heart. 'No. I won't.'

Grant's eyes closed briefly. 'What about the seals?'

She shook her head again and spoke, flat and despondent. 'My research findings will have to stand in their own right. It might not be complete without a significant site but it's still valid. The Atlas seals will just have to take their chances with the next owner.'

Grant frowned. 'There's *nothing* we can do?'

She lifted her eyes to his. 'Yes. You can keep the farm.'

Frustration hissed out of him. 'I can't, Kate. This was my father's life.'

'So honour it.'

Pools of anguished green glittered at her. 'I'm trying to honour it by leaving it intact.'

'Then stay and run it as a farm.'

The pools darkened dangerously. 'I think we both know I'm no farmer.'

'You just need training.'

'I have a six-figure job in the city. Responsibilities.'

'Which you seem to have managed just fine via the internet.' He'd not had to make a single trip into the city since arriving as far as she knew.

'It's not the same. I'm only working a few cases. Technically I'm on long leave.'

'But it is doable?'

'I'm a senior partner, Kate.'

'What, they've bought your soul as well as your expertise?'

'I'm not good at it, Kate!' All the seals including the bolshy male lurched off the rock shelf and disappeared into the frigid water, leaving only the sounds of Grant's explosion echoing around the now empty cove.

Kate took a couple of slow breaths to give him time to compose himself. 'At farming?'

'At any of it. It just doesn't interest me. It never did.' His whole body language shifted. Those broad shoulders that looked like they could support the world slumped along with his hanging head. His fists clenched. 'I'm not a farmer.'

Kate lowered her voice to match his. 'What does interest you? The law?'

He took an age to answer. 'The law is what I do. I respect it. I owe it my living.'

'But?'

'But I would hope there's more to me than that.'

Kate frowned. 'OK. Imagine all of this was over and you'd sold your stake in the law firm and money was no object. What would you do?'

Grant lifted his head, blinked at her. 'I have no idea. There's always been the firm. I worked so hard to get there.'

'Let me ask this another way.' She thought for a moment. 'What's on your magazine stand?'

His laugh was raw. 'Wow, this seriously is armchair psychology.'

She arched one brow. 'You do read more than contracts, I presume?'

'I have a huge collection of journals. Alphabetised.'

Why doesn't that surprise me? 'On what?'

He shrugged again. 'Civil engineering. Construction. Architectural wonders.'

'Why?'

He frowned at her, clearly frustrated with her needling. 'Because it's interesting, building things. I spend my days looking for loopholes that will tear contracts down. It's nice to think about building things instead. Things that last.'

Things that last—like the heritage of a family. 'Then build something, Grant. Don't worry about being a farmer.'

'You're talking about developing Tulloquay? You?'

'I'm talking about *strengthening* Tulloquay. Making the most out of it. Build an environment centre. Build a school. Build a museum.'

'Tulloquay has always been a farm.'

Why was he so fixated on the past?

'So farm something else. You don't have to run sheep just because your father did. The old sheds down the back were originally for cattle.' If you asked Kate, neither was particularly suited to this blustery, exposed site where even the good parts took a hammering from the…

'Wind!'

Grant's eyes narrowed. Kate twisted and grabbed both his hands. 'You could build a wind farm.'

The laugh that barked out of him was more than insulting. 'Do I strike you as the hippy type?'

Like her and her team? But she didn't bite. 'I don't believe for a minute that a man with racks of engineering journals wouldn't see the worth in alternative energies. Or the suitability of this coastal zone to wind farming.'

Again, his body language changed. His eyes narrowed

slightly. His spine straightened. 'That doesn't sound cheap,' he muttered, holding his interest in check.

Digging for loopholes?

'I'm sure it's not. But it's lucrative.' *Or there wouldn't be similar outfits up and down the coast.* 'Can you imagine how Mayor Sefton would fall over himself to have the state's first one-hundred-percent wind-powered town? And with interest comes funding. And a project like that would probably meet the Conservation Commission's definition of conservation purposes, even though its also development. You'd have to come inland a bit to get them away from the seal sites but you could revegetate thickly beneath them. Fulfil the requirements of the buffer.'

OK now he really was interested. Either that or his pupils were having another nonepenepherine surge. But somehow, dressed in her best lab whites and completely un-made-up, she didn't think so.

He tipped his head to look up at the top of the cliffs where the wind blew a permanent gale. But, as she watched, his bright eyes dulled. The high flush dropped from his cheekbones. His head started to shake. 'No. Tulloquay is a sheep farm. That's how Dad meant it to be. That's how it needs to stay.'

'What if you sell it to someone who puts a factory on it in five years?'

He practically blanched. 'I won't let that happen. I'll tie it up in the contract.'

'Who's going to sign a contract with that kind of encumbrance? You might as well put the buffer zone in.'

He pushed away from the rock face, from her, and dropped down onto the rock shelf. Kate scrabbled after him.

'My father died trying to make Tulloquay a success, Kate. I won't undo all that work.'

'Leo was going to allow the buffer.'

He shook his head and marched onwards. 'No. He must have had a plan. He just didn't get to see it through.'

'He was dying, Grant. Maybe he wanted to make something of his life before it was too late?'

Grant practically spat back over his shoulder. 'He *had* a life. He was a farmer.'

And a father. Although he wasn't much good at either, it seemed. Her heart squeezed at what he didn't say.

'According to John Pickering he was a closet fisherman! What if he was only running the farm because he felt he had to?'

Grant spun and she smacked straight into his angry, broad chest. 'Kate, stop it. I know what you're doing.'

She frowned up at him. 'What am I doing?'

'Sowing seeds of doubt. Pushing for your project.'

'The only thing I'm pushing for is for you to let go of this stupid obsession with Tulloquay's *destiny* and try and look at this situation rationally.'

She saw the words strike his soul the moment they slipped from her careless lips. His eyes frosted over.

'Stupid?'

'Grant, no, that's not what I—'

'It was a mistake bringing you here,' he ground out starting off again, his long legs making short work of the horror climb back up the cliff path. 'I should have known what choice you'd make.'

Oh, what perfect timing for a comment like that. Here on the path where she couldn't catch up with him, couldn't drag him to a halt and make him listen. The climb stole her breath anyway, so she hurried up the narrow, deadly path in silence. This argument was not worth plunging over the side for. But once they emerged at the top, shoved their way through the thick, nasty shrubs, she was free to respond. She lifted her voice over the buffet of the wind, spoke between heavy breaths. 'I meant what I said, Grant. I will not force your hand. I just wanted you to see you had options.'

He turned back to her when he got to the Jeep. 'After

everything you've just said you expect me to believe you're not going to use this information? The find of your career?'

Kate's stomach clenched. 'No, I'm not. And, yes.' She knew her eyes would betray her if she let him see into them. How would he miss the feelings she was sure simmered visibly there? 'I do.'

'Why would I believe that?'

Tight, aching heat boiled up like reflux. 'Because name me *one* time since we met that I've done a single thing that would be at home at one of your negotiating tables.'

'You got yourself time. You got yourself the mayor as an ally. You got my father on side.'

'I didn't *get* those things, Grant. I worked hard for them. Perfectly honestly.'

'Then give me your word, if you're so honest.'

She froze.

He continued. 'That your decision is not to go to the Conservation Commission with the breeding site. Your word, if you want me to believe it.'

'Are you testing me, the way you tested your father?' Kate barrelled on. 'Tell me, if I say nothing, do I pass the Grant McMurtrie loyalty test?'

His nostrils flared. 'What do you mean?'

'You walked away from Leo when you were sixteen, Grant. How long did you secretly wait for him to beg you to come back? How disappointed were you that he never did?'

His colour surged. 'Kate, don't go there.'

But she was way beyond caring. 'Why not? Either I betray you or I betray my team. Myself. The seals.' The very thought sickened her. 'What do I possibly have to lose at this point?'

'How about the lab? Your accommodations?'

'Take them. They mean nothing compared to—' She only just caught herself in time.

'Compared to?'

Her lab smock rose and fell with her heavy, silent breaths. 'Compared to your belief in me.' It was a half-truth at least.

Grant didn't speak for an age. 'Why is that so important to you?'

No way. She wasn't giving him that only to have him rip it out from under her they way he'd done with the breeding site, knowing she wouldn't use it against him. 'Because I'm a good person, Grant. I'm just trying to find a solution that means neither one of us has to lose everything. But you're treating me like I'm a mega-corporation trying to screw you out of your fortune.'

'This isn't about whether you're a good person or not.'

'You know what? I *get* that you have guilt issues about Leo. I *get* that the two of you had a fractured relationship. I *get* that you've chosen a career which exploits your natural suspicion about everyone on this planet. But I'm asking you to trust *me*. Believe in *me*...'

Her voice cracked horribly on the last word and Kate snapped her mouth shut. She busied herself opening the door so that he wouldn't see the sparkle gathering in her eyes.

'Kate...' His voice was low, cautious.

'Just drive me home, Grant.'

He didn't. He sat there in silence for thirty agonising seconds, thinking. Finally, her eyes dragged up to his, as dry as she could make them.

'That was quite a speech,' he said. 'But it was missing something.'

Exhaustion dragged at her like a diving belt. 'What?'

'Your word.'

A sink-hole opened up below her, leaving her feet hanging perilously over a giant, dark void. Just like Grant McMurtrie's heart. A dozen back-paddock curses spun through her mind, gathered for a bonfire in her wounded chest: that he'd missed the implication of what she was saying. That he'd harbour such suspicion about her integrity. Her own personal ethics.

That he could possibly, for one moment, believe that she'd screw over someone she loved.

And she did. That had begun to dawn on her down on the rock shelf as she had filled her lungs with his smell. As he'd shielded her with his body. The absolute irony that she'd fallen for the one man she could never have. That *he* was what her soul should decide to come out of hibernation for.

For what good it did.

Her eyes sank, deadened, into her skull. Getting words past the football pressing out from inside her chest was going to be a challenge. 'You have my word, Grant. I will not tell the Conservation Commission about the breeding site. I will not stall your sale. You will have everything you want.'

But she would be damned if she was going to leave it out of her research when this was over. It might be the only chance she and the seals ever got. And she would be damned if she was going to stay in the house of a man who held such a low opinion of her too. She'd sleep in her car. They were close enough to the shut-out date that the samples could sit on ice in her city lab until she had nowhere else to be but there.

There simply was no good reason to stay in Grant's orbit a day longer. And so many reasons not to.

She turned her face away from him and stared out of the window, swiping angrily at the single tear that defied her iron will.

She was done crying for the McMurtrie men.

For ever.

CHAPTER ELEVEN

THE offices of Castleridge Shire Council reminded Grant enough of corporate receptions everywhere to start his foot tapping a staccato on the tiled floor. The receptionist glanced pointedly at it for the third time. He pressed his business shoe flat and still.

Again.

A moment later an inner door opened and a middle-aged woman with a pile of files left, looking intensely relieved and just a little bit pleased with herself. It was a momentary reminder that to the rest of the world meetings like this one were something to get nervous about. Like Kate had been, the first time he'd met her. She'd practically rattled with nerves, but had hidden it bravely.

He'd been doing business for other people for so long he'd forgotten what it felt like to have something to lose himself.

The receptionist unfolded from her station to her feet, looking entirely thankful to see the back of Grant and his tap-dancing foot. 'Mayor Sefton will see you now.'

You bet he will. And he'd better have some answers. Still, Grant spared her his best receptionist's smile as he passed which went a long way to undoing the purse of her ancient lips.

'Grant, good to see you.' Alan stepped out from behind his desk and extended his right hand for a shake while his left rested more casually on Grant's shoulder. Business with heart—something else he wasn't used to. Maybe that was what made Alan a good mayor.

'I was going to give you a call or come out and visit,' the mayor said. 'See what you've done with the place.'

Grant slid into the comfortable single-seater across from the mayoral throne. That was the only word for it, a gaudy overly ornate thing that looked like the gold-sprayed macaroni art he'd done in third grade. The art that had sat on his father's fridge long after he'd stopped eating macaroni. The image struck him as incongruous against the rest of his childhood memories.

'Nothing dramatic,' he said.

'You define setting up a research lab as nothing dramatic?'

'Small town.'

'I hear everything.' Alan's body language may have been relaxed and his smile wide but Grant had a sense that he meant it. A man didn't survive this long in regional politics if he didn't have a thriving network of informants. 'I'm pleased you decided to work with Kate instead of against her.'

'I'm not working with her. It was just more practical. She has a lot to do.'

'Was coming to her rescue in the Castleridge Arms practical too?'

Grant shook his head. 'How long did that one take to get to you?'

Alan laughed. 'Pretty sure you were still having dinner. I heard things got a bit personal. I'm glad you were there to pull Kate out. She would hate to have any of them see that they got to her.'

It was Grant's turn to laugh. 'Kate was doing just fine on her own.'

'Don't bet on it. I've never met a woman with better camouflage skills.' He shifted in the throne and Grant recognised the commencement of their official meeting. Even the mayor's voice changed. 'So, what have you decided to do about Tulloquay?'

'I'm selling it.'

Alan stared at him. 'To whom?'

'To whoever is prepared to run it as a going concern.'

The mayor nodded. His eyes stayed blank. 'Could be hard to do with the buffer declaration.'

'There will be no buffer decree.'

His brows lifted. 'You seem confident.'

Kate had given her word. 'I am.'

'Then why are you here?'

'As dad's executor, I'd like you to give me forty-eight hours' notice of the probate settlement. Give me a chance to get all my ducks in a row. I figure it'll take them about that long to finalise the documents after you sign them.'

Alan thought about it. 'I'm sure as the sole beneficiary that's not an inappropriate request. But it's not going to buy you much time.'

'Enough. I only need ownership to sign the final documentation. There's nothing stopping me getting the ball rolling.'

Alan stared at him. 'You're going to put it on the market early.' It wasn't a question.

'Already have.' He'd visited the estate agent before coming here, just in case Kate wasn't as good as her word. Just in case she wasn't the woman he'd convinced himself she was.

Tulloquay was officially for sale.

His gut had been hollow since the moment he'd put pen to paper, imagining Kate's face when the sign went up out on the highway.

'And the two days?'

'Will let me finalise documentation ready for my signature the moment Tulloquay passes to me.'

Alan frowned and folded his hands in his lap. 'I guess I shouldn't be surprised.'

'By what?'

'By your haste to get rid of the place you hate.'

The place where he'd been born. Where his mother had died. Where he'd grown up. 'I don't hate Tulloquay. If I hated it I'd be putting a pesticide factory on it.' Kate's own words about a future buyer doing that echoed ominously in his ears. 'I want Tulloquay to remain a farm. A *stock* farm,' he added, for good measure.

Alan laughed. 'As opposed to…?'

He waved a dismissive hand. 'Kate has some crazy idea of using the buffer zone to establish a wind farm. She wants to see a forest of turbines up along the coast.'

Alan sat bolt upright in his seat. 'Really?'

Grant was tired of indulging the fantasies of everyone but himself. 'Don't get excited, Mayor. I've already said no. There will be no buffer. There will be no wind farm.'

Regardless of the breeding site.

Regardless of Kate.

The mayor frowned. 'Why not? It's a terrific use of the degraded land. And green-power initiatives like that come bundled with rehabilitation funding. You could revegetate the entire coastal strip.'

Was he the only person on the planet that wanted Tulloquay to keep its soul?

'My father didn't work his fingers to the bone building a sheep farm for all his life only to have windmills erected all over his grazing land.'

Alan considered him silently. 'Grant, you were little more than a boy when you left and your contact with Leo was so reduced in the years since. How are you so confident you know what your father wanted? You barely knew him.'

Grant curled his hands around the armchair. Another old buddy about to tell him what his father was actually all about. 'I know enough. I know he said goodbye to my mother there. I know he tried to raise me in his image and hated that I wasn't.' He swallowed hard against the painful memories. 'I know what he said the day I packed and left.'

I would trade you for her in a heartbeat.

Alan frowned. 'He was angry.'

'For the son I never was, I know. He resented everything about me. Being left to raise me, me having no aptitude for livestock. No interest. Me eventually leaving.'

The mayor shifted forward, his eyes softening. 'Yes. It took him a long time to accept what you'd done. What he never had the courage to do.'

Grant's eyes dropped briefly, then found Alan's again. 'What?'

'That you left, son. That you'd had the gumption and self-belief to walk away from what you didn't want.'

An icy chill rattled through him. 'Are you saying he didn't?'

'You don't know?' Alan's frown doubled and then cleared as he realised, speaking almost to himself. 'Of course you don't.'

'I know about his cancer.'

The mayoral eyes folded. 'Ah.'

But now was not the time for that discussion. 'So what other skeletons were in Dad's closet?'

Sefton considered his words. 'It was no secret around here how he felt about the hand life had dealt him. He lost your mother, then you.'

'If that bothered him he never did anything about it. He never tried to change the situation.'

How disappointed were you that he never begged you to come back? His stomach churned at the truth in Kate's hastily thrown out words. How could she read him so clearly when he barely recognised it himself? He'd waited days, then weeks, then eventually months for his father to make the first move. To call him up and ask him to come home. But he never had. He'd never got his wife back, but he'd traded his lost-cause son in without so much as a backwards glance.

'No, he wouldn't have,' Alan continued. 'He wasn't about to drag you back into a life you didn't want any more than he did. But he still resented the hell out of you for making the hard choice, when he hadn't had he courage.'

What?

The word wouldn't come. He couldn't do more than form the very beginning of it on silent lips. A life you didn't want any more than he did.

Goosebumps bubbled up under his fine suit. 'Dad wanted to be a fisherman.'

Alan's smile was bittersweet. 'Perhaps you knew him more than I thought.'

'Then why didn't he?'

'Because his father raised him to be a farmer. It was expected.'

A whooshing sound swirled around each of the mayor's words. Escalating. Amplifying. Expected.

'And he never stood up against *his* father, against the heritage,' Alan said. 'And that ate at him his whole life, that he hadn't had the courage. And then a scrawny bit of a kid did what he'd been wanting to do his whole life.'

Oxygen had to elbow its way past the tightness of Grant's lungs. His father hadn't wanted to be a farmer. He'd never had the courage to walk away.

But his son had.

'He wasn't angry at me?'

Alan's kindly eyes wrinkled at the corners. 'No, son. He was angry at himself for a long, long time. And by the time he finally worked all his issues through the damage was too deep-seated to undo. He'd lost you.'

Grant sat ramrod straight in his chair, his heart sucking back into itself, as the mayor continued. 'But he always had such satisfaction knowing what a success you were making of your life. How you'd turned your life into something you wanted.'

'But why didn't he just give it all up? Become a fisherman when there was no reason not to?'

'Because his father had worked all his life to build Tulloquay up. He felt he couldn't walk away from all that his forebears had done. Everything they'd tried to make the farm.' Kind eyes softened. 'Sound familiar?'

Grant swallowed hard.

His father had died admiring him for having the courage to stand up for what he wanted. Not hating him for it.

Not hating him.

He lifted his head. 'Then why didn't he leave me instructions in his will, if he wanted Kate's buffer to go through? It would have saved everyone a heck of a lot of pain.'

Alan lifted his hands. 'I tried to persuade him. But he didn't want to impose his wants and needs on you. He let you walk away from your only family years before rather than tie you to a life the way he'd been tied. Leaving you specific instructions would only have forced your hand.'

He hadn't failed. His father was disappointed with his own failings, not his son's.

Sorrow for a lifetime lost swamped over him like a tidal surge. Emotions he hadn't allowed for years all bubbled up from the mud that swilled around him and burst, fresh and raw. Every part of him ached.

'I need to—'

He stammered to a halt and frowned. Where did he start? There was too much to think about. So many things to filter, dissect. A lifetime of misunderstanding to sift through, like Kate with her lanternfish ear-bones. His head came up as all of those thoughts, feelings and regrets all lined up and made a three-dimensional letter in his imagination.

The letter K.

His eyes fell onto Alan's patient ones. 'I think I need to see Kate.'

'Going somewhere?'

Grant filled the entrance to her lab—her ex-lab—large and rock-solid, as if he was part of the building. Amazing ho quickly she'd grown used to seeing him amongst all the technical equipment they used on this project. Equipment that now lay dismantled around her. Of course, he'd never actually been in, not since the day he'd helped her move. The door was usually as far as he came.

She'd been stupid not to see that for what it was—proof that he didn't really support her. Or her research. She barely paused before turning her focus back to the data-logger computer. Lucky she'd kept all the cable ties handy. Maybe on some level she knew she wouldn't be here long.

'Coming here was a mistake,' she said. 'I'm just correcting it.'

Behind her, his voice grew pensive. 'You're leaving?'

She levered a recalcitrant cable back and forth, trying to prize it free. 'You can't expect me to stay.'

'Don't make any rash decisions, Kate.'

Pain lanced through her. 'You think I'm overreacting?' The cable finally yanked away from its housing on her indelicate grunt. 'I don't like being coerced.'

'By who?'

She spun to face him, heart racing. 'I believed you when you said you were tired of being the bad guy. I felt sorry for the man who'd view himself that way. I let you put the responsibility for the decision squarely onto me because I thought it would make it easier on you.'

She struggled against the tears that wanted to express her hurt, swallowing them back. 'You dressed it up as trust but that was one-hundred-percent pure strategy. You *knew* I wouldn't do the wrong thing by you. You *knew* I wouldn't prioritise myself over you. And you were right.'

She slammed something valuable into its box without a care for what it was. 'I'm not ashamed of that. I got my values from my parents and they are the one thing of theirs that I got to keep. But it doesn't mean I don't realise when I'm being manipulated. It doesn't mean I like being backed against the wall by a shark.'

Just one more word she could add to the litany of names she'd called him since this morning.

'What are you going to do?'

She shouldn't tell him. He was the enemy. Her mind knew it even if her body was in denial—her heart. 'I'm cutting my losses, Grant. I'll finish up at Dave's Cove and head back to the city.'

'You still have three weeks.'

'No.' Her lips tightened. 'I'm not doing this on your schedule.' *Like some starved dog grateful for whatever scraps you might throw me.* Pulling out on her own terms was the last thing she could do to control her own environment.

'But your research?'

Her voice thickened. 'Is finished. It had to end one day.'

His frown cut down between those eyes she knew she'd be dreaming about for years. She turned away, back to her equipment, unable to bear looking at him.

It hurt too much.

'My father hated the farm, Kate.'

His quiet words stopped her cold. 'What?'

'At least, he hated farming. I'm sure he loved the coastal position. You were right. He wanted to be a fisherman. You were right about all of it.'

She turned her eyes back towards the hollow, defeated tone of his voice. Sorrow swelled up inside her. Being right had never felt less satisfying. 'How do you know?'

'Mayor Sefton. They were friends.'

Kate nodded, itching to cross to him but conscious that he hadn't stepped forward. If he needed her, wanted her, he would have come to her, not stop just short, hovering in the doorway as usual. Her chest tightened. Actions meant so much more than words. Nothing had really changed.

But he did come to you, a little voice nagged. *He's here now.*

'You've been protecting a mirage.' She didn't say it to be unkind, but she saw the impact of her words in his expression: Pained. Raw. But still he didn't move.

While she burned to.

'A mirage,' he repeated, nodding. 'All the heritage I thought I was preserving. None of it was real. None of this has been real.'

She swallowed. '*I'm* real.'

His hands braced, white-knuckled, on the frame of the doorway to the lab. She ached to move, to take even a few steps towards him. But she anchored herself against the lab table and stayed put. He had to come to her.

'But I'm not,' he gritted out. 'I've spent my life persevering in a field I don't much like because I chose it. Because I threw away my family to be the furthest thing from a farmer that I could. Because pulling out would render that sacrifice meaningless.'

'Is that why your father kept on at Tulloquay after you'd gone? To justify all the loss?'

Was it a case of like father like son?

Grant shrugged. 'We'll never know. Something kept him on this land.'

Kate eyed him hard. Took a risk. 'What will keep you here?'

He missed her pointed look, shook his head. 'I fought to be in the boardrooms of the city. That's where I belong. For better or for worse.'

'Why? Because you don't believe in starting again? What if your future is here?'

He looked around. 'I feel like a ghost here.'

Sudden anger blazed through her. Would he still not accept

that there was a heritage in coming home—even if that home wasn't everything you expected? 'You are a ghost, Grant. You just stand there in the doorway and keep yourself removed from the reality of all of this. Refusing to become tangible. Refusing to take a single action that will make this real.'

Refusing even to step forward.

I'm right here, Grant. I'm real.

His eyes flicked over the corners of the lab before finally resting on hers. The fluorescent lights bounced off what she suddenly realised was a sheen of sweat on his skin. 'I can't come in.'

Frustration made her hiss. 'Why not?'

'This is where I found my father.'

The frustration and anger twisted over and over in an urgent ball and then plummeted to the depths of her belly. Horror should have torn at her skin. Fury. But all Kate could think about was how comfortable she always was in this room. And how it was the only place other than Dave's Cove that she didn't feel alone. How Grant had only managed to step foot in here once. So briefly. It made an unearthly kind of sense.

Leo had died here. Grant had found him right here.

She looked around.

Hello, Kate, the walls almost whispered.

His pain was contagious and it swelled and pressed against her chest. She put down the computer she was dismantling and quietly crossed to the doorway, conscious she was breaking her own sanction—going to him. *Again.* But doing anything less was in breach of the person she was. That was as pointless as Grant denying his heritage.

She stood on the step below his, slipped her hand into his icy-cold one…and pulled. His eyes flickered down into hers, his fingers tightening but not entirely with resistance. She ran her thumb over the back of his palm—encouraging, fortifying—and stepped back down into the sunken garage. 'Come on. You did this before.' Albeit brief and painfully rushed.

It was step out or topple down onto her. Grant's foot eased forward onto the lower step.

'It's just a room, Grant.'

And then he was there. Standing in the space his father had taken his last breath in. His grip was like a vice on her hand… But he was there.

Pride surged through her. 'How do you feel?'

He looked around, thinking. Confused lines splayed out from the corners of his eyes. 'I feel nothing.'

Not exactly what she'd been hoping to inspire.

His fingers tightened. 'No, not nothing. *Blank*.' His eyes found hers and focussed, as though he was really seeing her at last. Her heart flip-flopped. 'Canvas blank. Like it's waiting. Like everything starts now.'

Kate's breath tripped in her throat. Her fingers threaded more firmly between his.

He shook his head. 'Saving this farm was the last useful thing I could do for my father.' Self-loathing stained a short, bitter laugh. 'And there was no need. The farm wasn't his life. The sea was.'

His free hand slid up to cup her cheek. She pressed into it, to warm it. Uncaring about the tears gathering in her eyes. 'I'm so sorry, Grant.'

'Don't be. You did nothing but be a friend to my father in his final days.' He glanced around. 'Maybe your project brought him the first real satisfaction of his life.'

Kate's watery laugh was half a sob. She glanced at Leo's old chair. 'I hope so. I wish so.'

Grant's thumb broke free of her jaw to wipe gently under her eye, catching the tiny tear that wobbled there. Kate blinked up at him, lost in his intense, green depths. He shifted his thumb lower, dragging it back and forth softly across her lips. Her heart rate gathered momentum. He looked as surprised as she was by the movement, almost as if his hand acted on its own accord.

'I'm not selling the farm.'

She gasped.

'I'll take it off the market tomorrow.'

When had he put it on? She ignored the question and asked one of her own. 'You'll stay on the farm?'

His eyes darkened. 'I don't think so. I'll think of something. But you can finish your research. Take whatever time you need.'

Her whole body shuddered.

He glanced around again. 'It was wrong of me to make you choose. Things have just been…complicated, clouded, since I arrived.'

Every protective urge in her body reached out to him to take his pain. 'You gave me the breeding site. It was my decision not to use the information. I had a choice.'

'Not much of a choice. You did that for me.'

Her heart had to be glowing in her eyes. Surely? She could only nod.

'That changes things between us.'

Her eyes longed to flutter shut but she held them long enough to peer up at him, her heart kicking into high gear. 'Us?'

'Now that it's all over. Now that there's no your side or my side. Now that there's not a giant, messy gulf separating us.' He traced the sensitive line of her top lip with his thumb. She pressed her mouth to the masculine pad of flesh. 'Can I finally kiss you again?'

The heavenly drug of desire thickened her words. 'That depends.'

He smiled. 'On what?'

Kate opened her lips and let his thumb slide between them, between her teeth. Then she released him and slipped her arms around his warm, very unghostly body. 'On whether this is a beginning or an end.'

Grant's eyes flickered like a pilot flame before bursting into bright life as they drew closer. Kate drowned in their green,

green depths. His lips, when they finally touched hers, were as soft and coaxing as the first time they'd kissed. Blood rushed thick and fast into her head, pooling behind the sensitive flesh where her mouth met his, thrumming with joy.

He lifted his head, barely, and murmured close against her skin. 'This feels like a beginning.'

His arms tightened around her, kept her close as his mouth worked over hers. His serpentine hold seemed to restrict her air intake and all she could suck in were fast, flimsy gasps between glorious, blazing kisses. It only added to her light-headedness but for once she didn't care. If she stumbled, he'd catch her. If she passed out, he'd keep her safe until she recovered.

If she loved him…

Maybe—*maybe*—he could love her back.

She'd felt it on intuition when she'd been tucked into him behind the boulder on the rock shelf at the breeding site—that Grant would be gentle and protective should he ever make love to her.

She was about to find out.

She tore her throbbing mouth from his and confessed through hoarse words. 'I packed up my bedroom.'

A gaze the colour of a rainforest mist settled down on her. She held her breath.

'That's OK,' he murmured, lowering his mouth again. 'We can use mine.'

'Protective' didn't really cut it.

Grant practically worshipped her during the twelve hours they were sequestered away in his bedroom. His touch was gentle, his whispers a dazzling, mind-altering caress. He'd borne his weight over her as gently as she could have wished, but he was as self-assured and powerful as she could have dreamed for.

And he filled corners of her soul she'd thought she'd surrendered for ever to cobwebs.

They'd emerged just once to re-fuel on chicken sandwiches, then fallen back into bed. His mobile had rung—they'd ignored it. His laptop had dinged—Grant had snapped it shut and then dived back under the covers. His mobile had gone off again—he'd tossed it across the room.

They'd laughed and loved and lazed until the sun poked experimental tentacles over the horizon. Kate watched the glorious golden glow spread across Tulloquay's paddocks from the safety of Grant's bedroom window. From the warmth of his embrace.

Her naked skin pressed back hotly against his and the feathered quilt wrapped them into a sacred cocoon. Grant nuzzled his way through the wild tangle of her unbound hair and pressed his lips into her nape—in case it was the solitary square inch of her body that he hadn't kissed overnight.

Even on less than two hours' sleep, Kate felt revitalised. Nothing was too complicated with Grant at her back. She'd finish her research, save the seals, make a difference. She'd find a way to help him with the farm. Life just felt brighter. Like anything was possible.

All totally under control. And she did not care if it wasn't.

Because she had him.

She shifted uncomfortably as the ring that hung on a leather thong around his neck bit into her spine. He retrieved it carefully and draped it over her shoulder. She stared at it.

'Who…?' She didn't want to ask. She didn't want to know if he had an ex-wife squirrelled away somewhere. Or, worse, a dead one that he'd never got over. A man didn't wear his old wedding ring near his heart for nothing.

He picked the ring up and fingered it. 'This was my mother's.'

'You've always worn it?'

'I took it the day I left. I think my father knew, but he never said a word.'

'Maybe he didn't need the ring to remember her by. Or recognised that you needed it more?'

Tension radiated out from his hard body. It was different to the exciting tension he'd carried all night. It was subtle, but there. 'This is all so new to me,' he eventually murmured into her hair.

Kate leaned back into his strength, still revelling in the beauty of his body against hers. She tipped her head up and around to look at him. His jaw was strong and defined and irresistibly close to her lips. She pressed them into his stubbled skin and murmured 'Which part?'

'Not the sex.' He smiled down at her and her heart skipped a beat or three.

Her chuckle turned throaty. 'I figured. No-one's that good on instinct.'

'I don't…' He pressed another worship against her temple, then whispered against her hot skin. 'I've kept myself separate for a long time. Haven't let myself feel…anything.'

Her heart picked up pace, and not just because of the blazing hands absently stroking up and down her ribs beneath the quilt. 'You've had a lot of loss.'

'So have you. But you've managed to come out a decent human being.'

She twisted back to look more closely at him. 'You don't think you're a good person?'

'I…' Two tiny lines appeared between his brows. 'I feel like everything I have is undeserved. Like I just lucked into it.'

'You've worked so hard. Why would you think you don't deserve it?'

He fingered the ring. 'The last person that valued me wore this ring.'

His mother. She turned in his hold and the move pressed her more fully against him. They fitted together so perfectly. That had to mean something, right? 'Your father valued you. He left you this farm.'

'Only by default. Who else was he going to leave it to? He didn't exactly move heaven and earth to get me back when I left.'

'Leo was nothing if not proud. And strong. It must have burned him not to come after you. Releasing you to find your own dreams. Doesn't that tell you something about how worthy you were to him?'

He stared at her. 'I exploit weakness for a living. Do you imagine he would have been proud of that?'

Kate rolled her eyes. He was determined to find weakness in himself. 'That's one way to look at it. You could just as easily say you fortify. To protect people, the people you work for.'

His nod was far away. 'If not for the fact I haven't built a contract in years. I only tear them down.'

Kate shrugged. 'Time for a change, then?'

Green eyes met brown. 'You make it sound so easy.'

'It doesn't have to be hard. You have plenty of money. You have a home here. I'm sure there's no shortage of ambitious people working under you who'd kill for your spot in the firm.'

His words were soft. 'I don't know who I'd be if I wasn't there.'

She stretched her arms up to press against his strength. To share some of hers. 'You can be anything at all that you want to be.' She pressed her lips against the pulse thumping visibly below his jaw. 'That's the beauty of having all the cards. You can deal them any way you want.'

'You think I have all the cards?'

'You have money, experience, property, looks, reputation…'

You have me.

'There's something missing from that list.'

'What?'

Green eyes blazed down into hers and he shifted against her, bringing them into even closer contact. 'Family.'

Kate's heart lurched wildly in her chest and every bit of moisture in her mouth abandoned her.

'So I guess I've still got a few cards to collect,' he said.

Just then a short chime sounded from somewhere beneath a pile of their hastily discarded clothes. Grant kissed her, lingering against her lips, and then extracted himself from the comfort of their feathery circle.

'I'm going to take a shower; I'll be back,' he said. 'Unless you'd like to join me?'

Kate threw him a wry look. They both knew Leo's shower was barely big enough for one, let alone two. Not if they both wanted to get wet.

'OK, point taken. I'll be five minutes. Keep a space warm for me.' He reached down to retrieve his mobile and all the muscles down one side of his body flexed deliciously. 'Then let's see who was so keen to get hold of me last night.'

He disappeared into the adjoining bathroom, loading up with clean clothes on the way, and Kate heard the hiss of the water bursting into life. She turned back to her beautiful sunrise.

How many sunrises like this had she missed while she'd been busy driving back and forth to his farm? How many sunsets? She'd have to hold this one in her head for ever once she went back to the city. Even though the word 'family' hung tantalisingly in the air, Grant hadn't invited her to stay longer than the end of her project. Tulloquay had come to feel like a second home since she'd first set foot on it. A hard-won, and therefore extra appreciated home. Something she hadn't had for a really long time. Even her apartment was just that, a place to put her head at night. It was too empty to be called a home.

Did Grant know what he was giving up by leaving Tulloquay? Now that he believed his father hadn't lived and died by the place, would he hold onto it or ultimately sell it as a going concern? Could she persuade him to stick around a bit longer?

A lot longer?

Or would it make no difference at all? He didn't want to farm it. He wouldn't want to stay on it. Just because he was asking questions about his future didn't necessarily mean it included her.

A cold trickle worked its way down her spine. In all those illicit murmurings last night he hadn't said anything about the future. About 'for ever'. About wanting anything more than right now. She'd written up an emotional contract the moment she'd followed him into this room but it remained bare of signatures.

This feels like a beginning. That was all. He could have meant the beginning of a great night of all-holds-barred loving. She flexed sore muscles. He'd certainly delivered, but there had been no other promises.

At least not from him. She'd made promises to herself all night. Promises to be open about her feelings, not to shut him out. To take the risk. Something about growing up without a family only made her value it more when she found it. She'd come within a breath of crying out that she loved him several times last night but something—an indefinable, base-instinct *something*—held her back.

She wanted to say it. She wanted him to know. She wanted to take a stick and write 'Kate Dickson loves Grant McMurtrie' in the dirt and watch the realisation on his face. She wanted to hear the reciprocal words in his gravelly voice. She wanted that first flush of revelation.

She wasn't going to get any of that if she didn't screw up the courage to tell him first.

She'd dealt with cranky Leo McMurtrie before he'd come around; surely confessing her love for his son couldn't be all that hard?

Could it?

She turned her head and traced an unfamiliar sound back to the bathroom. Was he singing? It was hardly bar-room karaoke but it was rich, deep and soft. And joyous.

The water pipes under the house clunked as Grant shut off

the shower, and Kate turned towards the bathroom door on a smile. She pictured him towelling that amazing body dry. Brushing his teeth. Spraying on the deodorant she loved to breathe in so much.

All the things she wanted to be part of for ever.

For ever.

Wow. That was a much bigger mouthful than just 'I love you'. For ever meant rings. And public declarations. And babies. *Family.* But the idea of a lean-legged, green-eyed little girl running around Tulloquay getting dirty didn't fill her with terror. It just made her smile even more.

Grant would make an amazing father.

The bathroom door opened and Kate looked up, certain every thought she'd just been having was still written on her face, but not caring. He'd know soon enough.

She silently opened the quilt to invite him back in to the warmth of her love.

It had been years since Grant had sung in the shower but this morning a tune practically fought its way out of him. He soaped up to its bass beat and rinsed off to the chorus.

He hummed. He smiled.

He shower-danced and nearly took the plastic curtain with him when he over-balanced during a Jackson Five heel spin with a head full of suds.

He prayed for the first time in…for ever. He closed his eyes and he thanked everything out there for the gift of Kate—a woman who could see him for who he should be, not who he had been. An intelligent woman who used her brain for more than just conniving business. A beautiful, loyal woman who wasn't afraid to share herself with him.

A woman that made him forget himself and talk about his mother. About wanting family. About his long, painful history.

A woman he could trust with his future. With his farm. With his heart.

Out of absolutely nowhere, this was the person he could see himself getting old with. Raising children with—doing a damn sight better job with his kids than Leo had done with him. Just when he'd begun to actually believe that he wasn't truly worthy of the love of a good woman any more than he'd been worthy of his father's.

Not that Kate had spoken of love, but her eyes had, and they both knew what a terrible poker face she had.

He killed the water and stepped out onto the mat, briskly drying off.

A few moments later he was dressed, combed and roughly shaved—any longer meant time away from Kate who was cooling her heels in his bedroom. Or maybe back in his bed, if he got lucky.

He smiled and reached for his phone, eager to get business out of the way just in case dressing truly had been premature. But somehow he found it hard to care this morning.

He flicked through a message from his phone-service provider offering to change his subscription, and his daily update from his broker, then his thumb wavered to a halt on the third message—from Mac Davis, his associate.

And his man in the city handling investigations into Tulloquay's conservation status.

Blood surged thick and hard through his heart in a series of painful beats. Twenty years of self-doubt instantly made him fear the contents of the message, instantly had his momentary joy curling up in a cringing ball. But then the memory of twenty hours with a bright, loving woman gave him the strength to suck it up, not to automatically assume the worst. Kate was not his father. He was worth her love.

And she was worth his. The woman he loved had given him her word.

He lowered his thumb and activated the message:

Conservation Commission ruling in: breeding site identified. Full coastal buffer-zone ratified. Property encumbered. Continue sale documentation? Pls advise.

His chest squeezed so hard it gripped him like the start of a cardiac arrest before releasing him into a pool of pain and recriminations so overwhelming the phone clattered from his senseless fingers into the sink.

Lies—every single thing she'd said.

A joke—every single thing he'd said.

How she must have been laughing at him quietly as he'd spoken of family, of his mother, of his fears. As she had taken him by the hand and pulled him into the room his father had died in. *Inspired.* Was it triumph and not love glittering so wildly in her eyes as he'd buried himself deeper and deeper in what he'd thought was her goodness? Her honesty?

Her loyalty.

The time stamp on Mac's message was last night. She must have waited all of an hour before notifying the Conservation Commission of the location of the breeding site.

If that.

He braced himself on the edge of the sink and lifted his eyes to the mirror. They blazed dark and furious back at him and he did nothing to mask them.

Let her see what she'd done.

Let her dream about this look on his face for the rest of her life.

The face of her betrayal.

CHAPTER TWELVE

KATE crumpled her arms back into her chest, covering her vulnerability with a feather shield, conscious of having nothing but skin beneath the quilt, while Grant stood fully dressed and seething, blocking the doorway.

For a man who'd just stepped out of a steaming-hot shower, he was awfully pale. His eyes raged darkly at her and he half-strangled the mobile phone in his hand.

What?

She wanted to ask, but couldn't. Words just wouldn't come past the certainty that everything she'd just dreamed about was about to dissolve down into the sort of thing she was used to scraping off the rock's at Dave's Cove.

She just stared and mangled the quilt.

Grant recovered his voice before she did. 'I've said it before, Kate. You have a terrible poker face. Given how pleased with yourself you looked as I came out of the bathroom, I hope you're not going to pretend not to know what's going on.'

She had to swallow twice before she could speak. 'I have no idea.'

He tossed his mobile phone at her. She had to drop a corner of the quilt to catch it, but she sagged with it to the ground rather than do this naked in front of a man that was rapidly feeling like a stranger. She scanned the message on the tiny screen.

Her chest squeezed as she sucked in a short breath.

Her seals were safe. But then her gut lurched and tumbled as she lifted her eyes to Grant's ice-cold ones. She was desperately glad to already be on the floor.

'Well played, Kate. I have to say, I fell for every moment. The protestations of loyalty. Innocence. You even stooped to the dead-family card.'

Pain speared through her.

'Those big brown eyes were enormously persuasive. Remind me to get an intern with similar—'

'You think I did this?' she croaked.

'Who else? Breeding site one day, buffer zone finalised the next. It's not that hard to connect the dots.'

'It's government, Grant. They don't move that fast. They would have had to have the paperwork finalised a week ago to send you a confirmation today. That means it was a done deal already.'

'Also your handiwork, I imagine,' he spat.

Her eyes fluttered shut. The Commission must have decided to ratify on the basis of her early research alone; it was the only possibility. It *was* her fault. She lifted her eyes again. He might hate her—fine—but he wasn't going to think she betrayed him. 'I did *not* tell the Conservation Commission about the breeding site.'

His nostrils flared and she noticed for the first time how tight his clenched knuckles were. As though he was enduring something unendurable. 'Irrelevant now. The encumbrance has been added to Tulloquay's title. The farm's unsellable.'

'Grant, I'm sorry…'

He wrapped one white-knuckled fist around the front of the quilt where she bunched it together and pulled her to her feet, closer to his fury. 'No, you're not. Or you wouldn't have done it.'

'I *didn't* do it.' She held out his phone. 'Not this. I gave you my word.'

'Which apparently is as valueless as this farm.'

The missile hit its target. Her stomach clenched and she

felt the courage leach from her face. He wanted to believe the worst. It probably fitted perfectly with his view of the world. It probably protected him. But being on her feet did more than just equalise them physically. She felt stronger. Angry.

'You'd already decided not to sell.'

'I'd decided not to sell just *yet*. Big difference.'

'So you weren't even planning to stick around at all? Then what was *this*?' She indicated the rumpled sheets around them, vividly recalling how every crease had been made.

He scooped up her lab uniform and tossed the ball of fabric at her. She let the clothes rebound off her like the insult they were.

'*This* was an error of judgement on my part.'

The air sucked out of the bedroom as Grant stalked out of it. Kate fumbled her lab trousers on, not caring that they were inside out. In under sixty seconds she was in pursuit, fully dressed. Completely dishevelled.

She followed the sound of crashing and slamming to the kitchen. 'Grant…'

She stumbled to a halt, unprepared for the ravages on his face as he spun violently. 'You must have been laughing behind my back, knowing what you were going to do. Is that why you were so…vigorous last night? Celebrating? You heard the messages coming in one by one and you knew what they'd be about. Is that what it takes to get the virtuous Dr Dickson hot?'

Ice water plunged over her. 'You'd like that, wouldn't you?'

He glared at her, shady and menacing. His enormous pupils virtually eclipsed the green that had once been there, as big and wild as they had been last night. Her treacherous body still found him beautiful.

She forced those feelings away. 'It suits you for me to be a liar and a user because you have no idea what to do with someone who's genuine. Who's not out to swindle you. You have no idea what to do with someone good, someone genuinely trying to find a solution that means neither of us had to lose. It's totally outside your experience. You've come to expect nothing but disappointment from life.'

'You betrayed me.' A wildly unsteady finger pointed at her. 'I gave you shelter. I gave you a lab. I let you in where no-one else got to go.' He banged his chest with an angry fist. 'I helped you.'

Her lip curled and it was about as foreign to her as the rage seething off the man in front of her. 'You helped *yourself.* Let's not dress this up—you gave me shelter so you could monitor my progress. You gave me lab space in the room your father suicided in rather than have to face the reality of what had happened in there. You revealed just enough of yourself to keep me wondering, to make me open up to you. Tell me *that* wasn't boardroom strategy.'

The hoarseness of his groan broke her momentum. 'I *trusted* you, Kate.'

'No, Grant.' Her voice cracked on his name and her heart followed a split second behind it. Living her pain, feeling his. 'You never trusted me. Or we wouldn't be having this discussion.'

She turned and walked down the hall towards the room where her belongings were already packed. She'd send for the lab gear later, or she'd sacrifice the lot. She just didn't care.

When she returned, her belongings in tow, he was standing exactly where she'd left him, a granite monolith simmering like a latent volcano. It helped her to be calm. Like the eye of a cyclone.

'Just so there's no misunderstanding…' she said, balancing her suitcase on its wheels and walking carefully up to him. She slid her hands resolutely up the warm, familiar arms that had held her so safe the night before and stared up at him hard. He kept staring straight over her head, his jaw rigid. 'I did not alert the Conservation Commission. I did not betray you. I—' Again, something stopped her. Something that clearly sensed which way the wind was blowing. 'I *care* for you too much to hurt you like that. But if you let me walk out of this house you will not see me again.' She squeezed his arms for emphasis. 'Ever.'

The eyes that she'd been dreaming about since she'd first met him remained locked on the far corner of the room for what felt like eternity. Then slowly—agonisingly slowly—they slid down to fix on hers.

'Don't.' His voice wavered. 'Don't you look at me like that.'

'Like what?'

'Like you care. Like you have anyone's interests but your own at heart.' He pried her hands off his forearms. 'I was wrong when I said last night was a beginning. This can only be an end.'

Kate's pulse burst from its relentless hammering and bled out in her throat.

He stepped away from her and threw the kill shot back over his shoulder, hoarse and low.

'I want you and your "I love you" eyes the hell out of my house.'

CHAPTER THIRTEEN

THREE weeks had changed nothing about Tulloquay except the shiny new padlock on the gate. Kate stared at it and struggled not to weep.

She might as well not have come at all.

But Grant had not responded to her emailed requests to provide a date for her movers to collect the lab equipment and he certainly hadn't boxed it up and shipped it himself. So what choice did she have? Having made the enormously painful decision to come and collect it personally, having driven three agonising hours, she wasn't about to let a locked gate stop her. She climbed back into her car, reverse-parked it hard against the road edge then locked it behind her. Then she wiggled her way over the top of the locked farm gate and dropped down the other side, glancing around nervously, convinced she should be wearing a black balaclava.

Except she was stealing her own property. From inside Grant's house—officially, now that probate had settled. Today, in fact. Tulloquay was Grant's, and the Atlas colony was off-limits. But at least they were protected. The conservation buffer had seen to that.

And—despite everything—that was still an enormous achievement. One she was not sure she deserved.

After all, she'd been prepared to compromise them for love. Probably not the craziest thing anyone had ever done for a man, but certainly most out of character for her. She just didn't put people before her work. Not usually. Her work was all she'd had for so long. It was certainly what was holding her together now.

Well, karma had certainly sorted her out, hadn't it?

She straightened her clothes and set off for the two-kilometre walk down the drive to the homestead. Fingers-crossed, Grant wouldn't have locked the house completely up so she could get a little packing done until he got home. The last thing she wanted to do was waste this entire journey just because McAss had somewhere better to be.

Just because she was too scared to call him.

Because she'd fall apart if she heard his voice.

She was counting on her Dickson pride saving her when she saw him in person, not letting her shed a single tear. She was counting on him still being so angry that he'd rile the beast inside her and she'd be too busy being furious to indulge the tears and tremors that she saved for under her pillow. That she tried to muffle even though she was totally alone in her apartment, the same way she'd cried in her first nights at Aunt Nancy's.

She picked up speed.

She was counting on it.

The south-coast sunshine streamed gently down on her as she jogged past paddocks devoid of sheep, the resulting grass longer than she'd ever seen it. Grant hadn't wasted any time in re-homing them—or butchering them. The man she left standing in the kitchen would be capable of it, for sure.

Figures. He didn't strike her as a man to wallow long. If at all.

Ten minutes brought her to Grant's locked front door. For the first time, she worried that he might not even be here. What if he'd gone back to the city right after she had? Maybe that was why the gate was locked. A horrible thought streaked across her consciousness. What if he'd sold it, after all, and the shiny new padlock belonged to shiny new owners?

What if she really, truly *was* trespassing?

Heart in her mouth, she crept around the side of the house, hoping that old habits might die hard. Grant's city existence meant he locked the front door religiously but he'd not even been able to find a key for the back door, so that almost always stood unsecured. Unless he'd had the locks changed.

Please, please…

The knob turned easily in her hand.

The moment the door swung open, Kate's eyes began to water. The closed-up house smelled just like the man living in it, with the residual hint of the older man that had lived there for seventy years. The two McMurtrie men.

Both lost to her.

Had old Leo really got so deeply under her skin? She knew his son had. She should be in there packing her gear right now, not mooching around the kitchen door sniffing walls.

Caring like this was so foreign.

She threw her shoulders back and pressed on through the house. Nothing had changed inside but, for the first time, she realised that Grant had never really *had* much of his own to display. He'd lived in the same few outfits. He'd resisted letting any part of himself get comfortable in his father's house.

Stepping into the garage, she sighed. Everything was exactly as she'd last seen it—no, not exactly. A number of items had been carefully packed up into boxes but the rest lay where she'd left them. As though someone had begun to pack for her but then thought better of it.

He'd probably decided she wasn't worth the trouble.

She pulled a flat-packed box from the stack wedged down the side of Leo's ancient beer-fridge and folded it out into shape. Then she criss-crossed tape on it, placed a steriliser neatly in its centre, and padded it out with lighter, protective items. She wanted it to be light, given she'd likely be carrying these boxes to her car alone. As soon as she could get her car close.

Several other boxes joined the first before she paused for

a break. Not that she was tired from the packing, but she was tired from not sleeping. She was tired from all the crying. Tired from her two-kilometre jog here. Tired from over-thinking everything. Of having nothing but her work to keep her warm at night.

She was tired of being alone.

She'd been so careful her whole life not to let herself come to rely on anyone, not to let anyone too close—close enough that she might come to care for them. Close enough that it might break her heart to lose them. It had all but torn free back when she was a child and had lost her parents. She'd been super-careful to encase it ever since.

But Grant had snuck up on her, wiggled in under her radar and nestled himself deep in her limping heart. In some ways he'd even started to heal it, careful scabs forming over the old wounds. Until he'd brutally finished the job three weeks ago with his ugly accusations.

But she hadn't counted on him being more damaged than she was. That he could believe her capable of betrayal.

Leo's old chair beckoned from the corner. Kate crawled up into it, curled into a comfortable lump, and set the chair to spinning with a foot braced against the onion-pickling table that had become her lab workbench. She spun and she spun, pushing beyond dizzy, her eyes drifting shut with the hypnotic movement.

'Leo...' She whispered to the empty space around her. 'Help him.'

Everything around her was silent.

Her words were little more than a croak. 'He's your son and he's hurting. *I'm* hurting. You raised him like this—untrusting and cautious—this is your mess to fix.'

Help him. I love him.

A single tear squeezed out from between clenched eyelids as she spun.

Immediately she was under water. Deep under water, where

the seals dived for the best, oiliest fish to sustain them through winter. She swam amongst the seals she knew so well—Stella, Dorset, Amy. She swam amongst their pups who'd grown big and lithe. All of them twisted and frolicked towards an underwater cave. She kicked out toward it.

Her face broke surface but it was dark inside the cave. Cold. The bitter air stung as it dried the salt water in her eyes and she searched around her for…what?

That man?

Suddenly there was an old man standing on the shore, with eyes as brilliant and green as the gems in the cave all around her. She swam towards him, towards shore, but never drew any closer. She grew exhausted from the exertion and still he just smiled. He radiated enormous rightness, standing on the shore of that hidden cove, a fish frying on a pan in the corner. Dry. Warm. At peace.

Leo.

His lips moved but she was too far to hear. Too much water filled her ears she was so far from him, yet she could see those eyes so clearly.

I can't hear you, Leo.

A pillar of bubbles surged to the surface. She was still underwater. Her lungs ached for the air she'd only dreamed she'd been taking in. Leo shook his head, unable to hear her. He smiled. Pointed up.

The seals called, high-pitched and luring, from the light above her.

Kate tipped her head back. A pinprick of light shone far above, far from the darkness of the deep sea. Too far to get to on what little oxygen she had left. She looked again at Leo.

His left hand pointed up. His right slid up over his heart.

She raised hers in farewell.

Seals twisted amongst her limbs, buffeting her, catching her up, surging with her to the surface. Salt water streamed past her eyes, blinding her, but she kept them focussed on the pinprick of light that grew as she powered to the surface, closer and brighter.

The blue of the sky, except golden. The gold of Tulloquay's empty paddocks.

A comforting warmth seeped through her, radiating outward from her shoulder. Its existence registered dimly in her unconscious mind but grew in confidence as she pressed for the surface. So close.

So close.

Her eyes opened.

'Hey.'

The verdant green of Grant's eyes were as warm as the whisper of his voice. Kate sucked in a huge breath and swiped at the salty tears running down her cheeks.

'Please don't cry, Kate.'

Her heart contracted. Grant.

Every unconscious, sleep-deprived cell in her wanted to lurch into his arms, regardless of everything. But her conscious mind raced to catch up, censored. She shuffled backwards in Leo's chair instead.

Grant leaned back on his heels and lifted his hands carefully to his side away from her shoulder. 'I'm sorry if I startled you.'

Her eyes felt like dinner plates in her head. 'Why are you here?'

'I live here.'

Right. Everything was muddled but she had no idea why. Had she been asleep? The last thing she remembered was spinning in Leo's old chair.

She frowned. *Leo.* Something about him…The harder she thought about it, the further away it slipped.

'Why are *you* here?' Those gentle eyes narrowed.

But her subconscious reminded her how un-gentle they could be. She struggled to her feet, her limbs heavy and stiff. She turned back to her packing. 'What time is it?'

Grant glanced at his watch. 'Just after six o'clock.'

Kate snapped her face back to his, still muddled. 'Six? I've been asleep for hours.'

'I saw your car by the gate. You didn't hear me come in. I called out. I'm glad you came.'

She stared at him warily. 'Why?'

'Because I have a lot to explain. Because I'm sorry about how we parted.'

But not *that* they'd parted?

Sense was slowly returning. 'I came for my gear. To pack.'

'I started it for you.'

'Yes. Thank you.'

'But it killed me. Packing up your life. I couldn't finish.'

Kate's breath caught. Not because he couldn't be bothered. Not because it was in the room his father had died in…

Because he couldn't pack her up out of his life.

The tiniest glow of hope glimmered to life deep in her soul. She wrapped metaphorical hands around it to keep it from growing naïvely bright. Or was it to prevent it from extinguishing completely now that it had flickered to life again? Having found love, she was loath to let it go entirely.

'I didn't alert the Conservation Commission.' For some reason that was still the most important thing for him to know.

He shook his head. 'It doesn't matter now.'

'It matters to me.'

'Why is it so important that I believe you?' he asked.

Because I love you. 'Because I honoured my word. I meant what I said about never wanting to tear someone's choices away from them. That means something to me.'

He frowned. 'You still carry that with you?'

Being torn away from her home and community…? 'Every day. It made me who I am.'

'And who are you?'

She blinked at him. 'Kate Dickson. Champion of seals.'

His smile was weak, but it was something. He dropped his eyes to his shoes for a moment, then lifted them back to hers—clear, open. As green as gems deep under the sea.

Again she frowned at the image her sub-conscious threw up.

'You were right about more than just my father, Kate. You were right about me. I've become so accustomed to sniffing out the weaknesses in contracts, the crack through which the roots of exploitation twist… It's skewed my vision.'

'You really believed I did it.'

'I think I look for deception where there is none.' His large hand settled against her cheek.

She leaned her face into its warmth. 'There's none here. I've tried so hard to be only honest with you.'

Grant stared at her. 'Alan Sefton told the Conservation Commission about the breeding site.'

The mayor? 'How did he know?'

'Dad. I was arrogant to imagine there was an inch of this property he didn't know intimately. He lived on it fifty years longer than I did. Dad told Alan when he was getting his affairs in order. He wanted you to have it if you didn't find it yourself.'

'Why would he not just tell me himself?'

'It seems he wanted you to find it. To give you that joy. Alan was just biding his time in case you *did* find it yourself.'

'Then he's known all along…' Lord, all the pain that might have been averted.

'Timing's everything when you're a politician. He did what he believes is best for Castleridge.'

She nodded and stared at him. 'It wasn't me.'

The grin dropped away. 'No. I think I knew that. Once I stopped and thought about it with my head instead of my heart.'

His damaged, fearful heart.

Relief rushed through her as fast and furious as her seals on the hunt. 'Thank you. That means—' *everything* '—a lot.' But then she pinned him with her gaze again. 'Why didn't you tell me? Why let me go on thinking…?'

That you hated me.

'I've made rather a specialty of pre-emptive strikes, Kate. It's an effective survival-tool. I cut Mum out of my heart. I left farming before Dad could tell me I sucked. I cut you free before you could hurt me.'

Kate's lips thinned. 'Is that your excuse?'

'No. But it's the truth. I didn't call you because I had no idea where to start to apologise for what I'd implied. For what I said.'

I want you and your 'I love you' eyes the hell out of my house.

'And now you do? Or have I forced your hand by being here?'

He stroked her hair from her damp face. 'You answered my prayers.'

'You don't pray.'

'I didn't use to. I find myself…talking here. Out loud.' He frowned. 'To someone.'

Kate stared at him gravely. 'Do they talk back?'

'No.' Those lips twisted again. 'The sheep did…sometimes.'

Laughter felt like a gift as it spilled over her lips. Her mind immediately filled with images of whooshing through the ocean at high speed, the water streaming weightlessly over her mouth, her eyes. But she couldn't for the life of her work out why.

Grant chuckled, too. Then sobered.

'So, you're still here?' she said after a long silence.

'I am. I'm considering my options. Figured this was as good a place as any to do it.'

'What options?'

'You accused me of repeating the mistakes of the past, Kate. I've thought about that a lot since you left.' His eyes suddenly seemed flat. Lifeless. 'I'm rotting at the firm. From the inside out. When I was younger, I never would have jumped to some of the conclusions I have with you. But I've stuck with law because I've put so much of my life into it.'

'Sometimes you have to walk away from a bad investment.'

He nodded. 'That's exactly it.'

'Are you going to become a farmer?'

He laughed. 'Uh, no. Not a conventional one, anyway. But something else you said has stayed with me, and lord knows it's stayed with the mayor, who has nagged me until my ears bled.'

Kate held her breath. 'The wind farm.'

He nodded, his eyes bright again. 'I spoke to some friends of mine—engineers. They believe we could accommodate two hundred turbines, long-term. More than enough to power Castleridge and have some left over to feed back into the coastal grid. And allowing for revegetation below it.'

Kate held her breath. 'Can you afford it?'

'No. But we can start small. A dozen. And between the profits and rebates we should be able to expand. Slowly. Gently. Over a lifetime.'

'It's a big risk.'

Grant shrugged. 'A risk shared…'

'Shared? Who with?'

He shuffled more comfortably in his squatted position. 'I'd provide the capital but I'd need a partner to provide the land. A local landholder.'

'Just how far are you planning on expanding?'

'Only to Tulloquay's borders.'

'Then who are you planning to partner with?'

Grant reached behind him and pulled out a document folder, flipped it open and turned it towards her. 'You, Kate.'

Kate frowned. She tried to read the document sideways, then grabbed it and spun it more fully around. 'This is the deed to Tulloquay.' She looked up at him. 'You only received this today.'

'And I signed it right over to you.'

'What…?' The breath sucked clean out of her chest. Her heart started up a furious thumping. 'How did you know I'd be here?'

'I didn't. But it was always going to be yours. Whether I was around or not.'

The pain of three awful weeks bled out of her on a disbelieving grunt. 'Since when?'

'Since I woke up the morning after you left and realised what I'd done. What it meant.'

What does it mean? She wanted to scream it at him but aloud she just said, 'Why me?'

'You once said that Tulloquay wasn't the same without a McMurtrie on it. I feel the same way.' His eyes blazed. 'This land is meaningless to me empty. Or filled with rambling sheep. It's just one hundred-and-seventy square kilometres of pasture.'

'Besides,' he went on. 'You're the only person I trust not to sell out to the land barons who want to build their pesticide factories on it.'

Trust. She began to hyperventilate and slumped back into Leo's chair.

Almost as if he read her mind, Grant added, 'I think Leo would have approved. He seemed to have taken a shine to you if half the town is to be believed. And giving Tulloquay back to the ocean is about as close as he'll ever get to giving himself to it.'

'You're giving me Tulloquay?'

'There are a couple of conditions—two compulsory, one optional. I had them written into the deed contract.'

Kate scanned the pages of legalese but the words swam, meaningless, on the page. 'What?'

'You have to live here. Make it the country home you lost all those years ago. That's the first compulsory one.'

Live here. On Tulloquay. With her seals. *For ever.* 'OK.' The reality hit her; her eyes glistened and a wobbly smile followed. 'I think I can manage that.'

His eyes narrowed. 'Are you sure? You haven't heard the other clause yet.'

She frowned, confused, overwhelmed. 'Is it about the wind farm?'

'No, that's entirely up to you, Kate. It's your title. You might want to build that environment centre instead. Or a museum. Or a school. I know you'll do the right thing by Leo. By the land.'

'Then what?'

'Whatever you choose to do with the property, or your children choose, or *their* children choose, it stays in your family. I don't want Tulloquay passing out of the McMurtrie name ever. No matter what it gets used for.'

The dream of having children, having a family and raising them here, on Tulloquay…Tears flooded her eyes.

Wait… Kate lifted her watery gaze to Grant's. 'McMurtrie?'

He blazed, bright and true. 'That was the optional clause. Again, your choice.'

Her breath ached and swelled in her chest like she was deep diving without scuba gear. Striving for something just out of reach underwater. 'What are you asking?'

'I was in town when you arrived, looking for something special.' He pulled a small, ornate box made by one of Castleridge's craftsmen from his pocket and placed it on the arm of the chair. 'A message I was going to leave you amongst your lab equipment. A message I hoped would bring you back to me.'

He took a deep shuddery breath. 'Except fate brought you back to me anyway.' He dropped into a squat beside her. 'I can't promise not to make mistakes, Kate. I can't promise that I won't be an ass again in the future and hurt you without meaning to.

I'm just not that good at this stuff.' He appealed to her. 'But I can promise you that I won't ever walk away from the challenge. From something I'm not good at. From things I don't understand. I'll worship you, and honour you, and trust you as long as you'll let me.'

He shifted more comfortably onto one knee. On bended knee. Kate's heart stopped. 'I'll respect your opinion and only disagree with you sometimes, and I'll believe in you when everyone else thinks you're crazy. I'll boil your eggs just how you like them and I'll carry your heaviest equipment. I'll even kiss you when you smell of seal poop. 'I will make love to you long and late into the night, or morning, or afternoon, or whenever you can spare three-and-a-half minutes.'

Kate laughed through her tears.

'And I will do all of this because I love you, Dr Kate Dickson. Desperately. Entirely. And I would love you even more if you would please, *please* say some thing sometime soon.'

Kate silenced him—and his uncertainty—with a kiss to his gorgeous lips. The lips she'd missed for so many weeks. The lips she'd expected never to see again except for the pained sneer of her memory.

Heat burbled through her. 'You love me?'

Grant nodded. 'Completely.'

'You want to marry me?'

'If you'll have me. And I understand why you might not…'

'But Tulloquay is mine regardless.'

A shaft of doubt shot across his eyes. 'Regardless.'

She tipped her head and thought about her dreams that morning in Grant's bedroom—the green-eyed little girl—before it all went so horribly wrong.

'I'd like to be a McMurtrie,' she said softly, finally, and saw Grant nearly sag against the chair. 'I'd like to have your children. I'd like them to have a home here regardless of what they choose to be later in life. Farmers, fishermen, scientists, politicians…'

'Contract lawyers?'

Kate smiled. 'Just as long as they're happy and always have somewhere safe to come home to. Somewhere like Tulloquay. Somewhere with a mother and a father who will always be there for them.'

'Always?'

'Until death rips us away when we're old and grey.' Her eyes widened on an afterthought. 'And I want the fauna protected.'

His eyes narrowed. 'Are you negotiating acceptance terms, Kate?'

'How badly do you want this merger?'

'No price too high. The wildlife will have whatever protections we can write in.'

She fell into his arms. 'Then, yes, Grant McMurtrie. I accept this deed of title. And I accept your proposal. Not that there actually has been one.'

He smiled. 'Let me rectify that technicality.' He lifted the lid off the tiny box and tipped a fine gold ring into his palm.

Kate's breath caught. 'Your mother's ring.'

'Yes.'

'You were sending it to me?'

'I can't imagine anyone else ever wearing it.'

'What if I'd said no?'

'Then you would have sent it back. But it always would have been yours in my mind. I would have put it back around my neck and kept you close to my heart.'

She wanted to smile, so badly. But if she did more than carefully speak, she was going to burst into tears. 'But you've worn that your whole life.'

He shrugged. 'Now I'll have you. And you'll have the ring.' His eyes grew serious. 'Katherine Dickson—will you marry me and give me a lifetime to make up for what a clutz I've been about everything?'

Kate held her breath. Every moment of every day since they'd met showered before her eyes in a three-D action replay. His first smile. Their first kiss. Every squeeze of her heart. Was this what love was all about? Knowing you could lose everything at any moment but knowing with blazing certainty that it was worth the risk? Those moments of pure connection. For the chance to make something beautiful and keep it for ever.

Was that what her parents had for a few blissful years? No matter that it had been so agonisingly short, had it been totally worth it?

Only one way to find out.

A ball tightened her throat. 'Yes. I will.'

Their kiss went on for ever, making up lost time, reacquainting their lips, promising a future. She clung to his strength and let the hurts and sorrows of the past few weeks dissolve away. She shivered as his hands trailed down over her hip, sliding under her tight T-shirt.

'My bedroom's all packed up,' she whispered, a sultry kind of déjà vu.

'That's ok,' he murmured. 'We can use mine.'

And, as she led the way into the house, out of the corner of her eye she saw her future husband—father of her future green-eyed little girl—standing in the room where his own father had given up on life, with his right hand on his heart and his left hand pointing to the sky, as if acknowledging the man that had brought the two of them together.

Thanking him.

Kate frowned at how familiar the image seemed. But then Grant turned and captured her eyes in jade, gave her the most heart-stoppingly, leg-crossingly radiant smile and reached for her hand.

And everything but the man she loved blew like fallen leaves from her mind.

and [illegible] in [illegible] [illegible] the [illegible]. That [illegible] of her [illegible]. [illegible] what [illegible] knowing [illegible] could [illegible] [illegible] [illegible] [illegible] was [illegible]. [illegible] [illegible] [illegible] something beautiful and [illegible].

[illegible] what her parents [illegible] a [illegible]. [illegible] that [illegible] [illegible] would [illegible]

[illegible] to find [illegible]

[illegible] her through [illegible]

[illegible] went on [illegible] up [illegible] [illegible] [illegible]. She [illegible] [illegible] her [illegible] [illegible] [illegible] down [illegible] her [illegible] her [illegible].

[illegible] said [illegible] [illegible] [illegible] [illegible] of [illegible]

[illegible] [illegible]. We [illegible].

And as she led [illegible] into the house, [illegible] of [illegible] her future husband. [illegible] her future [illegible] [illegible] in the [illegible] where [illegible] had [illegible] with his right hand on [illegible] and his left hand [illegible] [illegible] [illegible] [illegible] [illegible] [illegible].

[illegible]

[illegible] [illegible] [illegible] [illegible] [illegible] [illegible] [illegible] [illegible] [illegible] [illegible]

[illegible] [illegible] [illegible] [illegible]

THE ARMY RANGER'S RETURN

BY

SORAYA LANE

DID YOU PURCHASE THIS BOOK WITHOUT A COVER?
If you did, you should be aware it is **stolen property** as it was reported *unsold and destroyed* by a retailer. Neither the author nor the publisher has received any payment for this book.

All the characters in this book have no existence outside the imagination of the author, and have no relation whatsoever to anyone bearing the same name or names. They are not even distantly inspired by any individual known or unknown to the author, and all the incidents are pure invention.

All Rights Reserved including the right of reproduction in whole or in part in any form. This edition is published by arrangement with Harlequin Enterprises II B.V./S.à.r.l. The text of this publication or any part thereof may not be reproduced or transmitted in any form or by any means, electronic or mechanical, including photocopying, recording, storage in an information retrieval system, or otherwise, without the written permission of the publisher.

This book is sold subject to the condition that it shall not, by way of trade or otherwise, be lent, resold, hired out or otherwise circulated without the prior consent of the publisher in any form of binding or cover other than that in which it is published and without a similar condition including this condition being imposed on the subsequent purchaser.

® and ™ are trademarks owned and used by the trademark owner and/or its licensee. Trademarks marked with ® are registered with the United Kingdom Patent Office and/or the Office for Harmonisation in the Internal Market and in other countries.

First published in Great Britain 2011
by Mills & Boon, an imprint of Harlequin (UK) Limited,
Eton House, 18-24 Paradise Road, Richmond, Surrey TW9 1SR

© Soraya Lane 2011

ISBN: 978 0 263 88894 2

23-0711

Harlequin (UK) policy is to use papers that are natural, renewable and recyclable products and made from wood grown in sustainable forests. The logging and manufacturing processes conform to the legal environmental regulations of the country of origin.

Printed and bound in Spain
by Blackprint CPI, Barcelona

Dear Reader,

I have always been captivated by the idea of a couple falling in love before meeting one another. What could be more romantic than writing letters to a stranger and then anxiously waiting to meet that person in real life almost one year later?

When United States Army Ranger Ryan meets cancer survivor Jessica, the bond they've formed on paper instantly translates into real life. But their romance is not as simple as falling in love. Ryan has a past to confront and a son to reconnect with, and Jessica needs to battle her own demons from the past.

This is my second book about a soldier returning from active duty, and it certainly won't be my last. There is something special about a man in uniform coming home with a wall around his heart and finding a woman to open him up and tame him.

I hope you enjoy this heart-warming story, and don't forget to visit me at www.sorayalane.com.

Soraya Lane

For Hamish, my husband and real-life hero.
You have always believed in me, and in my writing,
and this book is for you.

Writing romance for Mills & Boon is truly a dream come true for **Soraya Lane.** An avid book reader and writer since her childhood, Soraya describes becoming a published author as 'the best job in the world', and hopes to be writing heart-warming, emotional romances for many years to come.

Soraya lives with her own real-life hero on a small farm in New Zealand, surrounded by animals and with an office overlooking a field where their horses graze.

Visit Soraya at www.sorayalane.com.

CHAPTER ONE

Dear Ryan,

It feels like we've been writing to one another forever, but it's only been a year. When I say only, a lot has happened in that time, but it makes our friendship sound insignificant somehow.

Of course you can come to see me. It would be weird not to meet you, after getting to know you so well, but strange in the same way to put a face to the name. When you are discharged, write to me, or maybe we could use more modern forms of communication once you're back in civilization.

Stay safe and I'll see you soon. It's unbelievable that you could be back here and we'd pass one another in the street without even knowing.

Jessica

JESSICA MITCHELL STARED out the window and started pacing, eyes never leaving the road. She'd been like this for almost an hour. Stupid, because it wasn't even time for him to arrive yet, and he was army. He would be exactly on time.

She knew that. Jessica knew he was punctual. She knew he would be knocking on her door at twelve-noon bang on.

She knew just about everything about him.

Ryan McAdams.

Up until now, he'd just been a name. A name that made her smile, that made her run to the mailbox every morning. But that's all it had been. Innocent letters, two people confiding in one another. Pen pals.

And yet here she was, pacing in her living room, waiting to meet the man in the flesh.

Jessica looked down and watched her hands shaking. They were quivering, her whole body was wired, and for what? He was her friend. Nothing more. A friend she'd never met before, but a friend nonetheless.

So why was she still walking obsessively up and down? She could just make a cup of coffee or read the paper. Take the dog for a walk and not worry if he had to wait on her doorstep for a few minutes.

Because she wanted this to be perfect. There was no use pretending. His letters had helped her through the last year, had stopped her from giving up when she could have hit rock bottom. And she wanted to say thank you to him in person.

The phone rang. Jessica pounced on it, her pulse thumping.

"Hello."

"Is he there yet?" her best friend asked.

Her heart stuttered then restarted again. She let out a breath. It wasn't him.

"Hi, Bella."

"I'm guessing the hunk hasn't arrived then."

Why had she ever told her friend about Ryan? Why couldn't she have kept it to herself? It was stupid even making a fuss like this. He was her *friend.*

"Jess?"

She flopped down onto the sofa.

"I'm a wreck. A nervous wreck," she admitted.

Bella laughed. "You'll be fine. Just remember to breathe, and if you don't phone me with an update I'm coming around to see him for myself."

"He could be overweight and unattractive."

Bella snorted down the line. Jess didn't even know why she'd said it. Since when did she even care what he looked like? Whatever he looked like didn't change the fact that his friendship had meant a lot to her this past year.

"Bella, I— Oh, my God."

She listened to the thump of footfalls on the porch. Heavy, solid men's feet that beat like a drum on timber.

"Jess? What's happening?" Bella squawked.

A knock echoed.

"He's here," she whispered. "He's *early*."

"You'll be fine, okay? Put down the phone, close your eyes for a few seconds, then go to the door. Okay? Just say 'okay.'"

"Okay." Jessica thought her head might fall off she was nodding so hard.

She placed the phone down without saying good-bye.

He was here. Ryan was actually here.

Waiting outside her front door.

How could she know this man almost as intimately as she knew her best friend, yet be terrified of meeting him?

She looked at the letter on the table, reached for it, then tucked it into her jeans pocket. She didn't need to open it to know what it said. She remembered every word he'd ever written to her.

Jessica squared her shoulders and shook her head to

push away the fear. Ryan was here, waiting for her, and she had to be brave. It felt like she was about to meet a lover she was so nervous, but it made her feel queasy even thinking that way. One of her closest friends was standing at the door, and for some reason she was paralyzed with fear.

Bella had gotten her all wound up in knots, and for what? She wasn't interested in meeting a man in *that* way, especially not now. And she didn't want Ryan to be anything more to her, no matter what he looked like. What she needed in her life were good friends, and he had proven that he was there for her when she needed someone.

Another knock made her jump.

This was it. There was nowhere she could go but forward, down the hall.

Unless she escaped out the back window…

A flash of brown streaked past her and she groaned. Hercules. She'd put him out the back with a bone and hoped he'd stay there, but he must have squeezed through the doggie door when he'd heard the knock.

At least he'd be a good distraction.

Ryan wondered if it were possible for fingers to sweat. His were curled around the paper-wrapped stems of a bunch of white roses, clenching and unclenching as he tried to figure out what to do with them. Out in front seemed too contrived, behind his back looked ridiculous and hanging at his sides just seemed more ridiculous, like he was trying too hard. Why flowers? Why had he felt the need to complicate things by bringing flowers?

He was going insane. He'd survived the trauma and heartache of years serving his country, and now a stupid bunch of flowers was tying him in tight coils. He was a United States Army Ranger. Practised, strong and unflappable. He'd never have made the special ops unit with nerves like this.

Clearly he was losing his touch.

Perhaps he should throw them into the garden? He looked over his shoulder, beyond the porch, then listened as the door clicked and a small dog started barking.

He was out of time. Ryan slowly, cautiously turned back toward the house. He wanted to squeeze his eyes shut, walk back down the steps and start all over. Without the flowers dangling awkwardly from one hand, and instead standing at ease on the doorstep in front of her.

Ryan spun around as the door swished open.

"Jessica."

He exhaled the word as if he'd been waiting a lifetime to say it. In a way he had.

Ryan was pleased he'd never asked her for a photograph. It couldn't have done justice to the reality of her features. Hair the color of rain-drizzled sand was tucked behind her ears, eyes the shade of the richest dark chocolate peeked out beneath dark lashes. She smiled like she was greeting her first date—nervously, expectantly, unsurely.

Worried. Just like he was.

After so many months of writing one another, meeting in person was kind of surreal.

He went to move and something tiny hit him in the knees and almost made him fall. By the time he looked down a small dog was doing laps around his feet, before disappearing back into the house with as much speed as he'd arrived with.

Ryan laughed then looked back to the woman waiting to meet him.

"Jessica." When he said it this time it made him smile naturally, rather than feeling like a word-stuck teenager. "It's so good to finally meet you."

She grinned as he walked toward her, then opened her arms to him.

"Ryan."

Even the way she said his name did something to his insides, but he pushed past it. He was a soldier. He was trained to deal with difficult situations.

"I'm really glad you made it, Ryan."

He let the flowers drop to the porch as he opened his own arms to hold her. Jessica stepped into his embrace as if she'd been made to fit there, firm against his chest, arms tight around him. She hugged him like someone who cared about him.

Like he hadn't been hugged in a long time.

It had been years since his wife had died. Years since he'd felt the genuine embrace of a woman, one that wasn't out of pity, but out of something deeper, warmer.

Ryan inhaled the scent of her—the tease of perfume that reminded him of coconuts on a beach. The soft caress of her hair that fell against his neck as she tucked into him.

It felt good. No...even better than good. It felt *great.*

He cleared his throat and stepped back, not wanting to make her uncomfortable by keeping hold of her too long. Jessica leapt back from him like a bear from a nest of hornets, her face alternating between happy and concerned.

"I…"

"We…"

They both laughed.

"You first," he said.

Jessica grinned at him and rocked back and forth, arms crossed over her chest.

"I don't remember what I was going to say!"

Ryan shook his head and laughed. Laughed like he thought he'd forgotten how to, cheeks aching as he watched her do the same.

He bent to collect the fallen flowers.

"These are for you."

She blushed. When had he last seen a grown woman blush? It made a goofy smile play across his lips.

"Me?"

He nodded.

"It's been a long time since anyone gave me flowers."

Ryan watched as she dipped her nose down to inhale them, her eyes dancing along the white silhouette of each rose.

It had been a long time since he'd *given* a woman flowers.

"Do they give me passage inside?"

Jessica looked up at him with an expression he'd only seen once before. His wife had looked up at him like that from her hospital bed, full of hope, happiness shining from her face.

He clenched his jaw and stamped the memory away, refusing to go there. This was Jessica, the woman who had made an effort to write to him when most Americans seemed to forget what U.S. troops were facing overseas. This was not a time to dwell on the past.

"Yes." She looked sideways, away and then back, but he didn't miss the twinkle in her eyes. "Yes, it does. So long as you're prepared to meet Hercules properly."

"I take it Hercules is the small fur-ball who almost bowled me over."

Jessica reached out to Ryan and grinned. "Maybe if I'd given him a more insignificant name he wouldn't be quite so full of self-importance."

Ryan took the hand she offered and let himself be led inside. It felt too normal to touch his skin to hers, too casual, but when she looked over her shoulder at him and smiled, her fingers trailing away from his until she was just a woman walking ahead of him, he felt the loss of her touch like a limb had just been torn from his body.

The shock of doing normal things was something hard to get used to, after months being surrounded by other men in the desert. Each day started to merge with the next one…and home seemed like just a scene on a postcard.

Being back here wasn't something he had looked forward to, it was something he'd feared and wished he didn't have to confront again. But Jessica had been there for him, eagerly writing him back so he'd had something positive to concentrate on.

When everything else was gone, snatched away from him, Jessica had been there.

She'd come into his life when he'd been losing his way. When he'd almost felt as though his soul had been defeated, like he had lost his purpose. It was Jessica who had held each piece of him together when he could have lost hope.

Maybe she could help him now he was home, too.

Because nothing else had fallen into place since he'd returned.

A man could only hope.

Jessica set the flowers to rest in a vase on her bench and turned back to her guest.

"Shall we have lunch here or go out for something?"

Ryan shrugged. "I don't mind."

"But…?"

She laughed as he squinted at her.

"How did you know there was a *but?*" he asked.

Jessica tapped her nose. "You'd be surprised what I know about you."

Ryan flopped down on the sofa and crossed his legs at the ankle. He looked at home here, comfortable in *her* home. Aside from her brother, she wasn't used to seeing men in her space.

She didn't want it to bother her, but it did. Having a man around had become foreign to her. It felt too intimate, being so close, seeing him so…at ease.

Funny, she had expected being back in America to be hard for him, but it seemed like she was the one struggling.

"Okay, you got me." He gave her a smile that made her almost want to look away, but she didn't. The way his mouth curved, his eyes creasing gently at the corners, was exactly as she'd imagined he would look. Hoped he might look.

Her stomach twisted, as if her organs had been flipped then dropped. She wasn't meant to be thinking about him like that. Not now, not ever.

"The sun's shining, the ground is still wet from the rain last night and I'm desperate to be outside in the open. You've got no idea how good it feels—smells—outside here," he said.

Jessica beamed at him. She was still nervous, but the quiver in her belly felt as if it were less from worry than excitement. A day out with someone with whom she could just be herself was exactly what she needed.

Besides, it would be easier being around him on neutral territory. Even if he was just a friend, she wasn't ready to see a man in her house, on her sofa, like that. Not after Mark. Not after what she'd gone through this last year.

It sent a shiver down her spine just thinking about the last twelve months.

"Give me five minutes, I'll get my handbag and we'll go to the park."

"I'm guessing we have to take the mutt?" he teased.

Jessica cringed as she heard paws racing on the timber floor in the kitchen. Hercules was like a missile, as if he'd known exactly what they'd been talking about.

He sprung through the door and leapt onto Ryan's lap, tongue frantically searching out his victim's face.

"Hercules! No!"

Ryan grabbed him and held him at a safe distance.

"Five minutes?" He raised an eyebrow, ignoring the wriggling dog.

She nodded. "Sorry about him."

Ryan stood, eyeing Hercules. "I'll start the clock now."

She turned sedately and walked toward her bedroom as slowly as she could manage. She wanted to run, to sprint to her room and grab her things and not miss a moment of being in his company.

Ryan. His name was circling her mind over and over, like a record she couldn't turn off. Ryan.

He was everything she'd imagined he would be and more. When they'd first started writing, he was just a soldier. He was a man serving their country and she felt good giving support to him. But when they'd realized they had grown up within ten minutes of one another, something had started stirring within her. Then when he'd made noises of coming back home to California, to Thousand Oaks, she'd started wondering. That despite her insecurities, despite her worries about herself, she had a connection with this man. A man who understood her and wanted to meet her. But a man she only knew on paper, who wouldn't feel pity for her or treat her like an almost-broken doll because of what she'd been through.

And he was hardly a disappointment. In the flesh, he was even more commanding than he was on paper. Well over six feet and built like a man who could protect her on a dark stormy night in the meanest streets of Los Angeles. A man with dark cropped, slightly disheveled hair that begged to be touched, ice-blue eyes that seemed to pierce straight through her body. And beautiful lips that, despite all he'd seen and experienced, still hovered with the hint of a smile as he spoke.

Jessica scolded herself. Smiling over mental pictures of him while she was alone was exactly what she *didn't* need to be doing. Ever. Until she reached the five-year mark, until she knew she was in complete remission, men were strictly off her radar.

Jessica stole a quick glance at herself in the mirror as she passed and fought the urge to cross her arms over her chest. She was still self-conscious, but it was getting better. After all they'd said to one another, all they'd shared, she hadn't told Ryan. Couldn't tell him. Not yet. It was still too fresh for her, too raw, to share with anyone.

And she wanted him to just like her for herself. Treat her like she was normal and not a fragile baby bird in need of extra care.

She picked up her purse, squirted an extra spray of perfume to her wrist and reached for a sweater. She didn't know why, but today felt like a fresh opportunity, a new chance. She wasn't going to let her insecurities ruin it. Not when she had a man like Ryan waiting to spend the day with her.

Even if she was scared to death.

She utterly refused to let her past ruin her future. Not now, not after all she'd been through.

Today was about starting over.

CHAPTER TWO

Dear Jessica,

I've become desensitized to what we have to see over here. I wait for my orders, I no longer cringe when an explosion echoes around me, and I automatically squeeze the trigger to take down the enemy. Does it make me a bad person that I no longer feel? I'm starting to think I like being here because it means I don't have to face reality. I can pretend my wife didn't die and that my son doesn't hate me. But I'll be coming home soon, after all this time, and I'm not going to have any more excuses.

Thanks for listening, Jessica. You don't know how much it means to me to be able to write to you, to be honest like this. I can't talk to anyone else, but you're always here for me.

Ryan

"SO HOW IS it you've managed to stay away for so long?"

Ryan shrugged and turned his body toward Jessica as they walked. He made himself look away from Hercules racing up and down the riverbank so he could give Jessica his full attention.

"I guess I became good at saying yes, and the army were pleased to have me wherever I was needed."

"What about this time?"

Ryan chuckled. After so long being in the company of men, he wasn't used to the way a woman could just fire questions. So candidly wanting to know everything at once.

"What's so funny?" she asked.

Jessica was…what? Pouting? No, not pouting but she was definitely pursing her lips.

"You're very inquisitive, that's all."

She gave him a nudge in the side and rolled her eyes. Ryan tried not to come to a complete standstill, forced his feet to keep moving. He wasn't used to that, either. Someone touching him so casually, with such ease.

He'd definitely been away too long.

"I write to you for months, and you can't tell me where you are or why you're suddenly coming home on such short notice. So spill," she ordered.

He followed Jessica toward the edge of the lake, the water so still it looked like the cover of a postcard. The park was beautiful, much more attractive than he'd remembered it being, but after so long seeing sand and little else, everything about America seemed beautiful. The smell of fresh rain on grass, the softer rays of sunlight, not burning so hot against your skin that it made you sweat. Things you took for granted until they were snatched away.

"I can't tell you where we've been, you know that, but what I can say is that our last, ah, assignment was successful."

Jessica waited. He'd give her that. She could talk his ear off, but she knew when to stay quiet. Seemed to sense that he needed a moment.

"I'm a marksman, Jess." He paused and watched her, made sure she didn't look too alarmed. "I entered the special forces as an expert in my field, and it's why I've been deployed so long."

"But you didn't want to come home," she said softly. "What made you come back now?"

Ryan sighed and looked out at the water. It was so much easier just keeping this sort of stuff in his head. But he didn't have to tell her everything. It wasn't like he'd planned to come home, more like his hand had been forced.

If he'd had it his way he would have stayed away forever. That's what he *had* done until now. Now he was home and he had to deal with being a single dad for real. Not to mention the fact his son didn't want to know him.

He didn't like admitting something was impossible, but repairing that relationship could be like trying to bring someone back from the dead. It was his own fault, his own battle to deal with, and he'd been a coward to wait so long before confronting the problem.

But one thing he'd promised himself was that he was going to be honest with this woman. She'd done something generous for him, helped him from the other side of the world through her constant letters, and he owed it to her to be real and candid with her now.

"I had an injury a while back and it never healed quite right." He moved to sit down on the grass, needing to collapse. It was hard being so open, just talking, and he couldn't go back. Couldn't put into words what had happened to him then, that day he'd realized he wasn't invincible. "I've had a lot of pain in my arm, so I had surgery in Germany on my way back home, and the army wants me on rest until the physio gives me the all clear."

Ryan gritted his teeth and forced his eyes to stay open as his memory tried to claw its way back. The smell of gunpowder, the pain making his arm feel like it was on fire, and not being able to stop. Making his arm work, pushing through, pulling the trigger over and over until his body had finally let him down.

He clamped his jaw down hard and looked at Jessica. She was sitting, too, right beside him, legs tucked up under her as she stared at the water. As if she was the troubled one. He could see it on her face. That she was either reacting to his pain, or harboring her own.

"Jess?"

She turned empty eyes toward him, bottom lip caught between her teeth.

"That means you're going back at some point."

He raised a brow. Had she thought he was home for good? Had he made her think he was staying by something he'd said?

"Ah, all going well, I'll be deployed wherever they need me," he confirmed.

It was wonderful being back here in some ways, but it was also extremely difficult. He'd do his best, try to make amends, but he was a soldier. That's what he did. What he was good at.

She nodded, over and over again, too vigorously. "Of course, of course you're going back. I don't know why I thought you wouldn't be."

"I'll be here a couple months at least, then I have to figure out what to do. I'm eligible to be discharged, they've offered me teaching positions, but I'm just not ready to walk away from my men. I don't know where

I'll be deployed yet but it's my job to go wherever they need me."

Sad eyes greeted him when he looked back at her. She smiled, but he could tell something had upset her. He hoped it wasn't his fault. Seeing those bright eyes cloud over was not something he wanted to be held accountable for.

"What about your son?" she asked quietly.

Ryan sighed. His son. George. Now that was a topic he and Jess could talk about all day. Or maybe not talk about at all, as he'd been home a week already and they'd hardly spoken a word to one another.

"I don't know if I'm just not cut out to be a father, or whether he truly wishes I was back with the army."

He didn't say what else he wondered. That maybe his son wished he were dead.

Ryan picked up a stone and stood, then reached his arm back and threw it into the water. He'd meant to skim it, but instead the stone went a little distance then landed with a plop.

He shut his eyes and pushed away the anger. He hated not being capable, losing the function in his strongest arm, but getting angry about it didn't help his progress and he knew it. Sometimes he just forgot about it, and then he'd surprise himself all over again by not having the control he wanted.

He looked down at Jessica, sitting still, eyes fixed in the distance.

"You okay?"

It was as if she had to snap out of a trance before she even noticed he was speaking.

"Yeah."

Ryan watched as she jumped to her feet and brushed the grass off her jeans. "Yeah, I'm fine."

Maybe he'd been away way too long, or maybe he'd just forgotten how sensitive women were. Because they'd only been at the park less than an hour and already he'd done something to upset her.

And he had no idea what.

"You still want to grab some lunch?" he asked.

She smiled at him, this time more openly. Or maybe more guardedly. He couldn't tell which.

"Sure. Let's go."

Jessica couldn't fathom why her stomach was twisting like a snake had taken ownership of it. Why did it even bother her? So he was going back to war? He was a soldier and that's what soldiers did. It was just that she hadn't *expected* him to be going back. When he'd written to her and told her he was coming home she'd thought it was for good.

It wasn't as if he'd promised her something and was now going back on his word. She had no right to even feel this way.

They were friends.

So why was she acting like her lover had come home and lied to her about his intentions? Or maybe she'd just dealt with too much loss to even comprehend the thought of losing anyone else from her life again. She knew firsthand what the consequences were of him not coming home, what the risks were.

"You *sure* you're all right?" he persisted.

Jessica's head swivelled so quickly it almost swung off.

"Me?"

He laughed and she watched as he pushed his hands into his jeans pockets.

"Yes, you."

She felt the flush of her cheeks as he made fun of her. She'd expected him to be the one clamming up and here she was like a nervous bunch of keys being jangled. She hadn't even realized how long they'd been walking in silence.

"I'm sorry Ryan, it's just…"

He shrugged. "I took you by surprise."

This was a man who'd been away from civilization for years, and yet he seemed to have her all figured out. That made a change.

Jessica sighed.

"I understand if you don't want to, you know, hear about war or anything. It's not exactly the most pleasant experience to discuss," he said.

She frowned at the look on his face. It took her a second, because she hesitated, but Jessica reached for his hand to give it a quick squeeze. She was being stupid and he was the one who needed her to act like normal. To listen to him like she had in all their letters. He had no idea why she was affected by what he'd said, and that's how it had to be. She'd lost too much, exposed those she loved to that loss as well, and it had struck a chord with her. But that was one musical instrument she had no intention of playing around him, and that meant she had to deal with it and move on. Fast.

"You can tell me all you like, honestly. I just didn't expect you to be going back there anytime soon," she explained. "It took me by surprise."

Ryan caught her hand before she could pull it away. His hand was strong, smooth. And the touch made a tingle start in her fingertips and ripple goose bumps up her forearm.

"You're the only person I've been able to talk to, apart from the guys, since I left."

She nodded. Words refused to form in her throat. It had been so long since a man had touched her. Since she'd even felt a spark of attraction that had made her heart beat like a hammer was thwacking it from side to side.

"If I can't talk to you, I've got no one," he added.

Jessica couldn't take her eyes off their hands. Ryan followed her gaze and seemed to realize what the problem was, opening his grip and slowly releasing her fingers.

"I'm sorry," he muttered.

"Don't be sorry."

She smiled up at him. Watched the way his eyes crinkled ever so gently at the sides as he smiled back at her.

"Oh, no!" she exclaimed.

Ryan jumped to attention, eyes scanning, like he was looking for an enemy, but Jessica was already moving back toward the park.

"What?"

"Where's Herc?" she gasped.

Her heart had gone from thumping out of desire to banging from terror. How could she have been that distracted? How could she not have noticed that he'd wandered off? Her baby, her best friend, her…

Hercules had been there for her through everything. When she was home recovering, cuddling up by her side as the chemo ravaged her body. Snuggling her when she couldn't force herself out of bed in the morning. Listening to her as she'd sobbed after surgery.

He'd probably just wandered off in search of more ducks, chasing mallards again, but still…

Jessica had huge hot tears that felt like balls of fire fighting to get free of her lashes, desperate to spill, but she gulped them back, moving as fast as she could back the way they'd come.

She jumped as a hand came down on her shoulder. A hand that seemed to distribute calm energy through her body, grounding her, telling her everything was going to be okay.

"I'll run ahead, you keep your eyes peeled." Ryan's deep voice was commanding as he took charge. "I'll get him, you just stay calm."

Jessica nodded. She wasn't capable of doing anything else. Herc always followed along beside her off the lead, but then she wasn't usually so distracted.

She watched Ryan thump gracefully down the sidewalk, his feet beating a steady rhythm as he jogged away from her.

"Herc!" Jessica called as loud as she could. "Come on, Herc!"

Ryan had never felt as if his heart was actually in his throat before. Maybe at the funeral, when he'd had to watch his son cry as his mother was lowered in a coffin into her grave. But that was a different kind of emotion. That was pure agony, mourning like he'd never known he could experience.

This? This was desperation, panic. Determination to find what he was looking for.

He'd settled into a quick steady jog and he was almost back to where they'd come from, searching with his eyes as he moved. The dog had been at their side when they'd left but the little rascal must have skipped off when something caught his nose.

Then Ryan spotted him. A brown bullet barking his head off as he chased ducks back and forth along the bank again. Completely oblivious to the fact he was alone and had found his way back solo.

Phew.

"Hercules!"

The dog ignored him. Ryan kept running, slowing only to scoop the bundle of fur into his arms.

Hercules jumped and wriggled, but Ryan held him firm.

"You gave us a fright, bud."

The dog just wriggled some more, tongue flapping as he tried to contort his little body around so he could lick him. Ryan held him in an iron-tight grip, just far enough away so he could avoid being slobbered all over.

"Come on, let's go find your mom."

He started jogging again, until he spotted Jessica ahead. He would have waved but he was determined not to let the dog go. He was writhing like a slippery fish again.

When she saw them, Jessica's entire face lit up, a smile stretching across her lips.

"Herc!"

Ryan slowed and grinned. "Told you I'd get him."

Now she was crying. Oh, no, he didn't do tears well. He went to hold the dog out but she threw herself into his arms instead, almost making him drop the little animal!

"Thank you, Ryan. Thank you, thank you, thank you."

He gave her a half hug back, the other arm still occupied by Hercules.

Ryan went to move at the same time as she kissed him on the cheek. His face turned too far and she got him on the side of his mouth.

He fought not to turn farther into her, his pulse racing at her mouth on his.

"Oh."

He grimaced. "Sorry."

Jessica was bright red again, like a piece of freshly snapped rhubarb.

"I—"

He stepped back, clipped the dog onto the leash hanging from her hand and put him down.

"How about we head back to your place? Get him out of trouble?" he suggested.

Jessica nodded, still flushed.

He didn't know what was happening here, but one thing he did know was that somehow they weren't behaving like long lost pen pals. When she'd held him before, it had felt too warm. Like someone had shone the sun itself between them. Like they were the only two people in the world.

And if it had been another time and another place, he'd have been tempted to never let her go.

But he was only here for a few months. Maybe less. He'd come looking for her because she'd been such a wonderful support to him. Helped him talk about his feelings, open up.

Without her, he doubted he'd have ever have had the strength to come home, to face his demons once and for all.

There was no chance he was going to stuff this up by letting his emotions get the better of him. Jessica was off limits romantically.

And that was nonnegotiable.

He had to maintain their friendship, repair his relationship with his son and summon the strength to open up to his own parents. Tell them how much he appreciated them and what they'd done for him.

He grimaced at the thought of what the coming months held.

He'd just have to take it all one step at a time.

CHAPTER THREE

Dear Ryan,

I know you feel like you can't come back home, but that's just fear talking. I'm not going to tell you that soldiers shouldn't be fearful, because a soldier is nothing more than a brave human being and you can't help how you feel. But you need to repair your relationship with your son while you can. And you need to face the fact that he will want to talk with you about his mother.

I don't know what you're going through, but I do understand pain and loss. I know what it feels like to grieve, and to want to hide away, but in the end you have to be honest with yourself. It's the only way forward.

Remember I'm here for you. If you need someone to hold your hand, that person can be me. No questions asked.

Jessica

JESSICA HAD BEHAVED like a brainless airhead. Since when could she forget her dog? And the way she'd shut out Ryan after he'd opened up to her was unacceptable. He must think she was some kind of a nutcase. Not the level-headed pen pal who was full of wisdom that he'd come to rely on.

Nothing about today had gone as planned.

Jessica smiled as he walked back into the room. She swallowed away her fear and pinched her hand.

"Ryan, I'm so sorry."

He looked confused. One eyebrow raised slightly higher than the other. "What about?"

She sighed. He was either really good at pretending, or men actually were incredibly good at just letting things go.

"About before. Can we just start over? Go back to when you arrived?"

Ryan chuckled. He actually chuckled, while she stood there all breathless and red-faced.

"Whatever you say."

Argh! Men could be so irritating. He was just like her brother. Or worse. Acting like something hadn't happened when it had. But if he wanted to forget about it then she wasn't going to argue with him. She'd behaved badly and now she had a chance to make things right.

"Okay, how about we actually have a cup of something hot and make some lunch then?"

He grinned and walked right up to her, stopping a few feet back. Ryan held out his hand.

"I'm Ryan, it's so good to finally meet you."

She glared at him and stuck her hands in her pockets.

"Not funny, Ryan." The expression on his face didn't change. It was so serious he almost made her laugh, but she felt like too much of an idiot to shrug it off. "I made a fool of myself back there and it wasn't me. I mean, I don't even know how to explain myself."

He smiled at her again, but this time she didn't feel mocked.

"I thought you wanted to start over?"

Jessica turned away from him.

"Look, I took you by surprise, that's all. Now let's have some food, okay? I'm starving. Unless you want to meet all over again, again?" he teased.

Jessica sighed and walked back into the kitchen. Her face still felt flushed, but she was starting to relax. Lucky this was a friendship where they already kind of knew one another. If it had been a first date she'd have been toast.

"Can I do anything?" he offered.

She shook her head.

"I'll make some sandwiches and meet you outside."

When he didn't move she made herself look up at him.

"Hercules would love to play ball if you're up for a game in the yard," she suggested.

He winked at her and sauntered out the door.

Jessica had to force her mouth to stay shut. It was in grave risk of dropping down and hitting her on the chest.

Something about that man had her all twisted in knots, and that wink hadn't helped. She was all hot, like she needed a fan, but she gulped down a glass of water instead.

And it didn't help her any.

Ten minutes later, and still hot under the collar, Jessica found Ryan sitting back on one of her chairs, eyes closed, basking in the sun. A very put-out-looking Hercules lay nearby, ball neglected between his front paws.

She leant over to put the tray of food and drinks on

the table when Ryan's eyes popped open. He looked lazy, comfortable.

Gorgeous.

She pushed the thought away as he ran a hand through his hair and then down his face, as if to wake himself up.

"You've got no idea how good this is, just sitting here."

"Sandwich?"

He took it happily and started eating. Jessica made herself do the same, even though swallowing was like forcing large chunks through a sieve.

They sat in silence for a bit. Eating. Watching the dog chase his tail then start stalking a bird.

"Don't get me wrong, Jess, but I could have sworn you had something other than my going back to war on your mind before."

This time she actually choked. Had to reach for her coffee and take a big gulp. What had happened to the stereotype of brooding soldier who hardly said a word and wasn't up with the whole feelings thing? She had expected him to be quiet and reserved, but the reality of him was anything but. He'd either come out of his shell big-time, or he was making a huge effort here.

And hadn't they put this behind them and started over?

"Sorry, went down the wrong way," she stuttered.

Ryan didn't look convinced, just reached for another sandwich.

"Whatever you say."

She sighed.

"It's true I've had a lot going on this past year, but I just wasn't expecting to have to worry about you going back on top of it all. That's all."

It wasn't technically a lie. She *would* worry about him when he was gone. But when he'd told her, her mind had wandered. To a place she didn't want to go and shouldn't have let herself be drawn back to.

"Jessica?"

She put on the brave face she had perfected over the months of treatment she'd received and turned back to him.

"I'm fine, honestly. Tell me about you. What do you want to do while you're home? Do you need somewhere to stay?"

She held her breath, hoping he'd say no. There was no way she could deal with him staying here. Not now. It was messing her head up just trying to be normal around him for an afternoon.

"Tempting offer, but no, thanks."

She tucked her feet up beneath her on the seat and turned to face him. It was comforting in a way to watch his face, but off-putting at the same time. Hard to fathom this man sitting here was the author of all those letters, the ones that had kept her going, even through the hard times. Given her something to look forward to and something to focus on.

His eyes softened as he smiled, laughter lines etched ever so slightly into his tanned skin.

"I've been hoping you might have some good advice to throw my way." He paused, taking a sip of his coffee. "On how to deal with a twelve-year-old boy who can't seem to bear the sight of me."

Her heart throbbed for a moment, feeling his pain. But she recovered without him noticing.

"When you say he can't bear the sight of you…"

Ryan grimaced. "I mean that he gets up and leaves the

room the moment he sees me, or suffers my presence at mealtime by sitting silently and not raising his eyes."

Oh. "And your parents?"

That brought the smile back to his face. "Thrilled to have their only son home and desperate for me to reconnect with my own boy."

She thought about it for a moment. The nice thing about already having a relationship with someone, even if it was on paper, was that silent stretches weren't uncomfortable. Or at least they weren't with Ryan.

She unfolded her legs and leaned toward him.

"I know it's going to sound like a cliché, saying that you just need to give him time, especially after all the time you've been away, but I think he'll come around. He's probably angry at you for leaving and staying away so long, and he wants answers. You need to let him know that when he does want to ask you questions you can be there for him, straight up, honest."

Ryan closed his eyes and sat back. She could see this was painful for him, but he was better to get it all off his chest with her.

Besides, talking about him was taking her mind off the fact that she was attracted to him. That his being there, beside her, was making her have feelings she'd long ago abandoned when it came to men. And it also made her push her memories back where they belonged. Locked in a box, out of mind's reach.

He smiled sadly. "You're right, but sometimes I wonder if he'd have been better off if I'd just stayed away."

Jessica shook her head. It wasn't true and he knew it.

"Why don't you practice on me," she suggested, voice soft. "You can pretend I'm George."

He nodded. She only just registered the incline of his head as he moved it.

Jessica took a deep breath. "Okay, I'll start." She paused. "Why did you really go back to war so soon? Why didn't you come home? Stay with me?"

He kept his eyes shut. "I can't answer that."

She sighed and sat back. On second thought she reached for his hand, wanting to give him strength even if it hurt her. "If you can't be honest with me, how are you going to be honest with a boy who wants the truth?"

She watched as Ryan's thumb traced her palm, holding her hand back. It felt so good it hurt, but she didn't dare pull her hand away. Couldn't. The tingle in her fingertips and the pulse at her neck were enough to make her stay put.

When he was ready to talk he dropped his hold and pulled his chair around to face her head-on. She forced herself to breathe, had to concentrate on every inhale and exhale of her lungs.

"Okay, let's do this."

She nodded, still off balance from touching him, from his skin connecting with hers. From wanting him to do it again and hating herself for even thinking about him like that.

Ryan squeezed his eyes shut one more time then focused, looking firmly into hers.

"I left because going away was easier than staying. I was a coward and I should have been here for you."

Jessica gulped silently as tears pooled in her eyes. This was what he'd been needing to say for so long. There was no disguising the pain in his voice.

"Go on," she urged huskily.

"I told myself that you would be better off without

me, and I felt guilty over your mom's death. Like if only I'd loved her more, been here for her more, she could have pulled through. Everyone thought we had this perfect life, and in many ways we did, but then when she got sick everything just went into free fall, and after a while it was easier to just stay away than deal with her death." He paused. "And with you."

Jessica stood and walked away a few steps. She couldn't help it. Tears hit her cheeks and trickled their way down her jaw. She'd known hurt before, known what it was like to be left, but she also knew what it was like to be the one who did the hurting.

"Jess?"

"I'm sorry, it's just…"

"Did I say something wrong?" He sounded concerned.

She reached her fingertips to her face and brushed the tears away. Before she could turn large hands fell on her arms, holding her from behind.

"I shouldn't have said all that, but once I started it…"

Jessica closed her eyes then turned back to face him. She'd tried not to let her own feelings intrude, but it was hard. Impossible even.

"I lost someone once, too, Ryan, that's all. Hearing you say all that kind of brought that back. I don't know why but it did."

His eyes questioned her but he didn't say anything. Instead it was as if a metal guard had been raised, shielding his gaze and putting a wall between them. A divide that hadn't been there before.

Jessica didn't want to think about her past. Probably as much as Ryan wanted to disclose his, if the look on his face right now was any indication. It did give them something in common. Not exactly the common element most people would wish for, but on some level she did understand him. And if she wanted to tell him, he'd probably feel the same about her. But she didn't want to, and the last thing she intended was burdening him with her problems, or letting her mind dwell on what could happen to her.

"You know what? I think maybe it's time for me to go," he said, suddenly looking like a startled animal within sight of a predator. As if he wanted to flee the scene.

"Okay." Now she was the one confused. "Do you want to maybe grab dinner tonight? Do that 'start over' thing again?"

He was smiling but it looked forced. Not like before.

"Can we take a rain check on that? Maybe tomorrow night?"

Ouch. She hadn't seen that one coming. She'd overreacted, not been able to keep her emotions in check, but she hadn't realized he'd react like that.

"How about you call me when you're free?" she suggested.

He nodded and turned back toward the house. "See you, bud."

At least he'd said goodbye to the dog.

"I'm sorry, Jess. It's just that I need to pick George up from school."

She shrugged. Even she knew that school didn't get out for a while yet. "I get it. We can catch up later."

She followed him back into the house, wondering what she would give to truly start over with him and be the strong girl from the letters. To go back to him standing on her doorstep and make the day turn out completely different.

His tall frame disappeared through the door and he didn't look back, his broad shoulders and dark hair fading from sight.

Jessica stood with her hands on her hips and surveyed the huge stretch of canvas on the floor in front of her. Not her best work, but the colors were brilliant. The organic paint took some getting used to, although if it meant no toxic fumes she had no intention of complaining.

She'd tried to focus on her new piece, but her mind kept wandering. Going to a place she didn't want to go back to but couldn't claw out from.

She found it was easier sometimes to pretend it hadn't happened. When you were surrounded by people who loved you or who had been the cause of grief, it sucked something from you. Pulled you into a world you didn't want to confront.

Like her cancer. She'd dealt with. Fought it. Survived it.

Yet her family treated her like she needed permanent wrapping in cotton wool just to survive each day now. Looked at her in a way that made her uncomfortable. And she hated it.

Was that how Ryan felt? The same way she did when she looked in the mirror and saw the reality of her body? Is that how he felt about being home? About the reality of what he'd gone through and then battled every day? How it was to come home and face something you'd run from for years?

Sometimes she felt like that, too. Sometimes she wished she could run away from what had happened and leave it all behind. But just like Ryan had had to return, so had she. To the reality of life as a cancer survivor.

She let her hand brush over the almost-hard contour of her breast, skimming the side of it, not caring that her fingers were covered in paint. Jessica sighed. She'd always mocked women with implants. Found it hard to fathom why breast augmentation was such an attraction.

She smiled with the irony. When she'd faced the reality of a double mastectomy, the first question she'd asked was what kind of reconstruction they could do. How they could give her her femininity back. Her breasts.

So now she had teardrop-shaped silicone implants that were better than nothing, but that still made her shake her head sometimes. That despite being diagnosed with cancer, facing chemo, knowing there was a chance she could die, all she'd wanted was to feel like a woman again. To know that even though they didn't feel soft when they'd once been natural, she still had her femininity, even if it had meant facing cosmetic reconstructive surgery to obtain them.

Maybe it was the same for Ryan. Without being a soldier, he would feel like less of a man, less of a human being. Maybe that was why he felt he had to go back, had to return to his unit. Had to offer himself up for redeployment.

If she could talk to him, explain to him how she felt, maybe it would help him. Help them both. But she couldn't do it.

She didn't want him to know. Couldn't tell him. Because then he'd start looking at her the same way everyone else did, and with Ryan, she just wanted to be Jessica. Not the girl with cancer. The girl in remission. Or the girl who'd already lost her sister to the disease.

Maybe he wouldn't look at her differently, or treat her like a different person, but she wasn't prepared to risk it. Not when she only had a limited time to enjoy having a friend like Ryan.

Or maybe she was too scared to tell him.

Either way, it was her secret and she had no intention of divulging it.

But after the way he'd left today, like he was fleeing a burning wreckage, she didn't know when they'd be seeing each other again. If ever.

"Jess?"

She looked up as Bella crossed her arms and leaned against the door of her studio. Jess sighed. Today had definitely not gone as planned.

"You have some serious explaining to do," her friend said.

CHAPTER FOUR

Jessica,
I don't know how you know so much about loss or dealing with pain, but you've helped me more than I could ever tell you. Having a friend to write to, someone to just hang out with in the normal world, makes all the difference to me. I love what I do, wouldn't give it up for the world, but sometimes it helps to have someone non-army to talk to.

You do realize I'm gonna owe you big-time when I come home. Dinner, drinks, whatever you want, but you writing to me has given me a boost, and that only makes me a better soldier. I was starting to think I was too old for war, but it's like I've been recharged.

So think about it. When I finally leave this place and come home, my shout. Whatever you want. And I promise not to talk about me or ask you for any more advice. Okay?
Ryan

RYAN SAT IN the car and watched the throng of kids as they spilled out from the building. He couldn't see George, but then that was hardly a surprise. The boy would probably hide in class to avoid having to get in the car with his dad.

But Ryan was patient. He'd wait here as long as he had to. Besides, it wasn't as if he didn't have enough on his mind to keep him occupied.

Jessica.

Today had started out so well and ended so…badly. He closed his eyes and leaned back into the seat. He thumped his hand on the wheel. Ow! Sometimes he forgot he was meant to be recuperating, that he couldn't use his arm like that. It hurt badly sometimes, ached, bothered him when he was uptight or unsure.

He hated not being strong and capable. It wasn't that he was weak, but he'd always been the tough guy, the one who could be counted on physically and mentally in the worst of situations.

And it wasn't like it was only his arm troubling him. His head was messed up, too, especially after his behavior earlier.

Somehow he'd managed to screw today up. Jessica was supposed to be the easy part, the simple meeting of a friend. How wrong he'd been.

Why was being back so hard? He was so good at being a soldier, it came so naturally to him. Ryan swallowed and looked out the window.

Being a dad had come naturally to him once, too.

So had being a husband.

But that felt like another lifetime ago. Like he could just hold on to it as a long-distant memory, but it was starting to fade. Fast.

Ryan jumped at a knock on the car window.

He cursed, then pushed the button to wind down the window and acknowledge George's teacher. "You frightened the life out of me!"

"Sorry." The young man smiled, holding out his hand.

Ryan opened the door and got out, shaking the teacher's hand and leaning against the side of his car.

"It's Shaun, right?"

The teacher nodded. Ryan had only met him once before, on his first day back, but he'd liked him straight away.

"I saw you sitting here and thought I'd see how you were getting on with George," Shaun said.

Ryan shrugged. What did he say to that?

"Not great." There seemed no point in not telling the truth.

"Anything I can do to help?"

"You know, once upon a time I knew exactly what to say to make him laugh, just to be there for him. You know?" he said.

Shaun gave him a kind smile.

"It's not so easy anymore. Figuring out what the right thing to do with him is hard work," Ryan admitted.

"I'm sure you're doing everything you can. Just stick with it and do what feels right."

Ryan nodded, shoulders heaving as he exhaled. He wasn't usually one to open up, to talk to someone about how he felt, but George seemed to genuinely like his teacher. And he appreciated the offer of help.

"I guess I've found it hard to know what to say to him since his mom died. Until now, I've taken the easy way out and let my parents do the hard work."

It had indeed been the coward's way out and he was man enough to admit it. Especially now he could see firsthand the effect it had had on his boy.

"What matters is that you're here now and you want to do something about it." The teacher held out his hand again and patted Ryan on the shoulder with the other.

"You'll get there, and if you need someone to talk to—either of you—I'm here. Okay?"

"Thanks."

Shaun gestured toward the door. "I saw him by his locker before, I'm sure he'll be out soon."

Ryan watched the teacher walk off and got back in the car.

When he'd been redeployed the last time, he was still grieving for his wife. He'd held his son at the airport, hugged him tight and then walked away. Seeing his own mother hold his boy had left an image in his mind that had never faded. An image that told him George would be happier without his dad. That a messed-up, grieving, unsure father was nothing compared to the steady, loving influence of grandparents.

And then every month he'd stayed away it had simply been easier to keep telling himself it was true. That it was better for George, and it was sure easier for him. Because he didn't have to see the similarities to his wife in his son's face on a daily basis. Didn't have to remember what it had been like when they'd been a family, the three of them. Happy and content.

But now… Now George was, well, not a little boy anymore. He'd gone from a sweet nine-year-old to an almost twelve-year-old with a voice on the verge of cracking and an attitude to boot. It was obvious he loved his grandparents, but his feelings toward his father were a whole other matter entirely.

If he even felt anything for his father anymore.

But what had Ryan expected? To come home and pick up where they'd left off? He'd been a fool to stay away so long, but he wasn't going to run away again. He was going to stand up, take it on the chin and accept the fact that he'd failed his son.

The car door opened. Ryan sat up straighter and looked into the eyes of his son.

George scowled at him and slammed the door, school bag on his knee.

"Hey."

George ignored him.

"Good day at school?"

Ryan received a shrug in return before George slumped down low and stared out the window.

He turned the ignition and pulled out into the traffic.

Part of Ryan wanted to explode. To pull over and grab his son and shake him until he listened. To tell him what he'd been through, how much he hurt, what he'd seen during wartime that had made his stomach turn.

"George…"

But he couldn't tell him off. Because his son had done nothing wrong. He was just behaving how any hurt child of his age would. By dishing out the silent treatment. So Ryan clenched all his fingers around the wheel and kept his eyes on the road and his mouth shut.

George didn't seem to have noticed he'd even been spoken to. But a letter every other week and a dad absent for almost two years since his last trip home meant that Ryan deserved the silent treatment. The short time he'd spent with him between deployments the last time had been strained and emotional, but George had been a lot younger then. More accepting and so excited to have his dad back.

So right now he needed to wait it out, or figure out a way to make amends. It wasn't as if he could jump up and down and insist the boy behave. George was on his way to becoming a young man, and if he didn't fix things between them soon, he might lose his chance forever.

But this wasn't the army. And George wasn't his subordinate.

He was a dad and he had a lot to prove before he deserved the title. Being a father wasn't something you could write on a name tag and lay claim to. He'd been anything *but* a dad these past few years, and it was embarrassing. Ryan had grown up in a loving family, his parents had been married thirty-seven years and his own father had been a shining role model.

Ryan felt his knuckles harden, like he was trying to squeeze the lifeblood from the steering wheel.

He'd let his own dad down, too, as much as he'd let himself down. After having the best example set for him, Ryan had ignored his instincts, that gut feeling that he was behaving badly. Had left it way too long to make amends.

Which is why part of him wanted to run back to the army and write this entire episode off as too hard. Hide again because it was easier.

But he'd promised himself he wouldn't do that. Because this time he had to face up to his past, to what had happened, and try to move forward. Instead of sticking his head in the sand like a stubborn ostrich.

Ryan flexed his jaw. The kid still hadn't made a noise.

"What do you think about grabbing something to eat?"

George didn't look at him, eyes still trained out the window, like he couldn't think of anything worse than being in an enclosed space with his father, let alone having to communicate with him.

"Or would you rather go home?" Ryan asked.

"Home."

Ryan nodded. At least he'd spoken. But he knew the

drill. They'd arrive home, George would kiss his grandmother on the cheek and grab a handful of her baking, then head to his room. He'd either push his headphones on and blast music through his eardrums like he was determined to be deaf before his eighteenth birthday, or go square-eyed playing video games.

He had intended on asking George if he wanted to do something tonight, but that clearly wasn't going to happen.

Which meant maybe, just maybe, he should call Jessica.

Jessica.

Now that was one word that was always sure to put a smile on his face. He had grinned like an idiot whenever a letter had arrived for him with her unmistakable handwriting on the back. And when he'd seen her today, he could barely wipe the smile from his lips.

He'd been rude earlier, hot then cold, and he had no idea why she'd rattled him so bad. Seeing her cry had done something to him, made him remember what it was like to see his wife cry. Years of her being the strong pillar of their marriage had fallen like dust to the ground that day they'd found out she'd had cancer. And seeing Jessica cry today had messed with his head in the same way.

But she had seemed on edge, too, before she'd broken down. Not herself, if that was even possible for him to know when he'd never met her before. But all those letters, all those words they'd shared, they counted for something. And deep down something was telling him that she would be just as annoyed with herself as he was with himself right now.

Which meant there was a glimmer of hope that she'd give him another chance and agree to the dinner she'd suggested before he'd blown cold and fled like a pride of lions was in pursuit of his soul.

Ryan sighed and pulled into the driveway of his parents' house.

He'd already made a mess of his relationship with his son, but he didn't have to ruin the one good thing in his life right now. Jessica was a great friend, *had* been a great friend, and he wasn't going to act like an idiot and face the prospect of going back to war somewhere without knowing her letters would follow him there.

Wherever in the world he'd been, wherever they'd sent him, her letters had always found him. And she had no idea how that had kept him going. Kept him alive when everything else had gone so wrong.

He glanced at George again and noticed his eyes had closed. Great, now he preferred being unconscious to being in the car with his dad.

There was no chance of them spending time together tonight, so he wasn't going to beat himself up about going out on a date.

Ryan clasped the wheel harder and stared straight ahead.

Not a date. Not in any way a date.

He was going to ask a friend for dinner. They'd already discussed it earlier.

Just because she looked incredible did not mean it was a date by any stretch of the word.

He ground his teeth together.

George leaped from the car with the most enthusiasm Ryan had seen from him all day as soon as they were stationary.

Dinner with Jessica was definitely his best option.

* * *

Jessica couldn't stop stirring her coffee. It was the only way she could continuously avoid her friend's stare.

"You can't avoid me forever."

That was the problem. Bella had been her best friend far too long to be put off so easily. But what could she tell her? The truth was she had no idea herself what had happened.

"So what did he look like?"

Jessica took a sip and ignored the way the liquid burned her mouth.

"He was, um, normal. You know? Just a regular guy."

She looked down again. If normal guys had frames that could fill doorways without an inch of fat covering their bones. Sharp blue eyes that made her want to blush every time they were turned her way, or tanned skin that seemed like the sun itself had fallen to earth to kiss it.

"Normal?" Bella didn't sound convinced.

Jess nodded.

And received a punch to the arm in response.

"You're lying." Then Bella poked her, hard. "You know you can't lie to me!"

Jess sighed. "Okay, so he was good-looking, but it doesn't matter anyway."

Bella started to laugh. "Mmm, so the fact that your soldier was hot didn't interest you at all?"

Jessica felt her cheeks burn. They heated up so fast it was as if a fire had been lit in her mouth.

"Bella, we both know I'm not interested. He's a friend, nothing more." She did her best to sound firm. Assertive.

It didn't come naturally to her. Not given the current subject matter.

"Did you like him, though? I mean, if you weren't all hung up on not getting involved with someone…"

Jessica didn't like where this conversation was going. Not at all.

"Theoretically, yes." She held up her hand as Bella got that look on her face. That look that made her appear like an overexcited Labrador dog. "But that's irrelevant because I'm *not* interested in men. Period."

Bella didn't seem put off. "Did you find out if he was being redeployed anywhere?"

Jessica felt her skin prickle, like a hedgehog had rolled over her arms, making goose pimples appear. She didn't want to think about Ryan being sent back to his unit. Wherever in the world that might be, she knew in her gut it would be dangerous.

She nodded. "Yeah, he's going back."

"So let me get this right." Bella grinned and shuffled her chair closer. "You're telling me that the guy was gorgeous, you were attracted to him and he's only here for a short time?"

Jess *definitely* didn't like where this was going. She didn't even bother replying. It wasn't as if Bella was about to start listening to her now. She never had before.

"So can you explain to me why you don't want to jump his bones?"

She sighed. Did that type of question even warrant a response? So she'd thought about him *like that*. He was attractive, yes. He was charming. He was, well, *nice*. Better than nice. Wonderful.

But it still didn't mean she was going to let something happen romantically. She'd promised herself no men, no complications, no romance.

So why would she consider breaking her rules now for him?

"Jess?"

She shook her head. "I'm just not interested in Ryan or anyone else for that matter. Not now."

"You're missing the point, Jess." Bella reached over the kitchen counter and took hold of her friend's hand. "We're talking about a guy who's only going to be here for a short time, *before he's sent miles away.* It's not like it would be something long-term." She paused. "You could let your hair down, forget all about what's happened and just live in the now for a while."

Jessica didn't want to hear this. She wished she could close her ears and sing loudly like a naughty child who refused to listen until her friend shut up. Only they weren't children and Bella kind of had a point. But it didn't matter what she said or how tempting it might sound. She was a cancer survivor. She had to focus on her health. On her future.

On protecting her heart.

And she didn't want to ruin her friendship with Ryan. What they had might be paper-based, but it meant a lot to her.

"Well?"

"No."

Bella rolled her eyes. "Give me one good reason?"

The phone rang. Jessica had never been so pleased for an interruption. Its shrill bleeping made her jump to her feet.

"Hello," she answered.

"Hey, Jess, it's Ryan."

The deep baritone that hit her eardrums sent a lick of excitement down her spine. She could curse Bella for putting ideas in her head!

"Hi, Ryan."

There was a pause. A silence that made her heart pound hard.

"I was, ah, wondering if you wanted to have dinner tonight after all?"

Jessica made the mistake of looking up at Bella. Her friend looked like she needed a paper bag, as if she were on the verge of hyperventilating.

"Is it him?" Bella was mouthing at her.

She nodded then turned her back. "Sure."

Now Bella was flapping her hands. She was in danger of becoming airborne.

"Quiet," Jess mouthed as she turned back, but her friend wasn't listening.

"Shall I pick you up around seven?"

"Sounds great. I'll see you then."

As she hung up Jessica looked at Bella.

"Well?"

Jess gulped. "We're going out for dinner."

"Yaaaaaay!"

She cringed at Bella's high pitch. She should never have told her.

"I can't believe you're finally back in the game." Her friend sighed with satisfaction. "Going out on a date."

Jess wished a hole would open up in the carpet and swallow her. Just suck her up and eat her whole. This was not a date. Absolutely *not* a date. No way.

"What are you going to wear?"

Jess groaned. Who was she kidding? This was absolutely a date. It didn't matter what she tried to pretend, or how she thought about it. She was a girl going out for dinner with a boy, her stomach was leaping around as if something with wings had taken ownership of it, and Ryan had sounded as unsure as she had felt herself on the phone.

Given that she'd promised herself there was to be no dating for five years, she'd broken her one rule pretty fast.

But maybe Bella was right. If something did happen between them, if she did want something to happen, would it be so bad? Ryan wasn't hanging around for long, there was no chance she could have her heart broken or get into something long-term, because he wouldn't even be here beyond a couple of months.

"Come on, let's get you ready."

She looked at Bella and tried not to get excited. Ryan would be here in a few hours. She'd be getting in his car, sitting across from him at a restaurant somewhere, looking into those sparkling blue eyes…

Jess groaned again, even more loudly.

So much for thinking of him as nothing more than a friend.

Jessica wished she could quell the inconsistent thudding of her heart, but she couldn't. It was no use.

She was nervous. Terrified. And for some reason there was nothing she could do to calm her nerves, her fear *or* her excitement.

If Bella hadn't kept insisting it was a date…

Argh. The word kept circling her brain like an eagle hunting prey. It wasn't a date. So why—the more she thought about the word—did it seem she was trying to convince herself of a cold-edged lie?

Jess parted the blinds to look out at the street. She watched as a couple of cars passed. The third one slowed then pulled up outside her house. Her hand dropped away, as if she'd been burned.

It was like this morning all over again.

Except this time she didn't want to run from the scene. This time she wanted to run into his arms.

She growled at herself. She needed to stop listening to Bella.

But despite all her reasoning to the contrary, her promises to herself, the truth was that she was tempted. He *was* going away again soon. And she *was* attracted to him. So if he was interested in her *like that* then didn't she owe it to herself to have a good time?

The logical part of her brain was telling her no. That his friendship meant too much to throw it all away. To even risk the possibility of something happening.

But the other part? That was telling her to have fun. To let her hair down for once. To enjoy the company of a man who didn't know any of her baggage, her past. Who didn't want to treat her as if broken glass was shattered over her skin, like he could hurt her.

That part knew that maybe, just maybe, this was an opportunity to be herself. A woman who wasn't afraid of moving forward and having fun. For the short term anyway.

Jess straightened her shoulders and ran her hands down her jeans. She wasn't going to wait for him to knock this time. Her poor heart couldn't handle it.

It had been a long time since Ryan had felt like he couldn't settle his nerves. His career depended on it. When he was deployed, he always kept calm, had a confidence and calmness that saw him through any scenario.

So when Jessica walked out onto the porch and gave him a half wave, before turning to lock the door, he was taken by surprise. It felt like someone had placed a steady hand around his throat and squeezed, just for a moment, to make him gasp for the next gulp of air. Made his mind scramble, as if he were incapable of utilizing the rational, functioning part of his brain.

Jessica had to fiddle with the lock and it gave him time to watch her. This girl who'd meant so much to him for so long.

He'd known he would feel close to her, but he hadn't expected this. He'd thought she would be a normal American girl, just another person in the world. The kind of girl you'd pass in the street and not necessarily notice.

How wrong he'd been.

Her hair was messy, as if she'd spent hours at the beach to put the wind through it and then played with each strand through her fingers. It was tousled and slightly curly, falling below her shoulders. Her skin was golden, as if the sun had just been allowed to skim it, and… He gulped.

Looking any further wasn't going to help him. The curve of her backside in her denim jeans, the silhouette of her upper half in her summery top.

He swallowed again, hard, when she turned to face him. Jessica was smiling, her full lips pulled back to show off white teeth, eyes slightly downcast as if she was a touch embarrassed.

Any thought of her being "just a friend" fled his mind.

It wasn't because he'd been away serving. It wasn't because he hadn't been around women in a long while.

It was simply Jessica.

She did something to him, scrambled his brain and made his body jump, like he'd never experienced before.

Ryan leaped from the car. He couldn't have moved faster if it had been on fire. It was like his brain and his body were finally capable of acting as one.

"Hey."

Jessica's cheeks were touched with the lightest of pink blushes.

"Hey," she said back.

He walked forward, wanted to kiss her on the cheek, but felt awkward. They stood, watched one another for a moment, before he stepped back.

Idiot.

"Let me get the door." Suddenly he was all nerves, more thumbs than fingers as he walked around to the passenger side.

She walked past him and ducked to get into the car. "Thanks."

He grinned at her, he could feel the goofy smile on his face and was incapable of doing anything to remove it.

Jessica looked up at him, her own face open, expectant.

"Let's go grab some dinner," he said.

She nodded at him, before he closed the door.

Ryan walked slowly back around to the driver's side and tried to pull himself together. He had possibly the most beautiful woman he'd ever met sitting in his car, waiting for him to be charming, expecting the person she'd met on paper, and he could hardly string a sentence together.

Jessica had looked good earlier today, but he hadn't had the chance to just watch her and drink her in.

He got in the car and pulled on his seat belt.

Ryan could feel her, smell her, sense her beside him. He made himself look over at her and smile. Ignored the insistent thump of his pulse, or his heart near beating from his chest and tried to act relaxed.

"We doing that 'start over' thing again?"

He smiled at Jessica's joking tone.

"We don't need to start over." He turned the ignition. "It was just, well, kind of weird meeting after knowing each other on paper for so long. Don't you think? We both sort of overreacted."

Jessica sighed. "Thank goodness we're on the same page."

He laughed at the same time she did. Their eyes met and they laughed some more. It was as if all the worry had vanished, the knot of uneasiness in his stomach had been untied. Just from hearing her laugh, knowing she felt the same way.

"Excuse the pun," Jessica managed to say, when they'd stopped laughing.

Ryan resisted the urge to reach for her hand, to make a connection with her. It was so unnatural for him to even think like that, but with Jessica it felt natural.

"We're going to have a good time tonight."

She leaned back in her seat, body angled to face him. "I think so, too."

Ryan chanced a quick glance at his passenger. She was looking out the window now.

He dragged his eyes back to the road.

Maybe coming home was the best thing he'd ever done.

Jessica smiled. She couldn't have wiped the grin from her face if she wanted to.

This morning, she'd been a bundle of nerves. She hadn't been much better this afternoon. But seeing Ryan again, being with him, something about it felt so right.

They shared an understanding, had a bond that was hard to describe.

And Bella had been right.

She *was* attracted to him.

It didn't mean she wanted something to happen between them. But maybe she did have to listen to her friend. She'd been celibate for well over a year now, had pledged not to put her heart in harm's reach or let someone else suffer because of what she might have to go through in the future.

But if Ryan was only here for a short time, who was she to say no to a romantic fling?

Jessica glanced over at Ryan, watched his strong hands grip the wheel, his jaw strong and angled and freshly shaved.

There was nothing not to like about him.

So if she couldn't get hurt or hurt him in return, what was the harm in admitting it?

CHAPTER FIVE

Dear Ryan,
I still can't believe we grew up so close together. Not much has changed here since you've been gone, well at least not that I can think of. I often wonder about traveling, but I'm such a homebody. I like being surrounded by family and doing the same old thing, but sometimes, well, sometimes I think it would be nice to run away for a bit, even for a week or two. Step out of my life and be someone else, just another traveler in a foreign place.
Jessica

"I THOUGHT YOU said nothing much had changed around here."

Ryan raised an eyebrow as he looked at her before diverting his gaze. He was looking at a new electronics store, which was certainly not the restaurant he'd been expecting.

"Hmmm, maybe I hadn't realized quite how long you'd been away." She bit her lip to stop from smiling.

"I can't believe the little Italian place has gone. It was my favorite." He sighed and put the car in gear again. "When I was away I'd dream of their bruschetta and pasta, or watching their pizzas come out of the oven while we waited."

Now he had her mouth watering.

But, hang on…

"Do you mean Luciano's?"

Ryan's eyes flashed. "Sure do."

Jessica fought the urge to laugh again. The look on his face was priceless. "It might not be as good, but do you mind if I choose where we go?"

Ryan shrugged. "Sure."

"Turn left up here, then keep going straight."

He obeyed, pulling the car back out into the traffic. "You go to this place often?"

Jessica shook her head. "No, but I've heard about it."

"Up here?"

"Yep, keep going and then pull into any spot past the next set of lights."

When the car was stationary Jessica grabbed her bag and opened the door. She had gotten the hint earlier that Ryan was a little old-fashioned about manners, but she couldn't wait to get out. To lead him to the restaurant. There was no time to wait for him to get her door.

"So where exactly are we heading?"

Ryan had one hand slipped into his jeans pocket. He looked strong, completely unflappable. He had dark eyebrows, and they were pulled together now, as if he was wondering what to say to her. His almost-black hair was tousled, just-got-out-of-bed messy. Not the cropped soldier look she had expected. There were two buttons of his shirt undone, the sleeves were rolled up to expose his forearms, and his tanned, soft skin was doing something to her insides. To her brain.

Jessica forced her eyes from him. Drinking in the sight of him was way too easy to do.

"This way."

He followed. They fell into step beside one another. It was weird, this feeling that she was out with a friend, yet the pair of them behaving somehow like it was more of a date than a casual outing.

"Ryan, can I ask you a question?"

He glanced at her as they walked. "Shoot."

"You've only just come back, but your hair is, well, normal. I thought you'd have a buzz cut."

Ryan laughed. "Not in special forces. Well, not all the time."

Now she was confused. "Huh?"

He had both hands pushed into his jeans pockets now, his long legs going slow so as not to outwalk her.

"We often have to look the part, you know, fit in wherever we're posted."

She liked how comfortable the air felt between them. Like they could talk about anything. That's how it had always felt when they wrote to one another, like they could open up about whatever was troubling them. No matter what.

"Let's just say you wouldn't have recognized me when I was away this time. I had a full beard and my hair was long and shaggy."

"What!"

"We often have to blend in. The last thing you want is your buzz cut marking you as U.S. Army. That way we're in less danger, because we're not likely to create attention. I have to go completely undercover as a sniper sometimes, and that usually means making sure no one notices me."

Jessica giggled. She couldn't help it.

"So you looked like a hobo?"

Ryan nudged her, bumped his arm into her shoulder.

Jessica kept her eyes downcast, was too afraid to look up. His touch, the strength of his upper arm as it skimmed hers, made her stomach flip.

"Slow down."

He did.

Jessica indulged in the pleasure of closing her hand over his forearm, let the warmth of his skin tingle through hers. It had been a long time since she'd touched a man, and even longer since the feel of another human being had made her feel like this.

"We're here."

The restaurant had a full glass frontage, a podium outside with the menu displayed and the unmistakable red-and-white checked tablecloths of an Italian restaurant.

"This isn't..."

Jessica squeezed his arm and dragged him inside.

"Luciano's."

Ryan stopped and stared into the restaurant. She loved the wide smile on his face, the way his eyes were dancing. Seeing happiness in another was something that never ceased to warm her heart.

"Wow."

"Not quite the little old restaurant you remembered, but let's hope the food hasn't changed."

She went to walk inside but Ryan's grip stopped her. Suddenly it was him holding her, his skin possessing hers rather than the other way around.

"Thank you."

Jessica refused to drop her eyes, to look at his hand. She made herself be brave, didn't let her nerves stop her.

Because she wanted this. She didn't want him to think she didn't.

"No problem."

Ryan stared at her, his eyes never leaving hers for what felt like forever.

"Table for two?"

Jessica turned, the spell broken. A waiter stood before them in the doorway, menus in hand.

"Ah, sure."

She felt Ryan follow her, his big body close behind hers.

She glanced at him as they sat at a small table in the corner, tucked near the window. He smiled.

And she knew then that everything had changed.

Because from the look on his face, the way his eyes looked like a storm was brewing but at the same time sunlight was shining through them, made her realize that maybe he was having the same internal battle she was.

That they were supposed to be friends and yet within a few hours the goalposts had moved.

But it wasn't just a new set of rules. It felt like a new game entirely.

One that she hadn't played before. Or at least not in a very long time.

Ryan sat back and studied Jessica.

He was confused. More than confused. He had no idea what he was doing or what he should do, and it wasn't a feeling he was used to.

This woman was doing something to him and he was helpless to stop it happening. In fact, he didn't want to stop it. With everything else that was going on, with his son and his arm, this was a pleasant distraction.

He watched as she glanced up, long lashes hiding her eyes when she quickly looked back down.

She was as nervous and uncertain as he was, there was no mistaking it, and it felt good. He liked that she was unsure, too. He was as confused as a guy could get over what was happening here, so he couldn't have handled her being Little Miss Confident. Her shyness made him want to step up and protect her, but not like it had been with his wife near the end.

He never wanted to feel helpless like that again. Like no matter what he did he couldn't protect the person he loved. That he was useless and not strong enough to make a difference, to save that someone.

With Jessica it was different. He wanted to protect her, the animal within him wanted to growl like a tiger and keep her to himself, but it wasn't because she needed protecting.

Jessica was strong. Healthy. Happy.

All he needed to do was enjoy her company, and humor the alpha inside of him that wanted to be released.

Ryan grinned when she glanced up at him again. "Seen anything you like the look of?"

He didn't miss the instant flush as it hit her cheeks.

"Ah…"

He shook his head. That had come out all wrong. From the look on her face, she liked what she saw as much as he did when he watched her.

"I'm going to go with good old spaghetti bolognese," he said.

Ryan watched as she let out a breath and placed her hands over the menu.

"Meatballs for me, please."

He raised an eyebrow. "Good choice."

They watched one another. For a heartbeat that seemed like forever. Until she spoke, as if scared to just sit there and not say anything.

"How did you get on with George this afternoon?"

Ryan shook his head. "Not great. He's still not talking to me."

She smiled. "You'll get there with him. Have faith."

Faith. He'd kept the faith his entire time away, but at times, well, when he thought about his late wife or the way he'd run from his family, he wondered if he had any at all. What he'd seen away serving, what he'd had to witness, had made him question everything he'd ever known or believed in.

But sitting here with this sweet, charming woman now…it made him want to believe all over again. That he could be the man he'd been before experiencing loss. Before serving his country for so long.

That maybe, just maybe, before he went back the next time to rejoin his unit, he could be the man he'd like to be again in the future.

"Jess, about earlier today…"

"Water under the bridge." She put her hand up. "I asked for a chance to start over already, now you've had one. Consider us even."

He smiled at her; it was all he ever seemed to do when he was with her.

"Seeing you, well, emotional like that, it reminded me of a time I usually try to forget. I shouldn't have reacted like that," he apologized.

She reached out to touch his hand, the softest of touches, but enough to tell him that she was there for him. That she understood. "You mean your wife?"

Ryan swallowed what felt like a solid piece of gum in his throat. It shouldn't be so hard to go back there in his mind, not after all this time, but whenever he thought of the end, of what had happened, it was as if his mind put up an impenetrable shield.

"What I saw my wife go through took something from me." He paused. Jessica's hand was still hovering. "I couldn't ever go through seeing someone I care about experience that kind of pain again. Cancer is like a snake, it sneaks up on you, and once you're in its grip I don't know if you can ever be released."

He watched as Jessica's face froze. Only for a second, but he saw it. Saw something cross her eyes and her mouth, something that he couldn't put his finger on.

Her hand rose then fell back to his again, before she pulled it back entirely. Her face was back to normal but something had made her waver.

"I didn't know your wife died of cancer," she said.

Ryan nodded. Had he never told her in all those letters how she'd died?

"Seeing someone you love battle with it, well, I can't think of anything worse a person could go through."

The smile she gave him was tight, strained, but he'd probably just made her uncomfortable. Bringing up terminal cancer as a subject made people react differently. He should have realized that.

"Ryan, didn't you mention something about bruschetta before?"

His mouth watered. "Sure did."

"Why don't we share it? See if it's as good as it used to be."

Ryan raised his glass, pleased to see the sparkle back in her eyes, that sweet, natural smile back on her lips.

"To old times," he said.

"To friendship."

They clinked their glasses together, before he took a long sip of red wine from his.

It was good. Better than good.

This whole night felt great.

"I'll only say yes to bruschetta if we can finish the night with gelato," he teased.

Jessica sat back, wineglass tucked in her hand. "You're lucky I like my food."

They both laughed.

He'd done the right thing, inviting her out tonight. If they stayed just friends, then he'd be happy. But if something more happened…Ryan took another sip of wine before leaning in closer to Jessica across the table.

If something else happened then he wasn't going to say no.

He'd have to be a stronger man to resist. And after years of not being interested like this in a woman, it felt seriously good.

Jessica smiled at Ryan as he attempted to cut a huge piece of bruschetta, piled high with tomato, onion and basil. Her insides felt kind of fluttery, her brain kept firing her warning signals that she was electing to ignore, but she was still enjoying herself.

Hearing Ryan open up about his wife, hearing the dreaded *C* word…it had rattled her. She knew he'd noticed the look on her face, seen the blood drain from her skin temporarily, but she'd managed to recover fast enough that he hadn't called her out on it.

But still. Cancer? Part of her was pleased she'd never told him. After the way he'd talked about what he'd gone through, talked about what he *never wanted to go through again,* it had been clear he might not be sitting with her right now if she'd been honest from the beginning. He might not have even wanted to write to her if she'd told him.

But her chance to confess, to share what she'd been through, had passed. There had been a moment, a tiny window of opportunity, where she could have stopped him and told him what had happened to her. But she hadn't.

And she had no intention of telling him now. Maybe not ever.

"Jessica?"

She looked up. Ryan was watching her.

"This is delicious."

Jess reached for the large piece of bruschetta he had sliced off for her. The smell of the balsamic alone had her mouth watering. She could feel him watching her as she took a bite, trying to be dainty but struggling given the portion size.

"Mmmmm." She finished her mouthful. "You're right, it is delicious."

When he smiled at her, before finishing what was left on his plate like it was no more than a snack, she knew deep down that she couldn't tell him. If he was only here for a short time, who was she to be the one responsible for turning that happy smile into a frown? Why should her problems—health problems she'd dealt with on her own—be a reason not to have fun with him?

It wasn't like she was embarking on a long-term future with the man. They were friends, and friends kept their secrets sometimes. It just so happened this was one she didn't want to share with anyone who didn't already know about it.

"More wine?"

Jessica internally shrugged off her fears and eliminated all thoughts of Ryan's earlier words.

This was about having fun. Enjoying herself with a handsome soldier who would be back with his unit before the year was out.

"Please," she said recklessly, holding up her glass.

Ryan tipped the bottle of red and filled her glass to the halfway mark.

She took a long, slow sip, and leaned across the table toward him. "Tell me all about the guys you serve with. I want to know what it'll be like for you going back to them."

Jessica twirled her fingers around the long stem of her glass as Ryan sat back, his body relaxed against the chair.

"I don't know how exciting a story it is," he protested.

She shook her head, laughing as he grimaced. "You're not getting off that easily, and we've got all night."

"So gelato, huh?"

Ryan laughed. He seemed to do a lot of that around her.

"Believe me, when you're hot and sticky in the desert, thinking about gelato is like torture."

"And now you finally get to indulge."

He passed her the waffle cone before reaching back for his own. They were only a few blocks from where the car was parked, close enough to walk.

"Good?"

"Mmmmm."

Jessica was too busy swirling her tongue around the Italian ice cream to answer. She just kept making the noise in her throat to indicate how tasty it was.

Ryan gulped and tried to focus on his own dessert. But dragging his eyes from her mouth, from her tongue and the way her eyes were dancing as she watched what she was eating…

She looked up.

Whoops. Caught out like a dog trying to sneak a leg of lamb from the kitchen bench.

He watched in fascination as this time her throat worked slowly, swallowing, running her tongue over her lips then letting her hand drop lower as if she'd forgotten the gelato completely.

Ryan wanted to look away. He tried, he really did. But he found his body moving instead, toward her. The look in her eyes tormented and taunted him, pulled him into her web. He had to fight not to drop his cone to the ground.

Ryan could hear his own breathing, and he could hear hers, too. It was as if there was nothing else in the world around them, like they were the only two people on the street, in this moment.

He raised his arm, high enough to reach out and touch her face, and wiped the tiniest bit of ice cream from Jessica's mouth. Maybe he had imagined it, maybe he'd gently wiped away nothing. Maybe he just wanted an excuse to get closer to her, to be pulled toward her like a magnet to metal.

His arm ached, he felt a dull throb as he held it up, but he didn't care. He'd felt worse, and she was worth it. Touching her was worth any lick of pain, no matter how bad.

"Thanks," she whispered, eyes flickering low then higher again.

Ryan stood there. He gave her the chance to walk away, to move back so their bodies weren't so close. When she didn't he closed in, stepped forward and leaned toward her. She was tall but not as tall as him, the top of her head just higher than his chin.

"Jess," he murmured.

She nodded.

He pushed her arm down slightly, so she had to move her cone away from her body. It allowed him to get closer. Their chests were close, hovering, but not pressed together.

Ryan dipped his head, waited in case she wanted to move away. But she didn't.

Jessica raised her chin, inclined it up toward him.

He took a deep breath, looked at her mouth, couldn't pull his eyes away, then dropped his mouth to hers. Gently, ever so gently, he brushed his lips across Jessica's.

She tasted sweet, intoxicating. Gelato mixed with the warmth of a woman who wasn't sure, who wasn't used to being kissed in the street on a first date.

Ryan couldn't pull away, couldn't force his feet back. Instead he pressed their bodies that little bit closer, and touched his lips to hers again, more firmly this time.

Jessica couldn't breathe. She was finding it hard enough staying upright, let alone making her lungs work.

His lips fell on hers again, brushing, teasing, tasting. She couldn't help the tiny moan that escaped her mouth. Ryan's lips were soft yet strong, gentle yet firm, and it was turning her body into jelly.

He slowly pulled his lips away, raised his head high enough to look into her eyes.

"Hey," he whispered.

"Hey," she managed to reply.

They stood like that, bodies pressed together, neither ready to back away.

Ryan cleared his throat.

"I think your gelato's dripping down my arm."

"Oh!" Jessica jumped back and worked to clean up her cone, to stop the drips.

"Napkin?"

She nodded.

He walked back over to the ice cream vendor and retrieved a handful of paper napkins.

They wiped at their cones and started to eat them again, standing like a pair of teenagers who had no idea what to say to one another after their first kiss.

Jessica's body was singing, talking to her like a record on repeat. Telling her how good that had felt.

She'd just been kissed like she'd never been kissed before in her life. Her body was tingling, her skin on fire, alive. And her lips were tender from the thorough way his lips had danced over hers.

When Ryan grinned at her she couldn't help but do the same back.

"Shall we head back to the car?" he asked her.

Jessica nodded. And when he reached for her hand and took it against his big palm, she didn't resist. His skin was smooth but worn, a testament to the work he did.

Now there was no mistaking it.

This was definitely, without a doubt, one hundred percent a date.

Jessica wondered if it was possible for a heart to beat so hard that it could pump right through a chest cavity.

It didn't matter what she did, hers was heaving away so madly she could barely concentrate. She only hoped Ryan couldn't hear it.

He walked around and opened the door. This time

when he'd pulled up, she'd sat there in her seat, hadn't moved. And now he was towering above her.

Jessica gulped and forced herself to step out. She was torn. Part of her wanted another breathtaking, spine-numbing kiss. For Ryan to hold her in his arms and cocoon her, wrap her tight against him and kiss the breath from her over and over again.

But the other part told her to scurry inside her house as fast as she could. To never look back and to forget what had happened. No letting herself hope. Or think about what he'd said in the restaurant. Because no matter how much she liked him or wanted to take things further, his words had echoed in her mind over and over, reminding her of what he'd been through, telling her to be careful.

Reminding her of what he never wanted to go through again.

And it made her feel like she was deceiving him.

"It was great seeing you tonight, Jess."

Ryan held out his hand and she took it. Tried to ignore the tingle she felt when their skin connected.

He didn't let go.

"I had a really good time." Her voice was failing her, going all soft and breathy, but she couldn't help it.

He twisted her hand gently so their palms fell together and pushed the door shut with his other.

Ryan walked her up the path to her front door, slowly. "Good enough that you don't want it to end?"

"Yeah," she admitted. Only she couldn't ask him in. She wasn't ready for what it might mean or what he might think it meant.

"Can I call you tomorrow?"

Jessica was relieved he wasn't going to ask if he could

come in. She would have been powerless to say no if he'd given her the option.

"Until tomorrow," she agreed.

"Well, I guess it's good night then," he murmured.

Jessica tried not to wriggle. He still had hold of her hand, was turning her palm over so her wrist was facing up.

"'Night," she whispered.

Ryan smiled at her, a lazy smile that made her heart start thumping wildly all over again.

He brought his lips down slowly to her wrist, pressed a kiss there, then turned her hand back over. The touch of his lips, soft and pillowy, left an emotional indent on her skin.

It was one of the most intimate touches she'd ever experienced.

Ryan walked a few steps backward while she stood there. Immobile. She looked up at him and for a moment, words refused to form in her throat.

Then he took her breath away. "You know, I think you might just be better in real life than you were on paper," he said and he laughed as he turned, hand raised up over his head in a wave goodbye.

Jessica laughed until tears sprang into her eyes and she didn't miss the cheeky grin on his face as he winked before driving off. *You are, too,* she thought. *You are so much better in real life than on paper, and I never could have imagined it.*

Tonight had been crazy. Amazing.

But scary too.

Because here she was, standing on her porch, watching the taillights of his car disappear down the road, feeling like she had maybe, just maybe, fallen head over heels in love with a man who wasn't within her reach.

If they'd met under different circumstances, maybe it would have been different. But she'd promised herself time to heal, to not let anyone else in, and here she was wishing things could be different.

And Ryan didn't want this, either. He might think he did, but he didn't. Not if he knew the truth about her.

He had told her what had happened with his wife, she knew how much it had hurt him, the demons it had created that he'd never truly been able to shake. And tonight, he'd made it clear he could never cope with cancer again. Had spoken of it like the hideous disease it was.

But cancer was still as much a part of her life right now as her family was. It wasn't something she could pretend she'd never had or might never have again in the future. She was in the safe zone now, but it didn't mean it wouldn't come back or haunt her again one day. Unlikely, given the fact she'd had an elective double mastectomy, but it still worried her every day.

She knew what losing someone was like—the disease had taken her sister, too. So she couldn't blame Ryan for how he felt.

So would it be lying if she didn't tell him? If she just enjoyed his company while he was here, before he was redeployed? Would that make her a bad person, after what he'd told her tonight?

Jessica wiped tears away as they fell, heavy on her cheeks. This time she wasn't laughing. This time her tears hurt.

She wasn't going to say no to fun, but what had happened tonight hadn't just felt like fun.

It had felt like the start of something great.

Jessica heard shuffling then scratching on the other side of the door. It brought the smile back to her face.

"Hey, Herc."

She unlocked the door and picked her scruffy little boy up, holding him close to her chest. He licked at her face, tucked tightly against her body.

"Hey, baby. Come on, let's go to bed."

Hercules wriggled to get down and danced down the hall, his tiny feet padding on the carpet. He looked up at her, waiting, happy about tucking up in bed beside her.

"At least I'll always have you, huh?"

His tongue lolled out, as if he was smiling up at her.

She felt tears well at the back of her eyes again, and she didn't try to stop them. Life could be so unfair sometimes. Just when you thought you'd been through enough, coped with all you could, something else came along to steal the breath from your lungs and the fight from your soul.

CHAPTER SIX

Dear Jessica,

It's funny what you've done to me. For all this time I've avoided coming home, and now that I want to I don't know how long it'll be before I can. If you believe I can make things right with my son, then I'll give you the benefit of the doubt. Let's hope we can sit together and laugh one day, and you can say I told you so.

Hope you're well and that you're not sick of writing to me yet. You've got no idea how your letters bring a smile to this soldier's face. I haven't had a lot to look forward to for a while, and your letters make a world of difference.

Here's to seeing you soon.

Ryan

"PUSH UP AS hard as you can then hold."

Ryan felt his mouth twist into a grimace. This was hard. Harder than last time, but then he was making himself work as much as he could physically endure.

The physio pushed down on him, forcing him to exert as much energy, as much power, as possible.

"Okay, and relax," she instructed.

He let his arm drop. The thud started again, the pain

that seemed to shoot through every inch of his skin on that side when he exercised too hard. He'd told her the pain wasn't bad because he wanted to go as hard as he could.

Maybe that hadn't been such a great idea.

Ryan wiped away the sweat that had formed on his forehead.

"You did good today."

He gave the physio what he hoped was an innocent smile. "Why don't we keep going? Another few reps?"

She shook her head, not fooled this time. "You going to tell me again that it doesn't hurt?"

Ryan reached for his workout towel and wiped it over his face. She had him there. Perhaps she'd seen through his bravado the entire time. Seen the pain in his face each time he pushed himself too far.

"I just want to get stronger again as fast as I can."

"And *I* want you to develop your strength slowly, so you can use your arm properly until you're an old man," she said tartly.

Ryan laughed. He couldn't argue with that.

"Can I ask you a personal question?"

He looked up at her. "Shoot."

"I was just wondering why you boys are always in such a hurry to get back to your unit? I get that you're all close, but isn't it nice having an excuse to be home for once?" she asked curiously.

Ryan understood what she was saying. Lots of people seemed to think that way, but they didn't get what it was like to have such an unbreakable bond with another group of men. To feel that closeness and not want to let your team down. The way he felt about his unit was indescribable. He could probably never find words to explain it.

Maybe if his wife was still alive he'd have finished up in the army already, but now…? Well, now the army was his focus, what kept him going.

"It's hard to explain," Ryan said, complying as she flexed his fingers back and stretched his muscles out. "There's something about not wanting to let your unit down, but it's also about wanting to do the right thing."

She smiled, but he didn't think she understood. Not really.

"It's not that I want to be redeployed more than being here, but I'm good at it. It's what I do best."

He was sure better at that than at being a dad.

"So you still want to get fixed up as soon as possible, right? Get back to wherever it is they want to send you."

He nodded. "Yes, ma'am."

She gave him a pat on the back. He could see she didn't truly get it, but his physio was great at her job. And truth be told, not many civilians *could* ever understand the bond and camaraderie a good soldier enjoyed with his unit.

"Same time on Tuesday. And don't leave here until you've stretched out some more."

Ryan watched as she walked away. He sat there, thinking, barely noticing the other people in the room.

He always felt so useless, so powerless when he was here, even though he knew he was making good progress. Because it didn't matter how hard he tried, he was never as strong as he wanted to be.

Ryan took a deep, long gulp of water before moving

to stretch out his muscles some more. He knew he'd be sore in the morning if he didn't do as she'd said.

He couldn't help but think that the only time lately he hadn't thought about his weakness, about what was holding him back physically, was when he'd been with Jessica. Last night he hadn't thought about his arm once. Even when it had ached as he'd lifted it to touch her face, the pain had been nothing.

Or nothing compared to not letting his skin brush against hers.

He liked that she made him smile. That she listened to him.

That she blushed every time they were close, or the way a smile hinted at the corners of her mouth when he spoke.

For a guy who had sworn to never let another woman close again he sure could have fooled himself. Because when he was with Jessica, close to her, beside her, there was no other place he wanted to be. He couldn't offer her a future, anything more than a friendship or short-term relationship really, but he'd been honest with her. He was only back for a short time. No matter how much he liked her, his duty was to his unit, and he would be back serving again as soon as he passed the physical.

Maybe one day in the future they could be something more, but right now he didn't know what his long-term future held. His timing was way off, but he wasn't going to let that stop him seeing her now.

If only he could repair his relationship with his son, he'd feel like he was making real progress being back here.

He stood and tried to ignore the pain as it twinged through his biceps.

Ryan smiled. He might have said no to the pain

medication his doctor had prescribed, but Jessica was purely organic and the best pain relief he could wish for. He dialed her number. He didn't care if asking her out again tonight was too soon. He wanted to see her and it wasn't like he had all the time in the world.

If she was up for some fun while he was here, then he wanted to spend as much time with her as he could. Whether that was just hanging out together or something more.

Jessica stretched back and closed her eyes. The sun felt good on her skin. Like it was soaking through her pores to warm her from the inside out.

Hercules's bark made her open her eyes. He was chasing Bella's daughter, Ruby, around the yard, running alongside her and bouncing up and down.

Jess laughed. "Better than any toy, right?"

Bella agreed. "Nothing makes her giggle like that dog of yours."

"You know it's funny, but I don't think I could ever tire of hearing that little girl laugh."

They both sat back to watch the game between dog and child.

Bella was like her sister. When her own sister had died, Bella had been there for her, unwavering in her support even though it had been a lot for another teenager to cope with. And now Jessica liked to be there for Ruby. It was her way of paying Bella back for all she'd done. In the past and when Jess had been sick, too. Bella had never let her down.

Jessica watched as her brother, Steven, pushed himself up off the grass and stretched out his legs. He'd been lying back, swigging on a beer with Bella's husband, but she figured the barbeque was calling him.

"Are Mom and Dad coming over?"

Steven dropped a kiss to her head as he passed. "Nope. They had some old-folks thing to go to."

They all laughed at him.

"They're not that old."

Steven shrugged. "When you choose bingo over a real night out, you're getting old."

Jessica made a noise in her throat but she could hardly reprimand him. Aside from the fact he was her older brother, Steven didn't mean a word of it. He loved their parents as much as she did.

"You wouldn't get me a beer would you?" he asked.

This time she stood up and thumped him on the arm. "If you weren't so charming I'd tell you to get it yourself."

Steven pouted and made them all laugh again. "Then who'd make you burgers?"

Jess stood up and walked inside. She liked it here. Steven's place was a bachelor pad, not exactly warm and cosy like her house, but it always felt good. They'd had plenty of good times here, fun times with friends and their little family. It was like her second home.

Jessica reached into the fridge for a six-pack of beer just as her phone rang, vibrating and singing in her jeans pocket.

"Ouch!" She hit her head and almost dropped the beer. Darn phone, she thought. "Hello?"

The voice on the other end made her close the fridge and lean against it.

"Hey, Jess, it's Ryan."

She took a moment to catch her breath. Ryan. How could the sound of his voice make her legs wobble like that? Her heart was pounding.

"Hey."

"I was wondering if you were free tonight?"

Heck. She could hardly bail on her brother and Bella, not when they'd been planning to all catch up together for weeks.

But an offer from Ryan was sure tempting.

"Ah, I'm actually out already. At a barbeque."

There was a beat of silence.

"Oh sure, no problem. Maybe another time."

Jess cringed. She didn't want to say no to him. Well, she did and she didn't, she couldn't decide, but right now saying no felt like the wrong answer. Especially after that kiss last night.

She sighed. *Kisses* plural, more like.

"Ryan, I…"

Jessica looked out the window at her brother goofing around, chasing her dog. Bella was sitting on her husband's knee, laughing as her daughter bounced up and down with excitement as she played.

Would it be so bad if she asked Ryan over?

"It's fine, really, we can just catch up some other time."

"No, I mean, why don't you come join me? It's only a few of us. Just casual," she said.

He went silent again. Jessica pressed her ear closer to the phone, harder, willing him to say yes and terrified at the same time.

"Are you sure? I don't want to intrude."

"I'd love to see you again. We're sitting around having a beer and waiting for my—" Jess paused and watched Steven entertain Ruby "—idiot brother to get started with the meat patties."

"I'll see you soon then."

Jessica gave him directions then hung up. She leaned

against the fridge again and tried to steady her thoughts. Had she done the right thing?

Probably not, but she was desperate to see him again. To be near him, to touch him and see whether she'd imagined what had happened yesterday. To see if maybe the connection hadn't been as strong as she'd remembered it to be.

Or whether it was even stronger.

To see whether he was worth the heartache that was sure to come when he left again in a couple of months' time. Because no matter how much she told herself she was okay with his leaving, she'd never allowed herself to get close to a man before without thinking there was a chance at some sort of future.

"You making the beer yourself, sis?"

Steven's call forced her to move her feet, reach back in for the beers and go outside.

He gave her a puzzled look when she walked out again. He dropped his cooking utensil and moved toward her but she put up her hand.

"I'm fine."

He was overprotective. Always worrying about her, especially after the cancer. But he'd already lost one sister, she could hardly blame him for wanting to keep her safe.

"You look like you've seen a ghost."

She waved her hand in the air and tried to relax. "I was just chatting to a friend on the phone." Jess gave Bella a sharp look, but her friend was already smiling. She had guessed exactly whom she'd been talking to.

"Oh." Steven looked unsure but he turned back to the meat.

"He's, ah, going to come over and join us soon, actually."

"He?" Steven growled.

Now Steven was holding his cooking utensil at a scary angle, like he was about to behead someone with it.

Jess gulped. She should have predicted this. "Yes, *he,*" she repeated, standing up to her brother. "I think I mentioned that I had a pen pal, a soldier who I wrote to."

The look on Steven's face spelt thunder. There was a possibility he could have summoned a hurricane just with his expression. "And he's coming here? *Now?*"

"He's a friend, Steven, nothing to get concerned about."

He grimaced then turned away from her. Bella was wriggling in her chair, but Jess shook her head. She didn't want this to become a big deal. Right now Ryan *was* just a friend, and the last thing she needed was Steven getting worked up over it.

"His name is Ryan, and he's back for a while to recover. He had surgery and as soon as he's better he'll be back with his unit, so there is *absolutely no reason* to overreact. It's not like he's even here for long," she told him.

Steven shrugged, but he didn't turn around. She could tell he wasn't happy about it. But then given her recent track record, she could hardly blame him.

"And I don't want him knowing about the cancer."

That made him turn. Now he looked like Neptune about to command the entire ocean. "What kind of friend do you have to keep your cancer from?"

She reached for the bottle opener and popped the top off a beer for Steven. She passed it to him.

"The kind of friend who doesn't need to know. Okay?"

He took the beer and tipped it up, draining a third of the bottle. "If he hurts you, I'll deck him."

She had no doubt that he'd try. Her only issue was that even with a less than perfect arm, Ryan could probably kill her brother with his bare hands.

Bella waved her over and Jess went to sit beside her.

"He only wants to protect you," Bella said quietly.

Jess knew that, she did. And she liked that he was always there for her. After what her ex had done to her, she couldn't blame her brother. She'd been left heartbroken, facing surgery and serious chemotherapy on her own. One moment she'd been looking forward to a wedding, and the next she'd been fighting for her life without the man she'd once loved by her side.

Ryan was different though. He'd been there for his wife, by her side, and she'd lost her battle. He might not want to go back to that dark place ever again, but it wasn't something she could fault him for. He was a different kind of man. Honorable. Dependable.

"Is it so bad that I don't want him to know?" she asked Bella in a low voice.

Her friend squeezed her hand and shook her head. "No. No, it's not."

"He's not going to be around long enough for it to matter, right?"

Bella sighed then shrugged. She didn't answer; it was a hypothetical question, anyway.

"You were right yesterday," Jessica told her. "It's time I let my hair down, enjoyed being in remission, being alive, and being in the company of a man." She took a tiny sip of beer and tucked her feet up under her on the chair. She liked Ryan. She didn't have to pretend otherwise. So why was she still trying to convince herself he was just another friend?

Because after what had happened last night, she knew that they were way beyond friends now.

Ryan pushed the button on his key to lock the car and walked toward the house. It was stupid, being nervous about meeting Jessica's friends, but it had been a long time since he'd done normal stuff like this.

And his latest argument with George was playing on his mind. Hard to ignore.

His son had finally found his tongue, but the words coming out weren't pretty. Ryan grimaced. Maybe George did genuinely hate him. And if he did, what on earth was he going to do about it?

He knocked at the door, sternly pushing back thoughts of his son. It swung back and Jessica grinned at him from inside.

"Hey, Ryan."

The warmth that spread through him, the smile he couldn't help but give her in return, somehow took away all the pain.

She was like his ray of sunshine on the gloomiest of days.

"Hi," he answered.

She beckoned with her hand. "Come on in."

Ryan hesitated for a second too long. He should have kissed her on the cheek, touched his hand to her arm, anything. But he'd waited too long. Now it would just be awkward. It was the second time he'd managed to do that and he vowed not to miss his chance again.

"So this is a friend's place?"

She shook her head. "My brother's."

Oh, dear. He'd walked in on a family do or something.

When she'd said her brother was on burger duty he hadn't realized it was his house.

"I don't want to intrude, if you're doing the whole family thing."

She laughed and tucked a strand of hair behind her ear, her expression shy. "It's just my brother and another couple of friends."

"If you're sure."

This time she was braver in reassuring him. This time she reached out and touched his arm, so lightly he could have missed it if he wasn't watching the way her skin connected with his.

"It's really nice to see you again."

Ryan felt the warmth spread through him, just like it had when he'd arrived. He'd thought of little else but her since last night, except for when he was trying to deal with his son, and being with her again, right now, sure seemed right.

But then maybe he'd been away so long he wasn't sure what he was feeling anymore.

"Come and meet everyone," she urged.

Ryan stepped out into the yard and looked up. But the smile fell from his face in an instant, leaving him cold. That warmth that had spread through him like cookies just taken from the oven died like ice had been poured on them.

It wasn't hard to pick out her brother. He was the one looking like he'd crush every bone in Ryan's body, given half a chance. He stood up straighter, lifted his chin. He understood protective. If he had a sister like Jessica he'd probably be the same. But she was a grown woman and she'd invited him over. And he wasn't the kind of guy easily intimidated—even if he did respect the big-brother macho act.

"Ryan, this is my friend Bella, and her husband, Bruce," Jess said, making the introductions.

Ryan turned his attention to the petite blonde sitting with a little girl on her lap. Her double-wattage smile made up for the deathlike stare of the brother. He took the few steps to shake her husband's hand.

"And little Ruby, of course."

He smiled at the pudgy-armed child wriggling to get down.

Jessica moved closer to Ryan when she turned to face her brother.

"And this is my big brother, Steve." He felt her stiffen as Steve walked over. "I promise he won't bite."

Ryan extended his hand and regretted it the moment the other man clasped it. His grip was tight, viselike, and his dodgy arm was barely up to matching his strength.

He tried not to scowl as pain shot up his arm. He was used to being the strongest, never losing an arm wrestle. Ryan clamped down his jaw and took the pain, refused to give in to it. Didn't let it show even though he was burning inside.

"Nice to meet you, Steve."

Jessica smiled sweetly in Ryan's direction before taking a step closer to her brother and kicking him in the shin.

"Ow!" Steve dropped his iron grip and stepped back.

"He can be a pain in the backside." Jessica smiled as her brother glared at her then went back to the barbeque. "It's not until we have company over that we realize how barbaric he really is."

Ryan smiled, but it was hard. His arm hurt like hell,

scorching hot. He hated the ache that was thumping under his skin.

"So, Ryan, Jess tells us you've not long been back."

He took the beer Jessica passed him and sat down in the nearest seat, looking over at her friend as she spoke.

"I'm home for a bit of rest and recovery, then hopefully back with my unit."

Jessica sat down on the grass nearby. He moved to stand, to give her his seat, but she shook her head and crossed her legs, Hercules tucking in beside her.

It was hard not to watch her. Not to ignore everyone else and just drink her in. The way her ponytail fell over one shoulder, her tanned skin soft against the white of her T-shirt. The scoop neck showed him just enough cleavage to make it hard to swallow his beer.

And that smile. The way she cast her eyes downward when her lips curved up. It made him wonder what he'd ever done to have that look directed his way. To deserve her attention.

"So you're not tempted to stay here, now you're home?"

Ryan forced his eyes from Jessica and focused his attention back on her friends. "Tempting, but no." He watched as Jessica played with a blade of grass, not looking up. "I need to be back with my unit."

Steve appeared next to him then. "So you're definitely leaving?"

Ryan nodded. Had he not made that clear?

Her brother gave Ryan what he guessed was a smile. It should have been easy to tell but it wasn't. Unsaid words hung between them. Was Steve wondering why he was bothering with Jess, because he was leaving?

"How are those burgers coming along?" Jessica asked, breaking the silence.

Steve turned back to the meat, putting his hands up like he was surrendering.

Ryan took another swig of beer.

Maybe staying home with George would have been easier than facing off with the brother.

Jessica went out to Ryan's car with him. It had been an interesting evening.

The fact it was only nine and the night was over told her it probably hadn't been that successful. But then she'd pushed her luck hoping it would be.

It had reinforced a few things in her mind, though.

Her brother was an idiot sometimes, but he loved her and did his best to protect her. Even if it annoyed her intensely sometimes, she got it.

The other thing she'd learned was that Ryan was the kind of guy she wished she'd met years ago. Instead of wasting all her time on her idiot ex. Ryan had stood up to her brother with ease, and he was up-front and honest.

Bella had been right. What harm was there in having a little fun with a nice guy, when there was no chance of having her heart broken or breaking his? If he was only here for a short time, they could have a blast, enjoy one another and say goodbye as friends.

They were only a few steps from his car.

Jessica willed her body to cooperate and took a deep breath. She fell back one step and reached for Ryan's hand, catching his wrist then letting her fingers glide down to his palm as he turned.

"Ryan, stop."

She registered the surprise in his eyes as he faced her, but she didn't let herself think about it. She'd been waiting to do this all night, wishing she had the courage. Jess kept hold of his hand and pulled him closer. His body obliged. Then she reached her other hand to cup his cheek, standing on tiptoe to kiss him.

"Jessica…" he murmured against her mouth.

She shook her head. "Just kiss me."

His lips met hers as if they'd been made to touch. But he only let her feather-light kiss brush him for a moment before he pushed closer to her, deepened their embrace and slipped his hand around her waist, pressing her gently against him.

His hold was tender but his kisses became more insistent, his mouth moving firmly over hers, his breath hot against her skin when he pulled away, before crushing her lips against his again.

Jessica sighed into his mouth, head cloudy, as if she was being swept away on a wave of happiness, floating with the tenderness of his touch and the way he'd responded to her.

"I'm not usually brave enough to do things like that," she whispered.

Ryan smiled down at her, touched his forehead to hers, still holding her, both his arms around her waist now. He raised a hand and oh, so gently let his fingers skim her face, caress her cheek.

"Well lucky me then, huh?"

When she smiled at him, her lower lip caught between her teeth, he spun her around, one arm tight around her back, then pressed her against the car. Almost rough, but she knew he wouldn't hurt her. That he wouldn't even think one bruise on her skin was acceptable. And then he was kissing her again. This time harder, more urgently.

Jess let her head dip back as he pressed into her, his

body hard against hers, fitted snugly against her shape. She moaned as he left her lips and traced a row of kisses down her neck, stopping with the last touch against the indent of her collarbone.

When he raised his eyes again, held her face with both his hands, she couldn't help but giggle. A tiny gurgling noise that rose in her throat.

"What's so funny?" he asked.

She smiled then sighed, letting her lower body press into his, as he moved his upper body back slightly to accommodate her.

"It's just…"

He nodded. "I know."

She wondered if he did. If he understood how conflicted she felt.

And still they stood there, bodies locked together.

"Can I make it up to you and cook you dinner this weekend?"

Ryan raised an eyebrow. "I must be missing something here."

"What?"

He dropped a kiss to her nose then took a step back. Jess shivered. She hadn't been ready to let any air between them yet, could have stood like that all night. Against his rock-hard, strong body, and melted against that soft, pillowy mouth of his all evening.

"What do you need to make up to me?" he asked.

"For the way my brother was. The way tonight turned out."

He caught her hand and traced a finger across her palm. "Believe me, sweetheart, you more than made up for his frostiness."

Jessica's entire body felt hot, clammy. She wasn't used to being so bold, and she certainly wasn't used to talking about her actions. "He's, well, protective over me. We lost my sister a few years back, and he's made it his personal mission to keep me safe."

She wasn't lying. The fact they'd lost their sister had made Steven protective. Her ending up with the same cancer had made him worse, spurred his "big bad wolf" routine into action, but keeping that part from Ryan wasn't the same as not telling the truth.

"I've met my share of tough guys, Jess, and your brother doesn't strike me as anything other than worried about his little sister making a bad choice. He just wants to keep you safe, right?"

She liked the kindness on Ryan's face, the way he looked so open. It was not how she'd expected him to be. The soldier who'd seemed so tortured on paper was surprisingly unmessed-up in real life. Or else he was just really good at disguising it.

"I still want to make it up to you."

He grinned. "I'd like that."

Jessica didn't know where to look. His eyes were shining at her, suggesting things she wasn't sure about. Things she might want but maybe wasn't ready for. Yet.

"So dinner Sunday night?" she offered.

"Yeah." Ryan squeezed her hand and opened his door. "Maybe you could tell me about your sister."

Jess felt a shiver trawl her spine, her pulse suddenly thumping. She didn't want to go there. Didn't want to tell him how her sister had died, without being able to admit what she'd been through.

It was too close. Still too real for her to open up to him. And if she told him the truth, about her sister dying and then her getting the same disease, he would know she'd been lying all this time. That she'd listened to him talk about his wife, listened to him say he didn't ever want to be in that position again, and pretended she was fine. When she hadn't been fine, and still might not be.

"Maybe."

He didn't seem put out. Relief washed through her as he casually shrugged. "I'll see you Sunday."

She pushed his car door shut when he put down the window.

"Sunday," she affirmed.

Ryan pulled away slowly from the curb.

She watched him for a moment, then walked back to the house. Even though she felt a little guilty, that she should have just told him from the very beginning what had happened to her last year, about the breast cancer, it was so nice that he didn't know.

Would he hold her the same if he knew? Or would he think her as breakable as a tiny bird? Would he want her so bad if he knew what she'd been through? Especially when his wife had battled something similar and lost. From what he'd so honestly told her, she already knew the answer to that.

Jessica looked up and found Steve leaning in the door frame, his body filling the space. She glared at him.

"How long have you been standing there?"

He shrugged, not even caring he'd been found out, that she'd caught him as good as spying on her. "Long enough."

She gave him a shove in the shoulder and walked past him.

Once upon a time he would have shoved her back, grabbed her and made her beg for mercy, the way they'd been as kids, play fighting at every opportunity.

Tonight he just shut the door and followed. "You really like this guy, don't you?"

"He's only here for a couple of months."

He grabbed her shoulder, his fingers firm enough to stop her. She didn't turn.

"That wasn't my question."

Jess spun around. "So what? So what if I do?"

His eyes crumpled, the creases at the side of his eyes, the ones that hadn't been there before she'd battled her cancer, appearing. Jessica hated seeing the way he'd aged.

She relaxed against his touch. "I'm sorry, I didn't mean to snap at you. I've just got a lot on my mind."

"I was going to say that he actually seemed like a nice guy."

Jessica let out a shuddering breath. "He is."

"And I can tell he likes you."

She closed her eyes, embarrassed. Had Steve seen the way she'd kissed him? "But…?"

"But he's going away soon and I don't want you to get hurt."

Argh. There he went again. Just when she was starting to think he wasn't going to interfere. But he was only telling her what she already knew.

"I know what I'm getting myself into, Steve."

She turned to walk away again, but his words made her stop.

"But does *he?*" Her brother paused. She could feel him behind her but he didn't touch her this time, didn't try to stop her from walking away. "You need to tell him, Jess. He needs to know."

Tears filled her eyes then, but she forced down the choke in her throat. Wouldn't let it take hold of her. "Or what?"

His voice softened. "I just don't want to see you get hurt, okay?"

Too late for that. Her heart had already been broken before, shattered into so many pieces she'd wondered if it could ever recover. She was in no danger of Ryan doing that to her.

"I don't want him to treat me any different, Steve. I just want him to like me for me."

Steve moved closer, touched both his hands to her shoulders, waiting until she spun around to face him. "He'll still want you, Jess. If he's half-decent it won't scare him, but you need to tell him."

"I can't," she whispered.

Steve couldn't understand, because she didn't want to tell him the whole story. The truth about Ryan's wife's death. And it wasn't her story to tell anyway.

"Come here." Steve pulled her into his embrace and held her as she cried. As the tears soaked the shoulder of his T-shirt.

He might be an ass sometimes, an overprotective oaf, but when she needed him he was always there for her. She leaned heavily against him, safe in his arms.

"He's not Mark, you know," he told her, holding her tight. "The way he looked at you tonight, the way he was around you, I can just tell."

She nodded against his shoulder and closed her eyes until the tears stopped.

"What if I want to be the old me for a little while? What if I want to enjoy his company and have fun while he's here? Does he really need to know?" she begged.

Steve stepped back. "You're not that kind of girl, Jess. If you were, your ex leaving you wouldn't have hit you so hard."

It was true. She'd never been interested in casual

relationships, but this was different. This was getting outside her comfort zone with a man who wasn't making her any promises, who was only here for a short time. Was it so bad that she wanted to be with him while she could?

"I don't want him to know, Steve. It's more complicated than I can explain."

"I'm not saying anything if you're not. It's your choice."

She kissed her brother on the cheek. "So if you liked him so much why were you so hard on him?"

That made him grin. "I had to test him. No point letting him off easy."

Jessica rolled her eyes. "You're terrible."

He linked arms with her and they walked back into the kitchen. "Nope, I'm your big brother. And it means I'm allowed to be the tough guy."

As much as she moaned about him, there sure was something nice about knowing she had Steve around to protect her.

Ryan sat on his bed and toyed with his dog tag. It comforted him, the weight of it, reminded him of all those nights he'd lain awake on the other side of the world. Thinking about what he'd done, what he should have done and what the future held.

Part of him was itching to be back with his unit, but the other part was feeling settled. Happy to be back home on American soil.

And spending time with a girl he was going crazy about.

But it wasn't helping him with his son. Jessica had helped him, plenty, but his feelings for her weren't making things right with George. Instead he was showing her the person he wanted to be without proving the same to his son.

Something was weird about being back under the same roof as his parents. About having his son down the hall yet not feeling brave enough to go into his room to try to talk to him.

When he'd gone back to war after his wife died, he hadn't had a choice. He had been granted emergency leave when she'd been diagnosed, and the army had been understanding when he'd kept extending it. But the reality was that he'd owed them more time, and even though it had been hard going away again after all that had happened, he'd done it.

Back then, he'd told his parents they could move into his house, to keep things less traumatic for George. Besides, their place had been small, and the home Ryan had shared with his wife was comfortable and much bigger.

Ryan had felt like his paying the mortgage, making sure his parents and son were financially okay, was enough. But it hadn't been enough and until a couple of weeks ago he hadn't truly understood that.

Jessica was helping him to clear his head. To realize what it meant to be a real father again. Somehow her letters and her compassion, the way she made him feel when they were together, were reminding him of the man he'd once been.

Because right now the man he was around her wasn't the same man he was around his son.

And it was fear holding him back. Because when his son refused to talk to him, he wasn't telling him he hated him. Ryan could still pretend that one day things might be okay again.

But unless he did something about it, he might lose his chance forever.

He smiled as he thought about Jessica. About the way she'd fallen into his arms tonight and kissed him like he'd almost forgotten how to. It had been a long time since he'd held a woman, and with her he felt like himself again.

It spurred him into action. If he was going to be that guy, he had to be him in every aspect of his life. And that meant making things right with George.

Now.

No more excuses.

He got up and opened the door, then walked down the hall. Light was still spilling out from beneath his son's door, even though it was late.

Ryan knocked softly. There was no response, so he opened it.

George was lying on his bed, earphones in his ears, iPod resting on his chest. The lamp was still on, even though he'd fallen asleep.

He stood there, towering over his boy as he slept. His face was so young in slumber. There was no trace of the sulky preteen, almost a hint of the face he'd known years ago, when they'd been so close.

Ryan bent to pick up the iPod and gently reached to take the earphones out.

George stirred. Then opened his eyes.

Ryan froze.

His son went to say something, went to move, but Ryan put his hand against George's chest and slowly bent his legs until he could sit on the bed. George didn't say a word.

There were questions in his son's eyes. Questions he

wished would come out in the open so he could tell him the truth, could tell him how sorry he was.

George pulled the cord so his ears were free. Then glared at him. Ryan went to move, to stand up again, but his son grabbed his hand. Made him stop. Then George burst into tears, his entire body shaking from the sobs deep in his chest.

"Come here." Ryan took his boy into his arms and held him, held him so tight he hoped he wasn't hurting him, and fought the emotions that were running through his own body, thrumming through him, desperate to escape. His eyes were burning, body tense as he held his son, the boy suddenly feeling so young and vulnerable in his arms. "Shhh, it's okay."

"You left me," George managed to say between sobs. "Why did you leave me?"

"I'm sorry," he said, holding him even tighter, never wanting to let him go. "I'm so, so sorry."

"Grams told me," George sobbed, "she said you would be leaving again soon."

Ryan squeezed his eyes shut and did his best to force away his own tears, to push them away and be strong for his son. It was like his heart was being pulled from his body to beat in the unforgiving heat of the desert sun. Left to wither, exposed to the world.

"I'll never leave you like that again, ever." Ryan said the words into his son's hair. "I promise."

"But you are going back?"

George pushed away from him to sit upright. His eyes full of hurt, questioning his father.

"I am going back," he said, knowing he had to be honest. There was no point in pretending otherwise. But it was also time for him to be honest with himself. He wasn't done with the army, not yet, and he'd already agreed to another term. But it was time to prioritize, and he'd given his country years of service. Had been a dedicated and loyal soldier.

Now maybe it was time to put that same amount of energy into being the father he'd once been. The father he'd always wanted to be. Maybe it wasn't just about his duty to the army anymore.

"This time will be my last tour," he said, knowing he was speaking the truth, even though he'd never decided, until right now, that it was going to be his final stint away. "I will go away one more time, then I'll be done. And this time I'll be there for you even though I'm away—we'll stay in touch properly, okay?"

George looked unsure, hesitant, but Ryan didn't care. Tonight had been a major breakthrough. And all it had taken was some courage on his behalf to take the first step. His son might not believe his words yet, but Ryan would see his promise through and show his son he could be trusted. It was up to him to give George a reason to trust in him.

"You promise?"

He nodded and pulled his boy in for another hug. "I promise, kid. I'm not going to let you down again."

George held him back hard, clinging on to his father, and Ryan sent a silent prayer skyward. He wouldn't trade anything for this moment. The pain in his arm, the hurt of his memories, nothing would be worth sacrificing for knowing his son was close. For feeling like forgiveness was possible.

For remembering what it was like to be a real dad again.

CHAPTER SEVEN

~~*Dear Ryan,*~~

~~*I guess you might be wondering just how I understand what you've gone through. Maybe you haven't thought about it, but I feel like we're close enough now that I need to tell you something—that I've gone through what you have. Lost someone close. Battled with my own health and my own demons. That I've had…*~~

JESSICA SAT OUTSIDE, one hand raised to shield her eyes from the sun. Hercules lay at her feet, her constant companion. She ran the toes of one foot across his fur, the touch comforting her.

She couldn't stop thinking about the letter she'd almost sent Ryan. The one in which she'd tried to tell him everything. The one that was her opening her heart and telling him what had happened in her past, and what she was scared might happen in her future.

But then she'd scrunched it up into a ball and thrown it out. Forgotten about it. Except for last night, when the words of that letter had played over and over in her mind. She hadn't even realized they'd be in her memory bank still, but they had been. Every single word. Keeping sleep from her and haunting her thoughts.

Maybe her brother was right. Maybe she should tell Ryan. Maybe it was the right thing to do.

But she wasn't going to. If she did, she'd have to end their romance. Right now. Or more likely he'd end it straight away before she had the chance.

If she didn't? They could continue on, enjoying themselves, and Ryan could go back to his unit oblivious to what she'd been through. And why should he know? He had enough of his own problems to deal with.

Jess stood and stretched. She needed to get back into her studio and paint, unwind and enjoy her creativity. There was no use worrying over something once you'd made a decision, and she had.

It didn't matter how many times she went over it.

Ryan wasn't going to find out, she wasn't going to tell him, and that was the end of it.

"Come on, mister."

Hercules yawned and padded after her.

They had Bella coming around to visit this afternoon, and she'd be able to talk the subject to death if she wanted. Right now, it was time to paint.

And there was going to be no thinking about the past or the future. It was about time she learned to live in the now.

Ryan knew he had Jess to thank for reconnecting with his son. They had a long way to go, but they'd made progress. When he'd left George's room last night, he'd felt lighter somehow, like the burden he'd carried all this time had been a weight on his shoulders, pushing him down, trying to cripple him.

Even his arm felt better, despite the pummelling it had taken last night when Jess's brother had nearly crushed his hand.

But it was all worth it. Having George on speaking terms with him again, listening to his son talk and watching him smile, it was the best reward he could ever have wished for.

And all it had taken was a little courage.

"You want to walk down for an ice cream or something?"

George looked up and put down the video game control. "Yeah, okay."

He was going to have to get used to those kind of responses. Kids didn't seem that enthusiastic over anything these days. But he wasn't complaining. Not while his son was actually talking to him.

"Let's go."

They stood up to leave. George walked close to him, but Ryan resisted the urge to sling his arm around his son's shoulder. They might have made progress, but it was going to be slow and he didn't want to push it.

Jessica sat at the café, Hercules's lead around her ankle. She couldn't stop laughing at Bella. Her friend was in a particularly entertaining mood. Even though Bella had left her daughter at home with her husband, she was all they talked about, and it made Jess feel good.

"You know, Mr. Soldier Stud and you would make beautiful babies, if I do say so myself."

Jess almost spat out her mouthful of coffee. "Babies?"

How had the subject swung around to her all of a sudden?

"Oh, come on," Bella said as she swatted her hand through the air. "Don't go telling me you don't want a family of your own one day."

Her heart seemed to twinge, like a small knife had

been thrown into it. She had always dreamed of being a mother, but the chance of that happening seemed less and less likely these days. It wasn't even the kind of thing she'd let herself think about this last year.

"Maybe, Bella, but not with Ryan."

Her friend snorted. "Why not Ryan? He's gorgeous, funny, buff, did I mention gorgeous?"

It wasn't like Jess didn't agree, but it just wasn't a possibility. "You forget that he's a widower, a father, and oh, that's right. A soldier. Who's returning to his unit soon."

"Okay, so I get the soldier part, but that's doable. Heaps of soldiers are great husbands." Bella paused. "The fact that he's a widower doesn't mean he can't fall in love again, and so what if he already has a son?"

"I know it sounds lame, but..."

There was no way Ryan would consider a relationship with her if he knew the truth, and she didn't want to get serious. She wasn't ready to trust someone like that again. To put all her love and dreams into another person only to have them sucked away forever. And she didn't intend on putting anyone through her getting sick again. It was unlikely, but not impossible, and she'd rather be alone until she at least hit the five-year remission mark.

Bella gestured at her to continue.

"It's nothing. Let's just talk about something else, okay?"

Her friend just laughed. Not the response she'd expected.

"Well, well. Look who's walking toward us."

Jess glanced up and didn't see anyone. "Where?"

"Over your shoulder." Bella smirked. "It's the stud himself."

Jessica scowled at Bella before turning. "You seriously need to get out more. You're getting tragic."

But she felt her own heart start to race—the flutter in her belly that started whenever she was around Ryan began tickling her over and over.

Ryan hadn't seen them. He was walking with a young boy, clearly his son, and they were talking. Talking!

The nervousness she'd felt at him walking toward her disappeared as she watched the two of them smiling and chatting. Something major must have happened last night.

He'd be over the moon to be spending time with George.

Jessica felt her cheeks ignite. She hoped the smile on his face still had something to do with their kiss, too. It sure had her heart racing again just thinking about it.

Bella kicked her under the table. "Well? Get up!"

She glared at Bella before rising. She raised one hand, hesitantly. An even wider smile crossed Ryan's face when he saw her. She watched as he touched his son on the shoulder and directed him their way.

"Hi, Ryan," Jessica called out as they came nearer, swallowing away her nervousness.

"Hi." He gave her a beamer of a smile back and put his hand back on the boy's shoulder. "Jess, I'd like you to meet my son, George."

The kid gave her an awkward smile. "Hey."

"Hi, George. I've heard so much about you."

"And this is Bella," Ryan said, gesturing toward her friend.

George nodded in Bella's direction.

"So where are you two off to?"

Ryan stepped back slightly from his son. She wanted to reach out and touch him, to reassure him that he was doing a good job, but she didn't dare move any closer. They were only friends, and his son didn't need any confusing messages sent his way. Not when he was finally on speaking terms with his father.

"We're going to grab an ice cream then walk back home."

She was dying to know what had happened. "Sounds like a plan. I'd invite you to join us but you two probably want to spend some time alone together, right?"

George was shuffling his feet, head down, awkward. She felt sorry for him.

"Yeah," said Ryan, obviously picking up on his son's discomfort. "We had better get going."

That made George look up.

"Nice to see you, Ryan," Jess said.

"Yeah, you, too. See you, Bella."

Bella waved and grinned back at him.

"Great to meet you, George. Have a nice afternoon," Jess said.

The boy met Jessica's gaze, and she wasn't sure what she saw there. A touch of happiness perhaps, but more uncertainty than anything. She wished she could help him, talk to him maybe, but Ryan would find his way with him. It looked like they'd made some good progress. And it wasn't about how they got there, it was about how well they connected along the way. Ryan was his father and no matter how hard he was finding it, George was his son and deep down he would want to let his dad in. No child wanted to feel alone.

They started to walk away, father and son, before Ryan turned back. His large frame against George's slight one brought a smile to her face all over again.

"We still on for tomorrow night?"

Jess nodded. "I'll see you around seven."

Ryan gave her a wink and turned away again, but she hardly noticed it. It didn't make her heart palpitate like it usually would. Because it was George's last look at her over his shoulder that registered in her brain. The look of horror that passed through his eyes, the disbelief, said it all.

She wanted to run after them, explain she was only friends with his dad, tell Ryan that he needed to talk to his son about them. But it was too late.

She could have been wrong, but from the extra distance now between them, and the despairing stoop of George's shoulders, she knew she was right.

He had gone from happy to be out with his father to wondering if his dad was trying to replace his mom. And if he thought Ryan had come home for her and not for him, his son, then they'd end up right back at square one all over again.

"You all right?"

Bella pulled her back to reality.

"Why does everything have to be so complicated?" Jess asked.

Hercules moaned at her feet, a big sigh that made her wish she could do the same, whinge then put her paws over her eyes to block out the world.

Bella had no idea what she was talking about, and Jessica didn't want to discuss it. The last thing she needed was something else to panic about.

"Tell me more about Ruby, okay? Just make me smile."

Bella frowned but didn't push the point. Sometimes even her best friend knew when not to pry.

Ryan was starting to feel like there was a pattern developing as he drove toward Jessica's house. His palms had started to clam up and he was getting nervous again. Not alarmingly nervous, but it was there, and it wasn't something he was used to feeling.

Today had been good, and yesterday had been even better. George had gone a little quiet on him after they'd bumped into Jess, but they'd had fun, hung out and started to get to know one another again.

And now he had something else to look forward to. An entire evening with Jess, at her place.

He grinned to himself as he drove. Even though he had his arm resting on the open window ledge, and it was throbbing with a hint of pain, he didn't care. There were too many good things going on his life to worry about something he had no control over. His physio had told him he was progressing well, there were no indications of it being a long-term problem, not after the surgery going so well, and he just needed to keep up his exercises.

So having fun with his son, and with a woman like Jessica, was something he could enjoy before he had to go back to work. As hard as it would be to return this time, he was looking forward to being with the guys again, and now that he'd decided it would be his last tour, he had to make the most of being back with his unit.

Ryan pulled onto her street.

He didn't know what exactly it was about her, but something about spending time with Jessica felt so right. After his wife had died, he'd never wanted to be close to another woman again. Never wanted to feel so helpless again, so weak. And until recently he'd thought he'd feel like that for the rest of his life.

But Jessica was quickly changing his feelings. He didn't know what she wanted, if she felt the same way as he did, but this was starting to feel real. Part of him wanted to take it slow, to stay as friends yet something more, but then he also wanted to make things happen more quickly. To make the most of his time back home and see if something special could happen between them.

Because in the span of a week, Jessica had gone from pen pal and good friend, to meaning a whole lot more to him than any other woman had since his wife.

And he liked it. Liked the way she made him feel, the effect she had on him. Whether she felt the same was another matter entirely, but from the way she'd kissed him the other night, he liked to think he could hope.

More than hope.

He liked to think he was in with a real chance.

If he was going to be coming back for good soon, then maybe that meant a chance at a future together.

Jessica fluffed around in the kitchen, knowing she had no purpose, yet not being able to stop herself from moving. It was just a casual dinner at her place, not exactly some grand dinner party, but she was like a ball of wool writhing to untangle. On edge.

She'd put together a simple pasta dish, lots of fresh ingredients tossed with olive oil and lemon juice in a pan, so there was hardly anything culinary to worry about. And dessert was a cake she'd made earlier in the day, but she still felt panicky.

The knock at the door came while she was eyeing up her glass of wine and deciding whether or not to drain it for courage. She was leaning on the counter, staring at it.

Jessica turned away from the glass. She didn't ever

drink more than a couple of glasses, and the last thing she needed was to make a fool of herself.

"Come in!" she called, hoping Ryan would hear her.

Hercules went bounding down the hall and a second later the door clicked.

Jess took a deep breath, ran her hands down her jeans, then stepped out to greet him. This was ridiculous. She'd seen Ryan a handful of times now. First-time nerves were one thing, but there was nothing to panic about tonight.

"Hi, Ryan."

He was crouched down giving Herc a scratch. When he looked up she temporarily lost the ability to move. His eyes locked on hers, bright blue, serious yet laughing, drawing her in as if she'd never be let back out again.

"Hi." He stood and they both watched as Hercules took off down the hall again. "You look great."

Jess looked down and felt awkward. She was only wearing jeans, an embellished T-shirt that dressed her outfit up and a pair of heels. Her cheeks were flushed, she could feel the heat in them—and her hands could have been shaking. She was so off balance she wasn't even sure.

She went to turn down the hall, but he stopped her with a hand to her wrist.

"Hey."

When she turned Ryan took a step forward and pressed a kiss to her cheek before putting space between them again.

"You act like no one ever gave you a compliment before."

His voice was low, almost a whisper, and it made a shiver lick its way down her spine. She swallowed, hard. "I'm not."

The last compliments she'd had had been from a man who told her what he thought she wanted to hear, but there'd never been any substance to his words. The reason she was embarrassed now was because from the look on his face, Ryan meant what he said.

"I don't say what I don't mean," he assured her.

She didn't doubt that. "I know, it's just…"

"Jess?"

She felt uncomfortable being scrutinized.

"I find you not receiving compliments by the bucket-load hard to swallow," he said. Ryan tucked his fingers beneath her chin and smiled down at her, his eyes locked on hers, body so close. "You look beautiful tonight and you need to believe it."

Jessica fought against the urge to pull away from him. Instead of giving in to her instincts she made herself smile, forced herself to behave like the grown-up woman she was. "Thanks," she whispered.

He grinned and let his fingers fall from her skin. "Much better."

She turned before he had the chance to do anything else. She was nervous, scared.

Exhilarated.

So much for telling herself this was going to be a casual dinner with a friend, that there was no need to panic. She doubted there was much *friend* left in the equation between her and Ryan anymore. Part of her had hoped he would want more, and the other part told her that friend was as good as it got. Even after their kisses.

Now she wasn't so sure she was ready for the something more.

Ryan was a hot-blooded male who had suddenly, just from looking at her, from touching her, made his intent very clear.

The way her body was reacting told her she felt the same, no matter how much she wanted to deny it.

Maybe that glass of wine hadn't been such a bad idea after all.

Jessica didn't taste a mouthful of her food. She opened her mouth, forked spaghetti in delicate twirls and forced herself to swallow. But the only sense she had was of the man sitting across from her.

She'd forgotten everything else. Had no control over her other senses. Or maybe she did and they were too overloaded on Ryan. She was drunk on the sight of him, the feel of him, the look of him.

The taste of him.

She remembered only too well what his lips felt like on hers, how her body had felt when she was tucked against him, wrapped in his embrace. And after the way he'd touched her in the hall before, the way he felt had been the only thing she'd thought about since.

"This is great."

At least Ryan seemed to be enjoying the food.

Jessica took another sip of wine. She was going to tell him not to be silly but she remembered only too well what he'd said earlier about taking a compliment.

"Thanks."

She wished she could say more, could come up with something more savvy and chic, but her brain just wasn't cooperating. Her tongue was swollen like it was bee-stung, not letting her communicate properly.

It was stupid. She was a confident, capable woman and there was no excuse. She had to get a grip. Jessica cleared her throat and set down her fork. "So tell me about George. You two looked like you were having a good time yesterday?"

Ryan's entire face seemed to light up.

"We had a fantastic time. It's like we've really connected."

She smiled. It was good to hear.

"But I have to thank you, you know."

Jess gulped. Her? "Why me?"

Ryan put his own fork down and reached for her hand across the table. "Because you gave me the confidence to make it happen. I don't think I could have done it without you."

Jessica forced herself to look up and meet his gaze. His hand over hers was doing something to her, making her body feel hot all over, every inch of it.

"I don't think I did anything, Ryan. I was just honest with you."

He squeezed her hand, his eyes never leaving hers. She could gaze into them all night, lose herself in the ocean-blue depths of them, become mesmerized. She wondered if anything had ever looked so beautiful before. The way he was looking at her, the softness she saw there.

The honesty.

All this time, she'd thought it would be impossible to ever truly trust a man again. Told herself it couldn't happen.

But the way Ryan was watching her, the genuine feeling he conveyed through his gaze, the way the skin around his eyes crinkled ever so lightly in the corners when he watched her, his smile upturned to match his expression: all of these things told her that trust and honesty *was* possible with a man.

She'd just chosen the wrong one before. And let herself believe that he represented the entire male population.

"I went to him, Jess. I went to him because you told me to, because you told me I had to confront the past and be honest with him."

She looked down, unable to match his stare any longer. "I told you what anyone else would have."

Ryan shook his head. "That's the problem." He dropped the contact with her hand and raised it to her cheek instead, his fingers resting against her skin.

Jess pushed in, lightly, toward his touch. Fought the urge to close her eyes and sigh into his caress.

"I've never told anyone else what I told you in my letters. You're the first person I've been honest with in a long while."

She glanced up at him again, her breath catching in silent hiccups in her throat.

"It started because I trusted you on paper, and now I know I can trust you in real life, too."

She didn't know what to say. But when Ryan kept the contact with her face and raised his body, leaning over the table toward her, she knew exactly what to do.

Jessica raised her face to meet his, parted her mouth for his kiss. For the brush of his lips that she knew were coming.

Ryan took her mouth, gently at first and then with a hunger that scared her. She was barely conscious of him standing, of the way he had moved closer, until he pulled away and left her lips tender and alone.

She stifled the moan that fought to be heard deep within her throat.

But Ryan didn't leave her alone for long. He stalked around the table like a big game animal on the hunt. His large frame towered above her, then he dropped to his knees in front of her. She parted her own knees slightly so he could move closer to her. He was so tall that even with her sitting on the chair he wasn't much lower than her.

Jess just watched him—the rise and fall of his chest, and the way his eyes fell to her lips. She tried not to think about the what-ifs. Fought against the voice in her head that told her to take things slow, to stop now before it went too far.

Because Jessica knew they had already crossed that line. They'd already gone too far and she was powerless to do anything about it.

"Ryan."

He circled his arms around her waist, making her feel safe. Wanted. She slowly raised her hands and let them flutter to his shoulders, not sure where to touch him, and then they found his hair. Jess ran her fingers through the soft strands then stopped, fingertips on the back of his head as she bravely urged him forward.

He waited for her. Hardly let out a breath as he watched her and waited. Like he was leaving it up to her, wanted her to tell him it was okay.

And she didn't disappoint him, was powerless to do anything but make the next move. Jessica kissed him like she'd never kissed a man before. Kept her hands on him, drawing him to her, pressing herself closer to him as their lips danced, his arms still wrapped around her.

She only dropped her hold when she knew he wasn't going to pull away, to run her hands down his arms, drawing in a sharp inhale as she found bare skin.

His lips became more insistent on hers. Teasing her. Showing her how much he wanted her. And oh, did she want him, too. More than she'd ever wanted to be close to a man before.

"Ryan," she said his name again. "Are you sure…"

He just kissed her more deeply, ignoring her words. She took his lack of reply as a yes.

Jessica let her fingers keep exploring, reached the hem of his T-shirt and pushed it up, letting one hand discover the contours of his hard stomach, muscles firm against her touch.

His belly quivered, but he didn't move. Only moaned against her mouth.

She took it as encouragement.

Jess tugged, breaking their kiss to pull his T-shirt over his head, and Ryan didn't resist.

He shrugged out of it in a second and had his arms back around her before she could properly drink in the sight of him.

But she pushed him back, lightly.

"You have a tattoo," she whispered.

Wow.

"Yeah." He shrugged.

If the sun-kissed golden skin and hard muscles weren't enough, hadn't already taken her breath away, the tattoo came as even more of a shock.

She'd never dated a guy with a tattoo before. Had always thought they were for bad boys, and she'd never gone for that type. But on Ryan? It looked incredible.

"You're staring." His voice was low, husky.

Jess gave him a sideways look and smiled. Shyly. "Does it mean anything special?"

The black ink carved out a beautiful eagle, wings open, covering his entire shoulder and down his upper biceps. She'd never liked the idea of a tattoo, but this was something else. Made him look even stronger, tougher. Exciting.

His response was another shrug. She hoped she hadn't made him self-conscious about it.

"It's a special forces thing. I got it after my initiation with all the other snipers."

She leaned forward, bent to touch her lips to his shoulder, kissing down every inch of the inky black image. She let her fingers trail over the small, dark pink scar that showed where his keyhole surgery had been.

Ryan moaned and tightened his hold on her. It made her smile, pleased that he liked it, that he wanted her touch.

"Jess."

The way he said her name made it sound like a warning. He tugged at her hair, gently, to pull her had back up. She ignored him, slowly running her lips up his neck, making him wait before she returned to his mouth.

She stopped, hovered her lips beside his before kissing him.

Ryan didn't hold back at all this time. He took her face in his hands, kissed her again, and then stood, lip still tangled, arms around her body.

He only had to look at her to ask her the question. To tell her what he wanted.

The way he watched her, touched her, caressed her, told her everything she needed to know. Left only one question between them.

"Yes," she whispered, tugging his hand.

He dropped a feather-light kiss to her lips. "Are you sure?"

She tucked in tight against him, nuzzled her mouth

to the tender spot between his shoulder and neck, before taking his hand and leading him to the stairs.

No, she wasn't sure. Showing her body to a man again had been something she'd feared since her operation. All she knew was that she wanted to be with this man, right now, more than anything else in the world.

And that meant swallowing her fears and taking a big step forward. Maybe he wouldn't notice the difference? she found herself wishing…

Ryan felt as if his whole body was on fire. He wanted this woman like he'd never wanted a woman ever before.

And he was too weak to do what he most wanted. To scoop her up into his arms and carry her to her bed, to make her feel light and wanted in his embrace. He hated not having the strength in his arm, but then if he hadn't been injured he wouldn't be here right now. And he knew where he'd rather be, given the choice.

But even though he couldn't lift her like he wanted to, he could enjoy the weight of her hand in his and the promise in her eyes as she sent a shy glance back over her shoulder at him.

He'd never been nervous before, not with a woman, not like this. But it had been a long time since… He tightened his jaw and pushed the thoughts away. Now was not the time to think about the past.

The problem with Jessica was that she wasn't just another girl. A one-night stand. He hadn't been with a woman he felt this serious about since his wife.

She was rather like his wife—not physically, but the same type of woman. He didn't want to hurt her in any way, do anything that might compromise what they had. Because she meant too much to him. But right now he was powerless to stop what was about to happen, and it was too late to start thinking about why this was a bad idea. He was the one who'd started it, and he certainly wasn't going to not follow through.

Jessica stopped at what he presumed was her bedroom and dropped his hand. She touched the door frame, looked over her shoulder and gave him an even shyer smile than before.

"You joining me?"

Ryan gave Jessica a brave grin back. "Yes."

It seemed to settle her, looked like relief crossed her eyes, softening her face.

He was going to ask her again whether she was sure, whether this was what she really wanted, but then she disappeared into the room. Ryan hesitated for a moment before following her in.

Jessica was standing, waiting for him, like she didn't know what to do. He hated seeing her look unsure, uncertain and nervous, but he knew what he could do to make her feel better. To make sure she knew how much he wanted her.

Ryan tried not to but he knew he stalked her across the room. He wrapped both arms around her, sweeping her to him, before walking her backward until her legs touched the base of the bed.

"Ryan…" His name caught in her throat, and it made him smile.

"Yes?" He arched an eyebrow before taking up on her neck again, where he'd last kissed her, letting his lips tease her skin.

She didn't say another word.

He already had his shirt off but Jessica was fully clothed. He tipped her back and gently let her fall, before moving to cover her, to lie half above her.

She blinked and kept her eyes downcast, but he tipped

her chin up and kissed her lightly on the nose then on her lips. At the same time he touched his other hand to her T-shirt, curling his fingers around it and raising it, pausing to give her the chance to say no.

Jessica responded by wriggling to rid herself of the top.

His gaze fell from her face to her skin, eyes dancing over her lacy red bra, the way her breasts filled it to almost overflowing.

"The light," she whispered.

Ryan shook his head. "No."

He stopped when he saw the panicked look on her face.

"Please." Her voice held urgency, desperation.

"Okay," he said as got up again, crossed the room and flicked off the switch. "Your call."

It didn't matter how much he wanted to watch her, to drink in the sight of her, he would do as she asked. He wasn't doing anything to compromise what was happening between them.

He stopped, in the dark, letting his eyes adjust.

Before using all of his willpower not to rush across the room and pin her down to devour her, piece by piece.

Jessica felt like she was blushing all the way down to her toes.

She wanted to stop him, to tell Ryan she couldn't go through with it, but if she told him that she'd be lying to herself.

She wanted him.

She just didn't want to know his reaction when he realized her breasts weren't natural.

It was the first time she'd been intimate with a man

since her reconstruction, since she'd gone through her treatment, and it scared her. She hadn't wanted him to see them bare, didn't want to see his reaction, either, but as soon as he touched them he'd surely know. They weren't soft and natural as they'd once been. Now there was the undisguisable firmness of silicone, and she was embarrassed about it.

Ryan's hand skimmed her arm then trailed slowly down the edge of her breast.

She took in a deep breath. This was it. The moment she'd dreaded for almost a year.

"You're beautiful."

Jessica closed her eyes and tried not to cry, fighting happiness and tears at the same time. As confused as she'd ever been.

She tried not to shake her head. Thank goodness the light was off so she didn't have to see the look on his face when he realized.

"You are. You're more beautiful than I ever could have imagined you'd be."

Jessica wanted to tell him she wasn't, admit what he'd find when he took off her final layer, but she held her words in, too scared to say them out loud.

Ryan stopped, as if he were questioning her, but Jess responded by staying still, waiting for him.

She held her breath. Terrified.

When his hand touched her bra, her entire body went stiff, rigid.

She couldn't do it.

"Stop."

His hand hovered then fell.

"I can't, Ryan," she whispered, distraught.

He dropped his hands to hers, and lowered himself to rest beside her. "Tell me what's wrong."

Jessica closed her eyes and pushed away the pain. Tried to figure out what exactly she could tell him.

"I have, well..."

He brushed the back of one hand gently across the side of her face, touching her cheek with the softness of a feather.

"We don't have to do anything you don't want to do."

Jessica smiled bravely at him. She did want to, that was the problem, but she didn't know how to deal with the embarrassment of what he was about to find.

Because even with the lights out, without being able to see, he would be able to feel. The scars were minor, the surgeon had done a great job, but the evidence was real and he would notice. There was no way not to.

She took a deep breath.

"Ryan, I have scars. I don't want..."

"Shhhh." He bent forward and kissed her, lips hovering over hers. "You don't have to explain anything to me."

She shook her head. "I do. My breasts, they're..."

He waited, fingers stroking her hair.

"I have scars because I had surgery. My breasts aren't real," she finally blurted out.

Ryan didn't say anything. He dropped another kiss to her lips before trailing his way down her neck, delicately across her collarbone, until he reached the lacy edge of her bra.

He paused and looked up at her. She could make out his face even in the dark.

"You're beautiful, Jessica, and I don't care what you've had done or about any scars."

With an incredible sense of relief exploding inside her, her body felt like it had turned into a marshmallow.

Her fears faded, and her body responded to his touch again. By his lack of reaction, he obviously just thought she'd had a breast augmentation. Realizing she'd managed to put off telling him the truth for a little longer, she trembled. Right now, he didn't need to know why she'd had cosmetic surgery. If he didn't care, then why should she?

Her body still thrummed with tension as he slipped off her underwear, but she forced herself to enjoy his touch. She couldn't help but stiffen when he kissed first one breast then the other, his fingers gliding softly over her skin.

"See, they're beautiful, just like I knew they'd be," he whispered. "Just like the rest of you."

Jessica finally relaxed into his touch, closed her eyes and sighed as his hands explored her body.

Tonight was about feeling good and enjoying herself. Losing herself in the moment. All this time she'd been terrified of showing someone her new body shape, worried what the reaction would be and if she'd even want to be intimate again.

But this—this was what she'd needed. To feel loved and wanted by a man like Ryan. A man who made her feel like she was the most beautiful woman in the world, like he truly wanted her.

Even if it was only just for tonight. Or until he went away again. Because if the light had been on, she could have looked into his eyes and seen his honesty, his integrity. Yet what she couldn't see in his eyes, she could feel in his touch.

When Ryan inched his way back up her body and started to kiss her again, she pushed away her barriers, made herself think of nothing but the way he was touching her. The way his fingers felt against her skin, and the way his lips brushed hers in a motion she'd never tire of.

If this wasn't heaven, then she didn't know what was.

CHAPTER EIGHT

Dear Jessica,
It's funny, now I know I'm coming home for sure and that we're going to meet. I should have asked you for a photo, but then we probably don't look like either of us expects.

You know, I've enjoyed this life for so long, but now the thought of coming back and sleeping in a comfortable bed, of not having to get up at the crack of dawn, sounds pretty appealing. I can hardly imagine what it will be like not to be with my unit, here in the desert, because it's been so long. But I'm sure looking forward to meeting you.

I'll see you soon.
Ryan

RYAN WOKE WITH a smile on his face. It had been a long while since he'd woken up grinning, but then it had also been a long time since his arm had been taken captive by a beautiful woman.

Jessica lay in the crook of his arm, face turned into him, cheek against the edge of his chest. Her mouth was slightly parted, her long hair falling over his skin and spilling out onto the white pillow.

He didn't move, hardly let himself even breathe. Ryan could have stayed there forever, watching her. Content in what had happened between them. In the way his trip home had turned out after so many months of dreading it, after years of denying himself the luxury of returning. Of putting up barriers and refusing to confront what he'd left.

When he'd promised his son that this tour of duty would be his last, it had been a decision he'd made as a father.

But now? Deep down, he knew that part of that decision had been influenced by how he felt about Jessica. He wanted to come back for his son, but he also wanted more from this woman lying in his arms. Part of his decision had been because he wanted a real chance at making a future with her, too.

And that meant he had to let her in. A week ago, he'd have never thought it possible, but now he wanted to open up to her. To tell her the final chapter he'd kept behind lock and key from everyone but himself until now.

Jessica stirred. He shifted his body to face her, looking at her face as she started to wake.

Her eyes opened slowly, fluttered, then her head dropped slightly as she realized he was watching her.

"Hey, you," he whispered, stroking his thumb across her cheek.

She smiled, but he could tell she was shy. "Hey."

Her voice was so low he only just heard her.

"What do you say I rustle up something for breakfast?" he offered.

She tucked her head down and snuggled against him, hair tickling his chest as she buried into his body and pulled the comforter farther over them in the process.

Jess planted a kiss to his collarbone and sighed into his skin.

He lay with her in his arms for a few minutes then dropped a kiss to the top of her head and wriggled back.

His stomach growled. Loud.

"As much as I want to stay like this, I think my body needs some fuel."

Jess laughed and rolled over.

"What's so funny?"

He propped himself up and looked down at her. She was still trying to hide from him, face partially covered, but she didn't look nervous any longer.

"Jess?"

She groaned then turned back toward him. "I probably shouldn't tell you, in case you change your mind."

He raised an eyebrow and watched her.

She groaned again. "You're the first guy to offer me breakfast in bed, okay?" She let her eyes meet his. "Here I was worried you'd make an excuse and bolt, and instead you offer to feed me."

Ryan leaned forward to kiss her, brushing the hair from her face so he could see her better. He liked that her trademark pink blush was starting to cover her cheeks again.

"I don't recall saying anything about breakfast in *bed* exactly, but it can be arranged. Although if I remember correctly, you never actually gave me dessert last night."

She responded by pushing him away and throwing a pillow at him. He caught it and grinned.

"Okay, okay! Your wish is my command."

He stood up and walked across the room. Most of his clothes were in a heap near the foot of the bed, but it was her silk robe hanging on the back of the door that caught his eye.

"Mind if I borrow this?" He plucked it from the hanger and held it up.

Jessica was blushing all over again but she nodded, sitting up with the sheet clutched to her chest.

He grinned and put it on, just managing to secure the pink satin with the flimsy tie. It barely covered him but it made her smile, laugh even, and right now he'd do anything to see those lips of hers upturned, those chocolate-brown eyes sparkling.

Even if he did have to make a fool of himself.

He was about to turn around and make a joke when he heard a phone ringing.

"Yours?"

She shook her head. "Nope. Your cell?"

It *was* his. He took off down the stairs and looked around for where he'd left it. Nowhere. He scanned the room and found it just as it stopped ringing.

When he flipped it open he saw he'd missed a few calls. All from the same number.

Ryan gulped.

His parents. Or his son. He hoped everything was okay. After so long being used to only thinking about himself, he should have at least phoned to tell them he wasn't going to make it home last night. Not that his parents would be worried, but George might be. He was going to have to change his habits if he was going to gain George's trust again.

He hit redial.

"Hello."

His son picked up almost immediately.

"Hey, George, it's your dad."

There was silence for a moment, before his son cleared his throat.

"I thought something had happened to you."

Ryan felt as though someone had reached into his chest and stuck a knife through his heart. If he was going to get this dad business sorted, he was going to have to start acting like a father, not a bachelor with no responsibilities.

"I, ah, ended up staying at a friend's place. I should have phoned."

There was silence on the other end.

"George?"

"Are you coming home soon?"

Ryan looked down at the pink robe, at his hairy legs poking out, and then turned to look at the stairs. He wanted to see his son, to be there for him, but he also didn't want to hurt Jess, and if he left now she'd think he'd used her. That he was as bad as the last guy who'd clearly broken her heart by not caring enough.

She deserved better than that. But then so did his son.

"I'm going to be a bit longer." He paused, cringing at the silence down the line. "But I'll be home soon, then we should grab some lunch, okay?"

"Yeah."

Ryan hated the way he felt when George hung up. Like he was being torn in two different directions. Yanked one way in his heart, then the other.

He sighed and put down the phone. Fifteen minutes ago he'd been on cloud nine, had felt like everything was going to work out perfectly, and now he was all messed up in his head again. He needed to do something to make things right, and that might mean talking to his boy about Jessica. Somehow.

"Is everything okay?"

Ryan turned to find Jessica standing nearby. He was pleased he'd put down the phone because it would have dropped from his hand and hit the floor.

She was wearing his T-shirt and what looked like nothing else. It only covered her down to the top of her thighs, and she had her ankles crossed, legs together, hair all mussed up and falling around her face. She must have found it while he was on the phone, which meant he'd missed seeing her walk into the room naked.

"Ryan?"

He realized he was standing there like an idiot, mouth hanging open. Her face was like an open question mark, eyes showing her confusion. He didn't like it. He liked what he saw, her big brown eyes watching him, so much skin on show apart from what was hidden beneath his shirt, but he hated that she was unsure of him.

Ryan crossed the room and wrapped his arms around her, smiling as he realized that she now smelled like his cologne. He kissed her neck, then her cheek, then her lips, hands buried in her hair.

"Everything is fine."

She pressed her face against his chest, fingers teasing his bare skin where her dressing gown didn't stretch enough to cover him.

"So where's breakfast then?"

He growled and slapped her bottom. Jess shrieked and jumped away from him.

"Any more naughty business and I'll take a photo of you like that," she threatened.

He followed her across the room, teasing her. "Oh, really?"

She giggled, darting away, one hand holding down his T-shirt. He couldn't help but smile at her modesty.

After the night they'd just had, here she was still innocent enough not to want him to see her bare in the daylight.

When she moved again he pounced, grabbing her wrists and pinning her against the wall.

"You win." She wriggled but didn't put up much of a fight.

Ryan held her, restrained her, taking the chance to kiss her before backing away.

"If I win, that means I get a prize."

He let go of her wrists and walked into the kitchen, taking a look in the pantry. Jess followed him, but she stopped to fill the jug.

"Coffee? That can be your reward."

He shook his head, reaching for a loaf of bread and the maple syrup.

"French toast?" he asked.

Jessica nodded.

"And my prize is that you say yes to lunch with me today."

She leaned back against the counter, eyes slanted slightly like she didn't believe him. "What's the catch?"

"My son's joining us."

Jessica gulped and watched Ryan's face. He wasn't kidding.

"Are you sure that's a good idea?"

He looked around. "Eggs?"

She went to the fridge and pulled out a tray, still waiting for him to respond.

Ryan nodded, but she could tell he was teetering on being unsure about it.

"I don't know if it's a good idea or not, to be honest.

But I'm not here long and I don't want to feel torn between the two of you. I want to enjoy you both and that means not keeping us a secret."

Us. She took a silent, deep breath.

She had no idea what that even meant. What they even were to one another. Last night had only further complicated her jumbled thoughts.

This was supposed to be fun, something casual, but it was starting to feel a whole lot more serious than that.

"When you say *us*..."

Ryan looked up as he cracked eggs into a dish.

"Jess, you mean a lot to me." He paused, before opening a drawer and reaching in and rummaging, emerging with the whisk. "I want George to know how much you helped me when I was away, and I don't know why I should have to keep that a secret. If I'm going to make things right with him, I need to be honest. About everything. And I think it might help to open up to him."

Okay. That sounded better. More like introducing her as a good friend.

"So when I meet him you'll tell him we're..."

He smiled. "Close friends."

Right. "I just don't want you to push it with him. If he thinks I'm your girlfriend it might make things difficult for you."

Ryan dipped the first slice of bread into the bowl and gave her one of his double-wattage grins.

"I'm not going to make this difficult for him. But I have to be honest about what's going on in my life if I want him to let me back in. Trust me again. I'll talk to him beforehand, explain myself so he understands." He paused. "I'm doing this for him. If I thought it wouldn't be the right thing for him, I wouldn't even suggest it."

Jessica sighed. She knew what he meant, she just

wasn't convinced, personally, that his son was ready to meet her.

"Do you have any fruit?"

Jessica moved back to the fridge again. He seemed set on them meeting, and she wasn't going to hurt his feelings by saying no to the lunch. But she hadn't missed the look on George's face the other day, and something told her it might not be the right thing to do. Even if Ryan was doing his best to evade her questions right now, they had to tread carefully.

But he sure was good at changing the subject. "Go back up to bed," Ryan told her, pausing and leaning toward her to plant a kiss on her forehead. "I'll bring breakfast up when it's ready."

Ryan watched as Jessica's fingers played across his chest as they lay side by side. Breakfast had been started and then somehow quickly forgotten about, but he wasn't complaining.

He sighed as she snuggled in closer to him.

"What?"

Ryan propped himself up on one elbow, looking down at her. She was so beautiful it took his breath away. So innocent and giving, so kind.

He wasn't sure if this was the right time to bring this up, but he needed to tell her. Needed to be real with her, be honest if they were going to have a chance at that future he was starting to think about.

"I'm scared, Jess."

She tucked even closer into him and kissed his jaw. "Why? What do you have to be scared of?"

He tried not to frown. He had everything to be scared of. That was the problem.

"Because part of me wonders if I can do this being a

normal person thing. I don't know if I can forget what I've seen, and forget what I've thought and just be a human being again."

"You've always been a human being, Ryan. You've just seen things that most of us would be too scared to confront," she said.

"Sometimes I wonder if being in the army, serving overseas, takes the humanity from you and makes you into some sort of machine. It stops you from feeling, it makes it okay to just treat each day as a new opportunity. But in real life, you need to look back, too. You need to remember."

"See this?" Jessica let her fingers dance along his cheek to wipe at a tear. "This makes you human."

He smiled, just, from the corner of his mouth on one side.

She kissed his lips, softly, so he could only just feel it. He leaned forward as she pulled away.

"That makes you human, too." She rolled over and reached inside her bedside table and pulled out a letter. "See this?"

He would recognize it anywhere. One of the letters he'd sent her. "You kept them?"

"Every one. My drawer is full of them."

He reached for it but she pulled it away and tucked it back again.

"I don't even know which letter that was, or why it was on the top of the pile, but those letters? Each one told me you were a man who knew how to love and how to lose. That you were a man who could help save our country, who could help his men, and now here you are at home trying to be a man and a dad and a civilian."

"And?"

"And now I know that you can do it."

"Why?"

She pressed her face into his chest. He had no idea why she had so much faith in him, but it gave him a strength he'd worried he didn't have.

"Because now you're helping me and it's working," she told him, her voice muffled by his skin.

He smiled and puller her closer. "You do know that whatever I'm not sure about, whatever I'm worried about, doesn't mean I'm not absolutely sure about what's happening between us, right?"

Jessica sighed as she lay in his arms.

Ryan nudged at her breast with his finger, circling over her skin and tracing back up to her face. It was as if he couldn't stop touching her, and she felt the same about him.

One day he'd ask her about her scars, what had led to her cosmetic surgery, but he didn't care. Plenty of women enhanced their breasts, and she had obviously had her reasons.

"You're my second chance, Jessica."

She pulled up so her head was resting on her hand, propped by the pillow. "I wasn't aware you needed a second chance."

He needed to tell her now. Take that step to let her in completely. "You're my chance to make things right."

"It wasn't your fault your wife died, Ryan."

He smiled, sadly. He hoped she'd understand. "No, but I didn't love her like she deserved to be loved. She was my best friend in school, and I loved her like only a best friend can."

He didn't say what he really wanted to. Tell her how he felt right now. Because it seemed too soon, too fast.

Now he knew what true love really felt like.

"Did she feel the same way?"

Ryan shook his head and played with her hair, his arm resting on her shoulder. This was the part he hated to admit, even to himself. Why he felt guilt like a crawling parasite over his skin sometimes. He'd always wondered if maybe he hadn't loved her enough to save her.

"She loved me deeply, I'd always known it. I could see it in her eyes every time she looked at me, even when she was in hospital with machines bleeping every time she so much as blinked."

He stopped and she just watched him. Ryan wished he could tell what she was thinking. "I never lied when I told her I loved her. We got married when we were eighteen, she was already pregnant with George, and we were happy. We never argued, and I told her every day that she meant the world to me. And she did."

"But?"

He leaned forward and kissed the tip of her nose. He wanted to ask Jessica if it made him a bad person for thinking he was so pleased to have met her. That finding her meant he could finally forgive Julia for leaving him. But he didn't. Because part of him wasn't ready to admit that out aloud yet. And he had a feeling that maybe Jessica wasn't ready to hear it.

But what he was sure about was how he felt about her. The last twenty-four hours had proven to him how special she was. "There's no but. I just want to say thank you, Jess. For everything."

She smiled as a tear escaped from the edge of her own eye. He kissed it away as she whispered back to him.

"You're welcome."

CHAPTER NINE

Dear Ryan,

I know by now that you probably torture yourself by thinking over things you should have done, but there's no point dwelling on the past. Especially on things you had no power to control. Before you come home, I think you need to forgive yourself, and let yourself move on.

Focus on what you have to do, stay safe and promise me that you'll write to your son more often. Even if you don't have much to say, just put pen to paper.

We write to one another so often now that you don't have any excuses not to write to him. Okay?

Jessica

JESSICA COULDN'T HELP the sigh that escaped her lips. She'd thought waiting for Ryan to arrive last night had been nerve-wracking. How wrong she'd been. Waiting to meet his son was far worse. The only consolation was that she wasn't meeting his parents, too.

She walked into the park, clutching Hercules's lead and telling herself it was worth it. They'd had a great time last night. Make that super. And if he needed her to meet his son, to keep things open and honest, and help to repair his relationship with George, then she didn't have much choice other than to go along with it.

But she was already feeling messed up in her head about what had happened. Not the physical side, but the way he'd opened up to her. She was starting to think that maybe he wanted more from her than she'd expected from him. The way he'd talked to her, the things he'd told her…

She'd told herself this thing with Ryan was meant to be casual. He was leaving soon. She was not available to the idea of anything serious, and yet it felt like they had gone from friends to something very serious, very fast.

Jess pushed her hair behind her ears and tried to shut off the voice in her brain telling her to run. No matter what happened today, she had to remember it was worth it. Ryan had made her feel incredible last night. He had made her realize that she could be wanted and loved again. Just because he was going away did not mean it wasn't worth every moment. Because it was.

She'd been so scared of showing a man her body, of opening up again and putting her heart out there. But Ryan had helped her through something she had thought was impossible to recover from. Once she'd gotten over the initial shock of him seeing her breasts, she hadn't thought about it again all night. After months of worrying, he'd made her thoughts vanish in less than a heartbeat.

Just thinking about him like that put a smile back on her face. Until she spotted them. And her anxiety came back like a troop of butterflies playing in her stomach.

Ryan raised a hand to wave. They were walking along

by the pond. She could see his son smiling, then watched as his face fell when he saw her. She wanted to run. But it was too late to back out now.

Instead she sucked up her courage and bent to let Hercules off the lead. The least she could do was let the dog have fun, chase some ducks while she tried not to find a hole to crawl and hide in.

"Jess!" Ryan called out and she mustered up a big smile again. Forced it on her face.

She waved back and watched as Hercules bounded up to them, before taking off to do laps back and forth along the water's edge.

"Hi, guys."

Ryan walked toward her and kissed her on the cheek. She tried to enjoy it, to experience that magical breathlessness she usually felt when his lips touched her. But instead all she saw was the flush of George's cheeks as he looked the other way.

"I was telling George what happened with your dog the last time we were here," Ryan said.

The boy nodded, face still stained a patchy red.

Jess shook herself out of the slump she was in. She was the adult here, the least she could do was make it as easy on George as she could.

"Little Herc means the world to me," she said, taking a step away from Ryan, needing the breathing space as his boy watched them. "I can't believe I was so caught up in getting to know your dad that I almost lost him."

"Why did you start writing to my dad?" The boy's face flushed a deep red just asking her.

"Well..." She paused and looked at Ryan. He nodded at her to continue. "I wanted to show that I cared about what our soldiers were doing for us, for our country. I heard about a pen-pal program that was being run with the army, and somehow I ended up writing to your father, out of all the soldiers serving overseas."

Ryan moved closer to his son, hand on his shoulder. "When I told you that Jess made a huge effort to write to me, I meant that she wrote to me all the time. Every week. She helped me to see why I needed to come back home."

George took a few steps back then turned to face the water again. "What did she tell you?"

Jessica didn't know what to say. She was uncomfortable being made to feel like she was somehow a surrogate mother for the day. It wasn't a role she wanted to fill. She wasn't ready to face that kind of commitment.

"She guided me through dealing with my problems, we talked about everything and it gave me the strength to face what I'd left behind," Ryan explained.

"Did you talk about Mom?" George asked.

Jessica wanted to back away but she couldn't. She just stood there, feeling like an intruder.

"Yeah, about you and your mom."

George turned away, like he didn't want to talk about it anymore. It hadn't gone down that badly, but it hadn't exactly been great, either.

"Lunch?" She made the suggestion as the air became stale between them all.

Ryan looked at her gratefully. "Yeah, good idea."

She sat beneath a nearby tree on the grass and Ryan did the same. George didn't move.

Jess didn't want to be here any more than she guessed the boy did. It felt like she was intruding on something she had no right to be a part of.

"I hope you like sushi."

She nodded. At least lunch was going to be good. "Show me what you've got."

Ryan gave her a relieved look, reaching out to squeeze her hand before calling to his son. "You joining us, George?"

He slowly turned toward them, his eyes telling his entire life story. They looked sad, haunted almost, and Jess fought the sudden tug deep inside her that made her want to hold him, to comfort this boy who was so confused.

He just shrugged, but she knew he probably wanted to cry. To yell at her and ask his dad why he had to meet her at all.

"Hey, George, why don't you go get Hercules for me?" she suggested.

There was a small light in his eyes as she gave him the Get Out of Jail Free card.

"Either throw sticks into the water for him, or just get hold of him and bring him back," she told him.

George went off straight away and Ryan reached for her knee, his hand closing over it. "Thanks for that."

She took a deep breath. "I don't know if meeting George today was the best idea."

Ryan grimaced. "I know, but I did have a big talk with him before we came. Explained why I wanted him to meet you." He paused. "Sometimes the hardest thing is the best thing to do, even if it doesn't feel like it at the time, right?"

"I think him having to deal with me when you guys are only just starting to sort things out is too much." But part of her felt dishonest—because maybe, just maybe, it was just too much for *her* and yet exactly the right thing for George.

Ryan shook his head, jaw suddenly clenched a bit tighter, making him look more determined. His hand hovered then came to rest on her cheek.

Jess sighed at his touch.

"You mean something to me, Jess, and I don't want to keep things from him."

She turned her face to kiss his palm, wishing things could be more simple between them. That he wasn't going away, and that she didn't have to keep huge secrets from him.

"Ryan, you're going away soon." Jessica paused. "There's no need to cause complications when they don't even need to exist."

Now it was Ryan shaking his head. "I should have told you that I'm not leaving for good, Jess. If I didn't think we had a chance, that this didn't mean something, I wouldn't have let things go this far between us."

She swallowed, hard.

"In fact, I've already decided that this will be my last tour."

Silence hung between them.

Oh, my.

Was he serious?

She hadn't seen this coming. He'd been so determined to continue on with his career in the army, had made that so clear to her in his letters, it was the only reason *she'd* let things go this far. He'd even told her as much that first day they'd met.

Ryan was being so honest with her, and here she was keeping guilty secrets from him. All this time she'd thought it was men she couldn't trust, yet right now she was the one lying by omission. Who wasn't being up front about what she wanted and what she had to give. And now he was telling her that maybe they had a chance at a future. The one thing she'd thought he didn't have to offer her.

"Ryan…"

She didn't know what to say.

"Do you really think I would have jeopardized our friendship by making love with you if I was going to walk away and never look back?" She saw a flash of anger, of disappointment in his eyes. "You've done so much for me, the last thing I want to do is hurt you."

And yet from the sound of it, she was going to be the one doing the hurting.

Did that mean he wanted more from her? That he thought this was going to develop into something she hadn't possibly thought it *could* turn into?

Tears stung, pricked at the back of her eyes, but she fought them. She was used to putting on a brave face, to keeping her emotions to herself.

She wasn't emotionally available for a relationship. And she'd lied to him. If she'd just told him about the cancer in the first place, things would never have gotten to this point. It was her fault and no one else's.

"I think what you need to do is focus on your son," she said instead.

Ryan's eyebrows knotted as he drew them together. "Without you I wouldn't even *have* a relationship with my son."

She disagreed. He would have found a way to reconnect with George even if she hadn't been there for him. She looked up as Hercules landed in her lap. She cleared her throat as George appeared.

"Hey, buddy." She swatted at her dog as he tried to kiss her.

Ryan stayed silent.

"Thanks, George, he can be a handful sometimes."

The boy smiled at her and sat down. Hercules went straight over to him and had him laughing within seconds.

Ryan looked back at her, confusion in his eyes. She gave him a tight smile back. There was a lot unsaid between them, and from the look on his face, she'd hurt the one man who had given her a glimpse of what she might one day have in the future. An honest, caring, kind man who deserved better than what she could give him right now.

When he found out what she'd kept from him, he'd be hurt beyond belief. So the only thing she could do was make sure he never, ever found out. Which meant she had to make a decision and stick to it. Maybe it was time to walk away. Either that or she had to brave up and give him the chance to accept her for who she really was. The very thought made her shiver with fear.

"Sushi, right?"

Ryan gave her a confused smile and took three trays out of the plastic bag he'd been carrying.

She smiled back, but inside she was crying a thousand tears. He'd opened up to her, and she'd let him, because as his friend she owed it to him to listen and be there for him. What she hadn't realized was that when he'd told her this morning that he hadn't loved his wife *enough,* that just maybe he'd been trying to tell her something else.

Except she wasn't ever going to put him through that kind of heartache ever again.

CHAPTER TEN

Dear Ryan,
Have you ever thought about coming home for good? I know you love what you do, but I often wonder how long a person can live away from their family. From their normal life.

Don't you miss being home? Or are you so focused on your task over there that you don't even let yourself think about what you're missing out on back here?

Whatever happens, even if we don't end up meeting, I want you to know that I think about you and your unit every day. And I pray for your safe return home one day soon.
Jessica

AFTER TOYING WITH her phone for what felt like forever, Jessica put the key back in her car's ignition and gripped the steering wheel.

Things hadn't gone well this afternoon. Not well at all.

Somehow the perfect morning, waking in the arms of a man like none other she'd met before, had turned into the most dismal afternoon on record.

And no amount of grocery shopping or busying herself at home had helped the way she was feeling.

She needed to deal with this properly.

Finally she'd met the kind of guy she'd always dreamed of. Enjoyed the company of a member of the opposite sex, had a night that she would remember forever and had a man open up to her and tell her that she meant something to him.

Yet she was the one who'd managed to blow things. She wasn't ready for a relationship, had never thought whatever it was she had with Ryan could even have the chance of turning into something serious. Not when she'd expected him to be away serving again for goodness only knew how long.

So she either had to hurt him by coming clean and telling him about her past, and break her own heart in the process, and convince him that she liked him back but that nothing could happen, or call things off right now.

But in all the hours that had passed since she'd left him this afternoon, she hadn't figured out what to do. She cringed and put her foot down on the accelerator a little harder.

The way she felt around him was…indescribable and made her *want* to tell him the truth about her past. Yet would calling things off now be easier on him than telling him the truth? It would certainly prevent her from ever hurting him again like he had been over his wife's death, if he wasn't around to see her in the event that she became sick again.

If she wasn't driving she'd have banged her head against the wheel. It was all such a mess. Even without the added complication of his son, it was too much, too soon. Yet here she was, looking for his house, determined to do *something* to make the afternoon turn out better than it had so far.

She owed it to both of them not to leave things like this.

Jess scanned the numbers on mailboxes until she saw 109. Phew. His car was in the driveway. And it appeared to be the only one in residence. He'd mentioned that his parents were away for the night, had gone off to visit friends. And his son was to be at a friend's place, too, or so he'd said earlier.

That meant it was now or never.

Jessica stepped from the car and walked up the path. It was a nice house, nothing flashy, but modern and solid. A small family home. She guessed it had been Ryan's when his wife was still alive. He'd told her that he owned it, but his parents lived there and took care of the place while he was gone.

Jess knocked on the door.

"Coming."

His voice hit her in the chest, pierced her in the gut.

Suddenly the idea of calling things off was definitely not an option. That left her with one possibility on her list: she could leave it up to him, tell him the truth and let him decide if he could face the possibility of the pain of cancer again.

The door swung back.

"Jess?"

She stood there, awkward, handbag clutched under her arm. Unsurprisingly, Ryan looked unsure. She'd bolted from the park straight after lunch, so he was probably wondering why she was even here.

"Can I come in?" she asked.

His face relaxed and he held out his hand. "Come here."

She softened at his touch, let him draw her in, hold her. Comfort her. Even though she didn't deserve it.

"I'm sorry about earlier," she mumbled against his chest.

Ryan kissed her forehead and stepped back. "My fault, not yours. It was too much, too soon, right?"

She nodded, eyes cloudy with tears. It felt so right to be tucked against him, to find comfort from his body, but she knew what she had done was wrong. For once she had to admit that her brother had been right. If she'd been honest from the start she wouldn't be in this position right now.

"George is out?"

Ryan took her hand and led her down the hall. "Yep, at his friend's house. He looked pleased to get out of here."

She relaxed. It was just the two of them. Time to finally clear the air and come clean.

She followed him into the living room, toying with her bag, before sitting down on the sofa. He sat down, too, falling beside her, knees knocking hers, thigh brushing against her own.

Jessica felt rotten. The look on his face was so open, so kind, and she was about to bring up something that she'd wanted so badly to keep hidden.

And in the process she was going to hurt him.

But when she looked at him, saw the honesty there, remembered the way he'd treated her last night, she owed him nothing less than the truth.

"Ryan, I need to talk to you about something."

"Sounds serious." He grinned and took her hand, fingers circling her palm.

Why did this have to be so hard?

"It's ah, about your wife. Sort of."

Ryan's hand fell away from hers. She wasn't sure if he was angry or just plain unsure.

"You told me that you couldn't go through that again. That what happened with your wife…"

His face had gone from soft to hard. Like steel, braced for impact. "Is this about what I said earlier? I'm sorry if I scared you off, I just wanted you to know how I felt, that I wouldn't be doing this, misleading you, if I didn't think we had something special between us."

Jessica sighed. She didn't even know if she was doing the right thing now. Had no idea how to continue. But she had to try. Maybe she hadn't completely ruined what chance they might have had at a future together. Maybe he would understand.

"You opened up to me this morning, Ryan, and I think I owe you an explanation. I need to tell you something."

Ryan was a soldier. His life was all about walking away from his own personal issues and fighting for a greater cause. And yet he'd been brave enough to talk to her, to tell her the truth.

There was only so long she could run and hide from what had happened.

"You can tell me anything, Jess." He smiled at her so genuinely she wanted to cry. "Whatever you need to say, you can."

Jessica gripped his hand harder. Her eyes locked on his.

"I know what it's like to keep things hidden inside. I…"

He held her hand back, tight. "You do?"

A noise startled them both.

Jessica turned at the same time as Ryan. And came face-to-face with his son.

"George?" Ryan said, startled.

George looked at them and walked through the room and into the kitchen.

Jessica felt her heart sink to her toes. From the way they were cuddled up close on the sofa George probably thought he'd walked in on something he shouldn't have.

"Jess, can we…"

She smiled. There was nothing else she could do. Except maybe fall in a heap and sob her heart out. "Where's your room? I'll go and give you two some privacy."

He pointed down the hall. "Third on the left."

She touched his arm and walked away. "Take all the time you need."

Jessica opened the door to Ryan's room and stepped in. She could hear the sound of his voice as he spoke, but it was muffled and she didn't want to hear anyway. Whatever he needed to say was between him and his son, and she had enough on her own mind than needing to stick her nose in where it wasn't welcome.

It was weird being in Ryan's own personal space, and there was something disturbing about being there for the first time on her own. It made her think about what she hadn't managed to tell him. What she'd come here to say.

What she didn't want to tell him but had to.

Ryan was like a huge grizzly bear with a heart of gold, a man who'd known heartache like she could only barely understand, despite what she'd been through. A man who could kill an enemy with his bare hands yet was prepared to admit that he'd been a bad father in the past, and be honest with her that he couldn't face losing another person he loved again.

A man she wanted to love so bad, but was too scared of being honest with. It had been so much easier writing letters, when she could imagine that one day they could meet, that maybe he'd like her.

But she'd never considered that he'd be the kind of man she could fall in love with.

And deep down she knew she had already.

The reality of what she was feeling was harder to deal with. The reality of Ryan was a man who could cocoon her in his arms and make her feel safe. Make her think he could protect her from anything, maybe even from cancer. A man whose smile could make her forget every worry she'd ever had in her mind.

A man she could imagine having a life with.

So why hadn't she just been honest with him from the start? Why hadn't she told him when he'd opened up to her about losing his wife that first night over dinner?

Jessica sat on Ryan's bed, waiting for him. It seemed silly to be hiding out in here while he tried to deal with his son, but he was the parent. He was doing his best and she wasn't exactly helping the father-son relationship any. In fact, if they were both honest about it, her being in his life was probably the only remaining wedge stuck between him and his son.

But for some reason they had a connection that meant he was prepared to cause himself further heartache, to allow something to develop between them. And that only made her feel worse.

She'd been dishonest. And she knew that whatever he told her, as honest as he'd been with her, he'd probably still run away once she told him the truth. And if, by some miracle, he didn't run, at the very least he'd be angry…no, furious with her.

Jessica fought the urge to lay back and cry. Instead she sat up straight and looked around her. Pushed her thoughts away. His scent was in the room, the bed still crumpled from where he'd slept the night before, but it wasn't a personal room.

Jessica stood and walked to the dresser. She let her eyes wander over a photo of George and a very old wedding photo of a Ryan she didn't recognize. It felt like she was already intruding, looking over his things like this, but she didn't stop. At least it was taking her mind off the way she'd behaved.

She moved to his wardrobe and stood in front of the door, fingers itching to open it. She listened. Just faintly, she could still hear the echo of voices in the living room.

Jessica looked at the closet, considering it as if it was a living, breathing thing. She opened the door so fast she couldn't change her mind, then staggered back, stumbling over her own feet.

Oh, my.

Ryan's U.S. Army camouflage pants and shirt hung from a thick, sturdy hanger. It was as if it was a person, the way his clothes hung with such a presence. The way they managed to steal the breath from her lungs, just hanging there like that. The uniform looked back at her like it had a soul of its own.

It was a part of Ryan, as much a part of his life as anything. It was the uniform he had worn when he'd been on tour last, what he'd no doubt been wearing when he'd sat and written to her. Maybe he'd even been wearing it when he'd read the letters she'd sent him.

It was a Ryan from another life, not the man she knew here.

Jessica wriggled her fingers, flexing them, before touching the fabric. Her fingers skimmed the strong, rough cotton of the camouflage shirt, nails tracing the nametag. McAdams. His name played in front of her eyes.

She touched down the legs. Same fabric, same feel. His boots, black and shiny, stood forlorn beneath the hanging uniform.

Jessica stepped closer, inhaling as she moved. It was clean, but not freshly laundered. She pulled it closer, hoping he'd never wear it again, then wishing she could stop herself from thinking that.

Tears stung her eyes. It was like a lump of wood was jammed in her throat, making swallowing impossible.

Why had it taken seeing his uniform to truly make her realize? The problem wasn't that she didn't want to be with Ryan, didn't want a future with him.

What she was scared of was losing him.

She'd never wanted it to be just a fling. To start with, she'd convinced herself that a few weeks or months with him was all she wanted. But from the moment they'd met…no, from the moment she'd felt the power of his words, she'd let herself hope that what they had could develop into something special.

She'd just been too scared to admit it to herself.

Deep down she didn't want him to go back at all. To leave her for even a moment. She wanted him to stay here, safe, to look after her instead of her country.

To protect *her.*

Something crinkled. Jessica let go and watched as the uniform swung back into place, like it was trained to hang straight, with perfection, like the way a soldier stands to attention. She looked over her shoulder, making sure she was still alone, then reached forward. Her hand connected with the front pocket of his shirt, and she heard the rustle again.

Something made her open it. Made her curious. Something told her she had to see what was there.

She undid the button and reached inside. It was a letter. Someone else might not have realized straight away, but she knew. Just like she knew instinctively that it was a letter for her.

After months of writing one another, she knew his handwriting almost as well as she knew her own. Even the way he folded his letters was precise, although this one was rumpled, like he'd been carrying it a long time.

The only difference was that this one wasn't in an envelope that had her name scrawled across the front. But when she unfolded the sheet, it had her name at the top of it.

She closed her eyes, wishing she could walk away from it, put it back and not read it. He hadn't given it to her, it felt wrong to look at it like this, but she couldn't *not* read it.

Turning away would be like denying a bee its pollen.

It was okay. If he didn't want her to read it, he wouldn't have been carrying it in his pocket, right? He'd probably just forgotten to post it, then he'd arrived home and he'd probably already told her what was written inside.

Or maybe not.

Either way she had to know what it said.

CHAPTER ELEVEN

Dear Jessica,

I've been sitting here since before sunrise, and now it's almost midday. There's only one thing I want to tell you. One thing I've been wanting to tell you, so I'm just going to come out and say it.

I think I love you, Jessica. I know I've never met you, I know it's impossible to say this when I could pass you in the street at this exact moment and not know you. But one day, when we do meet, I know I'll look at you and still feel the same.

A stranger might say that when we meet it won't be the same, but something tells me it will be. That there's a reason we managed to find each other even though we're on opposite sides of the world. I want to come home, and I think the reason is you.

I love you, Jessica.

Ryan

JESSICA CAREFULLY REFOLDED the letter. She couldn't breathe. She couldn't blink. She could barely move.

She forced herself to put the letter back in his

breast pocket, fumbled with the button, then closed the closet door.

No.

He couldn't love her. He couldn't.

Now that he'd met her, did he still feel that way?

Could he truly feel that way about her now?

Love her?

But in her heart, she knew the answer to that. Just like she knew that, without a shadow of doubt, she loved him back with all her heart. She'd fallen in love with him about the time she'd been released from hospital. When she'd realized that his letters were what had helped her pull through. Had given her the strength to recover.

All this time she'd been denying it, telling herself she was okay with a casual fling, with him going away again when she'd been in love with him since before he'd even arrived home.

But he couldn't love her back. He couldn't. And she wasn't going to wait around to find out.

He'd made it clear he couldn't live through the pain of losing a wife again. And even if he accepted what had happened to her, what she'd hidden from him, it wasn't fair to put him in that position again when even she didn't know what was going to happen to her.

Jessica grabbed her sweater and tried not to run. She walked out of his room, moving as quietly as she could, and made for the back door. He'd be better off forgetting her. If he knew the truth he'd be devastated, and he deserved better. If she left now, before things went any further, he'd hurt less than finding out the truth later on. A slightly broken heart was better than him knowing she had cancer and having to deal with what might happen to her in the future. What could reoccur.

She should have ended things before they got this far.

Should never have considered telling him about what she'd battled. It would be better for both of them, her leaving.

So why was it so hard walking away?

Tears fell down her cheeks like oversize raindrops falling from the sky to touch her. Shudders ran back and forth along the planes of her skin. Her bottom lip quivered like it was an instrument being played. But she kept on walking, until she was outside, and she didn't stop until she got in the car.

It was over. It had to be.

She only wished she could have said goodbye to him first.

When she walked back into her house, even the smile and waggy tail that Hercules threw her way couldn't make her happy, not even for a heartbeat.

"Come here."

She hardly had to whisper for Hercules to come to her. It was like he knew the power of his fur, knew how much she'd come to need him, to crave the warmth of his little body and the way he cuddled into her when she held him.

Jessica scooped him up and pressed him tight to her chest, her face falling to kiss his little head.

She tried not to think about Ryan but no matter what she thought of, his eyes were in her mind and the words of his final letter to her were ringing in her ears.

"Who's been phoning us, huh?"

She smiled at her loyal companion through her tears, walking with him in her arms to hit the flashing light on the machine.

"Hey, sis, haven't heard from you in a while. Call

around for a drink tonight if you're free, or whenever. See you later."

Jess smiled and hit delete. Steven might be overprotective and overbearing sometimes, but he was a great brother. And she knew that no matter what happened, how right he might have been, that he'd never say *I told you so.*

There was one more message.

She leant back on the counter and snuggled Herc.

"Ah, Jessica…"

She jerked forward, almost losing Hercules in the process. She would know that voice anywhere. It was her doctor.

"I'd hoped to speak to you in person but I haven't been able to get hold of you. Your test results came back and we're going to need to do some follow-ups. Please don't worry, it might not mean anything but as you know we need to be overcautious."

Jessica hit delete immediately.

She gently placed Hercules down on the ground and let her shaky hand reach for the glass in the sink. She turned the faucet on and filled the glass, drinking a few mouthfuls, before turning the water back on to let the cool liquid run over her wrists.

This couldn't be happening.

She eyed the telephone and wished she didn't know the doctor's number by heart.

Jessica sat down at the table, pen in hand. It didn't matter how she felt about Ryan, but what she wanted to say, it was just so hard to get it out, to make the words form in her brain and force them out in the open. The only way she truly knew how to communicate with him was on paper.

The words ran like the credits of a movie over and over, around and around in her mind, a well of dialogue she couldn't deny. Writing to Ryan came so naturally, usually, but no other letter had ever been so hard to write.

The doctor was right, it might be nothing, but she still had to tell Ryan. She owed him more than a lie now. She hoped he wouldn't think that he had to be there for her, that he couldn't walk away, even if he really wanted to. That somehow her cancer was his problem, too, when it wasn't.

Because unlike her ex, Ryan would probably feel obliged to be there for her now, if something was wrong, and she didn't want to be a pity case.

She needed to tell him the truth, and there was only one way she knew how to.

Jessica started to write.

Dear Ryan,

I don't know how we got here, or what we did to deserve this, but there's something you need to know about me that I never told you. Something that will no doubt make you want to run and never see me again.

When I started writing to you, I was in the hospital. I should have told you, but then I never thought I'd actually ever meet you. I never thought you would have to be the one supporting me. You were the soldier, the man away at war, and helping you made me feel better. You were the only person in my life who didn't treat me like a bird with broken wings. I could be myself, talk to you, laugh, without any strings.

But something happened when you arrived

here, into my life. Suddenly you weren't just a soldier, a faceless person who needed a friend. You were a man and I was a woman. So I didn't tell you about my cancer.

Before you, cancer was all I thought about. Then I thought I'd beaten it. Maybe I still have, but I don't know for certain yet. Either way I owe you an explanation for why I ran out on you earlier today, and why I'm going to disappear from your life forever.

I need to go back and see my specialist, Ryan, and so I think it's best we don't see each other again. You have George to deal with, and my being with you was complicated enough even before I plucked up the courage to tell you about my past.

You mean so much to me, but I can't put you through this, not after what you've seen. What you've gone through in the past with your wife, and what you made so clear you could never cope with living through again. I should have come clean then, been honest with you, but I was scared you'd walk away, and I wasn't ready to lose you so soon after meeting you. I wanted to enjoy your company while you were here, enjoy our friendship, although I can see now that was selfish of me.

Please know that I love you, Ryan. If we'd met in another lifetime, maybe we could have had something amazing together. I'm sorry, for what it's worth, and I will never forget you so long as there is breath in my body.

Yours always,
Jessica

Jessica wiped at the tears falling in a steady stream down her cheeks, but one still managed to plop onto the paper. It didn't matter. In her heart she knew he'd probably shed his own tears when he found her note, and she deserved to feel bad over what she'd done to him.

What she'd kept from him.

She picked up the letter, folded it, then placed it in an envelope. Jessica scrawled his name across it and picked it up, her bag in the other hand.

Earlier he'd phoned, telling her he wasn't sure what had happened before but that he'd be around later tonight to see her. To make sure she was okay.

Jessica dialed her brother's number.

"You okay?"

She smiled into the earpiece. Her brother meant the world to her. "The specialist has agreed to see me in the morning."

"You want me to come with you?"

"No, I'll be fine." She hoped. "If it's okay with you I'm going to come over soon with Herc so he can hang out with you tomorrow while I'm gone."

"You want to stay here the night?"

She tried not to cry. "Yeah, if that doesn't mess up your evening."

"Get in the car, sis, I'll have dinner waiting."

She hung up and picked up her keys.

Hercules was at her heel and followed her outside. Jessica only paused to lock the door and tape the envelope to the timber, just below the handle. She was glad she wasn't going to be around to see the look on Ryan's face. Just walking away from what she'd written was like a stake was being forced through her heart.

* * *

Ryan held his son tight and gave him a pat on the back. Man-to-man kind of stuff.

George smiled when he released him.

He hated that Jessica had had to leave, that his heart-to-heart with George had taken so long, but he'd have time to explain himself to her tonight. What mattered was that he'd been honest with George about his feelings for Jess, and now he had to be honest with her about them, too.

"You sure you don't mind if I leave you here for a bit?"

George shook his head. "Nah, go see her."

"Because if you'd rather me stay here I will."

His son rolled his eyes. "I get it. Just go, all right?"

Ryan gave him another slap on the back and stood, feeling good about how things were turning out. Finally.

"Guess I need to stop running for good, right?"

George just watched him.

"It's time for me to put down my roots again here, son. You know I meant it the other night when I said this would be my last tour, didn't you?"

He received a nod in return. Ryan gave George one final look, to reassure himself he'd be okay, then pulled on his jacket and found his car keys.

He'd finally found out what it meant to be a father again, and he wanted to be there for George. Had spent the better part of the afternoon opening his heart up to him and making sure he understood what his priorities were. Made sure he knew that his bringing Jessica into their lives was because what he felt for her was real. And what she'd done for them, the way she'd helped him man up to his son, was why he was prepared to fight for his right to be in both of their lives.

If there was one thing this injury had taught him, it was that he wasn't invincible. Or immortal.

He was desperate to speak to Jessica now. Whatever she'd been upset about telling him couldn't change his mind, even if she was nervous about getting something off her chest.

Opening his soul to her had been less painful than he'd thought, and after having a long talk with George, he had no intention of mucking up a future with Jess. Not now that his son understood what she meant to him.

It was now or never.

Ryan pulled up outside Jessica's house and walked up the path. There were no lights on inside and the curtains weren't drawn.

Maybe she hadn't got his message? His stomach flipped, anxiously. He hoped nothing had happened to her.

Ryan decided to go and knock anyway. She could be taking a nap, reading in her room without the light on. He wasn't going to back down now, not when he'd mustered the courage to open up to her. To tell her what she needed to know about him, and to admit how he really felt about her.

As he neared the door, he saw something white moving ever so slightly in the breeze. He squinted. It was almost dark, but he could tell it was an envelope. He'd waited for enough of them over the last year to know the exact size of the stationery she used.

Ryan stopped a foot from the door and reached out to touch it. Jessica's soft, scrawly handwriting stood out and beckoned him, called to him as it always did.

He'd loved receiving her letters when he was away, had treasured every one, but this one felt different.

This time when he saw his name, it made him want to drop it. Why would she have left him a letter? She could have called or waited for him, or scribbled a note on the door telling him when she'd be back.

The formality of this one felt all wrong. His name on the outside. The envelope. The darkness of the house in contrast to the white of the paper.

Ryan pushed his thumb beneath the seal and slowly took the letter from it. He walked back to the car so he'd have enough light to read it. There was no point knocking on her door, she'd clearly left this for him, and she wouldn't have pinned it there if she'd been inside.

He opened his car door and dropped into the driver's seat, feet still firmly planted on the road. He flicked the interior light on and held the note up.

Ryan felt the kick of betrayal, of pain, the moment he read her words. They hit him like a heavy man's fist to his stomach.

Jessica had lied to him.

She'd lied to him and she didn't even have the guts to tell him to his face.

He finished her words, eyes first skimming then rereading more slowly what she'd written. What she'd written on paper rather than tell him to his face.

Ryan dropped the letter then bent to retrieve it, screwing it up into a tight ball and throwing it out onto the sidewalk, not even able to bear having it in the car with him.

He sat, he couldn't do anything else.

Why? Why hadn't she just told him? What had he done to make her think she had to hide herself from him? To think she had to deal with all his problems yet not share her own?

Ryan tried to calm himself down. Tried to put his training in place and stay collected, to keep his mind settled.

But he couldn't. Fury charged within him like a tornado that built itself up to rip homes from the ground and spit them out again all torn and broken. His face was burning hot, fists clenched at his sides.

No! He was *not* going to let her just walk away like this. He'd finally opened up, acted like the man he so wanted to believe he was, and she'd just disappeared.

Ryan swallowed, over and over, trying to fight something he hadn't felt in so long. Sadness. Gut-wrenching, heart-breaking sadness. Guilt and pain like he'd thought he'd never have to experience again.

Tears stung in his eyes but he was powerless to stop them. They wet his cheeks then streamed down his jaw. He wiped at them, furious, but he couldn't stop the way he felt, or the way his body was reacting.

He wasn't the kind of guy who cried, for heaven's sake!

Ryan pulled his arm back and made a fist, pummelling the steering wheel. His fingers and wrist exploded with pain upon impact, his upper arm and shoulder throbbing within seconds.

His physio was going to kill him, but he didn't care.

What he cared about right now, right at this moment, was the woman who'd run from him. Who'd thought he wasn't man enough to deal with her past, when she'd been so caring about his.

He hung his head, nursing his arm against his chest, and ordered himself to stop crying.

He couldn't lose her. Not now. If she didn't want him, if he didn't mean to her what she did to him, then fine. But he was not going to lose another person he loved, however long they might have together. He wasn't going to live with any regrets this time. *If* her cancer had returned, if she was that sick, then he was going to suck up his memories and his pain and deal with it. He was going to be there for her.

Now all he had to do was find her and tell her that.

Ryan got out of the car, slammed the door shut and wiped at his face. His hand and arm still hurt but he didn't care. He stood, fists clenched, trying to figure out what to do.

He didn't care if she'd had cancer. He didn't care how angry he was, or how much he wanted to shake her and tell her how stupid she'd been. He no longer even cared that she'd lied to him. He realized she had thought it was the right thing to do, just like he'd thought staying away from home so long was the right thing to do.

He would do anything for Jessica, and even if it meant facing his biggest fear, he would be there. This was his chance to prove himself to her once and for all.

He had two options. Find Bella. Or turn up at her brother's place.

Bella was the easier option, and probably the more logical one, but if confronting her brother was what he had to do, then he'd turn up on his doorstep and not leave until he had an answer. He didn't care what it took. What he had to do. Even if her brother gave him a black eye for upsetting her and making her run.

Ryan was going to find her and tell her how he felt. Whatever the consequences.

CHAPTER TWELVE

Dear Ryan,
Everything is fine here. Nothing really to report. Your letters are always so much more interesting than mine! I'm just busy with my painting and life in general, sorry I can't entertain you with anything more exciting.

Not long now until you're home, right? You must be so looking forward to stepping off that plane.
Jessica

JESSICA KNEW WHY she was feeling guilty. She knew why she had had to run, because she was scared of feeling like she had once before.

In love. With no power over her future.

Scared.

She couldn't deal with feeling like that, not now. Her focus had to be on healing herself, on *protecting* herself. And that's why she'd had to spend the night at her brother's place. She didn't have the strength to deal with being back here at the hospital and facing Ryan, too.

It was like she was only half the woman she'd been. The cancer had done that to her. Stripped away her hopes and dreams for the future and made her question her every move. It had taken away the part of her that made her feel like a woman. And she just didn't want to put another human being through what she'd seen her family go through.

Yes, Ryan had made her realize that her cosmetic concerns were unfounded, but the reality of him dealing with her past, with her *cancer,* meant she'd had no choice other than to leave him.

To see the look in another person's eyes that said they thought they were going to lose her was more than she could deal with. And to cry herself to sleep with another person in her mind who she couldn't bear the thought of never seeing again—that was what she was truly frightened of.

If the cancer came back.

Every day she lived with that. The worry that slowly ate at her brain and her thoughts like a termite gnawing on wood. She was a cancer survivor, she'd beaten the odds once, but there was always the chance that it could come back.

Since Ryan had stepped into her life in all his physical glory, she'd almost forgotten, almost felt normal for the first time in what seemed like forever. But then reality had come crashing down.

Her family would be heartbroken if she'd relapsed. No, they were already heartbroken that she'd gone through what she had. It would shatter their entire beings piece by piece if it had come back.

Jessica walked faster, moving as quickly as she could—as if doing so would make her heart heal. Or her mind forget the man she'd just walked out on last night. But the reality that confronted her was a sterile waiting room, and the smell of hospital that she'd grown to hate.

She should have brought someone with her. Bella. Her brother. Anyone. No matter how strong she tried to be, there was nothing worse than being alone.

Ryan felt like his head had been in a car crash. It was pounding, throbbing with a pain all of its own. He should have stopped to get a sling for his arm, too, but instead he'd swallowed a couple of pain relief pills he had in the car from the physio, and he was driving like a madman.

Bella had been a pain in the backside last night, refusing to tell him where he could find Jessica, but when he'd turned up at Steven's place this morning and told him the truth about how he felt, her brother had told him everything.

He was almost at the hospital.

Ryan had gotten over the fact that she'd written him a letter instead of telling him to his face. He'd gotten over the fact that she hadn't trusted him enough to tell him, to really let him in. He knew why she'd done it. He'd told her himself that he never wanted to see a loved one battle cancer, that he was scared of being truly heartbroken again, not knowing how much his words would have pierced her to the core. The last thing he wanted was to deal with her being sick, with anyone close facing something like cancer, but he certainly wasn't going to turn his back on Jessica. It wasn't her fault she'd been ill.

Once upon a time he'd thought he couldn't be strong enough to be there for someone again like he'd had to be there for his wife, but it didn't mean he wouldn't pull himself together for Jessica. Given the choice, he'd help her battle anything if it truly meant a future with her. Even just the chance at a future.

Maybe she was right not to have told him before. Maybe he would have run if he'd known about her cancer that first day he'd come back. To be honest, he probably would have avoided getting close to her at all, even via letters, had he known about her illness.

But this was *Jessica*. The woman he had now grown to love through letters and in person, who meant so much to him, that he couldn't be without her for however long they had together.

He pumped the accelerator a little harder, increasing his speed. If she told him to leave, he would. But he wasn't giving up without a fight. Without at least proving to her that he deserved a chance to be with her. To love her.

Jessica walked down the corridor. They wanted to keep her for a few hours, do some tests, and she needed to retrieve some things from the car. She knew how long these things could take, and she wanted to grab her book and sketch paper to draw on.

Heavy footsteps echoed out behind her but she didn't bother to turn. The hospital was full of noise, and even though she hated the place she felt safe here. So long as she didn't see too many cancer patients being pushed through the wards.

"Jessica!"

She stopped. Her feet actually stopped moving at the command, even though she didn't want them to. She squeezed her eyes shut for a nanosecond then started walking faster.

Ryan. She would know that voice anywhere and it was not one she wanted to hear. Not now. Maybe if she didn't turn around he'd figure it wasn't her. How had he found her anyway?

"Jessica!"

His voice was deep, strong, even more commanding this time.

She kept moving, head down. She wasn't going to let herself turn. Couldn't deal with him right now.

"Stop! Just stop."

The footfalls were right behind her. Running away wasn't an option. She had to stop. She forced her feet to a halt. Her shoulders heaved.

Why now? She didn't have the strength to deal with Ryan. Couldn't face him and see the hurt she knew she'd find there. The betrayal she knew he must be feeling. Why had he come?

"Jessica, look at me."

His voice was still commanding, but it was starting to crack.

"Look at me."

It was a whisper this time, barely audible. She still didn't move, not until his hand curled around her forearm and made her turn.

She could feel his big body behind her, so close all she wanted to do was lean back into him, to seek comfort from him.

But she couldn't. Not now. Not after what she'd done to him. If she'd just been honest from the beginning, instead of enjoying the fact that she could correspond with a friend who never asked her how she was coping, never reminded her of what she'd been through, she never would have had to face this kind of pain right now.

If she hadn't kept writing to him and pretending everything was normal, when she was actually in hospital and recovering…

Ryan's fingers traced up her arm, across her shoulder

and cupped her chin to make her turn properly. He gently tilted her face to look up at his.

Jessica opened her eyes, let him see her as the damaged, emotional mess she had become.

"Jessica, I love you."

His words almost made her crumple to the ground. No. He couldn't love her. Not after what she'd done, the way she'd deceived him, what she'd told him in her letter. He was saying it because he felt sorry for her, because he felt he had to care for her after what she'd been through.

The only thing worse than a man running out on you when you thought he loved you, was a man who was so honorable he felt he had to stay.

"Did you hear me?" Ryan's eyes flickered, searching her gaze. "I love you, Jessica."

She shook her head. "It's not enough." Her voice wobbled.

"Not enough?"

He stepped back, his hand leaving her skin to run through his hair. He looked like he was going to turn and storm off, like he didn't know what to do, but instead he propelled himself forward. She stepped back but he grabbed her, held her in place.

"I've been waiting for you my entire life, Jessica." His voice dropped as he reached both hands to her cheeks, holding her face. "It's like I've been living in slow motion, like my life has been building to this moment, like I've been waiting to meet you, to be with you, every day of my existence."

Tears started falling again, beating down her cheeks and curling into her mouth, their salty taste making it even harder to swallow. To say anything at all back to him.

She couldn't believe him.

"I don't want to hurt you." She stuttered the words out.

"Don't want to? Or are you afraid to let me in?"

She'd never seen him like this, so intense. One moment he looked broken, the next like the soldier he was. The powerful man she knew he must be when he was on duty. In uniform.

"I know what hurt is, Jessica." He stepped back again, like he needed distance from her to regain his strength. "I've seen men die, I've pulled triggers and thrown grenades and done plenty of things to hurt myself and others. I watched my wife die, in a hospital not unlike this, and I've had my heart break into so many pieces that I thought it would never heal."

Her tears ceased. She stood, arms hanging at her sides, face angled toward him. After pushing him away, and hoping he wouldn't come back, now she wanted to grab him and never let go.

"Despite everything I've already been through, do you know when I realized that I'd never truly known hurt before?" he asked.

She shook her head.

"When you told me in a letter you loved me, but then ran away from me. When I thought that maybe you might die, and I wouldn't be at your side to help fight it with you."

"Ryan."

"No." He put his hand up and started walking backward down the corridor as she followed him. "Don't pity me, or tell me you're sorry. Just don't."

He stopped when she did. Jessica wiped at her cheeks and took a deep breath. She'd tried to save him the pain of her problems and instead she'd done the opposite. His eyes were like the pathway to his soul. Big blue pools that blazed with hurt and betrayal. His skin was pale, so unlike its usual sun-tanned gold. Like all the blood had drained away.

There was only one thing she could tell him. And that was the truth. There was no point hiding behind her pride or her fear any longer. If he was prepared to put his own heart on the line, could honestly tell her that he felt for her so deeply that he'd face any battle with her, then she had to be honest with him in return.

If he was brave enough to deal with her cancer, then she owed it to him to face her own fears. To take a chance. To risk her own heart.

"I love you, too, Ryan." She only whispered but he'd heard her. Of course he'd heard her. "I'm sorry and I love you."

He didn't move. His feet were planted shoulder-width apart, like he was awaiting orders, and his face was frozen.

"Ryan?"

He blinked and looked back at her. "I think I fell in love with you before we even met."

Jessica started to cry again as she ran the distance between them. He opened his arms as she propelled herself forward, catching her as she landed against his chest. His hands circled her waist and hoisted her in the air, legs winding around his torso as she clung on to him like she'd never held anything in her life before.

The words from his letter, that last letter she'd found, played through her mind. It still seemed too good to be true, but she couldn't fight the way she felt any longer.

"I love you, Ryan. I love you so much it hurts."

Why hadn't she given him the chance to be here? To

hold her and protect her? Why had she not let it be his decision?

He pulled his face away from her neck, buried against her hair, to look at her. She leaned back in his arms, safe in his strong hold.

"Promise you'll never leave me again. Promise you'll never walk away again," he said urgently.

She nodded. "I promise."

Ryan watched her eyes, his now filled with tears, just like her own. He tipped her forward until their foreheads touched, before a big smile made his mouth twitch.

"We can fight anything together, Jessica. I promise."

She didn't have the chance to say it back. To tell him that she agreed. His lips searched for hers, his smooth skin whispering across hers as she clung on to him so hard her fingers dug into his shoulders. Ryan pulled her tighter against his body, one hand holding her, the other pressed into the back of her head as his lips continued their hungry assault on hers.

He was right. It was as if they'd been waiting their entire lives for one another.

And this was only just the beginning.

CHAPTER THIRTEEN

Dear Jessica,
Do you ever think about how your life turned out? If you've made decisions, done things that you should maybe have done differently? I often wonder how it was I ended up here, whether I was always destined to this life, even though I love what I do. Maybe it's just my injury making me think things like this, because I'm already sick of being laid up and waiting for surgery.

Anyway, see you soon, okay? Maybe it's our destiny to meet, or maybe I'm just getting carried away. You decide.
Ryan

JESSICA LOOKED UP at Ryan as he cocooned her in his arms. They were sitting on the grass as Hercules played his duck-chasing game. She leaned back into Ryan, her body fitting snugly between his legs so she could rest on his chest.

"What are you thinking about?" Ryan asked, nuzzling her neck, his lips making goose pimples appear on her skin.

"I'm wondering how neither of us realized that

we were writing love letters all this time," she said, smiling.

He wrapped his arms around her tighter. "Maybe we did and we just didn't want to admit it to ourselves."

She turned her body to face him, arms circling him as she sat between his legs still but pressing her chest to him now instead. She wrapped her legs around him, too.

"Have you told George about my cancer yet?"

Ryan dropped a kiss to her forehead. "Yeah."

She sat up straighter. "What did he say? What did you tell him?"

Ryan pulled her closer. "I haven't told him all the details yet, but I told him that you were in remission." He paused then sighed. "It was tough telling him, but he asked me a few questions and I did my best to answer honestly."

"Maybe I should say something to him. Talk to him about it."

Ryan shook his head. "No, I think *we* can talk about it as a couple with him. Make sure he understands how unlikely it is that it could come back, explain about the mastectomy, cover everything."

Jessica nodded.

"The last thing I want is for him to be scared of losing his future stepmom, too."

She snuggled into his shoulder, but Ryan pulled her back.

"What's wrong?"

Jessica squeezed her eyes shut before looking up at Ryan. Worry lines covered his face, brows pulled together.

"I'm scared about you going away again."

He closed his eyes as she tucked her face back into his neck.

"I have to go."

It sounded like the words were painful for him, like he didn't want to admit that he was going to be leaving her.

"I know, it's just…"

Ryan held her away from him and leaned back, his eyes searching hers. "I've got a lot to live for. Nothing's going to happen to me. I'm going to be back here before you know it, okay?"

She admired his bravery. "Okay."

"Your letters kept me alive on my last tour," he reminded her.

Jess laughed. "Yeah?"

"Yeah." Ryan pulled her back into him, his lips covering hers. "I'll be back here in a few months. Any sooner and you'd probably be sick of me."

Jessica just shook her head and pulled him closer. She doubted that could ever happen. "Just shut up and kiss me."

Ryan tipped her back onto the grass and pinned her down, hands above her head. He leaned over her, his shoulders blocking the sun from her eyes.

She giggled as he growled, his mouth moving closer to hers.

"You should know better than to give orders to a soldier."

Jessica sighed against his lips. If this was her punishment, she intended on ordering him around more often.

EPILOGUE

Dear Jessica,
I can't believe it's been six months since we were last together. Would you believe me if I said they were the longest six months of my life? Every day I think of you, not a day goes past when I don't think about what I have to come home to.

Not long ago, the word home *scared me. Now it makes me smile. Have I told you that you saved me? I know you'll say I saved myself, but you've made me whole. You gave me the strength to fight for what I believed in, what I wanted in my life, and somehow I managed to fight hard enough for you too.*

Before you ask, my arm is fine. But I'm not cut out for this any more. My heart's not in it, and for the first time in my life I'm looking forward to a desk job.

I promised you this would be my last tour, and I had the papers through today to confirm it. When you see me next, I'll be yours forever. I promise I'll never leave you again.

All my love, now and forever.
Ryan

* * *

JESSICA COULDN'T STAND still. She shifted her weight from foot to foot, gripping George's hand tight and grinning as he squeezed back.

"That kind of hurts."

She laughed. "Sorry. It's just..."

"I know."

Jessica watched as the first of the soldiers came through the gate. Her mouth was dry, heart hammering so loud she was struggling to hear herself think.

She had hated Ryan being away, but it had been good in a way. Jessica pulled George against her and his arm found her waist. He was as nervous and excited as she was. But he was also her friend. All these months with Ryan away had brought them closer, made them develop a bond that she knew would never be broken.

She couldn't wait to see the look on Ryan's face.

"Jess, do you..."

Suddenly she couldn't hear what George was saying. Her eyes were transfixed, body humming as she recognized the man walking through the gates and toward them.

Tousled dark hair, shorter than before he'd left, but unmistakably his. Tanned skin, broad shoulders, eyes that could find hers in any crowd.

Ryan.

She knew George had left her side, that he'd already seen his dad. But she was powerless to move. She didn't know whether to leap in the air and squeal with excitement or cry her eyes out that he was actually here. Alive. Whole.

She drunk in the sight of him in his combat uniform. Camouflage pants and shirt, the same uniform she'd seen hanging in his closet that day. He looked good enough to eat and he was almost standing in front of her now, his son by his side.

"Hey, baby," he said.

She couldn't move. Words stuck in her throat.

But he didn't care. His smile lit up his entire face as he dropped his bag and grabbed her around the waist, swinging her up in the air and kissing her so hard she almost lost her breath.

"Ryan…" His name came out a whisper, like she couldn't truly believe he was back.

He kissed her again, his lips soft against hers this time, like he was whispering back to her. He only pulled away to put his other arm around his son.

"I've been waiting for this day for six months, and I'm never leaving either of you again. Okay?"

George nodded and all Jessica could do was grin up at him, feeling giddy with the sight of him before her, with the strength of him beneath her touch.

"Welcome home, Dad."

She reached for George and the three of them hugged, snuggled up close together.

"I'm so lucky to have you guys as my family." Jessica almost choked on her words but she had to say them. She *was* lucky. To have a man like Ryan by her side and a boy like George in her life.

"We're the lucky ones, right, bud?" Ryan asked his son.

George laughed and stepped back, quickly rubbing at his face to hide his tears.

But Jessica knew better. She was the lucky one.

She'd fought cancer, she'd faced heartache and loss, and yet she'd still managed to find Ryan. He'd made everything right again.

Today was like the start of their new life together.

He'd returned home safely from war. She'd passed all her tests with flying colors. And George had finally accepted her like they'd known one another all their lives.

"Shall we go home?" she asked.

Ryan laughed and George nudged him in the side.

"You got it?" Ryan asked his son.

George blocked Jessica and gave his father something from his pocket.

"What's going on?" she asked curiously.

Ryan passed his son his kit bag and they grinned at one another, before he turned to face her, reaching for one of her hands.

"This time when I was away, I wrote to George, too, as often as I wrote to you."

Jessica nodded. She knew that already.

"So that's how I knew all your tests had gone fine, and that George was coping okay. That he wasn't scared of losing you, too, now that the two of you had become so close."

She wasn't sure where this was going. "I know, Ryan. George and I talk about everything, we don't have any secrets."

George laughed.

She turned to glare at his cheeky response but he just shrugged.

"There is something he's been keeping secret." He paused. "In one of my last letters, I asked George a question." Ryan smiled over at his son again, before dropping to one knee.

Suddenly the noise of the airport, the hustle and bustle around them, disappeared. She could hardly see straight, could only focus on Ryan on one knee before her. Surely not?

Her heart started to thump. Hard.

"I know it's tradition to ask the bride's family for permission first, but in this case I thought it was George's permission we needed."

Oh, my. Her mouth was dry, she couldn't move. Bride? Had she heard him right?

"Jessica, will you do me the honor of becoming my wife? Of becoming George's stepmum?" Ryan asked huskily.

Jessica couldn't help the excited squeal as it left her lips. "Yes!" She grinned as Ryan rose. "Yes, yes, yes."

He leaned in and kissed her, touching his nose to hers, his forehead pressed against hers.

"Are you sure?" he whispered.

"I've never been more sure of anything in my life."

Ryan stepped back and held up her left hand, opening his other palm to reveal a ring. She watched as he raised it and placed it on her finger. A single solitaire on a platinum band.

"I can't believe you were in on this." Jessica turned to George, who was blushing from ear to ear. He just shrugged, obviously thrilled to have surprised her.

Jess turned her attention back to the ring, holding it up to the light to watch it sparkle.

"Do you like it?" Ryan asked anxiously.

She reached for him and held him tight, never wanting to let him go. "I love it."

He kissed her on the top of her head and took her hand.

"Let's go home, family."

Jessica reached for George's hand with her free one as they walked from the airport.

Home had never sounded so good.

On sale from 15th July 2011
Don't miss out!

Available at WHSmith, Tesco, ASDA, Eason
and all good bookshops

www.millsandboon.co.uk

NOT-SO-PERFECT PRINCESS *by Melissa McClone*

Princess Julianna's attraction to rebel prince Alejandro is instant—but her intended is his brother! Can she remain dutiful, or is it time to follow her heart?

THE HEART OF A HERO *by Barbara Wallace*

All Zoe wants is time to heal her post-divorce wounds in peace. Until her new neighbour, ex-army captain Jake Meyers, helps her open her heart.

RESCUED BY THE BROODING TYCOON *by Lucy Gordon*

Harriet is content with her life. She doesn't need the upstart tycoon whose life she saved ruining it all! Yet can Darius make her see that she might need rescuing too?

FIXED UP WITH MR RIGHT? *by Marie Ferrarella*

After lawyer Kate's prince turned into a frog, she didn't want a new relationship—especially not with a client. Then sexy Jackson strode into her life...

WANTED: ONE MUMMY *by Cathy Gillen Thacker*

Take-charge CEO Jack loves his little girl with all his heart—but he doesn't believe in happy endings. Could wedding planner Caroline change his mind?

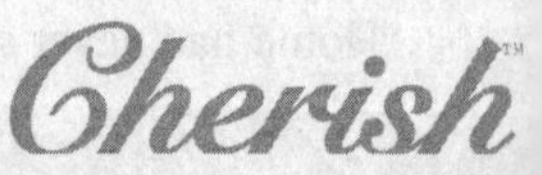

0711/023a

On sale from 5th August 2011
Don't miss out!

Available at WHSmith, Tesco, ASDA, Eason
and all good bookshops

www.millsandboon.co.uk

THE DEPUTY'S LOST AND FOUND *by Stella Bagwell*

Brady couldn't hide his fascination with the amnesiac woman he'd discovered. He wanted to claim Lass as his own—but what if she was already spoken for?

HER SECOND CHANCE COP *by Jeanie London*

Widow Riley's made herself a promise: no more romantic entanglements with police officers. So what is she going to do when seriously gorgeous cop Scott offers her his help?

AUSTRALIA'S MAVERICK MILLIONAIRE
by Margaret Way

Clio's the one woman who always saw the bravery beneath Josh's bravado. Now he's ready to prove to her that he's worthy of her love and trust.

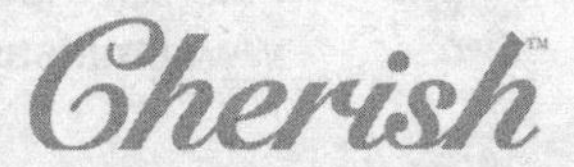

0711/023b

MILLS & BOON

Book of the Month

We love this book because...

Maisey Yates has an incredible talent for writing intense, emotional romance with a sexy, sassy edge. In *The Highest Price to Pay*, she creates a world of high fashion and even higher stakes!

On sale 15th July

Visit us Online

Find out more at
www.millsandboon.co.uk/BOTM

0711/BOTM

Special Offers

Every month we put together collections and longer reads written by your favourite authors.

Here are some of next month's highlights—don't miss our fabulous discount online!

On sale 15th July

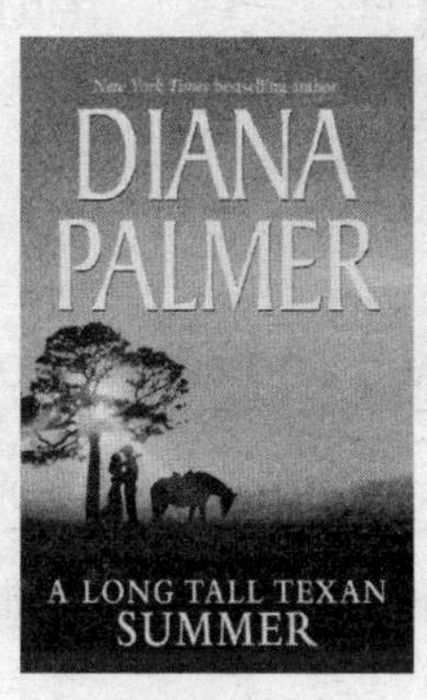

On sale 15th July

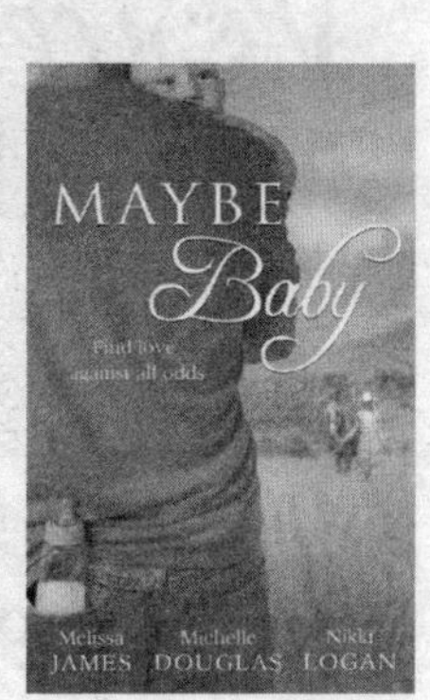

On sale 5th August

Find out more at
www.millsandboon.co.uk/specialreleases

Visit us Online

0711/ST/MB346

New Voices is back!

New Voices

returns on
13th September 2011!

For sneak previews and exclusives:

 Like us on facebook.com/romancehq

 Follow us on twitter.com/MillsandBoonUK

Last year your votes helped Leah Ashton win New Voices 2010 with her fabulous story *Secrets & Speed Dating*!

Who will you be voting for this year?

Visit us Online

Find out more at
www.romanceisnotdead.com

NEW_VOICES

711/06

There's Something About a Rebel...
by Anne Oliver
Why does sexy, brooding Blake Everett have to come back into Lissa's life when she's at a low point? Yet there's something about this rebel—he's irresistible!

The Crown Affair
by Lucy King
Laura spent an amazing night with the gorgeous stranger next door before starting a job on a Mediterranean island. But the island's new king is Laura's guy-next-door! Crown affairs have never been so hot...

Swept Off Her Stilettos
by Fiona Harper
Coreen Fraser's film-star style gives her any man she wants! Adam is the only man who knows the girl underneath the skyscraper heels. Is she brave enough to go barefoot?

Mr Right There All Along
by Jackie Braun
Chloe McDaniels has always depended on Simon Ford, even while he makes her heart flutter! But now Simon plans to show Chloe that love is worth the risk...

On sale from 5th August 2011
Don't miss out!

Available at WHSmith, Tesco, ASDA, Eason and all good bookshops

www.millsandboon.co.uk

WEB/M&B/RTL3

Discover Pure Reading Pleasure with

Visit the Mills & Boon website for all the latest in romance

- **Buy** all the latest releases, backlist and eBooks
- **Join** our community and chat to authors and other readers
- **Win** with our fantastic online competitions
- **Tell us** what you think by signing up to our reader panel
- **Find out** more about our authors and their books
- **Free** online reads from your favourite authors
- **Sign** up for our free monthly eNewsletter
- **Rate** and review books with our star system

www.millsandboon.co.uk

Follow us at twitter.com/millsandboonuk

Become a fan at facebook.com/romancehq

)711_S1ZED

2 FREE BOOKS
AND A SURPRISE GIFT

We would like to take this opportunity to thank you for reading this Mills & Boon® book by offering you the chance to take TWO more specially selected books from the Cherish™ series absolutely FREE! We're also making this offer to introduce you to the benefits of the Mills & Boon® Book Club™—

- **FREE home delivery**
- **FREE gifts and competitions**
- **FREE monthly Newsletter**
- **Exclusive Mills & Boon Book Club offers**
- **Books available before they're in the shops**

Accepting these FREE books and gift places you under no obligation to buy, you may cancel at any time, even after receiving your free books. Simply complete your details below and return the entire page to the address below. You don't even need a stamp!

YES Please send me 2 free Cherish books and a surprise gift. I understand that unless you hear from me, I will receive 5 superb new stories every month, including two 2-in-1 books priced at £5.30 each, and a single book priced at £3.30, postage and packing free. I am under no obligation to purchase any books and may cancel my subscription at any time. The free books and gift will be mine to keep in any case.

Ms/Mrs/Miss/Mr ________________ Initials ________________

____

Surname ____

Address ____

____

________________________________ Postcode ________________

E-mail ____

Send this whole page to: Mills & Boon Book Club, Free Book Offer, FREEPOST NAT 10298, Richmond, TW9 1BR

Offer valid in UK only and is not available to current Mills & Boon Book Club subscribers to this series. Overseas and Eire please write for details. We reserve the right to refuse an application and applicants must be aged 18 years or over. Only one application per household. Terms and prices subject to change without notice. Offer expires 30th September 2011. As a result of this application, you may receive offers from Harlequin (UK) and other carefully selected companies. If you would prefer not to share in this opportunity please write to The Data Manager, PO Box 676, Richmond, TW9 1WU.

Mills & Boon® is a registered trademark owned by Harlequin (UK) Limited.
Cherish™ is being used as a trademark.
The Mills & Boon® Book Club™ is being used as a trademark.

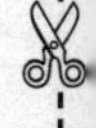